CU00712404

Acknowledgement

I thank the Almighty God for his love, gifts, guidance and never-ceasing mercy.
I thank my most beautiful wife for being the best. You're my first editor, darling and soulmate. Thanks for being there through so much.
I also thank my dad and mum for being the most wonderful parents. I am so thankful I was born into your care.

Rod Young and Seni, thanks for some of the technical assistance.
I thank the man known as M.O. for his unrelenting guidance.
The publisher is grateful to Cindy Davis for her experienced editing and input.

The writer thanks Microsoft. A few times I thought I had lost parts of the script due to my own fault only for Microsoft Word to recover the files. Thanks guys.

The publisher is grateful to the US FAA Civil Aviation Registry for providing information.
The publisher is also grateful to the Captain of the Three Fleets at British Airways for granting Rod Young's assistance.

Elizabeth Huddleston, Sam Wall, Cathi Stevenson and Bruce Emmett, thanks for your contributions in editorial and design.

My Father, My Trouble

John Golden

Paul Books Ltd

Paul Books Ltd
42 Pedley Road Dagenham
Essex. RM8 1XE

First Edition 2010

Published in the United Kingdom by Paul Books Ltd.

ISBN 978-0-9544791-2-1

1

The black Jeep with tinted windows screeched to a halt in Chevy Chase, an opulent suburb of Washington DC where most of the houses were mansions and estates. The driver was a big man who looked like a thug. 'There,' he growled at his passenger, pointing to a huge, black gate on which was written, **RESTRICTED PROPERTY—KEEP OFF**. 'That's the place.'

Leroy got out of the Jeep and walked to the wrought iron gate.

Bugsy, a burly, unshaven biker-type stood guard. He wore faded jeans and a white T-shirt. A gleaming .357 Magnum stuck out of his ageing belt. Bugsy handed Leroy a radio. 'All right?'

'Yeah,' Leroy grunted and clipped the radio to his belt.

'Gun?'

Leroy flapped open his jacket to reveal an Uzi nestled in an out-size concealment holster beneath his dark blue jacket, and a Glock 9 mm pistol tucked into his belt.

Satisfied, Bugsy pressed a button on the wall. The gate

slid open and Leroy walked into the grounds of The Starving Parrot, the home of the Director of the CIA.

Leroy stopped and looked around. The Director's Edwardian mansion stood seventy yards away, hidden from the outside world. He had never been here but from now on, this would be his new station. He admired the magnificent white mansion, set on three acres of plush manicured lawn, interspersed with beds of brightly coloured flowers: marigolds, snapdragons, roses and blue bells. The late afternoon air smelt strongly of freshly cut grass and flowers. A private road led from the gate to the patio.

He walked towards the mansion. For some reason the surroundings triggered the memory of a dream from a few days back. In it he was cozying up with this really pretty girl in a shoe shop. The owner of the shop emerged, wielding a butcher's knife. Leroy woke just as they fled the shop. He laughed. Weird dream.

He crossed the patio, rubber soled shoes silent on the exquisite red marble. He knocked on the huge, carved front door.

Ann Cagley opened the door.

He froze. She was slim and delightfully attractive; the kind of girl you see in beauty pageants, and on the catwalks. Those full pink lips, sparkling emerald green eyes and long, beautiful nose... Enticing. She wore a yellow waist-length jacket over a yellow knee-length dress that clung sweetly to her hourglass figure. She reminded him of Marilyn Monroe, only she beat the blonde bombshell by a mile. No, ten miles.

He didn't believe in dreams, and had never believed in them. How weird was this? Ann Cagley was the same girl he'd been hugging in his dream!

He cocked his head slightly to one side, and stared at her, amazed.

She frowned. 'Can I help you?

Leroy backed a step, realizing she thought he'd been gawking at her ample breasts. 'Er, yes. Hi, I'm your father's new guard.

2

My name's Leroy. Leroy Delgado. Call me Skinner. I'll be patrolling the grounds.' He stretched out his hand towards her.

She ignored it.

Who did he think he was, looking her over as if she was a chunk of meat? From his spiky, black hair, military-type face and fancy goatee beard, he gave off vibes like he owned the place. Was he too cool to behave like the other guards who called her, "Ma'am" and kept their distance? He was either dumb or fearless. His deep-blue suit was probably borrowed. Likewise those dirty, second-hand things he called shoes. And that cheap ten-cent silver bracelet, on which was engraved, "28 years old and still kicking."

'If you don't mind!' She stepped back and slammed the door—almost in his face.

'What's up with her?' He saw the funny side of it as he turned away, smiling. 'Ass.'

Ann Cagley was a firecracker. He found that extremely exciting.

What about the dream?

Weird, but maybe it was a sign from heaven.

Interesting prospect, the thought of getting to know her better.

But she was the daughter of the Director of the CIA, and CIA rules expressly prohibited CIA guards from any form of relationship with a subject in their care.

But, hey, rules were made to be broken, weren't they? He grinned and strode away.

On the other side of the door a frown screwed over Ann's pretty face. 'Jerk. When my dad finds out that your eyes have been walking all over my chest he'll break every bone in your body. Every single one.'

She reached for the phone.

2

Korea, 1952

'Halt!' Sergeant Ken's command echoed between the tall pine trees in the dull Korean forest. 'We take a rest.'

Sergeant Ken, a former brawler from the docks of Chicago snatched the water bottle of the soldier nearest to him and drank from it. When he finished he handed back the empty bottle. 'Your water tastes like shit.' He spat on the ground. He turned to the other men. 'Mileface, you take first watch!'

Mileface—his real name was Stanislaus—stuck a reefer between his lips. Here in the forest, any dry leaf rolled in paper would do. His face was long and thin, hence his nickname. Carrying his huge, black machine gun, he trained his bloodshot eyes into the forest.

'Petrowicz, you watch our rear!' Sergeant Ken ordered. 'And don't kill anything without me saying so!'

'Yes, sergeant,' Petrowicz muttered, his blue, dilated eyes sunk deep into his gaunt face. The war had taken its toll on Petrowicz. He had become a psychopath. So far, he had shot three people, two dogs, and a wild pig for absolutely no reason.

'Cagley, keep your eye on that girlie-prisoner! Rest of you, fall out!'

Michael Cagley, the youngest soldier in Squad 2 sat against a pine tree. The injured Korean girl-prisoner sat very close. The other soldiers huddled in a group, ten yards away. Water from last night's rain dripped off the trees. The girl-prisoner was shivering. He took off his green army shirt and draped it over her shoulders.

4

She looked up gratefully. '*Gamsahabnida.*' Thank you.

He nodded and smiled. Her voice was as soft as air and it made him feel soft inside. Soo Min Ji was seventeen, the same age as him. She was raw and beautiful, a wild rose. Her white dress was torn in a few places—the forest was never kind to clothes. She had big, bright eyes and though, fearful, they sparkled. Her long black hair had fallen forward to partially cover her face. He tenderly brushed off a few brown ants that wove in and around the shiny strands. She didn't seem offended that he touched her. She had long realised she was safe with him. He was the only American soldier out of this murderous bunch who treated her better than a dog.

Cagley brought out the last bits of his rations and split it in two. 'Take. Eat.'

She accepted the two dried biscuits and half a bar of chocolate and leaned back against the tree trunk to nibble first on the chocolate.

'Cagley is giving the girl his rations again,' Mileface grumbled to the sergeant. He was supposed to be on watch but his penchant for mischief often took over. He had a gift for inciting trouble. 'Don't know what's wrong with that boy. He keeps drooling over the commie bitch. Like he's never seen a woman before or something.'

'Yeah,' Putka agreed, reloading his rifle. 'He's a shit head. You know what? This morning, when my hand went up her dress he punched me in the face.' He rubbed his chin, the memory still clear.

Ever since they captured the female prisoner Putka harboured filthy intentions towards her. He had already raped six women in this war. That was his speciality. 'Just look at them,' he snarled. Cagley and the prisoner were smiling at each other. 'They make me sick!'

'Last night, when the gooks were shooting at us, she was so scared she froze,' Mileface added. 'Cagley had to pull her down. She stuck out her butt as she crawled, wailing like a doggone hyena. That gave away Cagley's position. Made the

5

gooks fire at 'em. She's gonna get Cagley killed—that bitch.'

'I think he likes her,' Wilshaw answered. He was a muscular black soldier from Harlem. 'I think she likes him too. She keeps close to him.'

Mileface groaned. He loaded an ammunition belt into his machine gun. 'We're right in the middle of a war, lost in a forest, and that American soldier is playing *love* games with the enemy!'

'She's not the enemy,' Wilshaw corrected. 'She's just a peasant girl who had the bad luck of running into us in this damned forest.'

Michael Cagley heard everything the other soldiers said. 'To hell with you all,' he muttered. 'I don't care what you think.'

The Korean War began in June 1950 when communist North Korea invaded South Korea. In just three days, the communists overran South Korea. Responding, the United States stepped in to bail out the beleaguered South Koreans. The Soviet Union and China took sides with North Korea, and together, they plunged into a savage war against South Korea, the United States and its allies.

At that time, Cagley was only fifteen. His days were spent helping out on his father's wheat farm in rural Kansas. He was the fifth of six children. He was content with the rural way of life and looked forward to someday having his own farm. At that time television was only just becoming popular in his part of Kansas, and when it came to his close-knit community of Little Wee Brook, his outlook changed. The Phillips black and white television flashed glamorous images of New York with its big cars, high life, skyscrapers, and trendy women.

Cagley was fascinated. So, there was a big city out there with buildings as tall as the sky? And women that looked like goddesses with painted lips, high heels and body-hugging skirts? New York was heaven on earth. The place to be! He began to nurture the dream of going to New York.

One day, young Cagley saw a US Army advert on TV. "See the world," it said. "New York! London! Paris! A whole new world full of fun and adventure!" The ad didn't mention anything about the men dying on the battlefield, however. Cagley packed his bags and, at the age of sixteen, walked into Fort Benning, the US Army base in Georgia.

'I wanna join,' he declared at the front gates in his Kansas farm accent. By then Uncle Sam needed all the help it could get. The guard promptly ushered the hillbilly into the camp where he had his basic training and MOS.

Now, here he was nine months later—not on the Empire State Building, not hanging out in Broadway—but deep in the Korean hills, serving with the 180th Battalion of the 45th Infantry Division. He was not with the Manhattan lasses but saddled with a Korean girl-prisoner. But he was thankful. He had fallen in love with her.

Cagley's face glowed as he remembered the very first time he set eyes on Soo Min Ji. It was three days ago. They had been on foot patrol at the edge of the forest. Cagley and the other soldiers of Squad 2 hid in a thicket, their guns at the ready, hoping to ambush the enemy. The crackling of twigs and swish of leaves told them someone was coming. They aimed their rifles, ready to shoot.

It was not an enemy soldier but a teenage Korean girl in a white dress limping painfully along the road. Blood caked her entire right foot.

Always eager for blood Petrowicz crept out of the thicket, his 8-inch hunting knife at the ready. He crouched stealthily behind her, grabbed her around the waist and hurled her to the ground. Petrowicz stifled her screams with a hand over her mouth. He pressed the blade into her skin ready to slice her throat.

The sergeant leaped from the thicket. 'No!'

Petrowicz reluctantly retracted his blade. Her eyes were wide as they gazed up at the pair of men. Putka approached now. He spoke some Korean (he was the platoon interpreter). He questioned her harshly then relayed to the sergeant, 'She says her name's Soo Min Ji. Age, seventeen. She lived with her parents in a tiny village called Kum To Nang, a few miles east of the forest. Her father farmed the rice paddies whilst her mother took care of the livestock. Her family was very poor. Their village generally kept out of the war, but two days ago, at about 1.00 am, her entire village was shaken out of sleep by gunfire. She doesn't know who attacked, whether Americans, KPA or the Chinese. All she saw was bright orange flames leaping out of the rifles in the dark of the night, and the rattling of machine guns. Then pandemonium. Then the screams, cries and wailing of dying villagers. She crawled out of her wooden hut in a panic just as somebody threw in a fire grenade. They shot at her and hit her in the foot.' He pointed to the inch-wide wound on her bare foot. 'She fled into the forest. When she dared returned to her village, everyone was dead. Burnt corpses. Her last memory is that of her mother engulfed by flames from the fire grenade. Everyone she knows is dead. She's all alone.'

'We'll take her with us,' the sergeant decided. 'She could be spinning a yarn, and could be an enemy informant.' The sergeant turned to Cagley. 'You watch her.' As the youngest soldier, he got the shitty jobs.

Cagley smiled. This was one shitty job he was glad to do. 'Yes, Sergeant!'

He held her hand. She had no shoes. The bullet wound was oozing pus. Cagley tenderly dressed it, wrapping it with one of the two remaining white bandages he carried in his chest pocket. Since then she had been with them.

Sitting against the pine tree, Cagley gazed at Soo Min Ji. He had never had such deep feelings for a woman. He no longer saw her as a prisoner. He saw her as his woman. He would get her out of this hellhole, and get her to America. He would give her everything she needed, send her to school, teach her English. And he would marry her! He ran his fingers through her hair, and smiled contentedly. *I'm so glad I'm in this war. Meeting her is the best thing that has ever happened to me.*

Sergeant Ken sat at the base of a nearby tree, smoking the

last of his cigarettes. He stared intensely at So Min Ji, his eyes tinted with lust. 'Wonder what she's got under that dress,' he drawled, exhaling a lungful of smoke.

'Me too,' Putka responded, churning smoke from some weed. 'Maybe we should go see.' For Putka, the chaos of war was an excuse to get laid. He had raped in every village they attacked.

'Y'know,' Mileface remarked, 'ever since that commie bitch's been around, Cagley does nothing but drool at her all day. Yo, Cagley!' he called, chuckling, 'You in love with the commie bitch or something?'

The other soldiers guffawed.

'Yo, Cagley, that wench is for me!' Sergeant Ken warned. 'To do as I please. That's why I keep her around.'

'I can't allow that, Sergeant,' Cagley replied boldly.

'You don't need to allow it, Private,' the sergeant drawled, asserting his superiority. 'The job I've given you is to watch her, so you watch her. She's for me. My plaything. When time's ripe, I'll come take her.' His eyes were dim.

'I hope no one intends to mess around with her or someone's gonna get hurt,' Cagley warned, clutching his rifle. This was the first time he had ever spoken back to a superior. 'This is my woman. She's the woman I love! The one I'm going to marry. I'll defend her with my life!'

The other soldiers glanced round at each other. Cagley had thrown down the gauntlet.

Sergeant Ken watched Cagley, his eyes sour. As sergeant, he had to be seen to be tough. Haggling with a private for a bush woman was just not respectable. At any rate, they had the primary duty of getting out of this creepy forest alive. He decided to play it cool, but he hated the fact that Cagley talked back. When sergeants talk, privates should do only one thing: shut-up!

He watched with steely eyes, and silent, jealous rage as Soo Min Ji tore off a fringe from her dress and used it as a hankie to wipe Cagley's face. She then placed her head on Cagley's shoulder and closed her eyes, her expression one of bliss.

Sergeant Ken got to his feet. 'Okay, you lot, let's get a move on. We gotta get out of this hellhole. I'll lead. Mileface, you watch the right flank. Petrowicz, take the left. Cagley, fall to the rear. And keep your eyes peeled!'

The soldiers of Squad 2 pushed deeper into the forest, slipping between the trees, rifles at the ready. The blue sky was far overhead but the tall trees kept out most of the light. The forest floor was littered with dead and rotten leaves. Water dripped from the tree canopy. Occasionally, grey squirrels appeared on the trees, chittered at the intrusion, then disappeared.

As they went through the forest Cagley's mind was hard at work. *When we get back to base I'll declare Soo Min Ji innocent, irrespective of what everyone else says. I'm confident she'll be set free. Then I'll get a South Korean soldier to interpret as I declare my love for her. Most likely, she'll say yes. She seems to have taken to me as well. I really love her! What if she says no?*

She won't say no. I can read it in her eyes. She loves me too. She'll say yes. She has no home, no family, nothing. She has no one...except me.

Now, how will I get her to America?

Simple. Marry her. That will be settled in the South Korean city of Seoul. Once she becomes my wife, she'll be ferried back to America by the Army. I'll send her to my mother.

Soo Min Ji's injured foot hurt severely; she could barely walk. Cagley helped her along. Whatever it took, he would do.

Tears filled Soo Min Ji's eyes. He was so gentle. She felt grateful and protected. He gave her a little hope, and she loved the way he smelled. She also liked his stony, grey eyes. There was something in them, something so natural and right.

Because of her foot Soo Min Ji and Cagley could not keep up with the pace of the other soldiers. Mileface looked back. 'Get a move on!' he yelled across the forest.

Cagley didn't wish to slow down or irritate the others, so he

10

held her by the waist. With her arms flung around his neck, he helped her along. Still they couldn't keep up.

After trudging another hundred yards Mileface looked back again. 'Hold up!' he yelled. Everyone stopped.

'What's going on?' Sergeant Ken bawled. He spoke with a lisp since he had lost his two front teeth.

'Cagley's fallen back,' Mileface answered.

Twenty yards behind, Cagley and Soo Min Ji were just coming around a tree.

Sergeant Ken stormed towards Cagley. 'What's keeping you?' As if he didn't see.

'She having trouble. The foot's infected now.' Cagley pointed at Soo Min Ji's bandaged foot, in case they'd all forgotten she'd been shot.

'I'll take care of that.' Sergeant Ken. He pulled out his pistol.

'No!' Cagley lunged at the sergeant.

The sergeant squeezed the trigger; his pistol went off with a bang.

3

Soo Min Ji slumped to the forest floor. The hole in her forehead oozed thick red blood. Her eyes were wide open and filled with fear. They peered up, seeing nothing.

Sergeant Ken swaggered away. 'Double up, Cagley,' he ordered. No emotion. No remorse.

It was as if Cagley had been pushed into an abyss. He stared in disbelief at his dream—now sprawled on the litter of leaves and twigs. All at once his knees buckled; he sank to the ground, landing on his butt beside his love. He took hold of her hand, and looked lovingly into her eyes, praying she would be okay. Yet, in his heart, he knew she was dead. Dead as Hector. 'My baby! My baby!'

He sat beside her body, and caressed her hair. She was still beautiful, even in death. Tears welled up. He held her hand, stroking it, sobbing uncontrollably.

The other members of Squad 2 had marched a number of yards away. As one, they turned and watched, aloof. 'Lighten up, Cagley,' someone drawled. Unconcerned. 'Gotta git the hell outta here.'

They didn't even care! They snuffed out her life and they didn't even care! To them she was just about as important as a dog. She was not a dog, damn it! She was the woman he loved. The three days he spent with her were the best days of his life. She was his soulmate, his true love. He knew it. He felt it. And they just snuffed out her life!

Cagley rocketed to his feet, grabbed his rifle—a long-barrelled, wooden carbine—and aimed at his colleagues. He squeezed the trigger. The rifle rattled; a few bullets whizzed

12

in the direction of Sergeant Ken and Mileface. Everyone scrambled for cover behind the trees.

'Are you crazy, Cag?' someone yelled from behind a tree. 'You shootin' at us?'

Cagley stormed forward. 'Where are ya?' He panned his rifle from side to side, looking earnestly between the tall trees, seeking the sergeant. 'You think you're so tough? What'd she do to ya? You killed my woman? I'm gonna kill you, bastard!'

But the sergeant had disappeared.

'Hold it right there, Cag!' Mileface yelled, pointing his machine gun at Cagley. 'Hold it right the hell there!'

'Screw you!' Cagley squeezed two shots at Mileface.

Mileface dived for cover. 'Bloody hell, Cag, that was close. That was damn close! Are you outta ya mind or something?'

Wilshaw peeped out from behind the needle-leaves of a spruce tree. 'Take it easy, Cag. Cool, man!'

'Halt!' Petrowicz the psychopath roared, training his gun on Cagley. 'Halt or I'll shoot!'

Cagley ignored Petrowicz. Instead, he searched the undergrowth, shooting randomly into any space he thought the sergeant might be hiding.

'Where are you, son of a one-cent whore?' Cagley yelled. He let out another shot. 'Think ya're tough?' He let off another shot. 'Come out here if ya're so tough. I'll kill ya, you slimy swine!'

'Drop the gun, Cagley!' Mileface aimed his machine gun. 'That's an order, Private!'

'Damn you!' Cagley fired three bullets at Mileface.

Mileface melted into the trees. He popped his head out a few seconds later. 'Drop it or I'll shoot!'

'Look, Cag, we didn't know she was that important to you,' Putka pleaded. 'Honest.'

'Drop the damn gun, dammit!' Mileface roared.

'Oh yeah?' Cagley squeezed another two shots at Mileface.

'Mama mia!' Mileface dove behind his tree. Cagley had to be disarmed yet Mileface could not bring himself to shoot

Cagley. He was just a kid for goodness sake.

Cagley discovered Sergeant Ken flattened behind a shrub, holding a .45 Chinese pistol, a souvenir he took off a Chinese captain he had killed. 'Drop it!'

Cagley squeezed the trigger. There was a click, and nothing happened. The rifle was empty.

The sergeant also heard the click. He knew Cagley's gun was empty. He felt a brief sense of safety, and lowered his pistol.

Cagley wasn't done. Letting out a huge battle cry he lunged at the sergeant, ramming the butt of his rifle into Sergeant Ken's head. The sergeant's helmet absorbed the impact but it jerked his head backwards.

Sergeant Ken groaned. The pistol dropped from his fingers. Blood seeped from his nose. Cagley went for him. For forty seconds, he battered Sergeant Ken with a flurry of kicks, and pounded him with the M1's stock. While Cagley's back was turned, the other soldiers rushed him. They wrestled him to the ground.

Sergeant Ken struggled to his feet. His flat nose had split in two. His rough face was bruised, lacerated and already swelling in a number of places. For a good minute, he wobbled, dazed from the battering. He staggered to a tree and leaned a hand on the rough bark, panting heavily, blood seeping from his nose and lips.

'Let go of me!' Cagley howled, grappling with Putka, Wilshaw and Petrowicz. But it was three against one. All three piled atop him, pinning him down to the ground.

With Cagley immobilized, Sergeant Ken knew he now had the upper hand. Half-dazed, and aching all over, he staggered to where Cagley lay. He picked up his Chinese pistol from where it had fallen.

'I killed your bitch,' he grunted, wiping blood off his swollen lips with the back of a hand. 'Now, I'm gonna kill you.' He pointed the weapon at Cagley's head.

'No, Sarge,' Mileface said. He turned his machine gun on the sergeant. 'You ain't killin' no American soldier.' His face was grim. Although he was a rabble-rouser he felt a little remorse that the sergeant had shot the girl-prisoner in cold blood.

The sergeant was taken aback. Mileface, his loyal deputy, had never opposed him. 'Stand down, corporal.'

'No, sergeant,' Mileface replied. 'You ain't killin' nobody else.'

'I said stand down!' the sergeant screamed.

Mileface shoved the barrel of his machine gun into the sergeant's chest with such force that the sergeant was thrown back a few feet.

Mileface was turning on him? He looked down the conical nozzle of the weapon. Mileface had his finger on the trigger. That gun would off-load eight hundred rounds in one minute.

Mileface looked the sergeant straight in the eye. He shook his head sternly. 'No.'

4

Leroy sweltered in the burning sun as he patrolled the grounds of The Starving Parrot, Cagley's three-acre estate. Sweat dripped from his forehead; his blue shirt was soaked. He wished he could take his jacket off but he could not. Like Secret Service agents who guarded the President, he had to keep his jacket on at all times to conceal his weapons.

The position of CIA Director had always been a sensitive one. Apart from heading the CIA, he was head of the Intelligence Community, an umbrella name for the intelligence bodies working for the United States, including those of the Army, Navy, Air Force, FBI and the super-secret National Security Agency. Because of this, the CIA Director had a 24-hour security detail: two armed officers accompanied him everywhere he went whilst two armed guards watched his home, whether he was there or not. The windows of his stately, white mansion were bulletproof. A ten-foot wire fence formed a perimeter around the entire estate.

Leroy let down his tie, and loosened his neck button. He wished he were at the beach wearing beach shorts and flip-flops, dipping into the cool surf. Or better still, racing atop the waves on a jet ski. Even better, lounging in the cool under a beach umbrella, tanking a Budweiser. And the best: cozying up with a smoking hot babe.

Four Roman columns on the patio supported the balcony above. It provided a refuge from the burning summer sun. As usual, he admired his boss' house. Nice mansion, surrounded on all sides by manicured lawns and brightly coloured flowers. It was very different from Brooklyn in New York where he grew up, where the skyline was littered with ageing six-storey apartment blocks. Here, in Chevy Chase, the houses were mostly mansions, surrounded by trees and exquisite lawns. And they had names instead of house numbers—names like The Weeping Willow; The Starving Parrot—which was Cagley's; Flushing Acres—which belonged to the Secretary of State.

Idle, he brought out his Glock and admired the grey firearm. He cocked it, squinted, and aimed a false shot at a nearby tree. His walkie-talkie suddenly came alive. 'Two-four, Skinner. Daisy two-four.'

That was Bugsy, the other guard stationed in the guardhouse, monitoring images from security cameras placed around the grounds. Security protocol demanded Bugsy alert him if anyone was coming into the house. Daisy was the code name for Ann. Daisy two-four meant Ann was on her way in.

'Roger,' Leroy responded.

He watched as Ann drove her blue Toyota up the drive and parked in front of the house. She stepped out of her car carrying a white handbag. She wore a white, linen blouse, a white cotton skirt, and pumps. He loved a woman in a skirt. Especially the knee-length ones with tiny slits in the back. He smiled, admiring her female form. Nice babe.

'Hi,' he said as she stepped onto the patio.

'Fool,' she muttered. 'Always ogling me like I'm a chunk of meat. Look at that ugly ash-grey suit he's wearing. Cheapskate. He probably got it from the charity shop.'

Not giving him an eye, she went into the house.

5

Korea, 1952

Turning your weapon on a superior was one of the gravest offences in the Army. Cagley was arraigned before a military court at the 45th division headquarters. The court was a converted elementary school classroom. Cagley stood bare-footed in the dock. His hat, belt, and shoes had been taken away. Two towering military police officers in white helmets stood guard behind him.

'We consider the fact that the sergeant, unprovoked, shot an unarmed female prisoner,' the Army judge, a bald, bored Lieutenant Colonel ruled in the cramped, makeshift court. 'We also consider that you, Private Cagley, confessed you were in love with the prisoner. I therefore consider this a crime of the heart. On those two counts, and this being your first offence, after much consideration, I sentence you to two weeks confinement.' The sergeant only got a nasty look.

Cagley was aghast. *Is that all? A nasty look? Is that all the punishment Sergeant Ken receives?* They didn't care. The Army didn't care. No one cared. Soo Min Ji was about as important as a dog to them.

He shook his head repeatedly. There was so much injustice in the world. So much!

Cagley was incarcerated in the 45th division's dingy guardroom for fourteen days. Every single minute of every day, he sat in the corner of the smelly room, thinking about his dead golden flower, Soo Min Ji. In those fourteen days, he lived an entire lifetime with her in his mind. He went shopping with her, had kids with her, went camping with her, went to the beach with her, and they died together, arm in arm. *I will never forgive the sergeant. One day, he'll pay.*

Whilst Cagley was in the guardroom the other sergeants in the 180th Infantry got to hear about the incident in the forest. 'What kind of sergeant are you?' they scoffed at Ken. 'You're a sissy sergeant, Ken. A wimp. You hid in the grass while a lousy private whacked your butt! Haw, haw. Haw!'

From then on, Sergeant Ken was nicknamed, Pussycat. Whenever Ken entered the Sergeant's Mess, the other sergeants mewed and purred like kittens. Ken hated being the laughing stock in the battalion. 'I will never forgive Cagley. I'm going to get even with him on this. Cagley's crossed the wrong man.' From then on he sought a way to salvage some pride. He sought a way to harm Cagley.

Now, at this time of war, the Army needed every man on the battlefield not in the dungeons. Short of treason and desertion you could get way with almost anything. Cagley was released from jail, but he was not allowed to rejoin Squad 2. He was seconded to Platoon 4, and resumed the war.

Four weeks later, the Chinese Army mounted a huge offensive to secure a hill east of Chumjamal. The US Army despatched the 180th Infantry and the 101 Armoured Corps to stop the Chinese. The battle raged for three days and three nights with heavy losses on both sides. Army HQ despatched an artillery battalion. Eventually the Chinese retreated.

Soon after, F, D and C companies of the 180th Infantry were ordered to mount extensive patrols into the surrounding countryside to ensure the Chinese did not return. Captain Wilson Tooley was in command of C Company. His units were depleted, and so he regrouped his men into squads, each led by a sergeant. Cagley fell into Squad 3, under his hated former Sergeant, Ken.

Cagley kept mum. He didn't trust the sergeant, neither did he feel safe with him. *If he comes near me, I'll shoot him. I don't mind going to jail thereafter. He had better keep away from me if he knows what's good for him!*

As they patrolled the countryside they walked through green fields in a shallow valley surrounded by bracken-covered hills. Cagley hated being anywhere near the sergeant and he made it show. He wore green Army shirt, combat trousers, and a green steel helmet. Rather than participate, he shouldered his rifle, lit a cigarette, and skulked behind.

The sergeant ignored him.

They arrived at the muddy banks of the Po River. Because of heavy rains of late, its waters were brown and swollen. Clouds hung thick and dark. It seemed like more rain was imminent. Sergeant Ken turned to his men. 'Duncan! Petrowicz, you take the right.' He gestured into the tall green grasses growing on a ridge at the riverbank. 'Walk down that ridge and see what you got.'

'Yes, sergeant.'

'Petrowicz?'

'Sergeant?'

'Take a couple of men and see what's in the bushes over there.'

'Yes, sergeant.'

'Cagley! Seluva! Davidson! Check out the field next to the rice paddy. Cagley in front. You two, hang ten paces behind.'

'Yes, sergeant!' Seluva and Davidson answered.

Cagley still kept mum. 'Mongrel,' he cursed. Frowning, he slid his rifle off his shoulder. Holding his weapon at the ready, he tromped into the overgrown field of fallow grass. A faint footpath ran all the way through it.

Davidson and Seluva stepped to follow, but the sergeant signalled them to wait, leaving Cagley all alone.

Cagley walked deeper into the field that extended for about two hundred yards. It terminated at the foot of a small hill. There didn't seem to be anything in the field except grass and a few grazing wild pigs.

Sergeant Ken watched with keen interest, a smirk on his face.

After thirty steps, Cagley stopped. He realised he was alone

20

in the field. No Seluva. No Davidson. All he could see were the battle helmets of the other soldiers as they crouched in the bushes, thirty yards behind, watching him.

What's going on? Is there—

He stopped, seeing a movement in the grass about a yard away. He clutched his rifle, but then he relaxed when he saw it was a wild pig. Wary of the nearby intruder, the pig sought safer quarters. The mud-covered animal lumbered fearlessly across his path, a mere one and a half feet away. The pig's hairy hoof stepped on a spot of earth twenty-four inches from Cagley's boots.

A brilliant flash and a huge bang that almost split his ear drums punctuated the stillness.

Land mine!

The pig was flung twenty feet into the air amidst white smoke and debris. A blast of hot air hit Cagley like a concrete wall, flinging him back. The shrapnel-laden air tore into his body like hundreds of sharp razor blades, cutting him open in a hundred and one places. He landed like a sack of spuds ten feet away, bleeding from his head, chest, thighs, and legs—everywhere. He couldn't move. He could not think. His eyes rolled back into his head. Then he felt the pain.

'Medic! Medic!' someone cried in the distance.

A medic wearing a red cross on his helmet appeared.

Lying on his back, and bleeding, he could barely make out outlines of the grey sky. Then a familiar face hovered above him. Sergeant Ken—wearing a triumphant smirk on his ugly brawler's face. The bastard had known the field was mined.

'Don't worry, pie face,' the sergeant scoffed. 'Look on the bright side. You die and your mother receives an American flag. Haw-Haw!'

The medic shoved the sergeant away from the bed.

Cagley felt weaker and weaker. He knew he was dying.

6

The sages say, 'Envy no one, not even the rich; you never know where they're hurting.'

True.

Ann lay on her bed, staring out at the night sky. She snivelled, and wiped the streaming tears off her cheeks.

She remembered what someone once said to her. "I admire you, Ann. You're beautiful, you're successful and you have a dream job. You live in a mansion and your father is Director of the Central Intelligence Agency. He's one of the most powerful men in America. You have the world at your feet."

The world at my feet?

If only they knew.

Ann was born into a relatively affluent home. Being an only child, Cagley and her mother invested much of their resources in her. At the age of two she had enough toys to fill a room. At ten, Cagley sent her to St Theresa's Catholic Girls School in Alexandria, which was run by a group of nuns. Their moral standards were high. As in England, they wore pinafores, and ties, and she got to learn such things as cricket, croquet, fencing and rugby. She was taught the values of God, resolving she would keep her chastity till marriage. By 16, she had matured into a beautiful, slim blonde. Boys flocked to her like pins to a magnet. The doctrines of St Theresa's always held her in check. Ann kept her chastity. Still, peer pressure made her stay out late, do some booze, try cigarettes, and even the occasional cigar. She had the occasional boyfriend but it was strictly no intimacy, take it or leave it.

It was at the age of twenty, in her final year at Yale, that she began to experience some unusual pain and discomfort in her lower abdomen. Most times the pain was bearable, but often it was so intense she could barely stand up. When the pain reached its worst, she decided to see a doctor at Woodlake Hospital, which was a security-cleared hospital in Bethesda. There, she went through a battery of tests, and an investigative laparoscopy.

Dr Cohen, the gynaecology consultant came into the sterile recovery room after the procedure. 'It's endometriosis, Ann,' he said sombrely.

She was startled. 'Endo-what?'

'Endometriosis,' the doctor repeated, scratching his thinning scalp. He looked so much like a whacky scientist.

'What exactly is that?' Ann nervously twisted her blue hospital gown.

'The lining of the womb is called the endometrium,' Dr Cohen explained. 'It's under the influence of female hormones. Somehow, similar endometrial-like tissues have appeared in other areas where they should not be such as your fallopian tubes and ovaries. Just like in the womb they respond to hormones. These tissues are causing a blockage in your tubes. That's what's giving you the pain.'

'What does that mean?'

'It means the eggs cannot move freely from your ovaries down your Fallopian tubes, where they can be fertilised.'

'What does that mean in plain language, doctor?'

Dr Cohen shook his head sadly. 'You may never conceive naturally.'

This wasn't the kind of news or diagnosis she had expected. In all her reckoning she assumed it was merely serious period pains. But that she may not be able to conceive? It was a bombshell. She tried to speak but could not. Her hands trembled.

Like all women she had planned her life meticulously. One major part of her plan was that she would get married to a good man, have kids, and raise those kids. Take them out, love them, discipline them, and help them be the best they could be. She even had a box in her room where she kept children's books, which she had been buying in anticipation. But now this? So all that would not happen now!

A million and one thoughts ran through her head. What if her husband wanted kids? Then it would have to be adoption. What if he wanted his own natural kids? What if she couldn't provide him with the kids he wanted? Would he then play the field with other women? And now, would she have to explain to every man who was interested in her that she may not be able to have kids? Would they stay with her after that or take to their heels?

'Is…isn't there something you can do?' Ann stuttered, her emerald eyes fixed on Dr Cohen.

'Yours is one of the most severe cases I have come across in my entire professional career. Now what's happening is that the human body—your body—is trying to cope with it. So, your body's soldiers, the white blood cells are prowling around in your womb, and treating any object in the womb as a foreign body, including semen, and instantly killing them off. Your womb is basically a hostile environment.'

Ann looked on in shocked silence, totally devastated.

'Because of the advanced lesions in your abdomen,' Dr. Cohen continued, 'I took the professional decision to use a laser to burn off all the growth…well as much as we could manage anyway, but the only problem is…' He paused, knowing full well, how difficult all this had to be for her. 'The only problem is, there is no lasting solution. Once you start your monthly cycle again, all the endometrium will also bleed when you have your periods. Of course, since they have no means of escaping the body like the rest of your periods, they will simply adhere to whatever surface they find, hence the whole cycle starts over. What we can do now is put you on the most effective treatment we have at our disposal. If you wish, we think we should embark on a drug-induced menopause for a few months.'

24

'Menopause?' Ann cried, aghast. What was he talking about? Menopause was for older women who were done with child bearing, not for young women like her who *wanted* children. She wanted kids! Didn't Dr Cohen understand that she wanted children?

'I don't want a menopause,' she cried, near tears. Then she realised Dr Cohen probably knew what he was talking about. 'Is-is there an alternative?'

'We'll see what we can do, Ann but I can't promise anything as your case is quite severe. You could be lucky and get pregnant, but the chances are slim. I'm sorry.'

Ann flopped back into her bed. Only twenty, her world had suddenly collapsed.

She might never be a mother. She sobbed for days.

From then on, the sad news made her see nursing mothers in a different light. Before, when she saw a mother with her baby, it hadn't meant much. But now, she took notice of young mothers. They had something she wanted. Children were so precious. Life was so valuable. Being able to get pregnant at all was a blessing, not a right. She would give anything to have a baby. Anything!

She shared her grief with her father. He was very consoling. 'Ann, don't worry about it. I'll be there for you. When you get married and you're doing the things you should with your husband, I'm sure something will happen.'

That always consoled her.

One day, Ann went shopping at Tyson's Corner, a huge shopping mall in McLean, northwest of Washington. She wore a grey skirt suit and grey suede pumps, and looked every inch a lady executive. She was trying out a pair of stilettos at *Trendy Maya's* when she observed a pudgy young mother in jeans staring at her. The young mother had two cute, bubbly boys in a pram. She pushed her pram over and smiled warmly.

'I've been looking at you,' she said. 'You look smart, you look beautiful, and you look successful. You must be a professional.'

Ann smiled warmly. 'Thanks.'

'I wish I had a good career like you. What do you do?'

'I'm in real estate. Nothing stops you from having a career if you want to.'

'Nothing? What can I do with these babies? They are a handful. I hate them!'

'What?' Ann glared at the young mother. 'You hate them? Give them to me then.'

'But you don't understand…my career.'

'Shut up!' Ann screeched. 'A career? You better count your blessings, young lady!'

Ann couldn't bear to be around the young mother for a second longer. She dashed out of the shoe shop. 'She envies me for things that are not valuable,' Ann muttered as she cut through the crowded mall. 'Oh God, what kind of life is this? What kind of woman is she? What is a career? Is it dedicating one's soul to building another person's business? What use is it being a professional? I'd give anything to be like her. I'd give anything to be a mother! Anything to hold a child in my arms. Anything!'

Heartbroken, and dejected, Ann sat in her car in the multi-storey car park. 'I want a child,' she sobbed, laying her head on the steering wheel. 'I want a child.'

She hurt to the depths of her soul. Then something broke within her. 'The doctors are mistaken,' she told herself, lifting her head and gazing blankly through the windshield. 'Yes, they are! What do doctors know anyway? Nothing. They tell me I won't have a child? What a bunch of jokers! Doctors are not gods. I will have a child. Not only that, I'll have many children. With or without the doctors. With or without endometriosis or whatever they call it. I don't need doctors to tell me how to have children. No. I know what I have to do!'

Her mind flashed to Marcus Fraser, the aspiring surgeon she was dating at the time. Marcus was virile. He fathered two children by two different women long before he met Ann. He'd let her know that right from the start. She was okay with it. After all, a virile man was helpful to her cause.

Marcus had been trying to get into her skirt for months. She always refused, vowing to be upright, and only give herself to the man she married. That was how she had been taught at St Theresa's.

She got out her phone and dialled Marcus. 'I'm ready,' she said softly. Regrettably.

She started her car, sobbing as she drove to his hospital. This was not what she wanted but she would go ahead with it anyway. They tried for fourteen months. The pregnancy test never turned blue.

The problem was not with Marcus, Ann knew. Marcus had fathered two children already. And whilst they were dating, Marcus was cheating, and had gotten one of his female Hispanic patients pregnant. That made him a father of three. The Hispanic patient felt Marcus was not giving her enough attention, and she lodged a complaint of misconduct against him with The DC Board of Medicine. The board sent down an attractive middle-aged female investigator to interview Marcus about the incident. The investigation degenerated into a farce as the investigator and Marcus seemed to have an eye for each other. She found him not at fault. A month or so later, as if to show his appreciation he gave her a present: he got her pregnant as well. So, he was now a father of four. The Hispanic woman returned to create a big scene in Marcus' surgery on account of child support payments, and had to be removed by the police. Gossiping staff then informed Ann.

The whole episode proved to Ann that the problem was certainly not with Marcus, who was getting everyone else pregnant, and scoring left, right and centre.

But not with her.

It finally sank in. The doctors were right. She would never have a child. For his antics, she split up with Marcus.

'Will I ever have a child?' she sobbed into her pillow. 'Will I ever get pregnant? Will I ever become a mother?'

7

It was now two years after she split up with Marcus. By now, Ann was slowly accepting that she may never have a baby. She tried not to worry too much about this. Instead, she channelled her energies into her work. Ann held the post of Vice President (Sales) at Denney Lee Associates, one of Washington DC's most reputable property firms. Her job involved checking out homes and property, which had been put up for sale, evaluating them, finding buyers and ensuring her company made a profit. Because of this, Ann was always on the move.

Today had been tough, but Ann was happy. She finally closed the sale on a $500,000 home in Hillcrest Heights, south of Washington. She arrived home in high spirits.

Sitting on her front porch was a conical package about two feet high, wrapped in elegant, blue wrapping paper.

What's this?

It was a giant bouquet of white carnations, tulips and roses, with her name boldly written on it.

Gosh! Someone's sent me flowers?

Her mood improved even more.

A rush of excitement built up inside her. She was twenty-four. There was no man in her life at the moment, so she was thrilled.

She smelt the flowers.

Who sent them?

Excited, she read the white card:

To a beautiful woman. Let's start talking.
- Leroy

Leroy watched with interest from afar, twiddling his goatee. What would she do? Smile? Say thanks? Or come over and plant a wet kiss on him?

She scowled. Then she dumped the bouquet in the trash can, and went indoors, slamming the door.

What? Leroy smiled. *Feisty?*

He knew how to deal with that. He went to her blue Toyota and deflated her tyre.

8

On Saturdays, Ann attended salsa dance lessons in Bethesda. Her instructor demanded her students dress the part, so, Ann wore a short, sexy, black Latin dance dress, and black Mary-Jane shoes. As required, her hair was styled in a formal updo. She stepped out of their mansion looking elegant and chic, like a model out of a men's magazine.

The sun was high in the sky. The marigolds, snapdragons, and bluebells bordering the front lawn were in full bloom. As she approached her car she saw that something was not quite right about it—one of the front tyres had gone flat.

'Trust my luck. Sweet. Just sweet. Now, I've got to change the wheel.'

She folded her arms and looked around the driveway. 'Sugar!' she swore, flustered.

Then she remembered she should call the breakdown service. She drew her cell phone from her bag and dialled Ramsay's Service. The dispatcher said, 'I'll send someone over but I'm sorry, we can't get to you for about an hour.'

'But I need to go out,' Ann protested.

'I'm sorry ma'am, but tyre replacement—at home—is not considered a priority. You're not stranded on the highway. Since you're at home you've got shelter.'

Bother. Ann switched off her phone. *I need to get to my dance class!* Their instructor was a grumpy little bitch. She whined when anyone was late. *Okay, you know what? I'll just change it myself. Everybody does.*

She opened the trunk. There was supposed to be something called a jack in there, and also, a spare tyre. She scavenged the trunk and found both. Ann brought out the jack. The jackscrew was lubricated with sticky grease. Dirty, oily thing. She held it gingerly between her thumb and index finger then let it drop to the ground. She attempted to lift out the spare tyre. It was heavy, cumbersome, and it soiled her hands.

'Sugar!'

'Do you need help?' a smooth masculine voice asked from behind.

Without turning she knew it was Leroy, the new guard, the irritating, ogling one who sent the flowers. His cologne wafted from his brown suit. *My goodness, he even wears a perfume. Do rodents do that?*

Armani or Gucci? she wondered vainly. *Nah, he's not that posh, probably air-freshener.*

'No,' she snapped, knowing fully well she needed help.

'Fine.' He shrugged and backed off.

As Leroy left, Ann knew her chance of getting help was slipping away. She hadn't even been able to lift the wheel out of the trunk, talk more of changing it. And bending over whilst wearing such a skimpy dress? The view would be totally X-rated. 'Er...okay, I need to get the wheel changed,' she conceded.

'Do you need help?' He wanted her to say it. He wanted to break that silly pride.

'Is it not obvious?' She flashed a you're-really-not-so-smart look across her pretty face.

'Yes or no?'

It was now clear Leroy was playing hardball. 'Okay, yes.' She frowned and folded her arms indignantly.

'Fine. Step back.'

He took off his brown jacket to reveal his huge outsize holster. A gleaming Uzi sub-machine gun nestled inside. He smiled within. Deflating her tyre was a superb idea. Damsel in distress. Knight to the rescue. Never mind if the knight created the distress. Taking liberties, he dumped his jacket inside her car then heaved the spare wheel out of the trunk.

31

She watched as he expertly changed the wheel. He was done in three minutes.

'You can fix this one at Tyrefit.' He tossed the bad wheel into the trunk effortlessly like some John Rambo. 'There's one on King Road, next to McDonald's.'

'Thanks, Skinner,' she said reluctantly, referring to him by his CIA code name.

'The name's Leroy,' he corrected, still playing hardball.

She forced a smile. *Hard nut*. 'Thanks, Leroy.'

He returned the smile.

He had a nice smile.

That evening, he placed another bouquet of flowers at her door.

9

Cagley was hooked up to a blood bag, drip, and other life support systems, and flown on a hospital plane to San Francisco. The hospital plane was a converted C-54. Its fuselage contained rows of trolley beds, occupied by injured soldiers, some with missing limbs, groaning from discomfort and pain. A doctor and a few nurses scampered around, attending to as many patients as they could. All through the journey, Cagley gasped and struggled for every breath as he fought to stay alive. His lungs were punctured. Numerous times he slipped in and out of consciousness.

Then his heart stopped. The monitor attached to his chest beeped.

A nurse shouted, 'Crash! Crash!'

Within seconds, the doctor and nurses surrounded his trolley. They resuscitated him, pumping on his heart, and chest.

After a tense minute, Cagley's heart regained function. Having been clutched from the hands of death, a nurse watched him at all times till the flight landed in San Francisco where a waiting ambulance took him straight to Letterman Army Hospital.

Army surgeons battled to save his life, performing three major operations to remove deeply embedded shrapnel from his body. Cagley was strong and took the treatment but it was three weeks before he was considered stable.

But his suffering was not over. For the next three months he battled pain with every breath. Three months of not being able to find a comfortable position to sleep. He had lots and lots of painkillers—till they became like food.

'Curse the sergeant,' he swore bitterly. 'Curse him for this. I hope he rots in hell. I'll never forgive him for this. Nurse!'

Slowly, he healed. After nine months he left the hospital with two visible scars on his face and several on his body. The Army awarded him a National Defense Service Medal, and he was given an honourable discharge. He returned home to Little Wee Brook in Kansas. When his mother saw him she cried non-stop for two hours.

While in Korea, Cagley learned many of life's lessons. The first was Love, which Soo Min Ji taught him. He thought of her often. She would always be a part of him. Always.

He had also learned to be wary of enemies, something Sergeant Ken so ruthlessly hammered into him. He had joined the Army as a life-loving boy—innocent, trusting, and full of hope— but because of his experiences in the hands of Sergeant Ken, he left it as a battered, sceptical man.

Korea also taught him the value of education. In Korea there was a world of difference between the officers and the men. The officers lived well, gave orders, and didn't die very often. The men lived rough, took orders, and died like fleas. He made a comparison between two 24-year-old soldiers, one a captain, the other a corporal. They both hailed from Missouri. The captain had a college degree; the corporal had nothing. So, education had to be the key.

He had to acquire an education.

New York with its skyscrapers and institutions was rumoured to be the land of opportunity, the place to get an education or make a fortune. It was also the place he always wished to go. Three months after returning home, despite his mother's pleas and tears, he packed his bags and went to New York. There, he rented a room in a grimy part of The Bronx.

He quickly saw that New York was not all it was hyped up to be. The land of opportunity? Rubbish! There were no opportunities except the ones you created yourself. The high-life? That was only on Broadway. The sophisticated girls? Mostly hookers, gold-diggers and girlfriends of gangsters. On the whole, New York was as congested as a stuffy nose. And someone got shot everyday.

With New York being such a letdown he kept his focus on his goal: an education. He studied during the day and worked nights as a porter at Manhattan's Winchester Hotel on 55th Street. By sheer determination, four years later he made it into Cornell University. He chose Cornell to prove that he could be as good as anyone else—if not better. He finished with a summa cum laude in Psychology with emphasis on Criminology.

After Cornell, the Washington DC Metropolitan Police Department offered him a job as a profile officer. He packed his belongings and moved to DC.

Something known as DC fever infects all who venture into Washington DC, America's seat of power. The sufferer often develops a craving for power, accompanied by a love of intrigue and politicking.

Cagley developed a chronic case of DC fever. Suddenly, working in the Police back office was not enough. Now, he wanted to be someone that mattered; someone that could get things done. Someone with power. He wanted to be a top dog. But he didn't want to be a politician. He hated politicians. They were hypocrites; a bunch of noisy zeroes and scumbags obtaining power by manipulating people.

The late fifties and early sixties were the height of the cold war in which Russia and the communists kept sabre rattling with America and its allies. The Central Intelligence Agency was at the forefront of the battle against the Russians. For Cagley, the CIA held unspoken mystery. He was enchanted by its eerie secrecy and its legendary, unseen power. The silent power was the most potent. Cagley chased his CIA dream and after only two years in the Metropolitan police he was accepted into the CIA. The first day he walked through the turnstiles in May 1964 was a great day for him.

On a very cold January morning in 1966, his Ford broke down near the Arlington National Cemetery. It was minus three degrees; the ponds were frozen and the trees were covered with snow and icicles. Cagley abandoned the car by the roadside and tried to hitch a ride. But the buses were not running since the roads were too dangerous. Cagley's toes had gone numb when an expensive Cadillac pulled over.

A petite young woman with flaming red hair rolled down the window. She looked so mild you could mistake her for an angel. 'Do you need a ride?' She had a trustworthy smile.

'Thanks,' he mumbled.

She reached across and opened the door. He got in. She had a picture of the Virgin Mary on the dashboard. Her name was Eunice, and she was the daughter of a wealthy factory owner in Virginia. She drove Cagley all the way to CIA headquarters at Langley.

They became friends. Eventually, he married her. She bore him a daughter—Ann.

Ambition is a dangerous thing. It has ruined many men, and changed countless more. Ambition drove Cagley through the ranks of the CIA. But a part of Korea stayed with him. His experiences in the hands of Sergeant Ken made him see his contemporaries as enemies, which had to be viciously liquidated or vanquished. They were obstacles barring his way to the top; to the position of CIA Director.

To overcome his contemporaries he studied the art of politicking. He learned the essentials: back-patting followed by back-stabbing. Soon, he became masterful at undermining his superiors. He became an expert at eliminating his contemporaries. Office politics, Washington politics, and power politics—he became adept at them all. He leaked information that should not be leaked whilst leaving traces that made his contemporaries look inadequate and ordinary. Worse, he enjoyed it; something most people didn't. He loved the thrill of it. Watching you own back, whilst exposing that of others; having no permanent friends, only permanent interests; saying nothing yet saying so much; saying so much and yet saying nothing.

'You're changing,' Eunice observed as she knotted his tie,

one day. She always did his tie for him. 'This isn't the Mike I used to know. My Mike was lovely. The Mike I'm seeing nowadays is mean-spirited, and will destroy anything that stands between him and what he wants. Why did you hide that dossier from Tom Summers?'

'I took the dossier, but what the hell? That's how the game is played, dammit. Every game has its rules. Learn the rules. That's how you survive.'

'You've become mean. Selfish. Almost evil.'

He only shrugged. 'It's a harsh world out there.'

'It's harsh because people make it harsh. People like you,' she said softly.

Again, he shrugged. He would be leaving the top secret dossier he took from Tom Summers' table on the train. Then he would get a little old lady to alert the police to its presence. Of course, the police would take the presence of a CIA folder on the train as a serious incident; there would be a massive uproar. Tom Summers would be accused of negligence and being careless with a classified document. He was on his way out of the agency.

Michael Cagley was now no longer the victim of injustice but a perpetrator of injustice. Cross him at your peril.

10

'Thanks for the flowers, Leroy. They were nice.' Ann smiled warmly as she got out of her car. The car, a gift from her father for her 21st birthday, was filled with brown grocery bags. She had been doing the household shopping since she turned sixteen. She had two credit cards charged to her father's account.

'I'm, glad you like them,' Leroy said.

'Carnations are my favourite. You got it right.'

'You know what, Ann? My mother often says, "If you truly appreciate something, show it, don't say it."'

She looked him in the eyes and smiled coyly. She knew he was up to something. 'How do I show appreciation for a bouquet of flowers?'

'By letting me take you to lunch at Sioux Place on Saturday.'

Ann tossed her blonde head back and laughed. She had not expected that. Smooth Operator. Hmmm. Sioux Place was a trendy restaurant in Silver Spring, north of Washington DC. They had the best rack of ribs on the planet. Their ribs were dipped in rich, thick, smoky barbecue sauce, and tender enough to peel off the bone with a toothpick. Thinking of those ribs, fries, and hot, buttered corn on the cob made her salivate.

'I'll think about it,' she said.

'In my books that means, yes. Saturday. Sioux Place. Two o'clock?'

'Er...er—'

'Think of those nice juicy ribs, Ann. Steak, fries, linguine, seafood, salad...'

'Sounds good but I'll have to decline. I'm sorry.'

He sensed she was interested yet she seemed to be holding back. 'Why? Don't you like good food?'

'I do.'

'You're not on a diet, are you?'

'It's not that, Leroy. I'm sorry.'

'So, what would it be?'

'You won't understand.'

'Try me.'

'Well…'

'Tell me.'

Since he was so persistent she took a chance, and opened up. 'My dad.'

'Your father?'

'Yes.'

'What has going to Sioux Place got to do with him?'

'He won't be happy with it. My dad can be awkward. He has this particular mind-set. Now that I'm twenty-four he reckons I should be looking to get married. His idea of a marriage is a Washington DC society marriage. If you're not the son of a general or a senator or the son of one of his big shot Washington friends he doesn't think you're good enough. You're one of his guards, his staff. He won't see it the way you do, you know, as two people trying to get together. He'll see it as betrayal. I don't want you getting in trouble. That's why.' She looked into Leroy's face. 'He could be dangerous. You never can tell what he's going to do.'

Leroy knew Ann was right about her father. Within the CIA Cagley was called many names such as Maniac, Psycho, Bulldog, Little Terror—and these were the nice ones. Cagley was greatly feared in the CIA. He had absolutely no regard for anyone; he was brash, ruthless, and routinely barked at staff. That was his style. Despite these traits he made good decisions and so commanded great respect. And the President—the only one who did matter—considered him a valuable ally. Leroy and Cagley had never crossed paths but Leroy knew a few people who had. His mind went to a security officer named

Doug Miller. Miller had been detailed to escort Cagley on a trip. Miller had terrible manners, which everyone complained about. Miller was in the car with Cagley when for some bizarre reason he decided to break wind. Cagley was so furious that he ordered his driver to stop the car. He ordered Miller out of his Cadillac and made the driver drive off! Not such a bad thing except they were in Arizona, right in the middle of the desert! Miller had to walk fifteen miles to the nearest town.

Leroy watched as Ann carried the shopping into the house. He was aware of her brazen father but that didn't stop him from being attracted to her. To begin with, he'd liked her good looks. Now, after guarding their mansion for a few weeks, her looks were no longer what he saw. It was her demeanour. She was sincere with a bubbly disposition. She was the kind of girl who could not hide what she felt. If she was happy she was gleeful; if she was sad she could not hide it. She was transparent and light-hearted, a woman that would be easy to get along with. There was also that subtle thing about her. It was intangible and inexplicable, but whatever it was, it made him want to be around her. Even if her father was the devil—that would not stop him from getting close to her.

'I'll take the risk,' he told her when she returned to the door.

'I don't want you in trouble, Leroy.' Her worried look indicated her words came from the depth of her heart.

He looked into her pretty face. She was decent. Polished. Refined. Talk about a clean woman. Not the kind of woman to be found drunk, stumbling out of a bar. She probably wouldn't even visit a bar. He could feel the depth of her concern.

'Let me worry about that, Ann.' He reached out and held her fingers. 'He doesn't have to know, does he? You're not going to tell him, are you?'

Looking into his face, she saw an option. True. Her father really didn't have to know. No one had asked her out on a date in a long time. Well, that wasn't true. Two guys had asked lately: one that dressed like a Harlem pimp, and the other—well, he just had to be a dope dealer. Washington seemed to be running out of decent, eligible men.

She smiled. 'Okay then. Sioux Place. Saturday. Can we do a late lunch—say 4 o'clock? I have salsa lessons at two.'

'Okay, it's a date.'

'Leroy? My dad must not find out,' she warned again. 'I can't tell what he'll do if he does.'

Leroy grinned. 'We'll keep it to ourselves. Our little secret. I'll pick you at the Little Mo on Connecticut Avenue.'

11

Ann hadn't had so much fun in a long time. Sioux Place had a cowboys and Indians theme, complete with tepees, stagecoaches, and sets of an eighteenth century cowboy town. The food was served by waiters dressed as cowboys, sheriffs and saloon keepers. They even had harlots in long pink, low-cut gowns complete with beauty moles on their faces.

Leroy and Ann had a great meal. They ate their way through two platters of smoky ribs, and sauce, and a mountain of fries. In the corner, a cowboy twanged fast-paced country music from a banjo. Leroy drank a Budweiser; Ann settled for sweet, red wine.

Ann saw that Leroy the bodyguard was very different from Leroy, the person. As a bodyguard he looked stern, wore dark Raybans and earpieces, and carried two guns. The day she first saw him he came across like a cocky, ogling pervert.

The real Leroy was surprisingly well-mannered, while at the same time a little artful. Okay, he opened doors for her but then he did ninety miles in a fifty mile-zone. What was it with men and reckless speed? Also, the real Leroy was a little deeper than she thought, and more responsible than he presented himself. She deduced this when his cell phone rang halfway through their meal. It was his mother. Ann couldn't help overhearing the conversation. Although Leroy tried to speak as discreetly as he could she still made out the fact that he always sent four hundred dollars to her in New York every month. That really impressed Ann. On the other hand when a cop pulled them over after they left Sioux Place because Leroy was speeding, he *forgot* a twenty-dollar bill between his driver's license and the registration card. Naughty Brooklyn boy. Naughty, naughty. He would do anything to get off the hook.

She had thought the date would end after Sioux Place but he took her on a speedboat ride on the Potomac. After that, they walked through the park and bought ice cream from a vendor. By now it was 6.30 in the evening, and having been together for a few hours the ice had long been broken, and they chatted freely as if they had been friends forever.

At 7 o'clock, she thought he would drop her off, but instead, holding her hand, he led her into a cinema. Talk about a marathon date.

After the movie he drove her to Connecticut Avenue, where she had left her car. His stereo was on full blast and they were both caterwauling *Long Time* by Arrow whilst raising their hands exuberantly through the sunroof of Leroy's red Honda Civic. He played one timeless sing-along party song after the other: *Set it Off* by Strafe, *It Takes Two* by Rob Base and E-Z Rock, *Curious* by Midnight Star, and *Finest* by SOS Band. The music brought back memories of the fun time she had at fraternity parties back at Yale.

She got home at ten. Her father wasn't home. Most Saturdays he was at a cottage known as Windwood near Baltimore, meeting up with Lizzy Bottagano. Ann thought it appropriate to call Leroy and thank him for the wonderful date. They ended up chatting till 4.00 am.

*　　*　　*

Cagley rose through the ranks of the CIA to become a section chief. He was posted to Egypt as Station Chief in 1973, and then to Brazil.

It was a rainy night in Brasilia in 1975. Cagley was working late at his office in the US Embassy. At that time, he was the CIA head of Station. It was sometime after 8 o'clock when he heard the Marine guards at the gate yelling out orders. Between Venetian blind slats he made out two women and two men. They stood outside the gates of the embassy. All four wore combat trousers and blue vests. They were trying to push their way into the embassy. The pair of Marine guards were trying to keep them out. The invaders were obviously unarmed, and not hostile.

Cagley and the Marines had seen it happen many times—people turning up at the embassy and demanding US protection or seeking asylum. As the most senior person on duty, he went downstairs to the gate. When he saw one of the women, a big-chested oriental woman, he stopped in his tracks. He didn't believe in ghosts but she looked so much like Soo Min Ji... The only difference was that this one had noticeably huge breasts. Otherwise, they were identical twins.

'Hold on,' he ordered the Marines. 'Take them into the gatehouse. I want to question them.'

'Sir!'

He questioned her. Her name was Lizzy, she told him. Lizzy Bottagano. She was a Bolivian, and was now disillusioned with the Bolivian Communist Guerrilla Revolutionary Movement of which she was a member. So many communist revolutionary groups pervaded South America in the seventies—from the Sandinistas in Nicaragua to FARC in Columbia. Lizzy said Communism had only succeeded in creating a new elite: the leadership. The comrades in power lived in luxury whilst the masses languished in depravation. So, she had deserted the communists. And they were now after her life. Therefore, she wanted asylum in the United States.

At first, Cagley thought he was being given another shot at life with Soo Min Ji. Using his CIA leverage he got her out of South America, and resettled her in the United States. The process took a few weeks. At the end he found he was living in fantasyland. This turned out not to be another shot at Soo Min Ji but a disaster. He had his hands full of two women! Lizzy was younger, voracious, and a bit of a wild rose but with nothing else to offer. And Eunice? Well, she was his ever-bearing, and ever-loving wife—mild, soft-spoken, responsible,

44

though not as voracious as he wanted.

What was he to do?

His ambition to become CIA Director helped him make a decision. A relationship with Lizzy would not help his cause if it became public knowledge. It would be a scandal. Eunice suited his ambitions, and so, it was settled. Lizzy had to go in the doghouse.

So, he bought Lizzy a car, provided her with a club membership, and put her on an allowance. But he didn't touch her; he kept her at a safe distance.

Cagley continued his rise up the CIA ladder. During the Beirut hostage crisis he returned to Langley HQ to take up post as chief of Counterintelligence.

In July 1978, Ann returned from school and discovered her ever-loving mother sprawled face down on the carpet, her flaming red hair spread all about her. She grabbed the phone and called her father. 'Dad, Dad! I just got back from school, and Mom's on the floor. She's not moving. There's blood on her head!'

'What? Call 911 now. I'm on my way!'

The doctors could not revive Eunice. She had tripped over the cord of the table lamp near the sofa and hit her head against the coffee table. It was evident from the deep gash on her forehead, and the fact that her foot was still entangled in the cable.

Cagley was strong and he quickly recovered.

Six months after Eunice's death he told Ann about Lizzy. 'I loved your mother. But now, she's dead. And I'm certainly not going to get castrated.' Cagley did not mince words.

Ann understood. Men were like broken down cars—always in need of servicing. So, Lizzy became his mistress. But he kept her away from his home. In fact, Ann did not know who she was.

After heading the counterintelligence division for four years, Cagley became Deputy Director (Operations) and eventually, Director.

Now aged fifty-seven, and standing a mere five feet, six inches tall, Michael Cagley was a harsh little man with a mop of grey hair flattened over his oblong skull. His eyes were narrow, grey and cold as tombstones. His lips were so thin they were virtually nonexistent. His face was a permanent scowl. His scowl betrayed two things about him: he was decisive and he was hard. Rather than speak, he mumbled. He was a tough cookie who smoked 40 Marlboros a day, the fearless one who berated the Vice President as "full of hot crap"—to his face. The Vice President could do nothing. The Director of the CIA answered to the President and Congress only, and in some regimes, held Cabinet rank.

Word within the CIA was that Cagley had only ever smiled once—when he got appointed CIA Director—and that smile wasn't even for joy. It was because he was now in a position to fire one of his office adversaries, a certain man named Neil Porter. Needless to say, Neil lost his job the next day.

It was now well over thirty-five years since Korea. Cagley had managed to get a lot of the things that happened in Korea out of his mind. Still, occasionally, Soo Min Ji popped into his mind. That had to happen, he knew. She had made such a big impact on him; every traumatic event in Korea happened directly because of her. She was a major milestone in his life. Every time he saw the scars left by the land mine, he thought of her. Often when he saw Lizzy, she reminded him of her. Besides, one never forgets a soul mate.

12

'Why don't you have a housekeeper?' Leroy watched Ann remove a tempting casserole from the oven. 'I thought you would have one.'

Leroy stood in the kitchen doorway at the rear of Cagley's mansion, looking into the big, modern kitchen. He did not enter. CIA rules prohibited him from stepping inside the actual mansion.

'You should ask my dad,' Ann replied, removing her oven gloves. 'We used to have a cook and a housekeeper, but he sent them away. On my twenty-first birthday.'

Leroy was amused. 'Strange gift, that.'

'He gave me a car and a credit card, which I really loved, but the same day he called me into the kitchen and said, "Ann, I love you, but it is my duty to train you. You're twenty-one today. You can't cook, and you're not keen to learn. Because of that I've fired Bovi and Carol. That's an oven; there's the food. Cook or starve!"'

'Your dad is hard nut!' Leroy cried, almost admiringly. 'A straight-talking hard nut.'

'He is. But I see his point. If he didn't fire Bovi I probably would never have learned. Now, I'm better prepared to cope with a home. I'm so good at it now that I don't spend much time in the kitchen,' she gloated.

'I love a woman who cooks. I love my food. I should thank your dad.'

'Is that what's important to you in a woman?' Ann asked, rolling her beautiful emerald eyes. 'Food only?'

She asked this question because she wanted to know what he

47

genuinely thought of her. After all, it was now four weeks since they went to Sioux Place. Despite that she hadn't been able to gauge exactly where he was going with their relationship. She didn't want to assume anything and then invest so much emotion only to be let down. She wanted to know now. Before things went too far. Already, unwittingly, her feelings were involved. He was having an impact on her life. She didn't realise how much till earlier that day when her boss, a bearded man named Jake, came into her office.

'Ann, you're not concentrating on your work lately.' Jake held out the evaluation figures she had calculated for a client. 'You got the figures wrong by one hundred thousand dollars.'

Ann could only blush. Such a catastrophic mistake.

Yes, Jake, she thought. *These days, my mind's never here. I keep looking forward to the evenings when I'll return home to the company of Leroy, my dad's bodyguard.*

'Why is that?'

I'm sorry, Jake. I was on the phone to...Leroy.

'Also, I noticed you no longer put in any extra hours these days. What's going on?'

Yes. I've got a life now. Sorry. Previously, I convinced myself that my job was all I needed. Now, I realise that work is just a ruse to cover what was really missing: a man.

Realising she was getting emotionally committed to Leroy, she asked herself the questions women ask: where was the relationship going? Why was he seeing her? Was it only to sow his wild oats or was it love? Or maybe he didn't even know what he wanted; a lot of men didn't. That was why she decided to ask, but ask cunningly.

'What do you mean?' Leroy asked.

'When you see a woman what are the key things you watch out for? Is it her looks, or her body? Is it her mind or her culinary skills? What do you look out for?'

'I would say her behaviour first,' he answered, thinking deep. 'Living with a pretty woman who has an ugly attitude is like living with an ogre. But a woman with a face like a pig who has a pleasant personality…well, you can get over the face. Her manners brighten the day.'

'And her body?' *Is he only after my body? Sex? Get his kicks and leave?*

'Important,' he answered.

'Why can't men simply love a woman for who she is? She's not just a body, you know.'

'Men are creatures of sight, Ann. That will never change. The first thing a man sees is a snapshot of how a woman looks, and behaves. That's the way it is. Once he gets past that then he considers other things.'

'No consideration whatsoever for her mind?'

'Do you pick up a book without being attracted to the cover?'

'No.'

'I rest my case then.'

She hadn't gotten any answers. She decided to go another route. 'Who was your first girlfriend?'

'Why do you ask?'

'You told me men are creatures of sight. I'll tell you something about women: we are creatures of the mind. Also, women, by nature, are insecure. Often, we try to hide it. Other times we try to show it, expecting men to pick up on it, and address it, but you guys just don't have a clue.'

'Oh yeah?'

'Yeah. We also like to be the best and to thrive. Women will tend to ask about your previous women, and your likes. It's not to persecute you but to make a comparison, to learn, and adjust.

'Well, it's a long story…'

'I've got my whole life. I'm listening.'

'Okay then.' He sighed. 'In my second year at Syracuse University I met a girl called Elaine Morris. She was from Cleveland and she studied Economics. We were the hottest couple on campus, inseparable. Everyone assumed we were destined for marriage. On Elaine's nineteenth birthday we decided to have a party. Deep into the night, the DJ played slow love songs. "It's time for the celebrant to have a spotlight dance with her man," he announced. I buttoned up my tuxedo. But guess what? Elaine was clinging to a guy named Trey. I was stunned. I thought she'd had too much to drink or something. I went to her. She turned and stared at me. "Who are you?" she asked. "It's me," I replied, and I tried to drag her away. Guess what happened next?'

'What?' Ann was all ears.

'She screamed, "I don't know you! Will someone save me from this lunatic?"'

'She said that?'

Leroy bit his lip. 'I was young, just twenty. I was just a kid from Brooklyn. She was my first girlfriend. I was so traumatised I didn't speak for two days. Not because I lost Elaine, it was the treachery. How could she date someone else behind my back? We hardly spent a day apart!'

Ann stared at him, gobsmacked.

'I thought I knew all her secrets!' Leroy cried. 'Never think you know a woman's secrets. How long had it been going on?'

'That must have been hard on you, Leroy. I'm really sorry about that.' She looked into his face. He looked forlorn and sad. It had been a traumatic experience for him. Aw, poor Leroy. He'd been hurt. Like many other people out there.

'It made me distrust women. I saw them as these deadly creatures that kept dark secrets. I didn't want to get into deep relationships. Purely platonic. And so, my evaluation of women became their bodies: how curvy, how pretty, and how voluptuous.'

'Aha!' she cried. 'Now, I know why sometimes when you're talking to me, your eyes keep straying to my chest. Breasts seem to be a man thing.'

He grinned. 'I do that?'

'Mm-hmm.'

'Not my fault. When a girl has 34-Ds or DDs—I don't know which size yours are...' He pointed gingerly at her ample bosom. 'And you sometimes wear these low cut things. What am I to do?'

'Leroy!' Ann protested sternly. 'Gawking at women's boobs is rude!'

'If you don't want it seen why show it? I mean, you're trying to get a decent conversation, and you've got these two round things staring into your face. Now, that's rude. I even learnt you ladies wear special bras to get them popping up. Is that true?'

'Who told you that?'

'We have our sources.'

She giggled. 'Those are top secret women's issues!'

'Not in my part of Brooklyn!'

'Is Brooklyn the good part of New York or the bad part?'

'The part with more men in the morgue than on the street.'

'What?'

Leroy laughed at the shock in her face. 'Posh kid,' he teased. 'You've lived all your life in a mansion, haven't you?'

'May be. Mansion life isn't always fun. My dad has always been strict. I'm sure your parents must have been strict as well, considering. Hmmm?' She nudged him playfully. 'You seem to have turned out pretty well.'

'My father was a soldier. I hardly knew him. He never returned from Vietnam. My mother is the one to be thanked. She's a darling.'

Ann saw a deep smile and twinkle as he mentioned his mum. 'All through my youth she slaved and laboured as a caretaker at Arcadia High School in Cypress Hills. All so I could go to Syracuse.'

'I don't understand why a trendy guy like you would study physics.' She rolled her green eyes. 'You don't look like a nerd to me. Why physics?' She just could not comprehend the sciences; she could not get her head around formulas. To her, those who studied the sciences were like aliens.

'My ambition was to be counted in the league of great physicists like Einstein and Faraday. Maybe even win the Nobel Prize. That was till I saw *Top Gun*, you know, with Tom Cruise. Then I decided to join the Navy but I got a ride in an F-14 at Career Day, and didn't like it much up there. I joined the CIA instead.'

'Hmmm. Since then you've been in DC, living the bachelor life?'

'Yeah, and hanging out with my no-good friends.'

'And your ambitions, Leroy? What do you aspire for?'

'Maybe get an MBA and move into the corporate world.'

Nice, Ann thought. Ambitious. 'What about settling down?'

Leroy checked his watch. 'Almost six. Your dad will be back soon. He shouldn't see us together.'

'I know. Just five more minutes,' she pleaded. She wanted him to linger with her. She thoroughly enjoyed his company. And his witty arguments. Still he hadn't answered her question. 'Have you had anything to eat?'

'No.'

'Let's share some dessert.' She dashed to the fridge and returned with a slice of chocolate cake.'

'You asked me about my ambitions,' Leroy recalled, his mouth stuffed with moist chocolate sponge, his lips smothered with chocolate icing.

'Yes.'

'What are your own ambitions?' he asked.

'To be a mother,' she answered without hesitating. 'Take care of my kids; be a wife—to the right man.'

'Am I the right man?' There was a mischievous twinkle in his eye.

'I'll know…after the first kiss… like Beauty…' she pointed to herself, 'and the Beast,' she pointed at him.

They laughed.

'So, see you tomorrow then? The usual place on Connecticut Avenue?'

'Yes. Leroy, please, this time we see a girlie movie.'

'Okay, fine. You have three choices: Wrestlemania, Terminator or Predator.'

'You're such a tyrant! Men just don't get it, do they?'

He laughed. 'No.'

*   *   *

The Perivale Golf Club was tucked away in the woods of Bethesda. It was a private club with twenty-seven holes, spread over an artificially created hilly terrain, and bordered on all sides by trees. The eighteenth century stone bungalow overlooking the golf course served as the clubhouse. Inside was an exclusive lounge and bar.

Michael Cagley was a member of The Perivale. Clad in green polo shirt and khakis, he entered the clubhouse accompanied by Ann and a bodyguard who carried his golf irons. The guard was Leroy Delgado. Because it was Sunday, the club brimmed with the *ol' boys*, the small cartel of politicians and bureaucrats that ruled America.

A full-bodied woman with oriental features sat in a corner of the cigar-choked clubhouse. She wore a black jumper and black slacks. She looked Korean or Japanese but in reality she was Bolivian. Cagley saw her and looked the other way. She saw him, and looked blankly past him. She was Lizzy Bottagano, his mistress. In public, Cagley and Lizzy never acknowledged each other in any way. That was the way Cagley wanted it: quiet and free of scandal. They would meet later at Windwood, Cagley's secret cottage tucked away in the woods near Baltimore.

Leroy, the security detail, hung back a few yards from Cagley, leaning against the clubhouse window. As the Director's security detail he had to be in clear sight of Cagley at all times. He kept the expected stern face, and watched everyone with an eagle eye.

Ann went to the bar to chat to a friend.

Cagley took a corner table with Brian Goldberg and Tom Deloitte, two of his friends. Tom Deloitte was a white-haired general in the Marines. He had a square jaw. Brian was a Supreme Court judge.

Brian turned to Cagley. 'I was gonna call you, Mike. I've been trying to buy my son a house. Something for his twenty-

53

eighth birthday. Your daughter is into property, right?'

Cagley nodded.

'Can you ask her to see me? She may be able to get me a good deal.'

'What exactly are you thinking of?' Cagley asked, interested. He was always on the lookout for sales leads for Ann.

'Apartment or house. Something really nice. Something Lenny will appreciate.'

'Got anything yet?' Cagley asked.

'Nope. The market's gone crazy.'

'Crazy's not the word,' Deloitte cut in, 'insane is. Homes no better than huts are going for well over a hundred thousand dollars!'

'Yeah,' Brian growled. 'I got a quarter of a million and can't get nothing better than a shack.'

'You know what, Brian?' Cagley pitched. 'My daughter should be able to sort you out. She's around here somewhere.' He looked around the bustling clubhouse. 'By the way, is Lenny still single?'

'Yep,' Brian growled, sipping his drink. 'A million girls in Washington and he can't find one. Don't know what he's waiting for.'

'Ann should be thinking of brooding as well. Why don't you run that by Lenny?'

Deloitte laughed. 'Lenny and Ann? Wedding of the year.'

Brian chuckled. 'Now you know why I'm getting Lenny the house.'

'In that case, you had better make it good,' Cagley quipped.

Brian and Deloitte laughed.

'Ann's around here somewhere.' Cagley peered around again. He saw Ann by the bar, chatting to Sarah Wilcox, daughter of the Secretary of Agriculture. Ann didn't seem interested in the conversation. Half the time, she was looking elsewhere. Cagley followed her gaze. She seemed to be looking in the direction of…the bodyguard.

Cagley finally caught her attention and gestured that she

should come over. Ann approached her father.

'Brian has an interesting proposition for you,' Cagley announced. 'He needs a house and he's willing to spend a quarter of a million.'

Ann smiled and took a seat next to Brian. She never let a sales opportunity slip by. 'I can get you the White House for that amount,' she said beginning a well-rehearsed sales pitch.

Cagley sat back and watched. Occasionally, she glanced in the direction of the bodyguard. She probably didn't know she was doing it. The clubhouse brimmed with senators, judges, generals from the Pentagon, senior staff in the White House, and top level government officials. For once he smiled. He had come a long way from the wheat farms of Kansas and the battlefields of Korea.

He was now a kingmaker.

Cagley watched his bodyguard. He seemed oblivious to the fact that Ann kept looking at him. He kept the usual stern face and watched the space around Cagley as he should. He was either not into Ann or he was damn good actor.

But why does Ann keep glancing at him? What is going on? I hope nothing. For his own sake, I hope nothing.

13

It was dusk. Leroy and Ann stood by the kitchen door at the rear of the Cagley mansion, chatting. They always met when Ann returned from work.

'Why do they call your house The Starving Parrot?' Leroy asked. He liked the orange skirt-suit she wore, and the orange lipstick, and her orange Alice band. Suited her green eyes. 'Weird name.'

'The rumour is that it belonged to a pirate captain called Two Machetes,' Ann answered. 'Two Machetes had a parrot that flew around the ship, listening to the crew and then divulging what they said to Two Machetes. Through the parrot, Two Machetes learnt in advance of plots of mutiny. As punishment he always made the plotters walk the plank.'

'Wow! Mean dude,' he exclaimed.

'The story's not finished. The first mate was a smart guy. He started feeding the parrot exotic food. The parrot switched sides and refused to inform Two Machetes of plans by his first mate to loot treasure, and get rid of Two Machetes. Anyway, the crew mutinied and cast Two Machetes adrift in a small boat in the Caribbean. He wandered the seas for many days till he was at the point of death, but eventually a passing slave ship picked him up.'

'He didn't die?' Leroy asked, feigning deep interest though his mind was on something else.

'He didn't die. The captain was English and didn't know Two Machetes' identity. He brought Two Machetes to Virginia. Two Machetes had hidden treasure in Williamsburg. He came here and bought this house. Then one day, he went to the market and what did he see? His old parrot—in a cage—on sale! He bought it against the parrot's loud protests, brought it home, and starved him to death!'

'Really?'

'So the story goes.'

'What happened after?' he asked, moving closer to Ann.

'Two Machetes was caught and put to death by—'

He could not help himself any longer. Without a word, he drew her close and kissed her full on the lips.

The suddenness of the kiss had a strange effect on her: shock. Still, the intensity of his passion held her mesmerised. There was a way in which he held her and claimed her. It was as if he owned her. He exerted such manly authority that it was overwhelming.

However, she didn't like the fact that she was being kissed without knowing it was coming, and worse, enjoying it. They'd been dating, and of course, she knew that first kiss would come but this one caught her out.

She tried to salvage some dignity. 'I'm not a cheap tart, Leroy.'

'And I don't think I look like a pimp,' he retorted. Then he kissed her again. Powerfully, and deeply.

That kiss sent sparks flying through her body. Against her will, she found herself breathing faster. It was futile, resisting it. She hungrily returned his kisses.

He slowly massaged her back. When his hands approached her buttocks alarm bells rang in her head. She was not a kid; she knew what men wanted. Especially Leroy. She could tell from the lustful, predatory glint in his eyes.

For her, sex was not an alternative form of entertainment. It was something intimate, which a woman gave a man she truly loved; a man that was hers. Even though over the past weeks she'd got to know him better, and seen that he was quite a great guy, she was not at that point yet. She would not give in to him, or indeed anyone. All her life she'd had only one lover, Marcus, the ultra-virile playboy. And she had only slept with him to prove the doctors wrong.

Then a thought popped into her mind: a child. She needed a child!

On that issue she was willing to do anything.

She knew deep in her mind that the problem was not with the man but with her. Still, should she give it a try? Could he give her a child? Could he get her pregnant?

She made a calculated decision.

She led him into the house.

14

The US Air Force 89th Wing is stationed at Andrews Air Force Base in Camp Springs, Maryland. Notably, the 89th saw to Air Force One, air transport for the President and Commander-in-chief of the United States. The 89th also provided air transport for executives of the US Treasury, State Department, FBI, National Security Agency and the CIA. Serving all these agencies, the 89th was very busy. To cope with the workload, the 89th operated a large fleet of executive type airplanes—private jets—ideal for ferrying small numbers of personnel. When these airplanes were not carrying US government executives around the world they were kept and maintained in hangars.

Hangar 22 was located southwest of Runway 1R. The building was made of steel and aluminium, and the size of a football field. The hangar's collapsible doors were fifty meters wide. Seven executive jets were grounded inside the hangar, in various stages of repair, their engine covers opened up, wings flapped down. In the far corner, a Gulfstream IV wore the circular stars and eagle emblem of the United States. Air Force mechanics in green jumpsuits milled around the aircraft, rectifying their faults. The compressor that worked their tools hissed like a fiery serpent. Now and again, a drill whirred as it bored into metal. Every few minutes, somebody applied hammer blows to some stubborn bolt. As if the noise wasn't enough, someone had his radio on full blast, blaring out Stevie Wonder's *Jammin*.

Sergeant Colin O'Donnell stood beneath an Air Force-designated C-22, replacing its landing gear actuator. He looked for his size 14 spanner. It was not on his tool trolley.

'Who the shit's been using my spanner?' he howled down the hangar. His face was squat and covered with skin flakes.

The other mechanics ignored him. The scum from Philadelphia was being uncouth as usual.

'Don't nobody be coming near my stuff no more.' O'Donnell banged a hammer onto his tool tray. 'You bunch of shit heads!'

Still, everyone ignored O'Donnell.

He looked at the instructions written on the job card belonging to the airplane he was meant to repair. 'Bah,' he grunted, and tossed the paperwork aside.

Aged forty, O'Donnell had served twenty-two years in the Air Force. He had a wealth of experience. As usual he disregarded the instructions on the job card. The job was to change the wheel actuator. He'd done that a hundred times. He didn't need any bookkeeping instructions from the pen pushers on how to do that. He rubbed his chin. The stubble was sharp. He ought to shave but he'd never shaved more than once a week, and he was not about to start now.

He looked for his wrench. Again, it was missing. 'Which son of a whore's been taking my wrench?' he howled at his colleagues, busy working on other airplanes in different sections of the hangar.

'Shut up, you old bastard!' someone yelled from the far corner of the hangar. 'Go smoke some hash, you stupid junkie!' They'd had enough of O'Donnell's foul mouth and bullying that morning.

True, O'Donnell's first love was something the Jamaicans call *ganja*, but he hated being called a junkie. That was reserved for people on real drugs like heroin and coke. Not him. As far as he was concerned, all he smoked—and had been smoking for fifteen years—was harmless weed. Harmless weed that was making him increasingly more irritable, and erratic.

'Your stinking mama, and your smelly grandma are the junkies!' He heaved a screwdriver in the direction of the back of the hangar.

'Get a bath,' someone yelled. 'You stink!'

True, O'Donnell had a body odour. He showered only once a week and smoked forty cigarettes a day.

'Ever heard of Colgate?' another added. O'Donnell's teeth were yellowish-brown.

'Like your mama ever heard of Colgate,' O'Donnell yelled back.

'You're the oldest dumbbell in the Air Force, O'Donnell!' someone jibed. 'Twenty-two years, and only three stripes!'

'I ain't no shithead like Farringdon who gets promoted and can't even use a screwdriver,' O'Donnell replied cockily.

'He's still your boss, dipstick.'

'Boss, my ass. I've been repairing B-29s when that piece of shit was still wearing diapers. I've got no time for him, and I've got no time for you—you piece of shit.'

Lieutenant Bailey, the chief mechanic entered the hangar. Bailey was tall and lanky. As usual, O'Donnell was having an insult-slinging match against everyone else in the hangar. He had seen that the hangar was descending into chaos. 'Ten Hup!'

All the mechanics came to attention. Bailey did that to restore sanity in the hangar. It was always like that when O'Donnell was around.

'Now, get to work,' Bailey ordered.

Everyone did as they were ordered.

O'Donnell set about his job. He stood on his green, steel toolbox underneath the airplane and continued work on the C-22. The actuator was mounted high up in the wheel bay— the huge cavity under the airplane where the wheels and the undercarriage were housed during flight.

Major David Farringdon was officer-in-charge, Hangar 22. His office was built on steel stilts, twenty feet high, to give him a clear view of the hangar. Farringdon had only been in his job for two months. Because of this he often walked around, getting familiar with his mechanics.

Farringdon was a graduate of the Air Force Academy in Colorado. His starched uniform was spotless, his black shoes polished well enough to reflect his face. The rear walls needed a paint job, he could see. He would have to call in the painter. He walked past a C-20 with a bunch of boys busy working on its engines. They came to attention and saluted.

'Morning, Sloane. Stand at ease. How are you?'

'Very well, sir.'

'How is your wife? Is she out of hospital now?'

'Yes, sir. Thanks, sir.'

'Poe?'

'Sir?'

'How are you, too?'

'Could be better, sir.'

'What's the problem?'

'Same problem, sir. Money. I need to buy milk formula for the baby but I'm broke.'

Farringdon knew his problem: he spent too much money on craps, chasing the never-coming big win. Still, he gave him ten dollars. Baby shouldn't suffer.

Poe grinned gratefully. 'Thanks, sir.'

Farringdon walked further into the hangar. He looked over a grey Gulfstream III turbojet. The operations people had been asking about it. Good thing it was almost finished. It still needed a couple of switches in the cockpit, though.

Major Farringdon walked up to the C-22 where O'Donnell was working. Farringdon mulled around the airplane, observing its fuselage.

O'Donnell had just dismounted the actuator arm when he caught sight of a pair of shiny black shoes, shuffling around his airplane. He knew it was Major Farringdon, that numbskull officer-in-charge. He was the only one who wore formal shoes and blue trousers. Every other person wore jumpsuits and safety boots.

A devious idea popped into O'Donnell's mind. Since he was about to replace the actuator he had closed the valves that carried hydraulic oil into the actuator. That way, hydraulic fluid wouldn't leak out when he removed the actuator arm.

O'Donnell banged on the pipe work to make it seem as though he was having a problem unscrewing a pipe. As he did, he intentionally opened the hydraulic fluid control valve. Red hydraulic fluid spurted out through the open pipes, spraying in all directions—especially on the Major's trousers and shoes.

'What the heck,' Major Farringdon cried, as he suddenly found himself dripping hydraulic oil.

He stormed away, livid.

'O'Donnell did that deliberately,' he mumbled knowingly. 'I'm gonna get that dumb son of a bitch,' Farringdon resolved. 'You just watch this space.'

O'Donnell laughed silently.

15

'My God, what is this?' Cagley pointed at the TV screen in the corner of his spacious office. He couldn't bear to watch a second longer. He ejected the offensive videotape from the recorder and hurled it across the room.

He banged his fist on his table. Damn!

Cagley paced, muttering, 'Skinner, one of my guards... without his pants on...right inside my own living room...on top of my daughter.'

Was he seeing right or was he mistaken?

The video couldn't lie.

The filthy images floated in his head. They made him feel like puking. His thick fingers trembled as he reached for a Marlboro. He dragged heavily on it and frowned as he exhaled thick, white smoke.

Heaving himself in the chair behind his desk he couldn't keep from quivering with rage.

He felt like going on a rampage and destroying everything in his path. Rip everything to pieces. Especially that audacious bodyguard, Skinner.

Skinner, the guard was getting intimate with his daughter!

Cagley thought back to the clubhouse the other day. She'd been intent on watching him. Skinner, the bastard, had acted like he barely knew Ann. Cagley recalled wondering if he was a good actor. Well, that question was answered.

He was dead. His mother had better go shopping for a black dress.

Fuming, Cagley pressed a button on his intercom. 'Yes, sir?' came his secretary's squeaky voice.

'Get me Schwartz, pronto!' Cagley snapped.
'Thomas Schwartz?'
'Schwartz, dammit!'
'Y-yes sir!'

16

Four miles away, Ann drove towards Woodlake Hospital in Bethesda. Woodlake was an eight-storey brick-clad complex set in the midst of a brightly flowered landscape, used mostly by top level US government employees and their families.

Since Ann had been diagnosed with endometriosis, a condition that prevents conception, she was required to see her consultant once every two months at Woodlake. She arrived for her usual consultation and was directed to an immaculate consulting room.

A nurse held out a sample bottle. 'Hello. Would you be able to give a urine sample?'

Ann collected the bottle. They took a sample every time she saw the consultant. She went into the adjoining lavatory and returned a few minutes later with the sample, which she handed to the nurse.

Dr Cohen, wearing a white lab coat, entered five minutes later. His hair was white and thin, and he looked like a whacky professor. 'Ann, how're you?'

'Good enough.'

Dr Cohen regarded her. 'You gave a sample?'

'Yes.'

'Can you give me another, please?'

'Another one?'

'Yes, please.'

Ann forced a dry laugh. 'I'll try my best, doc. I don't know if I have any more to give right now.'

Dr Cohen smiled. 'Please, try.'

The doctor spoke into an intercom. The nurse entered and

handed Ann another sample bottle. Ann went into the toilet and returned with a little liquid in the sample bottle. 'I busted my gut doing that.'

'I'll have it sent to the lab,' Dr Cohen said. 'Take a seat. Only be a few minutes.'

After twenty minutes Ann began to fidget. She had a client appointment to get to. She picked up her handbag, ready to leave but just then the doctor returned. The strange look on his face stopped her departure. It seemed he had diagnosed a grievous ailment.

'Sorry for keeping you. I need to ask you some questions.'

'Sure.'

'How do you feel generally?'

'Fine. That is apart from the endometriosis.'

'Any signs of lethargy?'

'No.'

'Headaches?'

'Sometimes, yes.'

'Nausea?'

'No.'

'Tiredness?'

Ann sighed apprehensively. Why was he asking so many questions? Usually it was always a case of "we'll keep an eye on things." Had he diagnosed another grievous ailment to add to the endometriosis?

'What is it, doctor?' she asked, starting to panic. 'Tell me, what is it?'

He looked straight into her eyes. 'It seems you're pregnant.'

She drew back. 'What did you say?'

'You're pregnant.'

Ann gazed around the consulting room. There must be someone else here. He had to be speaking to someone else. But there was no one else in the room.

'You're pregnant, Ann. Congratulations!'

'I'm pregnant?' It still didn't sink in. 'You're kidding.' Her hopes had been dashed so many times that she found it difficult to comprehend the good news.

'No, I'm not,' Dr Cohen replied. 'Isn't that what you've always wanted? You don't look very happy.'

'Yes, there's nothing I want more than that.'

'Then you are, my dear.'

'Are you sure? Really sure?'

'Yes, yes,' Dr Cohen answered enthusiastically. 'That's why I ran a second test—to be doubly sure.'

Then it sank in. Although, it was what she wanted most, the pessimistic side of human nature had convinced her it would never happen. After all, she had tried for well over fourteen months with Mr Virile, her cheating ex-boyfriend, who had managed to knock up four women including a fifty year old mama, while she ran a dud.

Me? Pregnant? Finally? Her emerald eyes lit up. 'I am?'

Dr Cohen nodded enthusiastically. 'Yes!'

She clasped her hands across her chest, still disbelieving. 'I am?'

'Yes, yes.' Dr Cohen grinned. 'Yes, my dear, you are.'

She screamed ecstatically. 'I'm pregnant! I'm pregnant. I'm pregnant. I'm pregnant!'

The doctor laughed. 'Shhh,' he cautioned. 'Let's not jump so much Ann, it's discomforting for the baby.'

Ann calmed immediately. 'Yes, yes.' Teary films of joy glazed over her eyes. She rubbed her yet-to-protrude stomach. 'Oh, baby, Mummy's so sorry.'

'Congratulations, Ann.' Dr Cohen offered a handshake.

'Thanks, doctor. Thank you. Thank you!'

'So, I'll give you an appointment to see me a week from now. We'll do a couple of tests, and may be prescribe a pregnancy supplement. We'll do a scan, and set up a schedule for antenatal appointments. He filled in the back of a white card. 'I'll give you an appointment for next week. Thursday, shall we say?'

'Yes. Thank you, doctor.' She gave him a hug. Her eyes dripped joyful tears. The tears rubbed on Dr. Cohen's face. 'I couldn't ask for better news.' She felt like she had won the lottery.

'Don't thank me, Ann. I didn't do anything. Thank God.'

Ann lifted her eyes to the ceiling. 'Thank you, God. Thank you.'

'Greetings to the baby's father.'

'Oh yes. Yes, I shall tell him. I shall tell Leroy.'

Oh, Leroy, the man of magic. Her heart warmed towards him. She got out her cell phone to call him.

'No, not in here, please,' Dr Cohen cautioned.

'Sorry, doctor.' She walked out of the consulting room.

In the corridor outside, her feet could hardly keep still. Trembling with joy, her eyes moist with tears of joy she dialled Leroy.

She wondered what he would say. How would he take the news?

17

Thomas Schwartz, CIA Deputy Director (Administration) was built like Santa Claus: chubby with a round face and puffy red cheeks. He was a family man who had been married for twenty-four years; his nineteen-year-old daughter, Michelle, was now in college. Schwartz had worked twenty years in the agency and was looking forward to his retirement in about two years.

Schwartz was on the phone, chatting to Michelle when his secretary popped her head around the door. He knew it had to be important or she would have waited for him to finish his call.

'Anita just phoned,' his secretary mouthed discreetly. 'The DCI wants you immediately.'

'Call you back, darling,' Schwartz said to his daughter and hung up. He donned his jacket and lumbered down the corridor. He passed a cubicle that housed the Director's guards, and walked into the Director's suite.

Cagley met Schwartz with a glare. 'One of my guards is sleeping with my daughter!' Cagley snarled, not bothering to say hello.

Schwartz stopped in his tracks. He stared blankly at his irate boss. 'C'mon, Mike, you're kidding me.'

'Kidding?' Cagley slammed his fist on the mahogany table, his face as black as thunder. 'Do I look like I'm kidding?' He poked an angry finger at Schwartz. 'The guy you detailed to guard me is not guarding me, he's been laying my daughter!'

'What? How could that happen?'

'If you must know, I'll tell you.' Cagley drew a Marlboro from a pack on his table. 'Last Saturday was when I knew something was going on and it must have been going on for quite a while. I was home and the guys from Operations had just brought in an update on the war situation in Somalia. I was reading the brief and Ann was watching TV on the sofa.'

Cagley walked slowly towards the window. 'There was something about Ann, you know...I think it was her body language.'

At the window, Cagley took a lighter from his pocket and lit up. 'For starters, she was sort of fidgety, and biting her nails, something she never does. She looked excited for no obvious reason and she kept glancing at the window. She didn't notice I'd picked up on it. I could tell something was up. Women can't hide these things. Also, she was wearing makeup, yet she wasn't going out.'

Cagley cast a cocky look at Schwartz, exhaling thick smoke from his nostrils. 'Does anyone wear makeup to watch TV?'

Cagley looked out of the window of his seventh floor office, at the tall magnolia trees that beautified CIA headquarters. 'I'm not sure, or maybe it was my imagination, but when the guard passed by the window doing his patrol, her eyes kept trailing him. Also, the TV was tuned to basketball. Ann abhors basketball. It's like me marrying the Convent Mother.'

'But that's nothing, Mike.'

'It is something! Can't you see? Her mind wasn't on the TV. It was on the guard outdoors!'

'So, what happened?'

'I decided to bait them. I asked Ann to go to the shop and buy me shaving gel. I watched to see what would happen. She went out of the front door to go to her car. It's only ten yards from the front door to her car. It would take twenty seconds at most to walk that distance. But she disappeared for a good five minutes! When she re-appeared she was re-adjusting her clothes, and her hair-do. I saw the guard walking away, wiping his lips. I became more suspicious. What was going on? Again, I recall some three weeks ago, at the golf club, I thought she was giving him just that bit of unusual attention.

71

So, I asked Bosworth to keep an eye on them. He took up post in the woods behind the house. Every evening they got cozy in the kitchen doorway. He asked my permission to set up a camera inside the living room. I gave him the permission. He came back with a tape.'

Paranoid asshole, Schwartz thought. *You are invading her privacy.*

Cagley knew what Schwartz was thinking. 'It's not an invasion of privacy.' Cagley bawled. 'It's my house. It's not a brothel for CIA guards. The guard is stationed there to do one job and one job only: protect me. My daughter does not come into the deal!'

'I agree,' Schwartz said softly.

'I don't want you to agree!' Cagley roared. 'I wanna know what you're gonna do about him! Tell me. He's your man, Schwartz. You're his boss. What the hell are you gonna do about him?'

'I'll start an investigation. I'll push him off your guard immediately.'

'You damn well will, dammit. He's going to get roasted for this, I promise you. That bastard was doing my daughter right in my own house. On my favourite sofa! Doesn't he have any fear? Where's the respect? Well if he has no respect, I'll teach him some; if he has no fear, I'll ensure he learns fear. He's—'

At that moment, Cagley's phone rang. 'John Hune,' Anita, his squeaky-voiced secretary said. 'Returning your call.'

'Ah, hello, John,' Cagley said.

'I was in a meeting, Mike,' Hune responded. 'How are you?'

Schwartz lumbered out of Cagley's office to accord Cagley some privacy on his call. He took a seat in Anita's office and read the papers.

'I need a favour from you, John,' Cagley continued after Schwartz had left. 'Someone's crossed me.' He paused, and spoke slowly. 'Violated my daughter. He needs to be taught a lesson.'

John Hune cleared his throat. He was governor at one of

Washington DC's penitentiaries. He was also a member of The Perivale, Cagley's golf club. By reason of his job, John Hune had access to lots of baddies, hoods, and thugs both in the prisons, and outside. In his position they were always eager to do him small favours.

'That's terrible, Mike. People have no respect these days, do they?' Hune drawled. 'So, this animal, is he in the penal system?'

'No.'

'Too bad, Mike, I would have made him sweat; send you his balls by DHL.'

That sounded good to Cagley. A good idea. And it was something he could do easily. 'I can get him inside,' Cagley said most assuredly. 'That's not a problem. Can your guys take care of him when he's in?'

'As a favour for you, Mike. Yes.'

'Thanks.'

'Does this animal have a name?'

'I don't have his real name. Skinner or something he's called.'

'Get me a name, Mike. If you can, get him in here. Then leave the rest to me.'

'Thanks, John. I owe you one.'

'You owe me nothing. What are friends for?'

Cagley had done a couple of favours for Hune in the past. Hune's wife was a pretty, long-legged model from Croatia but she was an illegal immigrant. Cagley had wangled a US passport for her in just three days.

Cagley hung up. He punched a button on his intercom. 'Is Schwartz still there?'

'Yes, sir, he's waiting.'

'Ask him to come in.'

Schwartz returned.

'I'm giving specific directions,' Cagley said, grim. By using the phrase, *specific directions*, he was using his executive powers to issue an order, which then had to be carried out

73

without fail, and without argument. 'I want you to arraign Skinner before the disciplinary committee. And I want the committee to recommend the case go before a judge.'

Schwartz scratched his bald head. 'I have reservations about that, Mike. You want to take this case to the county judge? It's gonna be funny putting an issue like that before the judge, more especially as Ann is of age. She's not exactly a minor, she's—what did you say—twenty-four? She was probably willing…and consenting.'

Schwartz knew he was pushing the boundary. Cagley had issued an executive directive. The decision was final. It was not something he should be contesting.

Cagley's face flushed red. 'What do you mean by *she was willing and consenting*? Of course, without her consent it's blatant rape! I wouldn't be here talking to you. I'd be at the district attorney's. But with her consent it's molestation. By CIA and Secret Service rules, a security officer cannot have intimate dealings with a subject he's supposed to protect. Those are the people I entrust my life to! Now, one of them goes behind my back to sleep with my daughter? It's a betrayal of trust! When suddenly did you become so righteous that you talk about consent?'

'Don't you think we're taking this too far? Skinner's just a silly boy who was probably fooling around. Besides, I would think you'd want it hush-hush.'

'Hush what?' Cagley howled. 'If you think I'm just gonna watch and do nothing while some bum ravages my daughter you're mistaken! Now let me paint this to you, Schwartz. Then tell me how you feel. You have a daughter named Michelle, right?'

'Right.'

'Good. Now, your driver is sleeping with her in your own house. How do you feel about that?' He stared deadpan at Schwartz.

'W-well, I feel—'

'Are you good with that?'

'Well, er –I-I.'

'It seems you would be. You'll probably buy him a cigar.'

'Of course not,' Schwartz conceded.

'Your daughter may not be as valuable to you as mine is to me. I don't know about you but I've spent all my life training her. I sent her to private schools; I sent her to Yale. I've invested all I have in her. She's my life's work. I am not going to stand around and let some low-life ruin her life!'

'Why don't you just fire him from the agency?'

'That's like letting him off. I'll keep him on…so I can stew him. Now, get on the job, and throw the book at Skinner. Any way. Any how!'

'Yes, sir.'

Cagley saw a silly I-can't-be-beaten-easily expression on Schwartz's face. He frowned, and tapped his pencil menacingly on the table. 'You do think I'm joking, right?'

'Er…'

'Well, I'm not.' He poked a warning finger at Schwartz. 'I'm giving you a specific order. I give you one week. One week only! If Skinner is not before a judge by this time next week, you won't be in a job this time next week. Do I make myself clear?'

Schwartz froze.

'I-I'll set up a disciplinary panel immediately,' Schwartz stuttered. 'We'll summon him right away.'

'Good.'

Frowning, his face bright red with rage, Cagley flopped into his executive chair, swivelled round, and turned his back on Schwartz. The meeting was over.

Schwartz plodded to the door.

'Schwartz?'

Schwartz stopped in the doorway. Cagley's back was still turned to him. 'Yes, Mike.'

'True, Ann was willing and consenting, but don't think for one moment she's getting away with it. I'll deal with her when I get home. You just deal with Skinner.'

'Yes, Mike.'

Schwartz left with his shoulders bowed. He knew Cagley always made good his threats. The CIA Director was tremendously powerful. Apart from having a budget of $30 billion he had command of 22,000 staff, and needed absolutely no reason to fire anyone in the CIA. He also had oversight of the National Security Agency and countless other US government agencies. With so much firepower at Cagley's disposal, Schwartz wondered what would become of Skinner.

As soon as Thomas Schwartz was out of his office, Cagley pressed a button on his intercom.

'Bosworth,' the person at the other end answered.

'I want you to do me a dossier on subject, CIA call sign Skinner. He's one of my home guards, the newest one. I want to know his real name, and what he's all about.'

'Skinner?'

'Yeah. I want it within the hour.'

'Er...' Bosworth protested.

'One hour!' Cagley switched off the intercom.

Next he dialled Judge Bloomsbury. 'Hello, Ed, I need a favour.'

18

As Leroy walked leisurely around the grounds of Cagley's estate his cell phone rang. He unclipped it from his belt. 'Yeah?'

'Leroy?'

He knew her voice. His manner softened. 'Ann? How are you doing?'

'Guess what, Leroy, guess what?'

'Er…er,' Leroy stuttered, a grin spreading across his face. Another intimate date he reckoned.

'I'm pregnant! I'm pregnant,' she squealed, unable to hold her excitement.

'What?'

He stopped dead in his tracks. The grin on his lips disappeared. For a brief moment his mind drew a blank. *She was pregnant?* His heart pounded inside his rib cage.

'Pregnant!' Ann squeaked. 'You're going to be a father.'

He was so astonished that for one long minute, he couldn't speak.

'Leroy? Are you there?'

'Er… er,' Leroy said again. He could not even think.

'Thank you. Thank you so much,' Ann babbled. 'I'm so delighted! You don't know what this means to me. Thank you so much!'

Thank you? She's thanking me?

For another minute he didn't speak.

'Are you there, Leroy?'

'Er…er.'

'Aren't you pleased with the news?'

'Er...er.' It was as if he'd been hit by a truck.

'I'm so happppy! I'm *soooo* happy.' She giggled girlishly.

He still could not find the words. Or the thoughts.

'You're such a gem, Leroy.'

It was only then it sank in.

What the hell? I'm not ready for a child!

Hillary Bosworth squeezed into Cagley's office. Bosworth was seriously obese with a massive 70-inch gut, which wobbled as he walked; the door was barely big enough to allow him through. He seemed as tall as the ceiling, being six feet and six inches tall, and weighing three hundred and fifty pounds. He held a blue CIA folder, and towered above Cagley's mahogany table. Bosworth was Special Assistant to the Director, CIA. Simply put, he was the Director's henchman.

'Sir, as you requested, I have the full dossier on subject, Skinner.' His voice was deep.

'Brief me!' Cagley ordered, not giving Bosworth a look.

Bosworth read from his file, 'Subject Skinner. Surname: Delgado. First names: Leroy, Alphonse—'

'His name's Leroy Alphonse Delgado?'

'Yes, sir.'

'Carry on.'

'Born third July, Nineteen sixty—'

'Skip the flimsy details,' Cagley snapped.

'Yes, sir. Native of Brooklyn, New York. Educated at Syracuse University—'

'Skip the details, Bosworth! Tell me something worthwhile!'

'Yes, sir. Family details: Father, Kenneth 'Ken' Delgado, formerly of the United States Army. Mother: Alicia—'

'Wait a minute!' Cagley eyed Bosworth.

Kenneth Delgado... That was a name he could never forget.

Kenneth Delgado? Ken Delgado? Sergeant Ken? Korea?

Probably not.

Still...

'Tell me about the father.'

Bosworth looked through his file. 'Born, first October 1930 in Chicago. Joined United States Army, March nineteen-forty-four. Deployed to the Eighth Army in Wake. Promoted corporal, nineteen-forty-eight. Deployed to Korea with the Forty-fifth Division, hundred and eightieth Infantry, C Company, Platoon three, Squad two. Promoted to sergeant—'

Cagley's ear picked out a few words: Korea. 45th Division. 180th Infantry. C Company. Platoon 3. Squad 2.

That was his unit in Korea.

There had been only one sergeant in Squad 2—Sergeant Ken, the bastard who murdered Soo Min Ji! Leroy Delgado was Sergeant Ken's son! Sergeant Ken, the murderer.

'Enough,' Cagley ordered.

Why the hell was the boss yelling? Bosworth wondered.

Cagley buried his head in his palms. Not looking up, he gestured that Bosworth should go away. Bosworth obediently shuffled out of Cagley's office.

Alone, Cagley shook his head a dozen times. An errant vein inside his skull thumped mercilessly against his brain culminating in a massive headache. The unthinkable had happened! Sergeant Ken's son was molesting his daughter!

Cagley's mind flashed to Leroy Delgado, the guard he had not bothered to know beyond his CIA call sign of Skinner. Yes, why had he never observed it? Leroy and Ken had the same eyes! Come to think of it, without his stubble he was a fair image of his father. He was.

Oh my God!

'Is it a curse?' Cagley said bitterly to himself. 'Will the Delgados never leave me alone? My only child! Are there no other women in the world? Why my baby?'

For the first time in almost forty years, Cagley wept. As he cried, memories of Korea flooded back. Korea. One part of his life he had tried to blot out of his mind. It was too painful to contemplate, too painful to think about. He remembered vividly how Soo Min Ji dropped onto the forest floor like a log of wood. He remembered her pretty but lifeless face. Once

79

again, he felt the same pain and anguish, and the same sense of injustice he felt on that horrific day. The day Soo Min Ji was murdered.

He lit a cigarette and dragged on it. *Why am I weeping like some shit-ass schoolboy? Maybe it's true no one can escape retribution. Or why else has fate suddenly dumped Sergeant Ken's son on my lap? Can it be that fate planned it all so that I can pay them back?*

I think so.

'Then it's time to get out the whip and scourge the Delgados. It's time to visit the iniquity of the father upon the children. It's bad enough my bodyguard is violating my daughter. But it's an atrocity when that scoundrel turns out to be the son of Sergeant Ken. The Delgados? I spit on that name!'

Unwittingly, Leroy Delgado had reopened an old wound.

Cagley punched a button on his phone. Bosworth answered at the other end. 'Where is Kenneth Delgado now?' Cagley boomed.

'Missing. Presumed dead, sir. Vietnam. Seventy-one.'

Stunned, Cagley hung up. Sergeant Ken was dead. He'd escaped retribution.

Sarge was dead.

Dead. He felt no pity. Only a great sense of injustice. Cagley had been cheated of vengeance.

Then his mind flashed to Leroy.

The devil's son. The hatred he had for Sergeant Ken translated to Leroy. Cagley lit another cigarette. *I need to pry Delgado's hands off my daughter. When that's done I'm gonna make him suffer, then I'm gonna put him in the grave. The Delgados have crossed me for the last time.*

Cagley punched a number into his phone. John Hune answered at the other end.

'John,' Cagley said. 'Can you talk?'

'Yes, sure.'

'You know that bastard I wanted you to take care of?'

'The guy who molested your daughter?'

'Yeah. Turns out he's a mole planted by my enemies to destroy me. His father is my arch enemy; made an attempt on my life a while back.'

'That's serious,' John Hune responded. 'I thought you were gonna get him sent down.'

'I'm working on that. But as you know I've got to make it legal. Make it clean. I've ordered he should be sent a summons to appear before a panel of inquiry on Monday, and to face the judge by Friday. Hopefully in about two weeks he should be inside. With you.'

'What did you say his name was?'

'Delgado...Leroy Alphonse.'

'I've written that down. He won't be bothering you any more after this.'

'Thanks, John.'

'Anytime.'

'And, John?'

'Yes?'

'Break all his bones. Every single one!'

John Hune laughed. 'And his balls as well.'

'I don't expect him to come out of it alive,' Cagley said firmly.

'In that case, send down a casket as well.'

'Thanks, buddy.'

'Anytime.'

Cagley hung up. His mind went to Leroy. *Damn! That murderer's son has been in my house all this while? I've been sharing my house with a viper.*

He dialled another number. 'Rambler, I give you ten minutes. I want that guard, Skinner off my property.' Rambler was the watch commander in charge of the guards.

'Er...' Cagley's request was unusual but Cagley was not a man to be argued with. 'Yes, sir.'

'Ten minutes!'

'Sir!'

Cagley dialled yet another number. 'Schwartz, have you sent

81

a summons to that bum?'

'You mean Delgado?'

'Whatever. He must be summoned today. And I mean today. Get your people to go and stick the letter of summons on his door.'

Schwartz knew Cagley was on the warpath, and there was no messing about. 'Yes, sir.'

Ann sashayed joyfully as she returned to her office at Denney Lee Associates. Denny Lee's office was on the 9th Floor of St Martin's house, a glass building in central DC, not too far from the Capitol. Three clients had been waiting to see her: a diplomat from the Namibian embassy; Florence Clohert, who was a lady member of Congress; and a Japanese man she didn't know, possibly a prospective client. All three waited patiently in the lobby.

'Hello!' Ann said unusually loud, acknowledging her clients, grinning widely. Her elation was difficult to conceal. Instead of a polite business handshake, she embraced each of her clients as if they were long lost friends. 'How are you, today? How's the family? Sorry to keep you. Would you like some coffee?'

It was very obvious to her three clients that their property agent must have hit the jackpot somewhere. In serious celebration mood, she gave her clients huge discounts she normally would not: five percent instead of two. What did it matter? She that had been told would never conceive was now pregnant. Blessed be the name of the Lord.

She finished with her clients at 2.45 pm. She refused to see any more clients. Instead, she spent the next thirty minutes calling *Motherworld* and the pregnancy hotline. There was so much to know about a safe pregnancy. Still trembling with excitement, and certainly not in the mood to work, she cleared her desk at 3.30. Then she drove to *Babyshop* in Georgetown, northwest of downtown DC. She bought a set of baby clothes, and ordered a crib.

She could barely wait to tell her father that she was pregnant.

After all the doctors said, and after all these years of crying on his shoulders he would be so happy for her. She would like to see the look on his face when he heard the news.

She left for home at 5.15 pm.

Leroy sat on the patio of Cagley's mansion, staring blankly into the plush, green lawn, his mind hard at work.

Ann was pregnant? Wasn't that something Ann and himself should have discussed and agreed?

Now, what could he do? What would he tell his mother?

Oh, she would be happy, no doubt. This child was a grandchild. But she was a staunch Catholic and her first question would be, "When are you marrying her?"

Marriage? He'd never considered that. He was still young, still having fun. A child had not been in the deal! Should he talk to her about getting rid of it?

But she seemed so excited. Why? Women were always excited about babies…that was why. *Did she do it deliberately to trap me?*

Now, he would have to start worrying about diapers and formula.

I suppose it was my fault, though. If you sleep with a woman, what do you expect? It's not rocket science that there's a chance that might happen. Now, what do I do?

His CIA-issued walkie-talkie buzzed alive. 'Skinner, come in for Rambler,' a gruff voice croaked from the handset. Leroy drew the handset from his jacket. 'Receiving you, Rambler.'

'Cagley requests you relinquish guard with immediate effect. Return to HQ immediately.'

'What?'

'Now!' Rambler roared. 'You have five minutes to get off the Director's property!'

That was unusual. Did Cagley know about the baby? Had Ann told him?

19

University Park, a middle-class suburb, north of Washington DC was always quiet. The neighbourhood was wooded and tall trees flourished around the houses. Leroy's whitewashed, three-bedroom house had a red roof and a big front lawn, which he groomed every week.

The Langley office of the CIA was well over fifteen miles away, so Leroy drove to work in his red Honda Civic. He returned home and parked his car in the driveway. As he approached the front door he noticed a white envelope stuck to his door. It was marked, Urgent.

It contained a letter written on CIA letter headed paper.

Dear Officer Delgado,

You are summoned to appear before a panel of inquiry in room 1223 CIA HQ on Monday 17th August 1991 to answer to the following charges:

1. Sexual molestation of a subject of trust, Ann Cagley on the 12th July 1991 at 1262 Maple Drive, Chevy Chase, Maryland.
2. Negligence in the pursuance of duty at the same time and place.
3. Unethical conduct, in the pursuance of duty.
4. Trespassing and unauthorised entry into US Government classified property 1262 Maple Drive without appropriate authorisation.

Maxwell Harley, head of investigations, will chair this panel. The panel is mandated to make findings, ascertain events, decide on wrongdoing, make recommendations, and initiate disciplinary actions if allegations are proven.

Be aware that any findings of felony will be referred to the District Judge and the Fairfax Police Department. Any findings of treason will be handed to the Federal Bureau of Investigation.

Hearing begins promptly at 09.30

You are directed to hand in your official weapons and passport, being property of the United States government.

Signed,

Jack Rooster

For the Deputy Director (Administration)

CIA

Leroy loosened his tie. Trouble was brewing. And it had everything to do with Ann. The bubble had burst.

Ann's father's armour-plated Cadillac was parked in the driveway when she returned home. That was odd. He was unusually early.

With a spring in her step and her heart bursting with song she pranced through the front door and into the living room.

Her father stood waiting, his face as pale as death.

'How're you, Dad?' Ann began excitedly, her face bright and radiant. 'You're back so early. I've got the best news ever!'

'I've got some news too. Do you know anyone called Delgado? Leroy Delgado?'

The cracking tone of his voice sent a chill down her spine. She stopped in her tracks, and her five-hour-old bubbly disposition evaporated into thin air. She glanced at her pint-sized father. His eyes were narrow, cold and hostile.

'Do you know him?' Cagley repeated, raising his voice.

That tone of voice spelt trouble. A sense of unease fell on her. She said nothing.

'I asked you a question, do you know Delgado?'

Slowly, Ann nodded.

'What is your relationship with him?'

'He's a friend.'

85

'Did it go beyond that?

'No,' Ann answered. 'Just friends.'

'You're lying,' Cagley barked. 'I learnt Delgado is not merely your friend but your lover.'

Ann's face flushed bright red. She could not look her father in the face; she stared at the carpet.

'Look at me.'

Ann raised her sullen blonde head, and looked into her father's displeased face.

'Have you asked yourself who you are? Have you asked yourself who your father is? Do you appreciate my position? I head the CIA. I deal in sensitive clandestine matters. Now, you've lied to me. Did you consider for a minute that you might have been caught on camera? You and him on the floor! Do you know how humiliating it is for you? How damaging it could be for me; for the United States?'

She cringed. *Caught on camera*? Oh gosh! No! 'B-but…'

'But what?' Cagley howled in her face. 'If you were from a filthy background, that would be expected, but your mother and I instilled some decency in you, dammit! I never dreamt I'd see the day my daughter would stoop so low—lower than an animal, being used on the living room carpet like a rag! What are you Ann, some low-life whore?' His voice dripped disgust.

Ann shrank back, hurt. She glared at her father. 'Dad, that's not fair!'

'To who?' Cagley boomed. 'Me or you?'

'To me. I'm not a whore!' Tears stung her eyes.

'You certainly acted like one. The whore only has more sense. At least, she makes some money in the process. As for you, you gained nothing! You lost everything: your pride, your chastity—everything!'

Again, Ann stared at the carpet, too ashamed to look at her father. Even at twenty-four, and a fully-grown woman, his words made her feel small. 'I'm sorry, Dad. I don't have an explanation. It was a mistake and I regret it. I'm sorry.' Her voice quavered, on the brink of tears. Shaky, she dropped her handbag on the leather sofa.

Cagley observed Ann was penitent. He calmed a little. He said his last word: 'Keep away from Delgado. Don't have anything to do with my personal staff or anyone in the CIA ever again. Business is business; family is family. The two do not mix.'

Ann nodded.

'We'll try and put this behind us,' Cagley said, wrapping up the conversation. 'Okay?'

Ann was relieved her father had said his bit and got it over with. But she knew she was pregnant. She knew she would have to tell him eventually—or at least her tummy would. 'Th-there's something I need to tell you.'

Cagley frowned. 'What's that?'

She summoned all her courage. 'I, er…I'm pregnant.'

The blood drained from Cagley's face. 'You're what?'

'Pregnant.'

'You mean you're carrying Delgado's child?'

She nodded bravely.

He poked a stubby finger in her chest. 'You'll have to wait till I'm dead before you do that.'

'But, Dad.'

'Are you crazy? You got pregnant?' It was as if he'd been hit by an express train. Ann was pregnant with Sergeant Ken's grandson? 'No, no, no! It can't be.' He stomped towards the mantelpiece.

'It—it was a mistake.' Ann knew she was lying. She had slept with him because she was desperate for a child. 'B-but it's the best thing that's happened to me—'

'Shut up,' Cagley howled. 'You got yourself knocked up by the hired help, and call that good? Are you crazy?'

'But I'm happy! Have you forgotten I have endometriosis? You know I'm not as lucky as other women. Can't you see this was a miracle?' she pleaded, trying desperately to get her father to understand.

'Yes, I know you have endometriosis. As I always told you:

87

we'll worry about that after you get married. But I'd rather you're barren than be pregnant by that scum!'

Now Ann knew something was seriously wrong. Her father had comforted her many times over the fact that she might never conceive. His contention was that when she got married and was routinely intimate with her husband, then something would happen. Even if it took medical intervention. It was only after then that there would be any cause for concern. She had never told him, however—and she never would—that in her despair and desperation she had gone all the way for fourteen months with virile Marcus, hoping to get pregnant. She had hoped he would share her joy. Instead, he was having none of it. He had been her life-long rock but now, he was turning his back on her. She knew she had to salvage the situation.

'Dad, I thought you always wanted a grandchild.'

'Yes, but not this one.'

'Not this one? What do you mean by that?' Ann was baffled. 'I thought you would be happy that I'm finally pregnant and that you were going to be a granddad.'

'A granddad to the seed of Delgado? Maybe when I'm dead.'

There was so much disgust in his voice when he mentioned the name, Delgado. 'Why? Is there anything wrong with Leroy…or with the name, Delgado?'

Cagley ignored her. 'Ann,' he called, looking her straight in the eye.

'Yes?'

'I want you to stop seeing that boy. I want you to break off the relationship immediately. He's most undesirable. He's not the one for you; you're not meant to be together.'

'B-but I can't stop seeing him. I just can't. I like him. Why do you think he's undesirable? Because he's a lowly bodyguard?'

Cagley looked away, pensive. Where could he begin to tell her the story? How could he explain to her how a part of him died when Sergeant Ken pulled that trigger? Korea was one part of his life he shielded from Ann, and her late mother. Would telling her a forty-year-old story change anything? It would not. So he decided not to say anything. Instead, he dug in. 'I'm not arguing with you, Ann. Neither am I asking you. I'm telling you. I don't want you seeing him any more. After, I'll see some doctors; we'll search for a way out.'

See some doctors? Was he talking about abortion?

'I don't want a way out, Dad!' Ann shook a warning finger at him. 'No. Never. You stay out of this. Don't you dare think about it. Leroy is good for me. He did what the doctors said would be impossible.'

'Leroy might be able to raise the dead for all I care, but you just keep away from him.'

Keep away from Leroy? Her father wanted her to keep away from the father of her miracle child? That was something she could not conceive in her mind. Besides, she didn't like the way her father imposed his control.

'I'm twenty-four years old. I can make my own decisions. I should choose my own man. It's my business who I see. If I want to date a donkey I should be free to.'

'You're free to date a donkey as long as it's not named, Delgado!'

Again, the resentment in his eyes and the bitter twist in his lips as he mentioned the name. 'What's wrong?' she asked, worried. 'Is there something between you and Leroy— something you're not telling me? Why are you so bitter towards him?'

He kept mum but his eyes were fiery, and full of hate.

'You're keeping me in the dark, Dad. I don't know what Leroy has ever done to you, but whatever he did is in the past. Please let it go.'

Cagley glared at Ann. 'Let it go? Are you kidding me? He's gonna pay for this dearly! I can guarantee that.' His mind flashed to John Hune.

Cagley sounded so lethal that Ann was unsettled. She recalled an incident two years ago, when her father made threats at three people. Within weeks one was in jail, the second was brutalised by a street gang, and the last inexplicably fled the country.

'I like him, Dad,' she cried. 'He's my man!'

'Your man? What a joke! You two wouldn't last three months.'

She resented her father's statement. She wasn't seeing Leroy for the short term, was she? Three months—was that what her father thought of her? It cut her deep. What gave him the right to make such judgement? What gave him the right to determine who she saw or not? It was a challenge to everything she was. She would prove him wrong.

'I'm not in this with Leroy for three months,' she declared defiantly. 'We're in this forever. And by the way, it's my business who I see. I'm free to do what I like.'

Cagley hated it when kids went out of line or used that phrase, "I'm free to do what I like." In whose domain? To him, it was a slap in the face, a slap that deserved a response. 'You can't do what you like while you're under my roof. You live with me, and you live by my rules. To live by your rules you have to leave this house. And my rules say no Delgado.'

'What?' Ann was so stunned that she took a step back. 'Are you asking me to choose between you and Leroy?'

'I certainly am.'

'In that case, I choose Leroy!' she said without hesitating.

'Well then, you've made your bed, so you lie in it,' Cagley roared. He pointed to the front door. 'Out! Get out,'

'What?'

Stunned, she stared disbelieving at her father for one long minute. *Get out?* 'Where do you expect me to go?' she asked, still stunned.

'I don't care!'

He didn't care? Now, Ann was annoyed. 'I don't ever intend to stop seeing Leroy, If you want me to leave, I'll leave,'

'I said get out!'

'I-I will.'

'Good luck. When you ditch that bozo you can come back home.'

'I won't ever.'

'We'll see where you're going to live, and how far you can get in DC on your own.'

'We shall see. And I'm never going to let you see the baby!' she yelled childishly to spite her father.

'I don't think I'm interested anyway!'

What—he said that? He wasn't even interested? He was so impossible!

Ann stormed up the winding staircase to her bedroom. Half an hour later, she packed her things into her Toyota and left home. It was only when she drove out of the gates of the Starving Parrot that she stopped.

Where would she go?

She thought of Marian Flench, her best friend. She lived a few miles away in Bethesda. Ann rang Marian but she wasn't home.

She mentally went through a list of the people she considered friends. There was none she felt comfortable enough to hang out with. That was when she realised that she didn't have as many friends as she thought.

Finally, she dialled Leroy.

20

Leroy was waiting as Ann pulled into his driveway. By then the sun was setting. Her car was laden with her belongings, obviously packed in a hurry. Dresses still on their hangers formed a huge pile on the front seat. Three suitcases lay on the back seat; her shoes formed two huge heaps on the rear foot mats. Jewellery, makeup, creams and lotions popped out of every crevasse in the car.

Leroy saw she was distressed. 'My dad is being an ass,' she ranted as she stepped out of her car. 'I don't know how but he learnt we're having an affair and he went mad. See…' Ann pointed inside her car. 'He kicked me out. I've got nowhere to go.'

He saw she was fighting to keep back the tears. 'Today was the best day of my life.' Her voice cracked. 'Till I got home and met him, waiting. My plan was that I would get home, tell him about the baby, he'd be happy and we'd celebrate. I even bought a bottle of champagne. Instead, look at me, I've got no home. He didn't even listen to what I had to say. He just kept barking at me.'

He held her close. 'Your dad kicked you out of home simply because we're seeing each other?'

She nodded, wiping a tear from her eye.

Leroy recognised now that Cagley was on the warpath. 'I've been summoned before the disciplinary panel as well.'

She looked up into his face. 'Why?'

'Same reason. Having an affair with you.'

'It's all my fault.' Ann realized her father was coming at them in different ways. In truth, however, she didn't regret anything. She had gotten what she wanted: a pregnancy. Every other thing was unimportant and totally irrelevant. 'So what can we do? Should we get a lawyer?'

'That's not gonna work.'

'Why not?'

'The CIA disciplinary panel is the CIA's form of a court martial. It's the first step when the agency wants to put someone away. They have to do it because the law demands it. It makes it legitimate but in reality, you're guilty for being asked to attend. Like the military, they do not go into arguments. They merely ask a series of questions to which you answer, yes or no. Then they establish a charge. From there it goes to the FBI, the police or a judge.'

'You haven't done anything outside the law, have you? Being with me?'

'That's not the way things work in Washington DC, Ann. The law is not the Constitution, it's the bureaucrats. Your dad is one very powerful bureaucrat. One phone call from Langley and the cops, the judiciary, and the FBI will be falling over themselves to do favours for your dad. Everyone on the disciplinary panel, and Ed Bloomsbury, who is the district judge, and the cops, the D.A., and the lawyers—everyone will be on your father's side! The entire system is stacked against you. If the establishment wants to screw you, they do.'

She sighed despondently. 'I see your point.'

'Look, all we did was make love. Two people attracted to each other, and what happens—a powerful man doesn't like it and the most common thing in America is being trumped into charges. Your dad is trying to get me locked up.'

'Don't speak like that,' Ann whispered, resolving in her heart that no harm would come to her child's father. 'We're in this together.'

'Thanks. I'll think up a way to get out of this web your dad's spinning around us.' He held her tenderly and kissed her cheek. She offered her lips.

'I half-expected something like this to happen,' Leroy

93

remarked later. 'I knew all along it was a bad idea messing with you, being Cagley's daughter and all.' He looked straight into her eyes. 'The truth is that from the moment I saw you I liked you. Right from the day I knocked on your door. You're one woman that makes my blood bubble. I was determined to get you, and I'm not regretting it one bit. Not one bit.'

'Aww, Leroy. That's sweet.' She kissed his cheek. 'Don't worry, we'll sort something out before Monday, me and you. Daddy's just being silly.' Ann looked towards her car. 'Can you help me move my stuff?' she asked girlishly, rubbing her yet-to-protrude stomach. 'I can't afford to do any strenuous labour. Baby needs to rest.'

'Okay,' Leroy agreed with a boyish smile. Within Leroy, he grumbled. Now, the issue of the baby…

21

'What's happening down there, Brodericks?' Cagley said into the secure red telephone on his desk at CIA headquarters. The sun shone brilliantly through the green-tinted window, lighting up the office. 'I gave you twenty-four hours to get me that information. Where the hell is Farar Aideed?'

'We don't know yet, sir,' Seth Brodericks, the CIA Head of Station, Somalia replied. Cagley was linked to Brodericks by satellite.

'You don't? What kind of unfruitful outfit are you running down there? Aideed is the man running the show down there, isn't he? He's the head of the most powerful militia. You should have him shadowed round the clock!'

'I don't have the resources to do that, sir. I'm desperately understaffed. We urgently need more officers in Somalia. We're being devastated down here. Three of my men have been killed within the last week. An RPG landed in one of the safe houses. It's a slaughterhouse down here. We're virtually depleted. I need more men. More men.'

'No way, Brodericks! I have no more men to put in your slaughterhouse!'

'But, sir.'

'No more!'

'I need more operatives,' Brodericks insisted. 'The job's gotta be done.'

'Then hire the damn locals.'

'They're not trained.'

'Train them, dammit.'

'I don't have the resources, and I don't have the time, sir.

The President demands the military move in within a couple of weeks. We need to back up the military, sir.'

'To hell with the military!' Cagley snapped.

'But, sir—'

'Brodericks, I expect valid intelligence on Farar Aideed's location in twenty-four hours. Goodbye.' He slammed down the phone.

Unruffled, Cagley reclined in his executive chair and loosened the buttons of his dark blue jacket. He lit a Marlboro. Brodericks was right. Somalia, a war-torn semi-arid country in North East Africa had now become a nagging headache for the CIA. Siad Barre, the dictator for over twenty years had finally been ousted in an armed uprising, sponsored by a coalition of his opponents. But after ousting Barre his opponents stopped co-operating. Each was power-hungry and they could not come to a consensus. Consequently, the coalition split into factions, along clan lines. Now, ten armed militias were engaged in a bitter war for control of the country. There was no Somali state. Instead there was anarchy, chaos, and death. The CNN constantly relayed gory footage of the carnage, suffering, and famine in Somalia, especially the sick and starving children with swollen heads and bellies. It was a humanitarian disaster. The President of the United States had taken a keen interest in Somalia, and decided to intervene to stop the war. Consequently, the White House, State Department, the generals in the Pentagon, and virtually all government agencies in Washington had now turned to the CIA for detailed intelligence and information.

Now, how could the CIA obtain all the information the President and the military were asking for when virtually all the CIA officers and agents in Somalia had been killed, deported or gone missing? Somalia was a perilous place! And now, Brodericks, the head of Somalia Station was demanding more support, and more officers, which meant more deaths and more body bags.

As Cagley thought about the Somalia problem, he glanced

at the framed photograph of Ann, propped on the right hand corner of his desk. It was five days since she left home.

When is my baby coming back home? I miss her.

They'd had disagreements before. He would have asked a couple of boys from the agency to locate her, but that really wasn't necessary. He fondly recalled when she caught the teenage bug in High School and started smoking and staying out till very late at night; generally, behaving like a degenerate. One day, she returned home at 4.00 in the morning. He put her back in line by locking her out of the house. It was winter, and it was zero degrees outdoors. She nearly froze to death—and she learned her lesson: Daddy would not tolerate any nonsense.

As he thought of her, his mind flashed to Leroy. He scowled. *I've given Maxwell Harley, the head of the disciplinary panel strict instructions. That punk will be arraigned before Ed Bloomsbury, the district judge. I've given Ed a call. That mongrel Delgado will soon be seeing the inside walls of John Hune's stinking penitentiary. I know John. He will organize a big, bloody surprise.*

The intercom on Cagley's desk beeped. Cagley pressed a button. 'Yes?'

'The DDA is here to see you, sir,' Anita said.

'Okay.' Cagley extinguished his cigarette as Thomas Schwartz entered. 'Any problem?' Cagley inquired seeing Schwartz was somewhat ruffled.

'Well, I won't say there's a problem in that sense, but I have news, and you may not like it.'

'Spill it,' Cagley grunted, nonchalant.

'It's the Delgado case.'

'Delgado?' Cagley sat up. His face turned harsh. 'What about him?'

Schwartz breathed deeply. 'Maxwell has dissolved the panel. Delgado's walking free.'

Cagley shot to his feet. 'What did you say?'

Schwartz swallowed hard. 'Delgado is walking free.'

Cagley's eyes turned dark. What kind of incompetent bums

97

did he have running things in Schwartz's directorate? They couldn't do the simplest things. Delgado was walking free? Free of trespassing, molestation, and other charges? That was not his instruction to Schwartz and the losers he had running things down there. They were supposed to have a hearing and then recommend the case—with or without merit—to the judge. And Ed, the judge, a friend, had agreed to find grounds to send Delgado to prison. So, now, the case was not even going to proceed to the judge at all?

Cagley was about to yell at Schwartz but he exercised a little discretion. If Maxwell and Schwartz, thick as they were, did something contrary to his instruction, they probably had a good reason. 'What happened?'

'He's got no case to answer.' Schwartz took a seat across the table from Cagley. 'The panel dismissed it.'

'Why, dammit?' Cagley growled.

Schwartz sighed. 'Delgado and your daughter caused a scene at the hearing.'

'Delgado and Ann?' On hearing Ann's name Cagley's countenance changed. Fully attentive, he leaned towards Schwartz. 'What happened?'

'I met with you last week and we agreed Delgado should face a disciplinary panel. I sent out a letter to Delgado the same day, hand delivered. Today, circumstances have changed.'

'How? What's changed?'

Schwartz breathed deeply. 'It seems Delgado and Ann are living together.' He looked Cagley straight in the eyes. 'Are you aware of that?'

Cagley drew back. 'Living together? Hell no!'

In all his thoughts, Cagley assumed Ann had moved in with Marian Flench, her best friend. Since high school, Marian's place was always her port of refuge when she was upset. Always.

'Delgado and your daughter flew to Las Vegas over the weekend,' Schwartz continued.

'What's that to do with the hearing?' Cagley asked, already

fearing Schwartz's reply.

'This morning, they came hand in hand to the hearing. Delgado walked to the table and dropped a certificate. "You can't charge a man for bedding his wife," he said. And your daughter added, "My child's not going to be a bastard." Without another word, they left.'

'What do you mean?'

'They got married. She's now his legal wife. The panel cannot touch him. Not on those grounds, anyway.'

Cagley's heart went into overdrive. For a brief moment it looked like he had seen a ghost. No it couldn't be true. 'They got married?'

Schwartz nodded.

'Are you sure?'

Schwartz nodded again.

Cagley sank into his seat. *Ann got married?* No, it couldn't be.

He looked at Schwartz. The grim look in his face told Cagley he was telling the truth.

Ann got married! *She got married without telling me?*

That was a scenario he had never bargained for. Give her a few days and she would come back home, he'd thought. That was the way it happened in families: voices are raised, people say what they ought not, everyone disagrees for a few days. Then things return to normal. Instead, Ann went and got married to that lousy son-of-a-bitch. She went and made her union with Sergeant Ken's son permanent.

To Cagley, it felt like a mortal blow.

He didn't like to lose or fail or made to feel like an idiot, but right now, Delgado's move made him feel like a loser and a completely incompetent fool. He stared grimly at the wall. And stared, and stared. *Delgado's stolen my daughter. The son of that bastard, Sergeant Ken has taken what's most important to me.*

Damn you, Delgado. Damn you. Now it's war!

Damn you.

99

'Just to let you know,' Schwartz said, 'I've moved Delgado out of the Office of Security. He's now in Intelligence. A desk job should keep him out of trouble.'

'Okay. Thanks, Schwartz,' Cagley said, drained. He waved Schwartz away.

Schwartz walked to the door. He stopped and cast a look at Cagley. Cagley was pensive and pale. 'I don't want to fire him,' Schwartz said softly. 'And it will be wise if you don't. Wife and baby will need the money.'

Cagley barely stirred.

'What are you gonna do now?'

22

The CIA lobby was overlaid with white and grey marble. Hillary Bosworth, Cagley's obese lackey held a key, which allowed him use the elevator reserved for the Director. Bosworth stood waiting for the Director's elevator to descend.

The shiny doors slid open. Bosworth expected the elevator to be empty but it was not. Cagley and one of his bodyguards were inside.

Bosworth stepped aside to allow Cagley to exit. Cagley didn't move. He merely stared at Bosworth. 'Get in,' Cagley said. 'I want to speak to you.'

Bosworth squeezed into the elevator, his enormous gut wobbling as he did. At six foot-six he towered above Cagley, who was five foot six.

Cagley turned to his bodyguard. 'Get out.' The guard promptly exited the elevator. The door closed.

'I gave you an assignment,' Cagley began. 'You haven't given me an update. How is my daughter doing?'

It was now three days after he learned Ann got married. Cagley looked straight ahead at the elevator door, and put a cigarette to his lips. He did not light up since smoking was not allowed in the elevators, corridors and offices of the CIA. Cagley routinely broke this law in his office, however.

'Sh-she's doing fine,' Bosworth babbled. 'They seem to get along very well.'

Cagley glared at him. 'I didn't ask for your opinion, Bosworth. And as far as I'm concerned, I hope they don't get on very well. I asked you to keep them under surveillance. So, just tell me what you saw. Tell me what you heard.'

'Er, they went to Las Vegas last Saturday, came back very late on Sunday.'

'I know that,' Cagley snapped.

'Delgado now works as military statistician in the Directorate of Intelligence, Middle East operations. His duty is cataloguing air power.'

'Tell me something I don't know.'

'They go to work. Delgado returns home at about six every day. She returns about five. She cooks. They watch TV. They talk a lot. Generally seem to have a good home-life together.'

'What do they talk about?'

'Many things: his past, her past. They also talk about the baby.'

Cagley yawned. 'Does she say anything about coming home?'

'No.'

Damn. Wasn't she missing him as much as he missed her? 'What else?'

'Ann asks him to talk to his friends, to tell them she has nice houses for sale.'

'That's nothing new, she's always doing that. She's a real estate agent. What else?'

'On Thursday, they linked up downtown and went to dinner at Amalfi's in Georgetown. I snapped a lot of shots of them together. I don't have any information from Thursday to Saturday. The listening device I planted in their living room lost power. I was only able to sort it out on Saturday, late at night after they went to bed.'

'Make sure they never find out about that,' Cagley warned.

'It's somewhere they'll never look. And I've masked the frequency.'

'Good. What other information do you have?'

'On Saturday they went to the movies. They were holding hands.'

'Holding hands? So, are you suggesting they…er, love each other?'

'If they're still holding hands after they hit the storms of life then we can tell.'

'Then let the storms begin, Bosworth. Let it begin. I want my daughter back home!'

The elevator door opened and Cagley walked out.

23

In Hangar 22 at Andrews Air Force Base, Maryland, twelve sensible mechanics laboured on their respective airplanes. One mechanic, Sergeant Colin O'Donnell sneaked into the lavatory and rolled himself a spliff. He dragged on it, and felt an all-familiar headache as the weed took effect.

Through the thick, white smoke that filled the lavatory, he saw fairies floating around near the ceiling. Pretty, tiny, golden things, carrying golden wands. They waved their wands at him. He tried to touch them but they melted into the ceiling. It was the weed making him hallucinate. He laughed raucously. With this high he could do anything. His mind flashed to the guy who'd sold him the grass, a Jamaican with dreadlocks, called Totay. 'Dis a good ganja, mon,' Totay had said. 'From d'jungle, mon.'

Totay was right. This was industrial strength weed. Some really serious shit. He dragged on the weed again. It hit his senses. 'Aaah. Balushaga!'

The smell of burning weed wafted out of the lavatory just as Major-General Tommy 'Slugger' Archibald, commander of the US Air Force 89th Wing walked briskly into the hangar. He was accompanied by Colonel Janolski, head of 89th Operations. General Archibald wore camouflage, and had greying hair.

Lieutenant Bailey, the tall and lanky chief mechanic, saw General Archibald first. 'Ten hup!' he bellowed.

All the mechanics stood to attention where they were.

'Easy,' Archibald said to Bailey. He was not always formal.

'Stand at ease!' Bailey yelled.

'Where's Major Farringdon?' Archibald asked.

'In his office, sir!' Bailey answered, smart and loud.

Farringdon had heard Bailey's voice as he ordered the men to attention. It often meant a senior officer was paying an impromptu visit. Farringdon shot out of his office and hurriedly climbed down the steel stairs. He met the general at the hangar door. He came to attention smartly and saluted.

'Easy, Major.' Archibald returned the salute. 'I was just passing by. You heard about the Air Force convention in Colorado?'

'Yes, sir.'

'I want you and Janolski to represent us there.'

'Yes, sir.'

'And by the way…' The general stopped and sniffed the air. 'What's that?'

The aroma was unmistakable. It hung thick in the air. Marijuana.

Farringdon cast a quick look around. All his mechanics were in there. Except that half-crazy one, O'Donnell.

What would the general think about the smell? Farringdon wondered. The general would think he could not control the hangar. This moron, O'Donnell was making him and the entire unit look bad. He had no respect for anyone or anything, and absolutely no regard for authority.

'Anyway,' General Archibald concluded. 'See you boys later.'

He walked out of Hangar 22. O'Donnell and Bailey saluted as he left. They held their salute till he entered his Jeep and drove off.

With the general gone there was now the other issue.

'O'Donnell!' Farringdon roared as he stormed towards the men's room.

Inside, O'Donnell was just coming out of a cubicle. The lavatory smelt strongly of weed. O'Donnell's eyes were glazed and bloodshot. Pot smoking was nothing new in the military but it was not done in the open.

'This is your last chance!' Farringdon roared, eyes ablaze,

poking his finger at O'Donnell. 'The next time you fall out of line, you'll regret you were ever born!'

Farringdon knew he wouldn't have to wait very long.

24

It was 3.00 am. The curtains in Leroy and Ann's bedroom were open. The streetlight outside their home flooded the bedroom with dull orange light. Leroy was fast asleep.

Ann lay beside him, wide awake. For some reason her stomach hurt severely. Something seemed to be gnawing away inside her. It felt like cramps but a lot worse. She groaned.

Leroy stirred out of sleep. 'Are you okay?' he mumbled, half awake.

'No!' she yelped as a bout of pain surged through her abdomen. She clutched her belly.

Startled, Leroy sat up. 'What is it? Are you okay?' He rubbed his eyes.

'No,' she screamed. 'No!'

Rattled, Leroy jumped out of bed. He flipped on the lights. The sight was sickening. Ann's nightie was stained with blood. There was blood on her thighs, blood on her underwear, blood on the bedspread.

'What the hell?'

Leroy dialled 911. A few minutes later he heard the blare of an ambulance siren.

Forty minutes later, Leroy paced anxiously around Woodlake Hospital's Emergency Unit.

What was wrong with Ann?

He'd given up smoking but right now he needed a cigarette. Clad in dark jeans, and T-shirt, he paced nervously round the Emergency Department reception. After an hour, a doctor finally appeared. He was Latino, and wore a ruffled, green surgery tunic. 'Mr Delgado?'

Leroy turned round. 'Yes.'

'I'm sorry, Mr Delgado,' the bespectacled doctor began, twiddling his stethoscope. 'There's no easy way to say this. Er, let me say it's mixed blessings right now.'

'Mixed blessings—what does that mean? Can you just tell me what's wrong with her; is she okay?'

'Calm down, Mr Delgado. Ann is okay. But as you are aware she was bleeding from the vagina. We don't know why that happened yet. Our main concern is to stem the bleeding. As you may be aware, she was pregnant.'

'Yes…'

'We're concerned…though we're still in the dark,' the doctor said as if he was holding something back. 'She'll see the consultant first thing in the morning. He'll explain everything to her.'

'Why can't you tell me?'

'We're not trying to hold back information, Mr Delgado. It's just that we haven't finished all the tests. Ann's sedated right now. Why don't you go home and get some rest then come back at about twelve noon?'

Leroy sensed some despair in the doctor's voice. 'All right. You said you're concerned… What about? What does that mean?'

The doctor's tone dropped low. 'Er, I'm sorry. I don't know how to say this but…she lost the baby.'

25

'I'm sorry, Ann,' Dr Cohen said. He sat behind his table inside the consulting room.

'I-I lost the baby? I lost the baby!' Tears flowed down her cheeks. 'That baby is—was—what I wanted most in life.'

He studied her for another minute. There was relative silence in the immaculate consulting room save for Ann's sniffing, and the humming air-conditioner.

'I'm really confused here…' Dr Cohen's voice thinned into a whisper. He peered at Ann suspiciously from behind his rimless glasses. 'I thought you were eager to get pregnant. Only a couple of weeks ago you were in this same room, rejoicing because you had conceived. You were so excited and you were jumping all over the place. Now, I don't understand it….What has changed, Ann? If you wanted a baby desperately why did you embark upon a termination?'

Ann raised her sullen head. 'T-termination?'

'Yes.'

She stared mortified at Dr Cohen. 'Y-you mean abortion?'

The grim look in Dr Cohen's face showed he meant what he said. 'Yes. You were brought here bleeding from the uterus. We have done an investigation and completed our tests. We found that the bleeding was a side effect of a pill-induced abortion.'

Ann stared vaguely at Dr Cohen. 'A pill-induced abortion?'

'Yes. From the lining of the uterus, your blood, and the urine tests, we are ninety-nine percent certain you took an abortion pill. It killed the foetus. That was what caused the pain and bleeding.'

She clutched her heart, horrified. 'No!'

'Yes. The lab boys did a test but it was such an advanced drug that it left virtually no trace. And the little residue they could find could not be identified as it was not in the pharmacopoeia. My guess is that it is a high-tech designer drug.'

Her eyes widened, horrified. 'A high-tech designer drug?'

'Yes.'

'I didn't take any drugs! I didn't!'

Dr Cohen studied her. Her eyes were wild and intense. She looked truthful enough, and he knew she wanted a baby very much. 'A pill that fits that specification is very rare. There are quite a few abortion pills like RU-486 and others, but you can always trace their type from blood and urine. But this one is quite expensive and very rare. A special make.'

Her eyes widened. 'Special make?'

Dr Cohen nodded. He saw from the intense look in Ann's eyes that she was eager for answers. He decided to volunteer information so as to get to the bottom of the mystery. 'Don't quote me,' he said, 'but I would say it's the type our boys use; the type the agency uses.'

Ann went numb. It was such a huge blow to her system that for a long while she could only stare at Dr Cohen. She understood precisely what Dr Cohen meant. She was not in an ordinary street-corner hospital; she was in Woodlake Hospital in Bethesda, Maryland. A hospital used by CIA and top security government employees. The CIA is essentially an organisation designed to spy on other countries on behalf of the US government. In the cause of that, sex and seduction played a major role. Quite often, information was cajoled from foreign nationals under the guise of love, and very often, in the cause of getting closer, agents and spies often became intimate with people they were trying to get information from. On the rare occasion, pregnancies occurred. But the CIA was only interested in information, not a baby brood. Consequently, there was a little white pill called ATK, which took care of that problem. All that was required was to slip it into the woman's drink. It dissolved without a trace, and flushed out the foetus.

110

The type the agency uses. ATK! The CIA pregnancy termination pill.

As if in a trance, Ann slowly stood up, and without saying a word, she walked out of Dr Cohen's consulting room. Without much control over herself, she left Woodlake Hospital. For the next thirty minutes, Ann wandered aimlessly around the wooded streets of Bethesda, looking fixedly ahead. *So, the reason I lost my hard-earned baby was because I ingested an abortion pill. ATK. Somebody spiked my meal or drink. That person deliberately killed my baby. My miracle baby!*

When she learnt she lost the pregnancy it hurt so much but she endured it. Now that she knew it was all some evil person's handiwork it hurt twice as much. As the truth fully dawned on her, she flopped against a lamppost by the roadside and sobbed uncontrollably.

As she wept her sorrow slowly changed to anger. *Who did it? Who in the CIA killed my baby?*

She had to get to the bottom of this. She asked herself some questions: *To begin with, who knew I was pregnant? Only someone who knew I was pregnant could have done it.*

She came up with answers: *Daddy, Leroy, Dr Cohen, and some staff at work. I didn't tell anyone else.*

Who amongst them has access to CIA pills? Who works with the CIA?

Only Daddy and Leroy. Dr Cohen too...but I don't see any interest he'd have in this. I am certain he was not involved. So, I've got just Daddy and Leroy.

Now, who didn't want the pregnancy?

Both of them. Daddy didn't like it. Leroy didn't sound happy about it at first.

Now, who can get close enough to me to feed me the pill? Only Leroy. Not Daddy.

Leroy? My husband? Would Leroy do that?

She recalled the first time she told him about the pregnancy. He was not enthusiastic at all. While she was screaming with joy all he said was, "Er...er."

Didn't he want the baby?

Maybe he was masquerading his true intentions. Maybe he never said anything...yet plotted to get rid of the baby.

She stopped. But it did not seem like the sort of thing he would do, though. *I trust him.*

But can you trust anyone?

Well, I...think I trust him.

But could he? She thought deep. Maybe. Maybe not.

Her mind went to her father. Could he?

She really doubted he would cross that line. He was mean, all right, but he was still her dad, and yes, he could be angry about certain things but when it came to harming her, she was certain he would not go that far.

Still, one of them had a hand in this. Was it her husband or her father? One did not want a child; the other did not want a child from her husband.

Seeking more information, she got out her phone and called Woodlake Hospital. She had Dr Cohen's direct number on her hospital card. Dr Cohen picked the phone.

'Hello, doctor, it's me, Ann Cagley.'

'Hello, Ann.'

'I just wanted to ask. This drug, ATK, how long does it take to act? How long after ingestion does it take effect?'

'Usually twenty-four to forty-eight hours.'

'Okay. Thank you.' She switched off.

Today is Thursday. That means I must have been doped on Monday or Tuesday.

She dragged her mind back to Monday and tried to think of everything that happened that day; everything she ate and drank.

On Monday, she didn't have breakfast till she got to work, and then she had toast and coffee, which she bought from *Biggs*, the breakfast kiosk. She took her regular pregnancy supplement. Nothing sinister about that, she'd been taking it for a couple of weeks now. She had more coffee at work but she made that herself, so no one could have spiked it. In the

112

afternoon she had lunch at a café. So, that was safe. In the evening… She thought hard. Yes, she made pasta, and had some Coca-Cola. She poured the Coke herself, so it couldn't have been spiked. That was about all for Monday.

Tuesday. As usual, she had breakfast at work, and had lunch near the Smithsonian when she went out on house valuation, so that was safe. Evening…

In the evening they ordered pizza. It was delivered.

Leroy got the drinks… *He got my drink, a Coke.*

Could it have been then?

On Wednesday, she didn't eat till she got to work. She skipped lunch, and…she was beginning to have stomach cramps by then. That meant the ATK was already working, though she'd had no inclination as to what it was. So, obviously it had been administered to her before then.

Looking over the last three days there was no time anyone could have had the chance to spike her drink except on Tuesday evening when they had pizza, and Leroy got the drinks.

Could it be then? It had to be then. There was no other time I took a drink that I did not get myself!

All indications pointed to Leroy.

Her eyes turned narrow, and vicious.

Leroy.

The coward. He did it.

Leroy did it. He killed my baby!

The grief that swept through her heart was almost palpable. She'd been a fool, trusting him, playing happy families with him when all along….

'Leroy! You, bastard!'

26

'You did it, didn't you?' Ann shrieked, standing in the doorway of their bedroom, wearing nothing but her white panties and a white nylon shirt, which bared her midriff. It was 7 o'clock in the morning. 'You did it, you rotten spook!'

'What's the matter?' Leroy asked.

She had been colder than ice ever since she returned from the hospital, yesterday. She'd only said three words to him since then, and that was when she snarled, "Don't touch me!"

What was up with her? He'd been trying to get her to talk but every time she locked herself in the bathroom. She refused to sleep in their bed, but stayed on the sofa downstairs. Well, at least now, she was talking. Or exploding.

'You're asking what the matter is?' she screeched, her fiery eyes tearing into him. 'Everything. You murderer! You killed my child. You killed my baby.'

Her words hit him like a sledgehammer. He frowned and drew back. His mind quickly put the pieces together and he knew in an instant what she meant. 'Are you talking about the miscarriage?'

'Yes! And it was you who arranged for me to lose my baby. You killed it right in my womb. You thought I'd never find out, didn't you? Well, I did. You fixed an abortion drug in my drink.'

'What?'

'How could you be so cruel, Leroy?' she scolded, wild eyed, her voice heavy with grief. 'So heartless. You are a monster!' Her eyes were wild. 'If you didn't want a child, then you should have been man enough to say so. How dare you use underhand CIA techniques with me, Leroy? How dare you use a CIA abortion pill on me?'

For one long minute Leroy didn't speak. What was she talking about? A part of him was livid at such an accusation and another part was sure she got her facts wrong. He couldn't believe what he was hearing. He looked into her face. The intense scowl on her face showed she was dead serious.

'What abortion pill are you talking about?'

'ATK!'

'ATK?' His eyes flew open. 'The CIA pill?'

'Yes.'

'Now, wait a minute. Are you saying you lost the baby because someone fixed ATK in your drink—and you think I did it?' He was grim.

'Yes. On Tuesday evening, I think.'

Tuesday evening? He thought back. Yes, on Tuesday, he got her some Coca-Cola. But all he did was open the can, pour its contents into a tall glass, then added some ice and lemon. That was all. An abortion pill? He couldn't believe she said that—or even dared to think it!

'Ann, I don't know where you got your story from but this tale about ATK or some abortion pill is way beyond me. Who told you it was ATK? How on earth did you hear about ATK in the first place?'

'My consultant at Woodlake said it was an abortion pill that was high-tech, untraceable and not in the pharmacopoeia—very likely ATK.'

Now, Leroy knew something had to be wrong. Woodlake was essentially the CIA hospital, and they had a good knowledge of CIA processes and medication. So, her information was probably valid.

'Ann, I'm really concerned. If anyone drugged you with any type of pill, I want to know who did it. I'd like to take it up and call the cops.'

'You don't fool me with such bravado, Leroy. Call the cops? Yes, I will call the cops. You can't get away with this. I'm certain you did it by spiking my drink. You're the only one that has access to me.'

'I had nothing to do with it.' The very fact that she thought he could stoop so low aggravated him. 'Why on earth will I want to do that? Where on earth would I get ATK? And why exactly would I want to kill our child?'

'I always knew you never wanted it. You were never enthusiastic about it!'

'True, it came as a shock at first. A big shock. But it's grown on me; I've accepted it, and I'm very keen on it. What makes you think I'd do such a thing as try to kill him, or her? I'm your husband for goodness sake!'

'Husband? Ha! I must be the luckiest girl in the world. I hitched Leroy, the murderer.'

He didn't wish to be provoked but her accusation made him angry. True, it hurt but he'd gotten over it, and she would also have to. Hurt as it may, the baby was lost. Nothing would bring it back. The only option was to have another.

'I didn't do it, okay? I'm sorry we lost the baby. I'm sorry—'

'Sorry? You ruined my life and all I get is sorry? I've waited so long to get pregnant. I wanted nothing more than that child.'

'I didn't do it!'

'You did! The doctors confirmed it was ATK. Who would have access to ATK except someone who works in the agency?'

'So, because I work for the CIA, I must be a cold, heartless killer, right?'

'I don't care! Someone who doesn't want me to be a mother has killed my child. The one chance I had—and somebody ruined it!'

'That person wasn't me, Ann.'

She said nothing. She hurt desperately. At a loss, she sat on the bed, buried her face in her palms and sobbed.

He hated to see her cry. It hurt him that she felt this way. He went to her. 'Ann, you know I love you.' He took hold of her shoulders. 'You must understand that I would not do anything to—'

She shrank back from him like he was a leper. 'Spare me

116

the sermon, Leroy. Just do shut up. I love you?' She laughed incredulously. 'Are three words gonna fix it? Is that gonna bring Jack back?' Full of hope that she would have had a son she had already given her expected baby the name, Jack.

'Ann,' he said softly. He used his thumbs to wipe the tears from her eyes. He knew she treasured that baby. Losing it must have been really hard on her. Right now, all he wanted was for her to be fine. He squatted in front of her. 'I know you've been through a lot. I understand how you feel. But you must understand, I had absolutely nothing to do with losing the baby. But don't worry about it. Everything will be fine. We had one, we can have another. C'mon, Ann, it's gonna be alright, huh?' He held her playfully. 'It's gonna be alright.'

She shoved him back.

He resisted playfully. 'C'mon, Ann, it's gonna be—'

Everything that happened had made Ann frustrated. She was like a steam boiler, waiting to explode. She had lost the one in a million chance she had to become a mother, and as far as she could see, Leroy was the culprit…and he was still acting playful?

She grabbed the first thing within arm's reach—a red, high-heeled, suede pump. She raised the shoe as high as she could and, mustering all her strength, smashed it, heel first into Leroy's skull.

The piercing sting shot all the way down his spine. 'Wh-what did you do that for?' he stuttered, staring shell-shocked at Ann, his head aching with every word. He saw this smug look on her face.

She said nothing. Instead, her hand flashed once more—so fast he never saw it coming. She smashed the shoe into his head once more. So hard, the heel broke.

Another piercing pain exploded inside Leroy's skull. Grimacing, he sank to the floor, both hands holding his head. He felt thick, warm fluid flowing between his fingers. He knew he was bleeding.

She watched for about ten seconds as he writhed on the

117

carpet. She glared at him then walked out of the bedroom, slamming the door behind her.

Leroy struggled to his feet, and staggered unsteadily across the bedroom. He caught a glimpse of himself in the mirror. Bright red blood seeped from two places on his scalp. It streamed down his face and dripped onto his white shirt, creating soggy, red patches.

The first thing that flashed into his mind was that snide look he had seen on Ann's face. That look was the very thing that infuriated him. She did all this and she wasn't even sorry? Who did she think she was?

'Stupid little bitch! You messed with the wrong man!'

In those few moments all the affection they had for each other disappeared down the drain. Suddenly, they were simply objects to each other. He was a despicable object whose head deserved to be hammered; she was an errant object that deserved to be taught a lesson. A big lesson.

He yanked his thick brown belt off his trousers and wound it tightly around his fist. Gritting his teeth, he bounded across the room. The blood was on his shirt, his shoes, the carpet, the bed— everywhere! The sight of it infuriated him even more.

He yanked open the bedroom door. Blood spilled over his eyelids. He swiped it off. He darted out of the bedroom, leaving a set of smudgy red fingerprints on the door. He bounded down the stairs, covering five steps at a time. He landed at the foot of the stairs with a thud.

'Stupid bitch. Where are you?' His eyes darted around, seeking her. She was not in the living room. Where the hell was she?

Then he saw her.

Although she was barely clothed, she was outside, heading towards her Toyota. He could see her skimpily-clad frame through the living room windows.

'Where the hell d'you think you're going?' He stormed towards the front door.

Ann heard Leroy's chilling voice reverberate through the

living room windows. Its sharp, hostile crack made her heart skip a beat. It was damn scary. Definitely murderous! She glanced back at the house. A reddish blur flashed past the living room windows. She knew it was Leroy. And he was neither calm nor tranquil. He was maniacal.

Swifter than a supercomputer, Ann's brain calculated the danger. It came up with only one solution: run! Her defences swung into action. Adrenaline surged into her bloodstream and she broke into a panicked run.

Leroy tried to open the front door but for some reason it wouldn't budge. Fuming, he struggled with the lock. Frustrated, he kicked at it.

Ann heard the violent banging behind her. She was now at the door to her car.

Back inside, Leroy remembered the reason the door wouldn't open was because the latch opened counter-clockwise. He had been turning the latch clockwise. His anger had caused disorientation, beclouding the commonest things. He swung the latch the correct way. The front door opened inwards, letting in a gust of cold air.

'Damn you, Ann!' he roared, cracking his thick belt. 'Damn you!'

Ann tried to jam the car key into the door lock. Trembling, her hand was unsteady. She fumbled and kept missing the obvious hole. She looked over her shoulder. Leroy was out of the front door, his body bathed in blood. There was blood on his hair; it streamed down his face. So much blood, even on his lips, in his mouth, between his gritted teeth. His eyes belched fire. He held a thick, murderous belt, tipped with a menacing brass buckle. He sprang towards the Toyota!

Ann finally got the key in the lock. She turned it. There was a click as the door locks bobbed up. She reached for the door lever and yanked it up. The door swung outwards. Faster than lightning, she jumped into the driver's seat.

Leroy was there. He grabbed hold of the door and pulled. Ann pulled too.

119

At times of danger, humans tend to develop more strength than they normally have. Ann snatched the door with all her might. Leroy had to let go or the door would have chopped his fingers off. She slammed the door shut.

Leroy lunged for the handle.

Inspiration came from nowhere; Ann pushed down the door lock. There was a whirr as all the four locks sank into the frames.

Leroy yanked at the handle but the car door would not open. Ann had locked herself in.

Ann shoved the key into the ignition and turned it. The car roared to life. Tyres screeching, she reversed onto the street and sped off.

As head of the CIA, Michael Cagley briefed the President every morning at 8.00.

At 7.15, Cagley emerged from his mansion and walked to the CIA Cadillac that would convey him to the White House. A bodyguard held the rear door open. He was about to step inside when a blue car approached the house from the front gates. He stopped momentarily. His two bodyguards also observed the approaching vehicle. For them, protecting Cagley was their livelihood. The bodyguards stepped around Cagley, creating a human shield. At the same time they yanked out their weapons, an Uzi and a Mac 10.

The car drew closer and Cagley recognised its occupant. 'It's all right, it's my daughter.'

Their guns reluctantly returned to the holsters under their jackets.

Ann pulled up beside Cagley's Cadillac. He stiffened. His daughter was practically naked, wearing nothing but a loose shirt and underwear. Worse, she looked battered. Her eyes were bloodshot and underlined with ugly, black bags. Her cheeks were lined with tears. It looked like she'd been through hell. It was evident she was hurting.

The natural paternal bond between father and child sprang

alive, strong as ever. Their petty squabbles paled into oblivion. Cagley hastened towards her. 'Are you alright?'

She didn't answer. Instead, she slipped into his comforting arms. Cagley held her close and stroked her hair. She opened her mouth to speak but instead sobbed.

'Come, tell Daddy about it. Whoever did this to you is gonna wish he'd never been born.'

Holding her, he led her into the house.

When Leroy regained his senses he trudged back indoors. He had lost a lot of blood. His head ached as if somebody had taken the drill to it. He washed the blood off his face, and changed his bloodstained clothes.

He downed a shot of tequila to calm his nerves. Then he drove to Woodlake Hospital in Bethesda.

'What happened?' the nurse asked at the Emergency Room.

'I was hit by falling roof tiles.'

A doctor stitched his head wounds and gave him some Tylenol.

Leroy left the hospital. At the traffic lights at the junction of Rockville and West Cedar Lane he debated whether to turn to the left and go to work or turn right, return home, and call-in sick. Merely thinking of home made him remember the ugly incident between himself and Ann. Work was a better option. It would help clear his head. He turned left.

27

After briefing the President, Cagley stormed out of the White House wearing a deep frown. He ordered his driver to head back to CIA headquarters.

Sitting in the back of his armour-plated Cadillac he scowled and cracked his knuckles. All through the seven-mile journey to Langley, not once did he look out of the window to watch Washington fly past as he usually did. His mind was occupied—not with issues of national security but with Ann, his daughter.

In a way, he was relieved. At last, Ann had returned home, and what bound Ann and Delgado together was broken. The baby was gone. Good for everyone.

Still, he was troubled. Deeply troubled. Ann was broken and shattered, and she had told him a weird little story about Delgado, ATK and how she lost her cherished baby. Cagley listened to everything she said but he found her story somewhat bizarre. True, the CIA had a drug called ATK, but it was only made available to HUMINT staff—spies—the actual guys who did the James Bond stuff in foreign countries. ATK was strictly controlled, however. Delgado was not a spy, and the agency would never issue them to him. How then could he acquire such drugs?

Earlier that morning when Ann was telling him her story she wept profusely, convinced Leroy was the culprit. But not five minutes later she turned and looked despairingly into his eyes, and asked, "Daddy, did you do it?"

'What?' he'd answered. 'What kind of stupid question is that? Of course not. I know nothing about it.'

If she was so certain Delgado was the culprit then she should not have asked him such a question.

As far as Cagley could see, Ann's story did not add up. Still, the issue was serious. Extremely serious. What if she had been given a poison pill, not an abortion pill? He didn't give a rat's ass about Delgado. All the better for him if Ann believed he was guilty. But what if it was some terrorist group scheming up a weird plot, and sending a message? What if they were hinting they could get to Ann? Or trying to prove they could get to him?

Ann was looking at things from a very narrow angle, but as head of the CIA he couldn't afford to take a similar chance. He couldn't afford to compromise his personal security or his daughter's safety. Something sinister was going on, and he had to get to the bottom of it. He picked up the car phone and punched in a number. Jim Lurkey, chief of CIA Medical Services, picked it up at CIA headquarters. 'Lurkey here.'

'Lurkey, there are some foul ups in your sub department,' Cagley fired off.

'Foul ups?'

'Yeah. But it's not administrative.'

'Oh.' Lurkey sighed.

'I want you to do an investigation for me—a thorough audit of ATK pills.'

'ATK?'

'Yeah, ATK. I want to know how many pills you ordered in the last year, how many you have in stock, and how many you issued to Operations. I want you to liase with them, and get an accurate count. I want to know everyone that has been given ATK in the past year. I want a tablet by tablet count. Each pill must bear a name.'

'Is there a problem?' Lurkey asked. Cagley's request was unusual.

'Don't worry about that. Just carry out my orders.'

Jim Lurkey was irritated. That hammerhead, Cagley always pissed him off. Still, if you hate the boss, you shouldn't let it

123

show. 'Yes, Mike.'

'I want the report in three days. I don't want any cover-ups. I want a straight clean report. If you hide something, I'll have your head. Do you understand?'

'Right.'

'I want that list, and I want it soonest.' Cagley hung up. That would take care of the ATK issue. He sat back in the plush leather seat, pensive, as his Cadillac sped past the tall magnolias on George Washington Memorial Parkway.

His mind switched to Leroy. 'Imbecile! I still have unfinished business with you, Leroy Delgado.' But in his mind he was talking straight at Leroy. 'Now that Ann is out of your grasp, it's time to take care of you. Permanently. I don't even need John Hune this time. I'm gonna do it myself. And do a better job than John Hune ever could.'

He smiled wickedly as a devious idea popped into his head. 'Someone had better call a hearse.'

Again, he picked up the phone. This time he dialled his secretary. 'Anita. Do a letter to the deputy directors of Intelligence and Operations and to the Office of Security.' He dictated his letter. By the time he got to Langley, Anita would have printed them and all he would have to do was sign them.

Leroy Delgado's fate was sealed.

But Cagley wasn't done. The last time, the son of a bitch was smart: he married Ann and beat the rap. This time there would be no escape. Cagley dialled yet another number. 'Rhodes,' he ordered, speaking to the top man in the Office of Security. 'Put together a team of security officers. Leroy Delgado is a subject the agency considers to be a prime security risk. You are directed to take him into custody by two o'clock.'

'Yes, sir!' Rhodes answered.

Cagley hung up. He smiled crookedly. At 2 o'clock Delgado would have a surprise.

Cagley arrived at his seventh floor office at 9.45am. Within an hour, he had signed the letter to the deputy directors, using his Special Executive Discretionary powers.

28

Air Force Major Farringdon sat in his elevated corner office at the rear of Hangar 22. His office was built on steel stilts, twenty feet high to give him a bird's eye view of the hangar. His phone rang. 'Farringdon, here.'

'Janolski,' the caller responded. Colonel Janolski was Head of Operations, 89th Wing.

'Morning, sir,' Farringdon said.

'Major. Have your boys finished repairs on my C-22?'

'No, sir.' Farringdon peeked through the reinforced window of his office, which looked down into the hangar. Two mechanics were still working on its engines. An avionics technician was in the cockpit, testing the instruments. Farringdon could barely hear himself speak: some nutcase was performing a full power test on a jet engine in the engine-testing bay, next door. The engine roar was deafening. The entire hangar vibrated. He sipped some coffee. A little spilled on his blue Air Force uniform.

'What do you have that's ready? I need two birds today. But if I can get one I'll be happy.'

Farringdon didn't have any airplane flagged as finished on his marker board, so he knew he had to fish around. 'Can I call you back in a minute, sir? See if I can get you something.'

'All right. And N219QY?'

'For Colorado?'

'Yep.'

The US Air Force was holding a convention for its officers at the Air Force Academy in Colorado. General Archibald had asked Farringdon and Janolski to attend.

125

'We're fitting the new pump, so it will be ready. How many of us are going?'

'Six. Madding and Krankoff will pilot.'

'Great.'

'I'll let you off now. Call me as soon as you've got something.'

'Yes, sir.'

Janolski hung up.

Next, Farringdon called the chief mechanic. 'Bailey, which bird's gonna be finished today?'

'Two-one-nine and two-five-eight should be ready,' Lieutenant Bailey answered, unsure.

'Get two-one-nine tested and ready by fifteen-hundred hours. We're taking it to Colorado.'

'Okay, sir.'

Bailey, a tall and lanky officer emerged from his tiny, grease-stained office, and entered the hangar. There were seven executive airplanes in the hangar. Bailey walked to the airplane O'Donnell was working on. 'O'Donnell!'

O'Donnell looked down from his gantry.

'How far have you gone with the pump? The major needs this bird out by fifteen-hundred hours.'

'Done, Lieutenant.'

'How many cards has it got?'

'One.'

One job card meant only one fault was reported. And that had been fixed by O'Donnell. Bailey was satisfied. 'You got the card?'

'Yep.'

O'Donnell whipped out a pen and put his initials, C.O., on the job card. He knew fully well he was supposed to sign it and print his full name. That was the rule. He didn't bother. He handed the card to Lieutenant Bailey who scrawled his signature across it and went to Farringdon's elevated corner office.

Farringdon sat behind his desk, his boots on the table. 'Your bird's ready.' He handed the job card to Farringdon.

Farringdon looked over the card. 'The mechanic has not signed off. This one's got C.O. scrawled on it. Who's working on the airplane?'

'O'Donnell, Major.'

O'Donnell, the errant one? 'Tell him to see me.'

'Yes, Major.'

Bailey went to O'Donnell. 'The major wanna see ya,' Bailey said, and walked away.

Immediately, O'Donnell developed his rebellious attitude. *Farringdon, the kid-Major was calling? Little prick. Let him wait.*

Sergeant O'Donnell waited a quarter of an hour before strolling into Farringdon's office, a hell of a long time to walk those fifty yards. O'Donnell didn't knock. He opened the door aggressively, and slammed it behind him. He didn't offer a complimentary salute neither did he offer a greeting. He kept mum, his dirty, oil-stained hands, dangling beside him. He also chewed gum, exaggerating his chew. It all portrayed a total lack of regard for Major Farringdon.

'Sergeant!' Farringdon yelled.

'Uh-huh?' O'Donnell mumbled.

'Go right back and knock on the damn door.'

O'Donnell let out a silly smile, and swaggered out of the office. He knocked feebly, entered Farringdon's office again and stood carelessly in the middle of the small floor. 'Uh-huh?'

Farringdon was fed up with this insolent twerp, O'Donnell. It was about time he sorted out the superiority issue. He pushed a button on his intercom. 'Saunders, report here on the double.'

O'Donnell stirred. *Saunders?* Lieutenant Saunders was of the Air Security, the Air Force's Military Police. O'Donnell had been in the can many times in his twenty-two years in the Air Force, mostly for indiscipline. This was one of the reasons why he had not been promoted beyond sergeant. He knew the military always punished insolence, yet he always pushed the boundary. Rough and crazy as he was, he knew Air Security hawked only two things: punishment and pain, and both he could frankly do without. So, he tried to salvage the situation. He offered a flat shabby salute. 'You called for me, huh?'

'You just keep standing right there,' Farringdon ordered.

'What'd I do?' O'Donnell protested, his dirty paws outstretched.

Farringdon looked away, angry.

'Sir, what'd I do?' O'Donnell protested. 'I didn't do nothing.'

The sound of size sixteen boots announced the approach of Lieutenant Saunders: a black guy, skinhead, six foot six and three hundred pounds of muscle. Saunders entered Farringdon's office cracking his knuckles.

'Sir!' Saunders boomed, coming to attention. The floor vibrated as he stamped his boots. Saunders saluted smartly.

'Lieutenant. Show the sergeant there must be discipline in the Force!'

Saunders cast a cold look at O'Donnell. 'Is he giving you grief, sir?'

Farringdon nodded. 'Serious grief.'

'Do you want to charge him, sir?'

'No, Lieutenant, but you must teach him to respect authority.' Saunders cracked his huge knuckles.

'Sir, what'd I do? I didn't do nothing,' O'Donnell protested.

Saunders shot a dirty look at O'Donnell. 'Sergeant! Shut up.' He reached for his baton. His voice was as loud as an exploding shell.

O'Donnell wisely kept silent.

Ordinarily, the Air Security ought to take a charge. That was the law. But that was theory, not practice. Saunders looked down at O'Donnell. Scrawny piece of smelly shit. 'Ten hup!' Saunders bawled.

O'Donnell snapped to attention.

'Sergeant, 'bout-turn! On the double. F'ward march! One-two one-two one-two one-two one-two!'

O'Donnell jogged out of Farringdon's office, followed by the hefty Lieutenant Saunders. And Saunders was one really sad, really bad dude. So bad that within the 89th he was known as Himmler.

Saunders marched O'Donnell outside into the burning sun. For an hour, he put O'Donnell through a rigorous drill—over stony ground, in the mud, and through prickly bushes. Then he made O'Donnell do leapfrog four times around the massive hangar. The drill ended back in Farringdon's office. O'Donnell was sweaty, dirty, and he groaned in pain.

'Sir, I believe he'll no longer be a headache,' Saunders vouched.

'Thanks, Lieutenant.' Farringdon turned to O'Donnell. 'Get the hell outta my office!'

Barely able to stand, O'Donnell snapped to attention. 'Yes, sir!' He wisely remembered to salute before staggering out of the office.

'Thanks.' Farringdon said to Saunders.

'Anytime, Major.' Saunders saluted and left.

O'Donnell cursed under his breath, and when he was out of hearing range of Farringdon and Saunders, he cursed aloud. O'Donnell returned to his airplane. He kicked at the wheels on the way past. 'I'm fed up with this lousy Air Force!' He flung one of his spanners down the hangar. 'Bunch of blood-sucking assholes!'

Full of hate, he sought a way to get his revenge on Major Farringdon. He knew Farringdon was scheduled to fly the T-120 with registration mark N219QY to Colorado. He would teach that twerp a lesson he would never forget.

O'Donnell marched up to aircraft N219QY, and opened the Number 1 engine pod. The copper pipes that carried hydraulic fluid were three millimetres thick. With his hacksaw, he etched a groove of two millimetres on one of the pipes, weakening it.

29

It was a little past 1.30 in the afternoon. Leroy sat forlorn at his desk in his new job in the Middle East office at the Directorate of Intelligence at CIA headquarters. The Middle East office was concerned with analysing information gathered by the CIA on Jordan, Syria, Iran, and other countries in the Middle East. The grey, windowless walls made the office feel like a sarcophagus. Every available inch of wall space was covered with maps of Arab countries, charts, and statistics. There were probably more computers in the room than in a computer shop. The unit supervisor was a hairy behemoth nicknamed 'The Bear'. And he holed up in a glass cubicle, ten yards away.

By now Leroy's anger was gone. He deeply regretted everything that happened that morning. *Ann must have been very distraught. That was why she hit me. I should not have lost my temper. That baby was what she wanted more than anything. I need to straighten things out with her. I'll call her... make sure she's okay.*

He dialled her cell phone. The call went straight to her voice mail. He decided not to leave a message. Next, he called Denney Lee & Associates, the property firm Ann worked for. A sweet-voiced lady informed him Ann had not come to work that morning.

Leroy was concerned. Ann wasn't answering her cell phone and she was not at work. Where could she be? He dialled their home in University Park. The phone rang numerous times but no one answered it. So, obviously she had not returned home.

She wasn't at their house; she wasn't at work, and she wasn't

130

picking her cell phone. Where could she be?

Then it dropped into his mind—and he knew he was right. She had returned to her father's house!

Would she really go there? She hadn't spoken to him since he kicked her out. Still, something told Leroy he was on the right path. He dialled Cagley's mansion. It was against CIA protocol to call the director's home, but right now, he didn't give a damn about protocol or the CIA.

The phone rang five times. Finally someone picked it. 'Hello,' a woman—not Ann—answered.

'Can I speak to Ann, please?'

'Who's this?'

'The name's Leroy.'

'Leroy?' the woman retorted. Her tone was filled with contempt. 'I'm sorry, Leroy, she's not receiving calls. Do you want to leave a message?'

Leave a message? She had to be joking. 'Give her the damn phone!'

'I'm sorry. I can't do that. She's in bad shape.'

'Who am I speaking with?' Leroy demanded.

'I'm Marian. Marian Flench.' Marian was Ann's bosom friend. Leroy had only met her once.

'Look, Marian, Ann is my wife. I need to speak to her.'

'She doesn't want to speak to you, Leroy.'

'Who made you the judge of that? What kind of friend are you? And when did you become the self-chosen wedge between my wife and I? Why are you meddling in our affairs?'

'I'm not meddling. She doesn't want to speak to you. Look, I gotta go.'

'If you hang up on me I'll never forgive you!' Leroy threatened.

'Leroy, please, you've got to understand, she—'

'The only thing I understand is that you are standing as a dividing wedge between my wife and I.'

'But, Leroy—'

'Look, let me tell you one thing, Marian. You may think

131

you're doing your friend a favour, but the truth is you're interfering. Maybe you should think about it. Couples do fight but they always make up. I'd like to know where you'll stand when Ann and I get back together. Because now, you've chosen sides and you're helping to split my marriage rather than fix it. If I don't get back with her I'll blame you, and I'll come looking for you.'

Leroy sounded so fierce Marian felt threatened. 'No, no, no. I'm not choosing sides. She just wants to be left alone.' But with Leroy threatening her she quickly realised it was unhealthy getting involved in their quarrel. She changed her tone. 'You know what? I don't want you guys blaming anything on me. Don't get me involved. It's your marriage. It's your lives. I'm not Ann's mouthpiece. You two settle it between yourselves. I'll hand her the phone.'

The line was silent for a good two minutes then it came alive again. 'Yes?'

'Ann, I've been so worried,' he said, his voice crackly. 'Are you all right?'

'I'm fine,' she retorted, cold as ice.

'Can we at least talk about it? I didn't do it. I swear. I did not.'

'There's nothing to talk about.'

'Let's straighten this out, Ann. We can work this out together.'

'Together? You're alone, Leroy, I'm out.'

'Don't talk that way. Don't even think that way. You're my wife. When we married I took my vows seriously and I meant it forever. I love you.'

'If you say that again I'll hang-up.' Ann's tone was sharp and uncompromising. 'Look, Leroy, it's over. I made a fundamental mistake marrying you. I'm rectifying that mistake. It's over. Don't waste your time.'

'You can't just dump me in the trash can. We can't just end it like this.'

'I am. Getting involved with you was a mistake.'

'Let's talk, baby. Please. Let's have dinner at Casablanca.'

Casablanca was Ann's favourite Spanish restaurant. 'Come on, honey, let's talk.'

Ann sighed. 'No.'

'Come on, please.' He used his little boy tone.

'No.'

'Come on baby, I love you, c'mon, *pleeease*.'

'No!'

'Remember the good times, Ann. We were perfect. We never had any friction except this once. I promise you it won't happen again. I know our relationship is young but it's been sweet. Look, I want you to be happy, Ann. I'm willing to do anything to make you happy. There isn't anything we can't get through together. There isn't anything we can't talk over. Just give me a chance. All I ask is that you give me the benefit of doubt. Just that one percent long shot. I didn't do it. I don't even understand why you think I did. I didn't do it. I swear to it.'

She paused for a while. 'Leroy, I've got to go, and I'll appreciate it if you don't call back.' She was resolute.

'Ann, *pleeeaasse* let's talk.'

'There's nothing to talk about!' she screamed.

Leroy was startled, but he said nothing.

Ann knew she had over-reacted. 'I'm sorry. I shouldn't have yelled. But just leave me alone, please.'

'Okay.' Leroy backed down.

'The issue is this: I've made a definite resolution not to come back. If there was a chance, I would, but there's absolutely no chance for us. It's not negotiable. I swear, Leroy, I'm out of this marriage! It's over.' She cleared her throat then spoke slowly and clearly. 'Don't call me, or I'll call the cops. I mean it.'

She hung up.

His mind tipped into limbo. It was over? Over for good? Was she serious about that? Really serious?

'But she really thinks I doped her,' he said to himself, perplexed. So, that was it? That was the end of it?

He slowly replaced the handset and checked his watch. 2.00 pm.

It was only then Leroy realised that four stern-looking men stood beside his desk, two on either side. Two wore dark blue uniforms identifying them as in-house CIA security officers. They were the ones who patrolled the grounds of the CIA headquarters at Langley, and manned the gatehouse, and access turnstiles. They also guarded the corridors, protected the archives and watched over anyone who was considered a risk within the CIA complex. If an employee was going to be arrested or walked out, they saw to it. The uniformed men carried pistols in their belts. The other two wore suits. One was blond, and the other had red hair. Both were about six feet-four, and huge. They were also armed. The butts of their pistols peeped out from under their jackets.

'Officer Delgado?' the red-haired one began. His voice was gruff.

'Yeah?'

He flashed a badge. 'Office of Security.'

'Can you stand up please?' one of the uniformed officers ordered.

Leroy was familiar with the procedure.

'Don't touch anything on the desk,' the security officer warned, placing his hand on his pistol.

Taken aback, Leroy stood up resignedly. The redhead in suit produced a letter. 'I have a warrant to take you into custody.'

'What's the charge?' Leroy asked.

'No charge as yet. We need to ask you a few questions. Can you come with us please?'

A few questions? Leroy looked suspiciously at the four men. *A few questions* was what they often said if an employee was suspected of leaking information.

Two female employees in his unit were staring horrified in the direction of his desk. The disgusted look on their faces indicated they had already decided he was a spy within. Hypocrites. He could imagine the gossip in the canteen. He decided he had better clear this up quickly. Besides, it was pointless to do anything but obey the security officers. 'All

134

right.'

'This way, please.'

Leroy was escorted out of the Middle East office. Something was wrong. Seriously wrong.

30

The phone on Major Farringdon's untidy desk rang sometime after 3.00 pm. It was Colonel Janolski again. 'I need a long-range airplane, Major,' Janolski said. 'One with a range of four thousand miles or more. I've got a request from the CIA. They need one for a courier.'

'I don't have any long rangers, sir.'

'What about N219QY?'

'That's the one we reserved for Colorado. O'Donnell's just about finished it.'

'N219QY has a forty-five hundred mile range, doesn't it?'

'Yes, sir.'

'Why don't we do a swap? I've got a C-21 that will make Colorado easily. We'll go on the C-21, and I'll send N219QY to the CIA. That way they get their long ranger and we still get a bird to Colorado. Everyone's happy.'

Farringdon thought briefly. Fair deal. 'Sure, sir. We'll let the CIA have N219QY instead.'

Cagley was about to have a meeting with the Director of the FBI in his office when his intercom beeped.

'We have taken Delgado into custody,' Rhodes reported.

'Good. Let Boltzman give him the surprise.'

31

The security officers led Leroy through a series of panel-clad corridors to the Operations briefing room on the second floor. Two guards were in front of Leroy, and two were behind. Leroy looked away from the prying eyes of curious staff.

A tall, dark, bald man with a deep scar on his octagonal face was waiting inside the briefing room. He gave Leroy a grim look-over. 'I'm Vince Boltzman, East Africa Operations. Grab a seat.'

Leroy sat. The security officers left the room, and waited outside the door.

The briefing room contained ten chairs. They all faced a white marker board. A massive political map of East Africa plastered the wall beside the marker board. The room was silent apart from the droning of the air conditioner.

'I have your warrant,' Boltzman said, holding up a letter as if Leroy might never have seen one before. 'I've been given orders, and they are to be carried out immediately. By executive powers conferred by Congress the agency is empowered at its discretion to place or deploy you to the role or station where its needs are best met. You have therefore been redeployed with immediate effect, Officer Delgado.'

Leroy stared at Boltzman blankly. 'Redeployed?'

Boltzman nodded. 'Yes, Officer Delgado, you are being transferred away from Langley.'

'Where to?'

'Somalia.'

Leroy gazed into oblivion. Where on earth was that? Then it clicked. Somalia! It was a war torn desert country in Africa.

That was the hellhole the CNN had been flashing in the news everyday. People were dying of famine and starvation in droves. The babies were as thin as rakes with massive, protruding bellies and huge, deformed heads. The flies hovering around them were the size of roaches. Bandits and militias ravaged the countryside. Drinking water was no better than mud, and temperatures were somewhere around forty degrees Celsius. In the last two months, three CIA officers, four agents and three contacts had been killed there. The casualty rate was so high that CIA officers called it Death Row.

Holy smokes! I'm gonna die down there.

'I will now brief you on your new station,' Boltzman said, blank-faced. He had served in Beirut, Russia, Cambodia and many hellholes around the world. He had also been shot in the face while doing a covert buy in Russia. So, he had long lost any feelings or emotions. As far as he was concerned, any CIA officer should be ready to redeploy into hell at a second's notice. Boltzman had briefed quite a few men in this room and sent them to Somalia. Today, only half were still breathing, the others killed on duty, one by a fanatical Islamic mob, one of heat stroke, another by a grenade, and another of unknown causes. Disease, perhaps.

'I don't need to reiterate the importance of CIA's presence in Somalia. You are being detailed to join Honey-badger, code name for our surveillance co-ordinating team in Mogadishu. You will be reporting to Big Ben, call sign for your unit leader. Your specific duties are to assist Big Ben in co-ordinating our agents on the field. To date, we have a hundred and fifty-one of them, the huge number because of the war circumstance in Somalia. I will fill you in with the details later.'

Leroy stared at Boltzman, deadpan. The ball was rolling so fast it was a blur. Only this morning he had a wife and a job in Washington. By afternoon he had no wife, and was being sent to a war-torn hellhole in Africa.

Africa! A place so far from his thoughts. A place that had never featured in his wildest dreams.

'There are no direct flights to Kenya tonight from any airport a hundred miles of Washington. Therefore, the logistics boys have pencilled you onto a routine courier flight out of Baltimore. Departure is twenty-three hundred hours. Be at the airport by twenty-two hundred. For security and cover you will carry a Zimbabwean passport. You are a Zimbabwean farmer returning home after a trip to Dallas to buy harvesters. Details are in this folder. Memorise it and leave it behind after the briefing.' Boltzman dropped a blue folder onto Leroy's lap.

'Your passport will be ready in an hour. The courier flight terminates in Kenya. Our man from the embassy will meet you at the airport in Nairobi. His code name is Memphis. He will carry a sign that says, Trust Bank Limited. He will put you in touch with your new unit. They will make arrangements to get you into Somalia. Now, for the operational details: Somalia is a desert country located here.' Boltzman pointed to huge patch on the map of East Africa. 'The people are mainly Moslem. It's a bit of a mess pot. Siad Barre, the ex-president, was deposed in an uprising staged by a coalition of his opponents. His opponents fell out after deposing Barre. Factions broke out, and we have a whole mess of warlords. The main guy is Farar Aideed. He has a militia, which we estimate to be ten thousand strong...'

Boltzman raved on for thirty minutes.

Boltzman's briefing ended at 4.00 pm. 'That's it,' he said. He opened the door of the briefing room. The security officers came to attention, then entered the briefing room. 'He's all yours, gentlemen.'

'But—' Leroy protested.

'Officer Delgado,' the red-haired security officer began, grim. 'Our orders are to keep you in custody and escort you to Baltimore to board a flight. Do you understand?'

Leroy frowned. 'Who the hell gave you such orders?' he demanded roughly, mounting a fight back.

'Our superiors.'

'Who the shit's that?'

'Michael Cagley. Remember him?'

'Cagley?'

Leroy's heart pounded into his ribs. Now he understood what was happening. Cagley had played a master card, and transferred him to the most dangerous place in the world for only one reason—so he would be killed. Or why else would this be happening? He was not a case officer; he had not been given the mandatory notice; he didn't have the experience; he wasn't even in Operations!

It was Cagley's vengeance. Little son of a bitch.

'No tricks, Officer Delgado,' the blond security officer warned as though reading his thoughts. 'Cagley says you're as slippery as a snake. He reckons you'll try to escape. That's why he's ordered us to take you into custody—to make sure you don't do that.' He brought out a gleaming pistol from his jacket. 'I've got a gun. Cagley ordered me to use it if necessary. And I really would love to.'

'We've got a van waiting,' the redhead officer added. 'We'll take you home to pack your stuff. Then we'll take you to BWI airport. You can go the easy way.' He gestured at the door. 'Or you can choose the hard way.' He brought out a pair of handcuffs. 'Make your choice.'

The blond was not so patronising. He jabbed his pistol in Leroy's back. 'Move it!'

With officers watching his every move and their guns drawn, Leroy was trapped. All four security men were armed. All four were bigger; and all four were fiercely loyal to Cagley. They led him to a waiting brown van on the ground floor.

The van drove out of CIA headquarters. It joined Georgetown Pike and headed towards the Capital Beltway.

As they headed east Leroy thought of Ann. Was it really over as she threatened? No, she was probably just very upset. Did she know what was happening to him? And the things her father was up to? Why would she care, anyway? Still he had the urge to call her, and let her know her father had made a dangerous move. He got out his mobile phone.

'You can't use that,' one of the uniformed security men ordered.

'Damn!' Leroy swore. He returned the phone to his jacket. 'Damn.'

He watched as the van sped down the Capital Beltway, the freeway, which encircled Washington. After about twenty miles the van turned into University Park. A few minutes later, they pulled up outside his house.

The redhead turned to Leroy. 'These guys are gonna go in with you. You have five minutes.'

One of the men opened the van. Leroy stepped out. Three men followed him into his house. Since the men weren't sure if Leroy had hidden weapons they drew their guns, cautious.

Leroy ignored them. He would find a way to escape. Sooner or later.

In the living room he looked around. The three men watched his every move. He went to the bedroom upstairs, followed by the guards. He got out a travelling bag and flung it on the bed. Not knowing what the future held he decided to fill it with clothes. He opened the closet.

He looked into the closet and froze. 'What the hell?'

The closet was half-empty. He quickly realised that all Ann's clothes were gone!

Taking no notice of the watching guards, he dashed to the small safe concealed behind the mirror on the wall. His certificates, some money, two pistols and other valuables were still there but Ann's documents and jewellery were gone. He looked around the room. Ann's shoes and cosmetics— everything that belonged to Ann was gone. But all his things were still intact. He realised what had happened: she had returned to gather her things when he was away at work.

So, she was serious; she was really out of the marriage. Disbelieving, and not knowing how to take it he flopped onto the bed.

'You are here to pack your bags,' one of the officers

remarked.

Leroy shot a cold look at that officer. It was one of the uniformed ones; tall and thin. 'You know, you really are beginning to piss me off,' Leroy warned, making a threatening gun gesture . 'Really pissing me off.'

The men glanced at each other. They didn't want a difficult situation, so they backed down. Leroy got off his bed and walked to his safe. He always kept cash in his safe.

'No tricks,' the blond in suit warned, spying the pistols in Leroy's safe.

Leroy took out a wad of bills. Five thousand dollars. He tossed it on the bed then looked each of the security men in the eye.

They cast a glance at the money.

'Let's talk about us,' Leroy pitched. Being from Brooklyn he was streetwise. 'How much?'

'For what?' the blond asked.

'To buy myself out of this shit!'

There was an uncomfortable silence in the room. The blond broke the silence. 'We don't deal, Delgado.'

'How about two grand apiece, and you guys look away?'

The two uniformed officers shot glances at each other. One swallowed the lump in his throat. 'No deal,' the blond answered.

'Look at it this way. It's a lot of dough. You guys can buy a whole load of shit with that kind of money.'

'Shut the hell up, buster. We're career officers; we don't do bribes.'

'Yeah. And we're also cool guys too,' the tall, thin security guard said. Leroy was certain he would have taken the money. 'We'll overlook your offer. But if you attempt it again, we'll charge you for it.'

'You know what, Leroy?' the blond added. 'You're really beginning to piss *me* off. Cagley says we should make sure you board the plane for Somalia. And now, we're really going to do just that. Now move your ass!'

Trapped, Leroy packed his bag. The future was suddenly not looking good.

32

It was night. The Atlantic Ocean blew a cool breeze over Baltimore Washington International Airport. Routinely, the roar of airplane engines disturbed the tranquillity of the night. Captain James Ridgeley sat leisurely in the cockpit of aircraft N219QY at a restricted section of the airport, sipping Coca-Cola from a can. His friends called him 'Car', short for caricature, since he used to be so thin. Now, a wife, a kid and many beers later, he had developed a big, round belly. He thought of his loving wife, Lorna, and his adorable daughter, Karen. He smiled. He had to remember to buy her a Hawaiian Barbie doll upon his return, as he promised.

His co-pilot on tonight's flight was thirty-year old Mark Harris. He had thick black hair like a Latino singer and a clipped moustache like Charlie Chaplin. He handed Ridgeley the flight plan. Destination: Kenya, via Dakar, Senegal. Ridgeley looked through the manifest. There were only two passengers on the flight: Paul Thorn and a Leroy Delgado.

At 10.45 pm, Ridgeley watched as a black Mercedes Benz sedan came to a halt beside the airplane. A lone man emerged carrying a stainless steel briefcase. Ridgeley knew it was Paul Thorn, the CIA courier, and that his briefcase contained top secret CIA documents, messages, and encryption codes which he delivered to CIA stations in Europe, Africa and South America every week. The briefcase was chained to Paul's wrist by a titanium bracelet, which looked like a single handcuff. Titanium is the hardest metal known to man. The easiest way to get that suitcase from Paul Thorn was to chop his arm off.

Paul Thorn clambered aboard the airplane. He wore the same

144

grey trench coat he always wore. His thick, brown moustache concealed his lips. 'Hey, James,' he muttered at the pilot. His breath reeked of Brandy. That was how he coped with flying out and back twice a week. It helped him sleep through the journey. He flopped into the plush leather seat across the aisle and shoved the top secret briefcase under his seat. He struggled with his seat belt for a good minute. When it finally clicked in place he turned his face to the window and shut his eyes.

A minute later, three men emerged from the darkness. The man in front had black hair; he carried a black travelling bag. Two men, a blond and a redhead, walked closely behind. The blond held a pistol. It was obvious the man in front was being forced at gunpoint towards the plane. Curious, Ridgeley watched through the airplane's open door as the men approached. The man with black hair tried to turn back. But the blond and the redhead were much bigger and they shoved him forward.

'Get in!' the blond yelled, shoving Leroy up the airplane's steps.

'No!' Leroy protested. 'I have a right to be where I want to be. I have a right to—'

'You've got no rights!' the blond prodded Leroy with his pistol. 'Just get in!'

It took five minutes of prodding, shoving, ordering and yelling before Leroy climbed the eight steps into the airplane, swearing angrily all the way. The guards ignored him, and stood at attention at the foot of the stairs.

'Hi. Can I help?' Captain Ridgeley asked when Leroy finally boarded the airplane.

'I'm supposed to be on this damn flight,' Leroy snarled.

Ridgeley knew better than to ask questions. This was a CIA mission plane. Anything could happen. Captain Ridgeley forced a polite smile. 'Your name, sir?'

'Leroy Delgado.'

'Welcome aboard.'

Leroy looked down the cabin to see if there was another

145

potential escape door. There were eight plush leather seats inside the cosy cabin, arranged four on each side of the narrow aisle. The interior was exquisite, laid in light brown carpet. Each seat had its own oval window. But there was no other door—the airplane had only one door—and that was manned by the blond and the redhead.

Seeing he was trapped, Leroy flopped resignedly into a seat across the aisle from Paul Thorn, who was fast asleep, snoring loudly. Captain Ridgeley closed the door of the airplane. The cabin fell silent, save for Thorn's periodic snoring and the mild humming of the engines.

'Drinks and sandwiches in there.' Captain Ridgeley pointed to a cabinet at the rear of the cabin. 'The bathroom is the little door right ahead.'

'Thanks,' Leroy mumbled, not looking at the captain.

Ridgeley entered the cockpit and closed the door. 'Have a pleasant flight.'

Leroy gritted his teeth. Damn Cagley! Damn him. Leroy looked through the window. The blond and the redhead stood on the tarmac, watching.

'Bastards,' Leroy cursed. He shook his fists at them. They responded with a rude gesture of the finger.

In the cockpit, the pilots applied more power and the engines' powerful vibrations pulsed through his body. The airplane taxied. Three minutes later they were airborne.

With seven hours of flying ahead, Leroy had little choice but to relax. He fell asleep an hour later.

The crackle of the cabin speakers jerked Leroy out of sleep. 'Morning gentlemen,' Captain Ridgeley's disembodied voice said. 'We're fifteen minutes to Dakar in Senegal. We will begin our descent into Leopold Senghor Airport where we'll make a brief stop to refuel. Please fasten your seatbelts. Hope you had a pleasant flight. Thank you.'

Blinding beams of sunlight streaked through the plane's oval windows. The airplane was floating above a gleaming expanse of white clouds. In between breaks in the clouds, Leroy could

146

see the bright-blue Atlantic beneath. On the horizon, a dull green African continent loomed, its distant coastline awash with frothy surf.

N219QY made a smooth landing in Dakar. Captain Ridgeley guided the airplane to an apron, away from the main terminal. The main airport terminal stood a distance away, its brown, control tower reaching to the sky. A field of tall, brown grasses bordered the tarmac, their metre-high blades swaying synchronously in the breeze. Leroy sighed.

Captain Ridgeley emerged from the cockpit. He unlatched the door handle. The electrically operated door slowly opened outward, unfolding into a sturdy staircase. Instantly, a blast of sweltering air swamped the cabin. It was probably about 40 degrees outside.

The heat stung Leroy's skin. 'Darn! It's an oven out here,' Leroy cried. 'I'm gonna get roasted out here. Oh my God.'

After refuelling, Captain Ridgeley boarded the airplane, and shut the door. The turbofan engines of N219QY whined to life again. The plane taxied out to the runway. It paused to allow an Air Afrique DC-10 passenger airplane to land. Shortly after, Captain Ridgeley received take-off clearance from the control tower. The airplane hurtled down the runway, turbofans screaming. It lifted off the ground, its high thrust engines lumbering as it gained altitude.

Dakar soon became a speck, miles below. The final destination was Nairobi, Kenya—three thousand nine hundred miles across the African continent—another seven hours flying time.

Leroy kept his face to the window, looking down at the African continent. Everything was so green down there. Miles and miles of thick forests. And so many rivers, snaking through the landscape! Exotic Africa—big game safaris, tropical fruits. What else?

33

Aircraft N219QY cruised eastward over the African continent at 38,000 feet. It was three hours after leaving Dakar, Senegal. Bright sunlight flooded the cockpit and its plethora of switches and flight controls as the airplane flew above the clouds. Captain Ridgeley sat back and watched the control column wiggle as the autopilot controlled the airplane.

In the cabin, Paul Thorn, the courier, was still fast asleep, curled up like a hibernating rodent, his top-secret briefcase still, chained to his wrist.

Leroy sat across the aisle his nose stuck in the oval window.

Inside the Number 1 engine of aircraft N219QY, the hydraulic pump worked perfectly as it pumped fluid at high pressure through the maze of copper pipes in the airplane. But the integrity of the pipe had been breached by Sergeant O'Donnell. The reinforced copper pipe cracked. Red hydraulic fluid spewed into the engine pod.

In the cockpit, First Officer Mark Harris opened a can of Coke. 'You know, that's one thing I like about airliners,' he moaned to Captain Ridgeley. 'They always offer relief crew.'

'C'mon, Harris,' Ridgeley contended. 'Commercial piloting is a drag, believe me, I've been there. You got all them noisy passeng—' Ridgeley stopped dead.

He leaned forward and studied the flight controls. After twelve years and having logged well over ten thousand flying hours in executive jets he had developed a certain familiarity with the flight controls. He knew how things ought to be on the instrument panel. If something was amiss, it stuck out. He gazed intently at the gauges, especially the altimeter, the fuel gauge and the N1 gauge. He did some calculations. They were cruising at 38,000 feet at 430 knots. Ridgeley considered the gross weight of the plane and concluded that the airplane was producing more power than expected at this altitude. Yet, the airplane maintained a constant speed. Evidently, something was creating drag, and the autothrottle was compensating for it by increasing engine thrust.

'Hey, Harris, check this out.' Ridgeley poked his thumb at the N1 gauge. 'What do you think?'

'Strange,' Harris croaked. 'Strange.' For the first time, he realised the airplane was consuming fuel at an alarming rate.

'Do an instrument check, will you?'

'Right, Cap'n.'

Harris ran the self-diagnostic test of the flight instruments. The result was good. The instruments were fine.

'Maybe it's the fuel,' Harris suggested.

Ridgeley shook his head. 'I don't think so.'

'What could it be then?'

'Faulty instruments or something. My guess is something could be wrong with the airframe. Maybe a flap or an aileron is faulty, y'know, something causing drag. Do me a favour, Harris, go to the midsection and check the wings; see if anything looks out of place. I'll watch the instruments. I have control.'

'Yeah, Cap'n.'

Inside the Number 1 engine pod, the copper pipe breached by O'Donnell broke in two. In the cockpit Captain Ridgeley felt a thud. It wasn't a noise. He didn't hear it; he felt it through the floor, from within the airframe. It was as if something had fallen loose. 'Wait!' he said to Harris.

Ridgeley looked at the hydraulic pressure gauge in the roof of the cockpit. He observed a shift in the needle. 'Check this,' Ridgeley said.

Harris looked up too. The indicator flickered and shifted a little to the left.

'Deselect autopilot,' Ridgeley ordered. 'Disengage

autothrottle. Reduce airspeed to three-hundred knots.'

'Aye, Cap'n.'

That moment N219QY entered the clouds. The airplane shuddered.

34

The airplane computer on N219QY detected a loss in hydraulic pressure. The computer switched off Hydraulic System 1, driven by the Number 1 engine, and started Hydraulic System 2, powered by the Number 2 engine.

A green light flashed in the cockpit. This alerted the pilots that Hydraulic System 2 was on and working fine. Captain Ridgeley sighed, relieved. The front instrument panel said the airspeed was steady at 300 knots; the fuel consumption had returned to normal and the N1 gauge showed the correct percentage.

Suddenly overhead, the hydraulic pressure warning light flashed on again. A warning horn blared in the cockpit. Harris and Ridgeley glanced at each other. Harris looked up at the hydraulic gauge. The gauge flickered, and its needle slowly swung towards zero.

'We're losing hydraulic pressure again!' Harris cried.

Ridgeley glanced at the N1 gauge. The engine seemed to be running fine. So, the problem was definitely with the hydraulics. The light was green on the Hydraulic System 2 indicator. It indicated that the System 2 pump was running, yet, it was not building pressure. O'Donnell had removed the oil filter and thrown a hand towel into the oil reservoir. This had clogged up the pipe.

'Reduce airspeed to two-fifty,' Ridgeley ordered as a precaution.

'Going to two-fifty,' Harris replied, bringing down the throttles.

Almost immediately, the airplane responded with a sharp

drop in altitude. Captain Ridgeley felt it and so did his first officer. Leroy also felt it in the cabin.

Air turbulence, Leroy thought. He ignored it.

Captain Ridgeley knew better. The first officer had pulled the throttle gently, and the plane had dropped. There was only one answer: there was a problem with the airframe's aerodynamics. It was very likely that the faulty hydraulics was making the elevators, ailerons and flaps automatically uncontrollable. Without hydraulics it would be difficult to control the ailerons, which were the moving sections on the wing that flap up and down to steer the plane.

Airplane designers put in plenty of backup systems to ensure safety, however. The airplane's computer detected that Hydraulic Systems 1 and 2 were not functioning. The computer shut down both systems and switched on Hydraulic System 3. Its pump was electrically driven and located inside the wheel bay. The pump would not start.

O'Donnell had removed its fuse. He had then bridged the circuits with low amperage wire, thereby deceiving the computer.

'Get on the satellite uplink!' Ridgeley ordered. 'I'll speak to Air Control.'

Harris switched to the satellite radio uplink, which provided a secure channel to the National Security Agency outpost in New York. Since they were on a security mission, it was mandatory to alert US agencies.

'Keron calling Kane, Keron calling Kane,' Harris called. Keron was the unique code name of the flight.

The radio hummed then a response. 'Kane reading you, Keron.'

'We got an emergency. I repeat, emergency.'

'Confirm emergency, over?'

'Affirmative! Affirmative!'

'Confirm location.'

'One-zero-zero from Jos at one-two-one degrees.'

'What's the problem, Keron?'

'We've lost hydraulics. Probably problems with the wing frame. We're—'

At that moment the airplane passed through a strong air draft. Since the hydraulics had failed, the ailerons wouldn't respond to the computer's stabilising controls. The air draft caused the airplane to roll sharply to the right. As it did the cockpit door jerked open. The sudden jolt startled Leroy. Because the door to the cockpit was open Leroy could see into the cockpit with all its controls and the two pilots. The pilots seemed ruffled.

'Pan-Pan, Pan-Pan, Pan-Pan. Jos, come in for Keron two-zero-two. Model T-one-two-zero at zero-nine-seven from Jos at one-two-zero degrees; eighteen thousand feet! We've lost hydraulics. We have difficulty with directional handling. Request permission to land immediately,' Ridgeley called.

Jos air control picked up Ridgeley's distress call. 'Keron two-zero-two, Jos receiving you. Confirm Pan-pan?'

'Roger.'

'Turn left to Jos at zero-five-zero. Diverting all air traffic away from your area.'

Leroy had heard enough. There was trouble. He tried to force himself to stay calm but it was useless. His heart pounded into his chest. He was alone in the cabin. Save for the courier, who was still snoring loudly. A great sense of loneliness came over him. There was no one to talk to. No one to share the panic with. He was alone!

'Hey, Hey,' Leroy yelled to the courier. 'Wake up. Wake up!' He reached across the aisle and shook Paul Thorn violently. 'Wake up, man. There's trouble. We're gonna crash!'

Thorn didn't open his eyes. He rolled over and let out a gentle snore.

Leroy shook Paul Thorn vigorously. 'Hey, this is serious, man. Wake up.'

Thorn would not budge. It was like trying to wake a corpse.

In the cockpit, Captain Ridgeley made an assessment. 'I don't see this getting any better. We'll have to take the bird down. Declare Mayday. I'll speak to the passengers.'

'Mayday. Mayday. Mayday!'

As Harris sent out the distress message, Ridgeley switched on the intercom. 'Gentlemen, this is your captain speaking. We seem to have a bit of trouble. Please fasten your seat belts. We may have to make an emergency landing. Your life jacket's under your seat. Pull it out and wear it—now! The emergency exits are at the front and on the wing, and marked red. I advise you move close to one...'

Leroy turned around and spotted the rear emergency hatch door. He loosened his seat belt, staggered down the aisle and settled himself next to the door. Under his seat he made out a bright yellow package containing the life vest. He yanked it out.

'Keep calm,' Ridgeley continued. 'Everything will be fine. We only want to take precautions. Thank you.'

Jos air control called in: 'Jos to Keron two-zero-two. You're cleared for immediate landing on Runway twenty-eight. Set course for nine degrees, five-three north by eight degrees five-one east!'

'Keron reading you, Jos,' Harris replied.

'What is your current location?'

'One-one-five at one-nine-five degrees of Jos—'

The rudder was also powered by hydraulics. Without hydraulics the rudder could not be controlled. It locked up in its last position. Without a corresponding adjustment from the ailerons, the airplane yawed sharply, and then it dipped and plunged into a dive. As it plummeted earthwards everyone inside the airplane felt a sense of weightlessness.

The air pressure crushed Leroy into his seat. He couldn't breathe. It was as if he was constricted by an invisible hand. His groin seemed to suck into his stomach. He clutched his seat till his knuckles bleached white. He opened his mouth but nothing came out. He felt like a prisoner: trapped, wanting to get out but could not. Fearful, he peeked through the window as the airplane hurtled down. The ground closed in faster and faster. The trees were so near he could tell one from the other.

A white cow grazed in a field. He would give anything to be on the ground right now, even swap places with that cow. He felt cold. His mind flashed to Ann, then to his mother and then to Cagley.

Cagley!

So this was his game. This was Cagley's way of settling the score. *Cagley deliberately set me up on this trip so I could have a crash and be killed!*

Leroy closed his eyes, awaiting the worst.

The airplane hurled towards the earth at enormous speed. The altimeter rolled like crazy. Captain Ridgeley tugged at the control column. The airplane failed to respond.

Harris pushed all the controls within arm's reach, hoping something would work and put the plane back under control. He pumped furiously on the rudder pedal. Air trapped in the hydraulics system built up enough pressure. The airplane slowly turned its nose up and sluggishly returned to level flight.

The ground was dangerously close.

'Drop to one-thirty,' Ridgeley ordered when he got his breath back.

Harris reduced throttle. The airplane slowed; it seemed to float like a glider. Again there was a rapid change in G-force. It was the change in pressure that jerked Paul Thorn out of his drink-induced sleep. He opened his eyes and looked around the shuddering cabin. Somehow, he knew something was wrong. He spied Leroy, cringing at the rear of the cabin, looking as pale as a ghost. 'What's going on, man?' he drawled.

The airplane shuddered violently and lurched to the left. The overhead plastic panels rattled. In the cockpit, Harris pumped on the rudder pedal.

Captain Ridgeley took stock of the state of his airplane. The hydraulics gauge indicated dead zero. He had six red lights together with a host of sirens and beepers, warning him of the poor state of his airplane. The on-board navigation system showed serious deviation from track. Ridgeley decided it was time to ditch the airplane.

155

The landing gear was also worked by hydraulics. However, it had a manual override, a steel wheel next to the first officer, which could be cranked to lower the undercarriage.

'Landing gear!' Ridgeley ordered.

Harris cranked the wheel. A green light on the instrument panel indicated the landing gear was fully lowered and locked into position.

'Jettison fuel from centre tanks,' Ridgeley ordered.

Harris obeyed, pushing the combinations. The altimeter indicated seven hundred feet.

Ridgeley searched out the terrain below. It was mostly savannah grassland and small forests. However, it was interspersed with massive rocks, some the size of mounds, some the size of trucks. Either would damage the airplane. He spied a silvery river to the right but it meandered so much it would be useless as a landing spot.

Then Captain Ridgeley smiled. He spied a massive green plain, miles away. It was completely free of trees, and rocks. He guided the airplane towards it.

Unfortunately, plains are flatlands, and flatlands are sources of wind. The wind gathering from the plain swayed the airplane and churned it from side to side. N219QY dipped to the left.

Captain Ridgeley applied more power to counter the wind. Rumbling and groaning, the airplane sluggishly pulled out of its left bank and headed towards the grass plain, rattling as if it would splinter.

Leroy seemed to be going through the process of breathing but he just couldn't seem to get enough air into his lungs. His head ached, his vision blurred.

In the cockpit, the altimeter indicated four hundred feet.

With the wind from the plains contending with the airplane's aerodynamics, the left aileron snapped up. The airplane tipped into a left bank at two hundred feet. Inside the cabin, it rumbled as if someone was working a giant pneumatic drill against the sides of the plane.

Paul Thorn made a sign of the cross. Leroy spied him and

did the same. 'Oh God, save me!' Leroy wailed.

Half gliding, N219QY rammed into a bushy canopy with a massive bang!

The cabin split open with a deafening, shrieking noise. Leroy screamed as jagged scraps of metal flew through the cabin like arrowheads. There was nowhere to hide from the carnage. A tree trunk swept through the cabin, crushing everything in its path—passenger seats ripped off with human bodies in them. Whatever remained of the airplane tumbled through the growth. It was like being in the company of rocks in a tumble dryer. Repugnant jet fuel filled the air.

Then there was silence.

And an awful lot of smoke.

35

The white telephone in Cagley's CIA Cadillac rang a few minutes after he left the White House. That particular phone had a ringer, and it clanged like a bicycle bell. It was the emergency hot line and only the four deputy directors of the CIA, the White House, the Pentagon, and a few members of the National Security Council had its number.

Cagley put the receiver to his ear. 'Trident.'

'Dog Fifty here, Mike.'

Dog Fifty was code name for Donald Billingham, CIA Deputy Director (Operations). He was Cagley's closest friend and ally in the CIA.

'Problem?' Cagley asked. It could be nothing else.

'Yes, Mike. We lost an airplane carrying encryption disks for African and Middle East operations. We're almost certain it crashed.'

'Security compromised?' he asked.

'Possibly. We can't make an assessment yet.'

'Can your people secure the crash site?'

'That's the problem. We don't know where it crashed.'

'You don't?'

'We don't. Somewhere in Africa.'

'Africa?'

'Yeah.'

'Not so bad. Could be worse: China? Russia?'

'It's bad, Mike. First, the disks contain our encryption codes.' He paused then threw the bombshell. 'They also contain our emergency codes in case of war or a nuclear strike.'

'What!'

'We need a situation meeting immediately.'

'I'll be in Langley in ten minutes.'

'Fine. I'll call the other DDs and SECO.'

'Okay.'

'Bye.'

The hot line went dead. 'Jones,' Cagley called to his driver. 'Step on it. Now!'

The situation meeting began at 9.40 am in a vaulted meeting room on the third floor at CIA headquarters. Cagley, three deputy directors, and eight departmental chiefs sat around a huge, hexagonal, glass table. There was also a secretary to take the minutes. Cagley sported his characteristic grey suit. He beckoned Thomas Schwartz to start the meeting.

'We lost an airplane somewhere over Africa this morning, carrying two crew and two active officers.' Schwartz mopped his fat face with a hankie. 'Paul Thorn, one of our courier boys, was on that flight. He was carrying two compact disks in a courier briefcase. The disks contain de-encrypting codes for our communications in the Indian Ocean environs. It must not fall into wrong hands. So, we have two problems: finding survivors and retrieving the disks.'

The directors murmured, and exchanged side comments.

Cagley turned to Bill Daniels, CIA chief of security. 'Bill, give us your assessment. What's the damage?'

'We have to look at it twofold,' Daniels answered, stroking his white, Amish-style beard. As chief of security it was his responsibility to ensure CIA security was never compromised. It was a job for which he was paid six-figures in wages and perks. 'First, we consider the human angle. We may have lost two officers, and two pilots. Second, we must consider how this affects national security. The courier was carrying top secret disks, which contain our communication codes, and so, our communications is potentially compromised. We have notified the out stations that the codes on those disks are no longer valid. However, the disks are invaluable for a few

159

reasons. First, they give a pattern of our communications. Second, we want to protect the technology. Third, a major disaster is brewing if the disks are duplicated. Remember the Ruminoff case when that crazy ex-comms guy at Romania station fabricated similar disks, and planted his own codes? When we transmitted, he heard everything. With modern technology and supercomputing capabilities, things can only get worse. Therefore, any crack in the network is not acceptable. One weak link and we're in danger of leakage or worse still, enemies could download a virus. Besides, we cannot leave such sensitive items lying around. Crucially, those disks contain our emergency codes in case of war or nuclear strike.' Daniels looked straight at Cagley. 'The disks must be found.'

'Can we get a precise bearing on location?' someone asked.

'No,' Schwartz answered. 'The last position from the pilot to Nigerian Air Control was seventy miles south of a town called Jos. This stands as longitude nine degrees, thirty north; latitude eight degrees, fifty-one east. It could be anywhere within a forty or fifty mile radius of there.'

'Satellite?' Cagley asked.

'The imagery boys have scanned the flight path twice,' Schwartz answered. 'There's no sign of the plane and no sign of the wreckage.'

'Any news from the Nigerians?'

'Only that it disappeared from their radar screens. They scrambled a Puma helicopter to search—'

'And that's something we really do not want!' Daniels interrupted.

All eyes turned on Daniels. 'Aren't you concerned about survivors?' someone asked. 'Finding survivors should be our priority, not some disk.'

'I agree but we must consider the implications of a third party getting hold of those disks. They contain our nuclear situation codes. What if falls into the hands of the Russians or the Chinese?'

'I don't believe there will be any survivors,' Schwartz added. 'I saw satellite images of the terrain down there. The whole place is littered with rocks. Should the plane hit any of them it would disintegrate. There may be no survivors, and there may be no disks.'

'We can't afford to take that chance,' Daniels debated.

'I agree with Schwartz. I doubt if the disks still exist,' Bradley, Deputy Director (Intelligence) said. He was ever one to seek the soft approach. 'Procedure demands that in a dangerous situation, the courier must destroy the disks. I doubt if there are any disks.'

'I'm certain that in a crash situation even the most experienced officer will never think of the disks,' Daniels argued. 'His priority will be his own survival, not the disks— and that's if he didn't die instantly. We must recover those disks, damaged or destroyed.'

'I agree with Daniels,' Cagley said. 'The disks could be lying somewhere. We have to find that plane. Worse, the courier would be wearing a handcuff and chain attached to the briefcase. A corpse or injured man chained to a briefcase will raise serious eyebrows.'

'I also agree,' Billingham, the spiffy Deputy Director (Operations) added. Billingham was built like a wrestler but he dressed like a GQ model. His suit, shirt, tie and silk pocket hankie were all Gucci. 'That chain and briefcase scenario puts us under more pressure. I had an update a few minutes ago. The Nigerians haven't found it yet. We've got to throw our hat in the ring, and quickly too. Since satellite imagery isn't yielding anything we must go conventional. We need low flying choppers to scan the area.'

'We can't do that easily,' Singleton, the chief of communications responded. 'It's gonna break the cover.' Singleton was fifty. His tweed suit also belonged in the fifties. 'The plane would have identified itself as a business jet to every air control station in its route. The Nigerian authorities will be alerted if we request to send so much equipment into their country for a business jet. They'll suspect something's up. International rules demand that the Nigerian authorities find the plane.'

Cagley turned to John Trash, the chief of Africa division. 'Trash, this is your turf. What do you say?'

'Choppers, first and foremost. Secondly, saturation—place as many agents as possible on foot and in vehicles around the zone. I have directed Ted Raleigh, Station Chief, Nigeria to redeploy to the crash zone.'

'We're overlooking one thing,' Daniels prompted. 'What if the Nigerians find it first?'

'We don't want that,' Cagley acknowledged. 'If they get their hands on the disks and realise their importance, it's gonna be a huge bargaining tool for them.'

'It could also be a blackmailing tool,' Daniels added. 'They'll hold all the aces.'

'So, we don't have much time,' Cagley said. 'We have to move fast.' He turned to J. Walter Smith, chief of Counterintelligence. 'Smith, see to misinformation. Send another airplane to Kenya with two dummy agents. Plead a delay. That way, things look normal.'

'Yes, sir,' Smith answered, taking notes.

Cagley turned to Schwartz. 'Inform the families of the concerned staff that the officers are being held up by fuel scarcity in Kenya. There's no fuel to fly the plane. They won't be back for another four days.'

'I checked it out,' Schwartz answered. 'Both officers listed their mothers as their next of kin. We don't have to say anything just yet.'

'Good,' Cagley said. 'That takes care of family pressure. I'm still not satisfied with the groundwork.' He turned to Bart Johanssen. Johanssen was the Science and Technology representative at the meeting. 'I want that entire zone rescanned. Every silly inch of ground. And I want it done within thirty minutes. Get your boys on it pronto.'

'Done,' Johanssen responded.

'We need a lot more than that,' Cagley continued. 'We need to search that entire area, and we need to figure out how to send choppers into someone else's country without all hell breaking lose.'

'I have an idea,' Ron Mayer said. Mayer was Acting chief of Logistics. He was mild mannered and soft-spoken. 'Peter Rudy may be in a position to help us.'

'Who's Peter Rudy?'

'He owns Barrow Helicopters, servicing some of the oil companies in Nigeria. We can talk to him. Maybe he could divert a couple of choppers to the crash zone.'

'This guy, Rudy, is he okay?'

'Yep. South African by birth but carries a Botswanan passport. He's a billionaire; owns many businesses, mostly oil servicing, supplies, the lot. We've got a tab on him.'

'Is he gonna play?' Singleton asked.

'Hopefully. Rudy does a lot of business with Sheikh Farouk, the Bahraini prince. I can get the Secretary of State to pull some strings, and speak to the sheikh. The sheikh will speak to Rudy. But then we'll owe Peter Rudy. He'll probably be losing loads of money, dumping his customers to help us.'

'Pay him double his bill as compensation,' Cagley ordered without batting an eye.

'Er, he's not one of those you'd want to pay, if you know what I mean,' Mayer replied thoughtfully. 'He's a billionaire. I don't think money will mean anything to him. Frankly, it will be disrespectful.'

Cagley reclined in his seat, and stared thoughtfully at Mayer. 'What do you suggest?'

'I'd say a man of his calibre should receive the executive handshake—and there is a strategic reason. As you know, South Africa's just opening up to the international community. The US will need friends in there. Powerful friends. People who know the country, and who have the connections. Peter Rudy is one of those. This is an opportunity to cultivate his friendship. If he's doing us a favour I think we should

163

reciprocate. I recommend we invite him over, host him, and get him to meet the President or the Vice-President or offer him a US passport, you know, a gesture. We need his friendship.'

'Good thinking, Mayer,' Cagley said. 'Do a thank you letter, and extend an invitation to him on behalf of the US government. We'll be glad to ask him to dinner.'

'Right.'

'One more thing: if you're using Peter Rudy's choppers, what's your story to the Nigerians?' Cagley queried.

'Remember, the courier flight flew in the guise of a business jet?'

'Yeah?'

'It flew under the guise of Keronoil. The plan is this: we formally inform the Nigerians the crashed plane was carrying Keronoil executives. They know already, since that was how the pilot identified himself to Air Control. We now inform the Nigerians that Keronoil is worried sick for the safety of its staff, and consequently, Keronoil is hiring two choppers from Barrow Helicopters to aid in the search. We still use Keronoil as a front. It's a perfect excuse.'

'Will Keronoil co-operate?'

'Let me say we have quite a few friends in the right places in the company.'

'Good,' Cagley said. 'So it's decided. We'll use Mayer's choppers.' Cagley tapped the glass table. 'I also think we have to hit the Nigerians below the belt.'

All eyes fixed on Cagley.

'Send out one of the Air Force Special Forces teams,' Cagley ordered. 'They should locate the Nigerian helicopter involved in the search, and disable it. They have to make it look like a technical fault. That way, the Nigerians don't suspect anything. Just make sure it doesn't fly. We need the coast clear as we search.'

'I won't recommend that approach, sir,' Trash advised. 'Nigeria is one of those countries we don't wanna mess with. They're too strategic to the region, and they're one of our closest allies in Africa. They're going to be alongside us in Somalia; we can't afford to rock the boat. My suggestion is that we come clean to the Nigerians; get the President to call the Nigerian Head of State and ask him to hold his people back. In exchange we'll supply intelligence on Libya. That's something they want.'

'Good point.' Cagley poked a finger towards Mayer. 'Meanwhile, you get those choppers in the air.'

'Yes, sir.'

Cagley rapped on the glass table. The house fell silent. 'The code name for this search operation is Stinger. Just so you all remember this is a major operation, we'll call it Major Stinger. I consider Major Stinger top priority. I want each one of you to come down here and give me an update on your progress at least once every hour.'

The attendees nodded.

Cagley turned to the chief of counterintelligence. 'Smith, you need to get to the root of the crash. I want to know what caused it. Give your findings to Billingham. I want a six-hourly update on your progress. A couple of your boys should ship out to Nigeria, pronto. I want to know why this happened. When the plane is found I want the black box.'

'Done,' Smith answered. 'But if it's a mission plane it may not be carrying a black box.'

'Get me the facts.'

'Sir.'

Cagley turned to John Trash. 'You cannot sit pretty up here, Trash. Africa is your turf. Take the next flight out to see to Major Stinger. Get your butt out within the hour.'

'Sir.'

Cagley stood up. It meant the meeting was over. The directors slowly filed out of the meeting room, but Thomas Schwartz waited behind.

'Yes, Schwartz?'

'I think you need to know the guys involved in the crash.'

'Who?'

'The courier is Paul Thorn. Thirty-eight, no family, sixteen years in the agency, on probation 'cause we suspect he's a bit of a drunk.'

'Uh-huh.'

'The other guy?'

'Uh huh?'

'Leroy Delgado.'

Cagley frowned. 'Delgado?'

'Yeah.'

'What was he doing on there?'

'The word is that you shipped him out to Africa, and it had to be done pronto. There was no direct flight to Kenya, so the logistics boys pencilled him on the courier flight.'

Cagley breathed deeply. 'Okay.'

Schwartz left the vaulted meeting room, leaving Cagley all alone.

So Delgado was aboard!

Putting him aboard that crashed plane was not exactly what he had in mind. He was supposed to be headed for Somalia— with the heat and the militias—a very slow death. Rotting in the desert.

Still good, anyway. Very likely Delgado was dead. That was sweet vengeance. That would settle his score with the Delgados. The Delgado chapter was now closed.

But what if he survived?

Cagley stiffened.

36

Ted Raleigh stood on the tarmac at Jos Airport, in the Plateau region of Nigeria, chain-smoking Marlboros. The terrain was beautiful with the flat land spreading for miles in all directions. The flat land invoked high winds, which tugged at everything in sight. Shrubs and tall grasses dominated the land. A number of white, humpbacked cattle grazed. The airport building was a sprawling two-storey complex. It had a huge concrete tarmac; beyond that was a 5000-foot runway. In the distance, a hill, which looked like a traffic cone sprouted from the earth.

Raleigh, a former White House intern had risen quickly through the ranks to become CIA chief of station, Nigeria. He was tall and muscular with brown hair, beard and moustache; his close buddies called him Solo since he vowed never to get married. Still, he went after anything in skirts.

Earlier in the day, signal had come in from CIA headquarters concerning a missing Air Force T-120 carrying two crew members and two CIA officers. It was top priority because one of the CIA officers was carrying highly classified CIA encryption disks. Raleigh had taken the first available flight out of Lagos and arrived in Jos at 4.00 pm. Since then he had hung around the tarmac, awaiting the two helicopters that would help in the search.

At 5.55, two clattering Agusta CH-133 helicopters appeared from the setting sun and touched down at Jos Airport. Raleigh scampered over to the Agustas. He had to stoop to avoid being blown away. The roar of their engines was deafening, and the downdraft from their rotors created a mini-hurricane. He opened the front door of the lead Agusta, a four-door helicopter.

167

'Hi,' Raleigh yelled to the pilot. 'I'm Ted, Services Manager, Keronoil,' he lied. That was his cover. 'Permission to board the craft?'

The pilot nodded. He was an ebony-skinned Nigerian with a squat, shaven skull. He wore the customary white shirt on black trousers of civil pilots, and huge, green headphones.

Raleigh climbed aboard. 'Have you been briefed on what's going on?' Raleigh asked, taking a seat beside the pilot.

'Yeah,' the pilot answered. 'The information we received is that one of your company jets went down and we're doing a search and rescue mission. Do you have its last known position?'

'Yeah, but we don't know how accurate it is.' Raleigh handed the pilot a piece of paper containing the set of coordinates CIA headquarters had relayed by radio.

The pilot studied the figures. 'Not too far, but we need to top up on fuel. Barrow four-eight?' he called into the microphone attached to his headset.

'Receiving, Barrow forty,' the pilot in the second Agusta answered.

'We have rendezvous. Tanking then setting course for one-eight-zero. Copy?'

'Copy.'

'Roger and out.'

After refuelling, the Agustas lifted off. Jos Airport gradually diminished as they gained altitude. The interior of the helicopter was similar to that of a car. It had two front seats and a long rear seat. A coil of communication cables hung from the roof. The joystick and the control column were between the pilot's legs. Raleigh watched as green fields, farms, and the vibrant savannah landscape whizzed past beneath the speeding chopper. He didn't particularly like flying; it gave him a sick feeling of floating in the air like there was nothing under him. It made him crave a cigarette.

After thirty minutes, the two Agusta helicopters arrived at the last known location of the crashed airplane. The choppers hovered above the spot at 200 feet, their rotor blades delivering powerful downdrafts that swayed the greenery below. The spot turned out to be a corn farm, overgrown with weeds. There was no wreckage on this patch of land, nor indeed, as far as the eye could see.

'Barrow four-eight,' Pilot Chuck called into his microphone, speaking to the pilot in the second helicopter. 'Nothing here. We'll have to scout round. Can you fly two miles north by two miles east along the flight plan course? I'll fly two south by two east.'

'Roger.'

'Maintain altitude at three hundred feet.'

'Roger.'

The choppers split up, skimming above the trees.

Savannah grasslands are normally endless miles of grass, shrubs and small trees, but the terrain in this region of Nigeria was unusual: it was interspersed with irregular rocks, some as small as cars, some as big as hills. As night fell, it became pitch-black, but darkness was not a hindrance to the Agustas. They were equipped with Forward Looking Infrared Radar (FLIR), and powerful searchlights, necessary to function in the Nigerian oilfields, most of which were located in swamps and jungles. As the Agustas skimmed over the dark savannah their FLIR and searchlights easily picked out rocks, which gleamed greenish-yellow in the searchlights. The searchlights flashed over silvery streams, farms and sleepy villages but there was no sign of the crashed plane.

At 8.00 pm, Raleigh placed a call to Langley on his radio. 'We can't find the plane. It's lost.'

37

Major-General Tommy 'Slugger' Archibald, commander of the US Air Force 89th Wing, stormed into Major Farringdon's elevated corner office inside Hangar 22. Colonel Janolski and Brigadier-General Fauster scurried behind. Janolski was head of the 89th Operations Group. Fauster was head of the 89th Logistics Unit.

'This has never happened. Never!' General Archibald howled. 'What the heck's going on here?'

Farringdon had been seating behind his paper-laden desk. He sighted the general and shot to his feet. 'Good morning, sir.' He saluted crisply.

'Don't you dare, major!' Archibald stormed over to Farringdon's table. 'What do you think I recalled you from Colorado for? Four people may be dead and you're only saying good morning? What's good about it, you incompetent fool? How on earth did that airplane get out of this hangar? The pilots said they had no hydraulics, and that airplane came into this hangar for hydraulics work just before the flight! Obviously then, someone in this unit screwed up big time! Who the hell's that?'

'I d-don't know, sir,' Farringdon stuttered.

'You don't?'

'N-no, sir.'

'Who did the job?' Janolski asked.

'Sergeant O'Donnell, sir.'

'Who was the supervising officer?' Fauster asked.

'Lieutenant Bailey, sir.'

Archibald turned to Colonel Janolski. 'I want you to start

an investigation right now.'

'Yes, sir.'

'Get Air Security on O'Donnell. Arrest him.'

'Yes, sir.'

'Detain Lieutenant Bailey as well.'

'Yes, sir.'

'When you've done that, overhaul this department. Restructure the entire procedure—from booking in airplanes, the schedule of maintenance, spare parts—the whole lot. And tighten the bookwork for putting an airplane back in service.'

'Yes, sir.'

'Get in touch with Westwind Aircraft. I want to know why their planes are so damn flimsy. Do a letter to the Pentagon. Cancel future orders from Westwind.'

'Yes, sir.'

'Put Major Farringdon on suspension, pending the outcome of your investigation.'

'Sir.'

Archibald turned to Janolski. 'Send a few boys to CIA. See if we can assist in any way.'

Archibald stormed out of Hangar 22.

38

It was late in the afternoon. Huge raindrops pelted the green-tinted windows of Cagley's office at CIA headquarters.

Jim Lurkey, chief of CIA medical division, walked into Cagley's office. 'Remember the investigation you ordered on ATK?'

Cagley looked up from his computer, his face sour, as usual. 'Yeah?'

'It's ready.' Lurkey handed Cagley a compact disk.

'Okay,' Cagley said in a dismissive tone. Lurkey got the message and left.

Cagley slotted the disk into his computer and opened the only document on it. It listed the names, units, dates, and quantity of ATK provided to each agent. Cagley searched for the name, Delgado. Nothing. Obviously then, Leroy Delgado had not collected ATK from agency supplies. That was inconclusive, Cagley decided. He could have gotten the ATK by other means; from friends or contacts.

Cagley pressed a button on his intercom. 'Anita, access the mainframe. Look up this subject: Delgado, Leroy Alphonse. See if his file mentions his friends and associates. I want a list of his associates who work for the agency.'

'Okay, sir.'

Anita called back over the intercom a few minutes later. 'Sir, the files list seven names.' She recited the names.

Cagley searched to see if any of Leroy's listed friends was named on the spreadsheet. None were.

'Strange,' Cagley said. 'Strange. Leroy Delgado has never been issued ATK and does not appear to have access to it, yet

Ann insists he used it on her. Strange.'

Seeking an alternative explanation, Cagley browsed through the spreadsheet. It listed the names of two thousand CIA agents, located all over the world. It was highly unlikely anyone overseas would be involved. Whoever used ATK on Ann was certainly in the United States, and in every likelihood would have collected it in the United States.

Manipulating the spreadsheet, Cagley sorted the names so that only those based in America were displayed. That narrowed it down to a hundred and fifty. He browsed through the names alphabetically. He stopped dead when he got to the letter B.

He pressed a button on his intercom. 'Anita, call SA-1 immediately!'

'He's not in today,' Anita replied.

'We pay you to do a lot more than hang around filing your nails all day long. Get your butt off that silly typewriter and make sure he walks into this office in thirty minutes!' He switched off the intercom.

Anita cursed. But since she didn't fancy joining the welfare queue just yet she made a string of phone calls. Sure enough, in twenty-five minutes, the SA-1 strode into Cagley's office.

Cagley regarded his special assistant coldly. 'I asked Jim Lurkey to do an audit of ATK pills. He's come back with the result. Your name's on it. Why is that?'

The SA-1 was Hillary Bosworth, Cagley's enormous, ginger-haired lackey. Bosworth only stared down at the grey carpet.

'Ann, my daughter, seems to have had some problems with ATK. I have confirmed you were very much involved in it. Why, Bosworth?' Cagley was being psychologically assertive, speaking as if he knew everything. Rather than ask, 'Did you do it?' he was asking, 'Why did you do it?' Police gimmick.

Bosworth didn't answer. Instead, his face became laden with guilt.

Cagley knew he'd hit home. 'Bosworth!'

'Sir?'

'You exceeded your orders. Why?'

'I was only following your orders, sir.'

'My orders?' Cagley scowled. 'I don't recall giving you instructions to give my daughter ATK.'

'Sir, when I met you in the elevator your orders to me were, "Let the storms begin, Bosworth. Let it begin. I want my daughter back home!"'

Cagley remembered saying those words.

'I-I thought Ann went away with Delgado only because of the baby. If the baby wasn't there she would have come back home.' Bosworth looked straight at Cagley. 'She did return home, sir. I entered their house and spiked her medication.'

'I don't understand.'

'She's been taking some pregnancy supplements. Pregnasupple. It's in red capsules. I opened one of them and replaced its contents with ATK.'

For one long minute Cagley didn't speak. *Bosworth was the culprit!*

Half of him was furious. Then he calmed. *Bosworth was only following my orders, wasn't he? I gave the orders that he should ensure Ann came home by any means, and he did what he had to do. So, strictly speaking, I am responsible for Ann being given ATK! I am responsible for the loss of Ann's child!*

For a moment he was pensive.

But what the heck? I don't want to be a granddad to a seed of Delgado anyway. Certainly not.

In actual fact, Bosworth has solved a very thorny problem for me. By getting rid of Ann's child, everything is back in place. Ann is back home, her so-called marriage to that undeserving twerp is as good as finished, and that twerp, Delgado is probably dead. Things couldn't be better, and it's all thanks to Bosworth!

For the first time in ages, Cagley smiled meaningfully. 'Thanks. You can go.'

Bosworth walked to the door.

'Bosworth,' Cagley called, his head abuzz with intrigue.

174

Bosworth turned around.

'I will be recommending you for promotion.'

Bosworth grinned. 'Thank you, sir.'

'You have shown that you have my back,' Cagley continued, seeing a chance to recruit a proven ally. 'You just keep watching my back and there will be rewards for you.'

'I've got your back, sir. If there's anything you need done just let me know. I'll take care of it.'

Cagley nodded. 'Thank you.'

'Thank you, sir.'

'Tell Anita to alter Delgado's file to say he did *not* use ATK for personal purposes. I don't like him but the truth should be said. It has already been entered into his file that he used ATK without authorisation. Ask Anita to put it in his file that he has been cleared of that charge, and that it was a mistake by a rookie pharmacist at Woodlake.'

'Okay, sir.'

Beaming, Bosworth walked out of Cagley's office.

Cagley sat back and pondered. So, indeed, Leroy Delgado did not use an abortion pill on Ann. Now, he was probably dead. He had paid an enormous price for trifling with his daughter.

Cagley sat back and recalled that hateful incident in his mind, thirty-something years ago when he was being dragged out of the minefield in Korea. "Don't worry, pie face," Leroy's father had scoffed. "Look on the bright side. You die, and your mother receives an American flag."

Bitter words.

'I've avenged the death of Soo Min Ji. I have avenged all the pains the Delgados—father, and son, put me through.' Satisfied, he poured himself some coffee. He took a sip then reclined back in his seat. Life couldn't be better.

Ann gradually accepted the fact that she had lost her cherished baby. It still hurt dreadfully; she'd cried a lot but she knew nothing would bring him back. Slowly, over the last three days, she pulled herself together. She had taken time off from work. This helped her unwind and she was feeling much better. She had also done a lot of thinking. A lot.

She curled in the living room, watching a TV movie when her father returned from work. 'Dad, you're back.' Ann gave him a warm a hug. 'How was your day?'

'Good. Very good.' With Delgado probably dead, everyday was a good day. 'How are you feeling?' He kissed her cheek.

She forced a smile. 'Getting there.'

He walked to the answering machine to check for messages.

'Dad,' Ann began.

Cagley turned and saw an all-familiar I'm-going-to-be-naughty-but-please-don't-be-offended look on her face. He knew that look.

'Yes, what is it?'

'Er… I've been thinking… Maybe I should call Leroy.'

Cagley's stone-grey eyes narrowed. *Call Leroy?* Leroy was something that should be off the menu. Her only link to Leroy should be the divorce court. 'Is there any reason why you want to do that?'

'Not really. You know, just to call. He called a few days ago. I didn't speak to him. But, now… well, I've been thinking… I guess we can't row forever.'

Her new stance surprised him. 'After what he did to you?' Cagley cried, deliberately bringing up the ATK issue to rekindle her anger.

Ann's spirits sank as she remembered the ATK thing. 'I really don't know, Dad,' she lamented. 'I really don't know what's going on. I was so angry and distraught I couldn't think straight. Now, I've calmed, I've thought a lot about it. Looking at it from another perspective, it's just not in his character. He's sometimes a fool, but…I don't know. Now, I'm not so certain he did it. You said you would do an investigation. How far has it gone?'

'Well,' Cagley drawled, doing some high-speed thinking. Delgado was probably dead, and Bosworth was the one that doped her. Now, Ann was changing her mind. Maybe it wasn't such a good day after all.

'Is it ready?' Ann badgered.

'Oh no. No! Not so fast. It could be another two or three weeks.' He changed the subject. 'Now, why don't you get your mind off that bozo? Relax. Enjoy the change of scene. I would suggest a holiday. Hawaii? Bermuda? Tahiti?'

'Maybe later, Dad, but I think I should call him. I hit him, Dad. He was bleeding! I want to know how he's doing.'

Cagley saw that Ann was really concerned. 'You can't do that, Ann. I put him on a top secret stake out in Chicago. He's incommunicado.'

'Chicago! Why?'

'Calm down, Ann. You see, I wish to do a thorough investigation, and I didn't want him getting in the way. You should be able to understand that.'

She nodded, reasoning along with her father.

'Why don't you try and get him off your mind?' He put his arm around her. 'Forget the past. Look at you. You're damn beautiful. Why don't you get a friend to take you around? There are thousand of guys who'd give a limb to date you. You're still young. You're pretty. You're free!'

'Dad, I'm still legally married to—'

'To an undeserving guy who used ATK on you?' Cagley interjected.

'We can't confirm as yet, Dad. We're still investigating!'

'Look at Harry, Senator Johnson's son. Now, that's a good man. He's on the presidential campaign train. Soon, he'll be in line for congress. Now that's a man who deserves you.'

'I like Leroy, Dad. I like him a lot. I hated him a few days ago, but now, I think I've just got to carry on. I miss him.'

She missed him? For Cagley, that was bad news.

Don't worry about it, he told himself. *That dimwit is dead.*

Dead or not, the very notion that she was still thinking about Leroy Delgado was not a good sign. He would put a stop to it. He knew what to do. Cagley drew away from Ann. He walked to the liquor cabinet, fixed himself a shot of whisky then walked to the mantelpiece. He sighed heavily, shook his head sadly, and stared down at the carpet, looking every bit downcast.

Ann detected the change in her father's countenance. 'What's the matter?'

'Nothing,' Cagley snapped, putting up a dejected countenance.

'C'mon, tell me.'

'No, there's nothing to tell. The past is behind us. Forget it.'

'Please, what is it? I mean, one moment you were okay, and the next you're looking really sad and withdrawn. Is there something wrong?'

Cagley shrugged. He sipped his whisky and sighed.

'Is it about me?'

Again, Cagley shrugged. He was whetting her curiosity. He knew how to manipulate the human mind.

'I've been through the worst, Dad. Tell me.'

'I guess you're right,' Cagley replied softly. 'You've been through a lot. There is no need adding to that. That would be cruelty.' He walked away from her.

'Come on, Dad. Tell me. Please,' Ann coaxed. The suspense was getting to her.

'Well....'

'Come on, tell me.'

'I don't want to hurt you, Ann.' He held her tenderly, looking every bit mournful. 'There's some indication…a very strong indication…'

'Is it Leroy?' She looked fearfully into his eyes. 'Did he do it?'

'I'm not saying anything about that.' He was playing the caring dad.

'Did he?' she whispered.

'Well, I did get a feedback on the investigation this afternoon.'

'But you said two or three weeks.'

'Yeah,' Cagley answered, looking sombrely into his glass.

178

'I was only trying to find a way to push back the bad news. You've been hurt too much. I didn't want to hurt you again.'

'Did he do it?'

Cagley looked away—a subtle, lying disposition, which suggested, *Yes*.

'So he did it!'

'Well, I didn't want to tell you, but it was confirmed he collected four tablets of ATK a week ago,' Cagley lied. 'But that doesn't mean he used it on you,' he added for good measure.

Ann sank into her father's arms.

'Now, you see why I didn't want to tell you?' He stroked her hair. 'I knew it would kill you. I'm sorry, I shouldn't have told you. I'm sorry.'

Ann looked up. There were no tears in her eyes. Instead, she was angry. On the day she packed out of Leroy's home, she had every intention of getting a divorce. Her father urged her to. He had hired Harrington & Hergoven a firm of top flight Washington lawyers, and they had drafted divorce papers within three hours. In it, she wanted nothing. No property, no alimony, only an amicable, uncontested divorce. It had been lying on the table since then.

She walked to the table and signed it.

39

The chopper floated at 15,000 feet. Ted Raleigh could see for miles around over a huge terrain of grassland, shrubs and small trees. The routine had been the same in the past five days as they searched for the crashed airplane. They took off from Jos airport then roamed around the vast Nigerian interior till their fuel got low. Then they went back to refuel and went out to search again. CIA headquarters kept them updated with maps, charts, computer simulation and satellite photos of the Nigerian terrain, sent daily from Langley. On the back seat, were a few dozen cans of Pepsi, mostly empty. The air was thin. It was hot, dry and dirty, and the chopper stank of stale, masculine sweat.

'Chuck,' Raleigh drawled to his pilot for the umpteenth time.

'Yep,' Chuck answered, peering through the windshield. Pilot Chuck was Nigerian. Ever since he came across *Flight* magazine in grammar school, he'd wanted to fly. His father wanted him to be a lawyer, but he wanted to be a pilot. Since his father adamantly refused to splash out any funds on piloting, he had to make do with Law School or no school. But Chuck could not overcome his love of flying, and after finishing his degree in Law, Chuck sold his books and headed to flight school in America.

'What would you do to find this plane?' Raleigh asked, sick of flying.

'Exactly what we are doing. Fly till we find it.' Chuck was content with cruising around in the air. It was something that assuaged his soul.

'Hey! I see something,' Chuck cried suddenly.

He took the chopper down and hovered above the trees. The rotor blew a draft that parted the vegetation to reveal the undergrowth. 'Thought I saw a reflection,' Chuck muttered. 'Damn! It's just water.' Chuck took the chopper up again.

Frustration makes people think, and Raleigh had been thinking. 'This is a vast country,' he said to Chuck. 'If we keep flying around we may never find it. Maybe we should send people into the villages on foot. Maybe the villagers have seen something or they know someone who has.' Raleigh picked up his walkie-talkie. 'AJ calling Rodney. Come in Rodney.'

The CIA had set up a temporary command centre in a room in a hotel in Jos. The search operation was coordinated from this hotel room by a CIA officer code-named Rodney.

'Receiving you, AJ,' Rodney crackled from the walkie-talkie.

'I got an idea,' Raleigh replied. 'Put out about ten guys to all the villages within a hundred mile radius. Say one guy to about twenty villages. Let them go in and make enquiries, you know, talk to the missionaries, village heads... Maybe they've seen something or they know someone who has. If we keep flying around we'll get nothing.'

'Sounds good, AJ,' Rodney replied. 'I'll get that done.'

'Roger and out.'

Ted Raleigh and Chuck continued their search. Raleigh reached for a Marlboro. Every time he lit a cigarette, he remembered the Surgeon General's warning.

40

In the abyss, a bell rang after ages of nothingness. His subconscious struggled gallantly to regain function, and eventually, he had leverage. Then he became aware of darkness. Cold, damp, darkness. Slowly, the darkness peeled away. He seemed to be inside a body once more. A numb body. He had no feeling of any part of it. After what seemed an eon his senses kicked in. The sense of sound—that was something familiar, something he used to know. The bells faded away. Then he heard something he seemed to identify with—the voices of humans. Soft, tender, female voices. But their sounds made no sense. They sounded different, exotic.

After a while he became aware of his eyes. He tried to see with them but couldn't. They felt heavy and seemed to be taped shut. He struggled with his eyelids; gradually they opened like stiff gates. What seemed like a white cloud loomed before him. The cloudy curtain slowly drew open and a blinding light caught him straight in the eyes. His eyes hurt, and he squinted in discomfort. Still, he couldn't see anything.

Then ugly, traumatic memories flooded his mind. The images were so vivid that it seemed he was living the incident all over again. He was inside some sort of vehicle, and he was in grave danger. There was no escape! Terrible air pressure ground him into his seat. An awful bang, as if a giant wrecking ball was ramming into the sides of his craft. The cabin was disintegrating around him, collapsing. Jagged pieces of metal flew at him from all directions. He remembered the acrid smell of smoke and burning fuel. He closed his eyes, giving himself to the worst. Finally, he remembered lying somewhere.

It was a long time before he realised the worst was over and he was in a different place. There was no noise. There was calmness and the sweet musical notes of chattering women. He opened his eyes and this time he could see clearly. He realised he was lying on his back inside a dome-shaped room that was made of mud and thatch. Bright sunlight streaked through the cracks in the thatched roof. The thatch kept out the heat whilst aerating the room. It was cool inside the hut.

He made out a movement in the room. A middle-aged woman, an African, stood at his feet. She had genial, motherly eyes with long black eyelashes. Her skin was light brown. She wore a yellow *boubou*, similar to a batik caftan, and a matching yellow head-tie with a red shawl draped around her shoulders. She was mopping his body with a piece of hot cloth. She dipped the cloth in steaming water, wrung it to squeeze out any excess water, and then applied the steaming cloth to his body. The heat stimulated his nervous system, and gradually, he regained some feeling. The first thing he felt was pain all over his body—horrendous pain. It was as if he was inside a grinding mill. He groaned.

Startled, the woman shrieked and jumped back. Then she gathered her wits. '*Fie sama, fie sama!*' She pointed at him gleefully.

He didn't understand her words, but from the smile on her face he could tell she was ecstatic that he had finally regained consciousness. Two other women appeared. They all gazed at him, their faces alight and pleased. They all wore brightly coloured *boubous* and shawls, and they babbled in a sweet-sounding intonation.

He groaned again. The women shrieked joyfully. He had finally come round.

Opening his eyes and seeing those women, their excitement and concern, their smiles and shrieks, it was that friendly human touch, the unfeigned smile and care of total strangers that did the trick. He snapped out of the other world and became fully conscious. He felt drained and tired. Then he

183

drifted off again, this time into restful sleep.

He woke up many hours later, still lying on his back inside the round thatched hut, which was about twelve feet in diameter. Outside, tender female voices sang in harmony. His right knee was bound between some sturdy bamboo sticks. It ached. Great pain raged through his body, especially his knee. He was also ravenously hungry. As if he had not eaten in days. He moaned.

Almost immediately, a woman appeared beside him. It was the same woman he had seen when he first regained consciousness. She was probably in her late forties and had kind eyes and a lovely, chiselled nose.

They gazed at each other, their eyes doing the talking. He seemed confused, and in pain. She seemed curious and sympathetic. '*O ma l' hawa?*' she asked softly.

He didn't understand. He nodded and forced a smile.

She could read the pain behind his smile. '*An u,*' she comforted. She was an instinctive mother. She felt his temperature and caressed his face. '*Ba na hawa mu je ka?*'

He shook his head, indicating he didn't understand.

At first she was at a loss then her face lit up. She hurried to the door. 'Tila. Tila!' she called.

A few moments later, a teenage African girl scurried into the hut. She was about fourteen years old, and very slim. Her complexion was chocolate brown and her hair was done in long braids. She wore a brown blouse and sarong. She gazed down at him. A wide grin built up on her face, showing a row of beautiful white teeth. She knelt beside him, holding his hand like he was some long lost friend. 'My name be Tila,' she began with a massive grin. 'You be Leroy?'

'How did you know that?'

She pointed to his bracelet. His name was engraved on it. 'Your aeroplane drop from sky into my daddy farm. This be my mummy,' she said, glancing at the genial lady. 'Her name be Mama Roda. She no speak English. I speak *smaaaall* English.'

She exaggerated the *small*, squinting.

'Where am I?' he asked.

'Our village. Dan Apali.'

'Dan... appalling?'

'Dan Apali,' she corrected, amused.

'What country?'

'Nigeria.'

Nigeria! That was deep inside Africa. West Africa.

Tila's mother spoke. Tila translated, 'Mummy say, how you feel?'

'Rough. Very rough.' He grimaced to emphasise the pain.

'Aww,' she said sympathetically. She conversed briefly with her mother in the local dialect then turned to Leroy. 'My mummy want to clean your wounds then she give you medicine. Medicine take pain away. Make you well quick.'

'Okay.'

Mama Roda loosened his bandages. He saw that there were so many of them—twenty cuts, bruises and lacerations in the least. The tiniest ones were surface wounds; the biggest a four-inch gash on his biceps. All his injuries had been carefully and evenly stitched, and they looked really neat. It had to have been done by someone with nimble hands and a lot of skill. She cleaned each wound carefully with an antiseptic then applied a yellow paste and fresh bandages.

He beckoned to Tila. 'I'm hungry. Can I have something to eat?'

She told her mother. A few minutes later, her mother brought in a porcelain bowl in which was some warm, brown pap. She added some sugar and a ground, green herb. Tila fed it to him off a carved, wooden spoon. It was tasty and he finished every bit of it.

The final moments of the crash swamped back into his mind. 'What about the others?' he asked.

'Others?' She didn't understand.

'Yes, the others. We were four in the aeroplane.'

She was still baffled. 'Four man...in aeroplane?'

He gestured weakly as he spoke.

'Oh!' she exclaimed when she finally understood. She shook her head sadly. 'They die. Three die. We bury them.'

Leroy was mournful. In a way, he felt guilty being the lone survivor. He knew he had been very lucky. The line between life and death was very thin. He could easily have crossed to the other side. Realising this, he felt grateful to be alive. Deep, deep within him, he felt as if he was being given another chance. 'Thank you, God,' he said from the depth of his heart.

Leroy seemed to hear a reply in his heart: 'You're welcome, son.'

'Where you from?' Tila asked.

'America,' Leroy answered.

'A-m-e-r-i-k-a?'

Leroy nodded.

'You know Michael Jackson?' she asked childishly.

'Sure.' Leroy smiled. 'Do you know him?'

'Yes. Our teacher bring him photo to our class. He dance plenty.' She imitated Michael Jackson's trademark pose of grabbing his crotch.

Leroy chuckled. As he did his right knee hurt terribly. 'I need to get to hospital. I need to see a doctor. I'm hurting. Ooh! Can you take me to hospital?'

'Ah!' Tila exclaimed, at a loss, arms outstretched. 'No hospital in village.'

'Where is the nearest one?'

'It be in Jos.'

'Can you ask your mother to take me there?'

'Jos...far. Very far.'

'Don't you have a car?'

'Car? No car in village.'

'Is there a place I can make a phone call?'

'Phone call?' Tila queried.

'Telephone, telephone.' Leroy imitated the posture of someone using the phone.

'Oh, Telefon, telefon,' she nodded, indicating she understood.

186

'No telefon in village. Telefon in Jos.'

These people didn't have anything. On deeper reflection, he realised this was probably a remote village, deep in the heart of Africa. How would anyone find him here?

'So, how do you people get to Jos?' he asked, concluding that Jos was probably the nearest big town or city.

'Big lorry come here one time every week. It bring cloth, slippers, sweets—plenty things from Jos. We send yam, corn, other food to Jos.'

'What if you become sick or have an accident?'

'Papa Zaki cure them.'

'Papa *what?*'

'Papa Zaki. Him name be Zaki. Him be old man, so we call him Papa. He be village doctor. He know plenty things. He cure everybody. He cure you.'

'I still want to see a doctor,' Leroy insisted.

'I tell my daddy, but you not feel good?'

'No. I want to do an X-ray. Make sure nothing's broken.'

'Papa Zaki say no bone break.'

'How can he know that?'

Tila shrugged. 'He know.' She pointed to his right leg. 'Your leg not break. It twist.'

Leroy understood she meant his knee was dislocated, not broken. He knew he was still relatively intact. Despite his pain, he could move every part of his body except his right knee, which was bound between the bamboo props. Fate had been kind to him, too kind.

'Tell your mother I'm very grateful,' he said, grimacing because of his pains.

'*O na kada bawa,*' Tila said to her mum.

Mama Roda smiled, curtsied and spoke to Tila. Tila interpreted: 'She say you not worry to say thank you. She ask, you feel pain?'

'Yes.' Leroy grunted.

Mama Roda poured a cup of light brown stuff that looked like tea. She handed it to Tila.

'Mummy say to give you drink,' Tila said. 'Name of drink is *chado*. You drink it, pain go away. Make you sleep.'

'Okay.'

Obviously tutored in motherly care, Tila raised Leroy's head and put the cup to his lips. It was warm and had a distant bitter taste. When he finished it, Tila translated for her mother: 'My Mummy say we go now, so you rest. We come back in evening. We bring Papa Zaki come see you.'

Tila adjusted his pillow while her mother placed a blanket over Leroy's feet. Then they both walked to the door. Tila turned around and looked back at Leroy. She smiled and winked.

Leroy smiled. Mischievous imp. When she was out of the hut, he laughed out loud. There was something he'd seen when Tila reached out to hold his hands. This Tila was a real imp. She had a tall, slim stature and she was certainly flat chested. When she bent over to hold his hands her blouse had sagged, and he'd caught sight of her bra. There were no breasts in them, instead, there were a couple of dried lemons which she'd packed in there to imitate breasts. He laughed and tears rolled down his face. Now, that was a new one.

41

Hillary Bosworth, Cagley's baby-faced henchman was a happy man. As promised, Cagley had given him a commendation, and now, if Cagley needed information on someone, Bosworth was his man. Once, when Cagley needed Cuban cigars, which were banned in the US, Bosworth sorted out that problem discreetly and without questions. Cagley had also given him a promotion. Now, Bosworth had two juniors working for him: Harry Fisher, an Irish boy from Newark, and Roy Dominguez, a sleek Hispanic from Rampart, Los Angeles.

Bosworth cherished his newfound status as the man who had the Director's back and he diligently pursued that role. Right now, there was one issue to be dealt with—the issue of Senator David Grant.

Senator Grant, a Democrat, was vice-chairman of one of the senate committees. He was the man that booed, and chanted, "Scumbag! Scumbag!" while Cagley addressed the Senate, last week. Cagley hadn't asked Bosworth to reprimand Senator Grant. Cagley need not. But Cagley had grumbled, "That bozo needs to be taught a lesson or two." So, it would be Cagley's wish.

Senator Grant had one weakness: slim, teenage girls.

Roy Dominguez had found a drugged-up teenage tart to do the job. It would cost just two hundred dollars. Senator Grant's hotel room had already been wired for sound and video.

'Do it tonight,' Bosworth ordered.

'Done,' Dominguez, the sleek Hispanic answered.

Senator Grant's downfall would grace tomorrow's papers.

189

42

It was a few days after Leroy regained consciousness. His wounds were healing, and he could move around with the aid of a walking stick. Eager to know more of his surroundings, he hobbled out of his hut. The village of Dan Apali was set at the edge of a huge grass plain that stretched for miles to the east. A silvery river snaked through the plain. Cattle grazed in the distance.

The sky was cloudless and bright blue. The air was clean and fresh. There were about a hundred dwellings in the village. Some were huts and some were bungalows. Exotic fruits blossomed on trees everywhere. Oranges, bananas, guavas, berries, tangerines, paw-paws, wild apples were everywhere—in the backyards, around the huts, on the farms, in the wild—everywhere. They didn't go to the shops; they walked to a tree. Sheep, goats, chickens and other livestock roamed freely. The people were of varying complexion, from very light-skinned to dark brown. Life was plain and simple; men and women went about their business leisurely. Old men lazed under the trees, smoking pipes. Women wore gowns known as boubous. Batik caftans. And shawls.

Tila had a geography textbook, which had a map of Africa. According to her, the village of Dan Apali was sixty miles away from the town called Jos. Leroy easily located Jos on the map. It was four hundred miles north of the nearest coastline, which was the Atlantic.

Nearby, a group of kids enjoyed a game of soccer. A middle-aged hunter walked past. He had a five-foot Dane-gun slung across his shoulder. A pipe dangled from his lips. He wore a

190

brown dashiki and knee-length shorts—the typical male dress in the village.

'*Agba*,' the hunter hailed, beaming. He continued on his way, the sharp smell of pure tobacco wafting after him.

By now, Leroy knew his hosts well. They lived in a large compound, which contained eight huts, a barn, livestock pens, and numerous fruit trees. Papa Roda was the head of the family. He was sixty, fair skinned and stumpy. The airplane had crashed into his farm. Mama Roda was genial, pretty, soft and warm. She was a great cook. Tila was the first daughter. She was 14, and extremely mischievous. Tila was the only one who spoke any English. She was therefore Leroy's closest friend.

Without much to do he had a lot of time to think. Often, his mind drifted to Ann and all that happened between them, and how it had brought him so close to death, and left him an injured man in a remote village, deep in the heart of Africa. Often, he was really annoyed with her: she'd been so damned convinced he was the culprit. She wouldn't even give him a chance to talk things through. She didn't care what happened to him, did she? All she cared for was that baby, he reckoned. Did she even know what her father had done? She didn't even care that he could be lying dead somewhere right in the middle of Africa, many thousands of miles away from home. She turned her back on their marriage without a thought. Well then, she could go to hell for all he cared.

And Cagley too.

A thought crossed his mind. Could Cagley have gone as far as engineering the crash?

Was it a set-up? All that was needed was a word in some aircraft engineer's ear. But then, what about the others on the flight? Expendable? Collateral damage?

Then there was Ann's mysteriously terminated pregnancy...

Different thoughts flew around in his head. Many questions. No answers.

Maybe getting to know Ann had been a big mistake.

He wasn't sure. But he did really like her. Now, it seemed

like a fatal attraction. A fool's errand. Liking what seemed to be costing him his life. Was she worth the hassle?

Damn, maybe divorce was a good idea. Maybe being away from her was best. Cut his losses. Or maybe even forget her... Find himself some other woman. *Yeah, that will be good. I'll find myself another babe. A smoking hot one.*

For now there was not much to do except get well, relax and enjoy the village of Dan Apali.

Somehow, he had a feeling that this place had a lot in store for him. He only hoped it was good.

It was eight days now. Eight hot, sweaty days in that cranky noise box called a helicopter—and the crashed plane was yet to be found. Ted Raleigh was sick to death of this fruitless search. He listened to the recorded conversation between New York and the pilots. The airplane's distress bearing was ten east by nine north. They had searched every inch of ground on that bearing. They also gave on allowance of twenty miles, to accommodate for errors, and after that, had extended the search ten miles in all directions. This gave a giant patch of three thousand, six hundred square miles. It was now worse than looking for the proverbial needle in the haystack. More like looking for a speck.

43

Leroy's hosts pampered him. Tila's mother fed him four times a day. For every meal she prepared three different dishes for him. If he didn't like the taste of the first, she offered a second or a third.

Early in the afternoon, after lunch, Tila came to Leroy's hut. She had just re-done her long braids, and she looked in high spirits. 'My mummy send me go Dai-wai,' she began, flashing her perfect set of white teeth. 'I want buy milk. Dai-wai is next village. You come with me?'

'Come with you?' He had never ventured out of the Roda Family compound. 'My knee still hurts, Tila. I should not be walking around.'

'Village doctor say you walk plenty. Walk good for your leg. Make it *strooong*.'

'Okay then.'

With the aid of his walking stick, and Tila by his side, he hobbled out of the Roda family compound. Since he had never ventured outside the premises he looked around curiously as they walked deeper into the village. Some of the huts in the village were made of thatch, some of clay, and some of cement blocks. The family huts were grouped together; each family had a compound. Tropical fruit trees blossomed everywhere. A network of sandy footpaths crisscrossed the village. The people were warm and friendly. The few villagers they met waved at them and he waved back.

They soon left Dan Apali behind, and followed the sandy footpath that led to the next village. A cool afternoon breeze blew; the sky was brilliant blue, and the moon was visible. The

193

birds chirped playfully as they hopped from shrub to shrub. The scent of brightly-coloured wildflowers filled the air.

Tila sang—a melodious traditional folk song. She skipped along, at peace with herself.

After a quarter of a mile, Leroy stopped. 'Tila. My knee hurts. Let's have a rest.'

'Sorry,' she said, compassionately. 'Come, sit.' She pointed to a pear tree nearby.

Leroy sat under the tree and rested his back on its smooth, grey bark. The tree offered a cool shade.

'You want pear?'

'No,' Leroy answered. 'Help yourself.'

Tila walked around, looking for ripe pears to pluck from the branches.

He watched Tila, smiling to himself. She had such warm personality. He admired her innocence, her playfulness, and the way she lived without a care in the world.

He was musing over Tila when he caught sight of a lady walking up the path. She wore a white linen outfit, and a white, transparent wrap. A strong wind tugged at her clothes while she frantically held on. Leroy watched, amused, as the wind lifted her shawl and blew it onto a shrub. She picked it up gracefully. She walked leisurely up the path whilst trying to re-fix her shawl. She was probably a cross between Arab and African. The wind blew back her long, black, wavy hair, making her appear somewhat glitzy. Leroy spied smooth shapely legs. Her gait was carefree, yet dignified. She was probably about five feet, nine inches tall. The first conspicuous thing about her was her nose. It was slightly convex and pointed. Her eyes seemed bright and alive, almost like fire. Her lips were a natural soft pink. Her arms and neck were slender and graceful. Her complexion was that of polished beech. There was something about her. Something extra. He couldn't tell what. Maybe it was the way she carried herself. She was that type of woman that strikes you, and lingers in the mind. She looked tender. Gentle. Pretty. She was just so feminine that she oozed it; you

194

could almost smell it.

At first, the lady didn't notice Leroy. She was busy fighting the wind for her clothes. When she saw him she stopped abruptly, astonished. That was understandable. Caucasians were nonexistent in these parts.

After a moment, she regained her composure. She curtsied, smiled and walked on. He studied her intently as she continued her journey. He could now see her from behind. Her hips were curved like a pair of parentheses, and they swayed lightly as she walked. She had this fantastic derriere, which oscillated with her steps, not carelessly in this case, but with firm dignity. His eyes stayed glued on her as she disappeared down the path. This girl would make Miss Universe envious.

'Tila,' Leroy called excitedly.

Tila popped out from behind the pear tree. 'You feel better now?'

'No. But did you see the girl that just passed?'

'Yes.' Tila disappeared behind the tree once again. 'Her name is Talata.'

44

In Dan Apali, everyone in the family had a role to play. The men hunted and farmed. They were the breadwinners. The women were mostly petty traders; they also kept the home. There was no pipe-borne water in the village, and the young girls had the duty of fetching water from the stream. So, everyday, as the sun set behind the trees, the girls trickled from their homes, carrying clay pots and headed to the stream, chatting and giggling. This daily chore gave them an opportunity to strut their stuff. They looked their best, and swayed their hips, knowing the boys always gathered to watch.

Tila also had to fetch water for her mother. She carried her brown clay pot, and went to Leroy, who was reclining in a wooden deck chair beside his thatched hut.

'You see stream yet?' Her long braids reached to her shoulders, complementing her slim, chocolate figure.

'No,' he replied lazily.

'Come, see stream. Stream very good. Come. I go get water.'

'Okay.' Leroy perceived that Tila was up to something. Her eyes sparkled mischievously.

'We go now.' Tila handed Leroy his walking stick.

The stream was fifty yards east of the village. It gushed out of a massive rock, ten feet high. The water was crystal clear, and flowed into a pool. There was a sense of orderliness in the way the villagers used the stream. Drinking water was collected upstream, near the source. The children bathed midstream, where it was wider. Clothes were washed downstream. In this very simple way, they avoided contamination.

Leroy's arrival caused a stir. He was a celebrity of sorts—

most had never seen a Caucasian. Leroy was *Kananu Naka Nu*, meaning the strange white man who fell from the sky and survived. An enigma. The village lasses could not help but giggle and wave.

'*Agba,*' they hailed.

'*Agba,*' Leroy responded. He had picked up this common greeting.

A few bold ones approached. They touched his skin curiously and fawned over him. Leroy grinned, enjoying the attention.

Tila pulled Leroy away. 'Come, I show you something.'

'Where are you taking me now?' Leroy protested.

'Come. I show you something.'

Spoilsport.

Insistent, Tila led Leroy to a part of the stream that was only a couple of feet wide. She found a plank and placed it across to create a small bridge. Leroy walked across. On the other side, a small path led through a wild bush. Beyond the bush, the scenery changed in a spectacular way. Suddenly, there were no more trees. Instead, the flat grass plain stretched as far as the eye could see. Apart from an isolated granite rock a few yards to the right, the lush grassland stretched out infinitely. Far away, was a distant range of hills, too hazy for the eye to see. The tall savannah grass swayed lazily in the evening breeze, rustling softly.

Leroy loved the scenery. It was beautiful. Paradise.

'Come,' Tila tugged at him. 'I show you something.'

She led Leroy towards the isolated granite rock, which was about six feet high and eight feet long. The front face of the granite rock looked out over the grassland. A bubbling brook flowed past and headed into the grassland. The brook was only about two feet wide, and was crystal clear.

'Come,' Tila said, leading Leroy around the rock. 'You see?'

'See what?'

'You not see?'

'What are you raving about?'

Tila grabbed Leroy's hand. 'Okay. Come. I show you.' She

shoved him around to the front face of the rock.

A lady sat on the grass at the foot of the rock, reading a book. He recognized her instantly. She was the ravishing damsel he'd seen two days back as he sat under the pear tree. Today, she wore a grey dress and a grey shawl. She was still beautiful. More beautiful.

'I know you like her,' Tila whispered mischievously. 'Go talk to her.'

Leroy had not expected this unsolicited blind date. The lady was not aware of Tila and Leroy. Leroy did not want any uncomfortable scenes. Since the lady was immersed in her book, he decided to retreat. He took a few steps back.

Tila blocked his way. 'Aunty Talata!' she called.

The lady looked up, startled.

Leroy waved sheepishly at her. 'Hi.'

'*Aunty, bobo kana rimin yin,*' Tila said to the lady.

The lady looked down, embarrassed, and shook her head resignedly.

Leroy turned to Tila. 'What did you tell her?'

'Nothing.'

Leroy was later to learn that Tila had said, 'Aunty, this man has been dreaming of you.'

Tila laughed and skipped out of sight, leaving two uncomfortable strangers in the company of each other. Now, Leroy was stuck in it. He initiated a friendly gesture and sat on the grass a couple of feet away from her. Close up, she was a pure natural beauty. Her skin was smooth and unblemished. The setting sun flattered her complexion, causing it to glow a lustrous golden tan. Her eyes sparkled, yet expressed an unspoken innocence. Her nose was the masterpiece of a master sculptor, defined, and delicately chiselled. Her nostrils were round and precise. Her lips crowned her beauty. They were soft, pink and perfect, not too thick, not too thin, and just good to look upon. She was unlike any woman he had ever seen.

'You're Tattler, huh?'

'Talata,' she corrected, watching him cautiously. She had

this tender, disarming voice. Soft and smooth.

'Tah-lah-tah.'

She nodded.

'So, what brings you to this lonely spot, Talata?' He could not think of anything better to say.

She shrugged. '*Ba turensin fa.*'

'Sorry?'

'*Ba turensin.*' She gestured in a manner, which meant she didn't speak English.

Leroy understood. He placed his hand on his chest. 'Leroy.' Then he pointed at her. 'Talata.'

She nodded. He gently rubbed his hand against her skin then pointed to the setting sun. 'Your skin is like the sun.'

He sensed a smile inside her. She pointed to Leroy's skin then pointed to a page of her book meaning, yours is white, a bit like the page of my book.

Leroy smiled. However, his mind was at work. How could he get across to a girl he couldn't communicate with? Maybe he should leave her in peace. But this girl was too gorgeous to leave in peace. She was a phenomenon. He had a desire to stay. He searched for ideas.

Tila peeped out from behind the rock and saw Leroy gesturing to Talata in sign language. 'She speak English!' Tila cried. 'She speak plenty English! She go school.'

Leroy read the disappointment in Talata's face. She glared at Tila. Tila grinned and stuck out her tongue.

'Silly girl!' Talata hissed.

Tila laughed contentedly, then skipped out of sight.

Then it clicked. She had been reading a book. Leroy took the book. Caught out, she didn't object. The cover of the book was torn, but the first words Leroy saw was Don Corleone.

He looked into her face. 'The Godfather, huh?'

She nodded.

'How do you find it?'

'Scary. But very good.'

'Guess so. Why did you pretend you didn't speak English?'

She shrugged and smiled mischievously. She had a sweet smile. She retrieved her book and continued reading. For the next few minutes neither of them spoke.

Leroy opted to leave rather than seat around sheepishly. He stood up. 'I know I'm boring company. I'll see you some other time. Do you live in the village?'

She nodded.

'See you around.'

She continued with her book.

Later, Leroy lay on the thatched mattress in his round hut, staring into space.

A small oil lamp in the corner burnt with an orange flame. It was nothing compared to the ember glowing within him. He tried to fight it but he was powerless. He tried to proffer all sorts of silly explanations for this insane attraction, and after a long while he knew he could only solve this problem by facing the truth. But what exactly was the truth?

It was this ravishing rural beauty called Talata. She had a huge effect on him. Her soft smile, her voice, her scent, her mannerisms—everything about her excited him. She oozed such distinct appeal, and yet, set a solid boundary. There was something about her, something within her. This village girl set new standards. Now, truly, the most beautiful women were not in the big cities, they were hidden in obscure villages in the middle of nowhere!

Talata sat imposing on his thoughts like the Statue of Liberty. At the same time, Ann, his wife or ex-wife—he didn't know which to call her—also came to mind. It was his conscience at work—it seemed to constantly bring Ann into the picture.

But we're getting divorced. She dumped me, and she's never coming back. She packed all her things and left! It's over.

Or maybe she didn't mean it. She was probably very upset at that time. She really didn't mean it.

His mind went to Talata. Angel Talata.

Again, Ann came.

Something within him wanted to get closer to Talata. The kind of thing that made men go after mistresses. Animal instincts? Maybe. The urge was strong.

And Ann?

She was the one who wanted out, not me. I'm getting on with my life.

So, it was settled. Come what may, tomorrow, he would make an appearance at the granite rock beside the bubbling brook.

The next day, Leroy woke with a sense of mission and when the sun lowered in the sky, he set off for the rock at the edge of the plains. The breeze swayed the tall grasses, causing them to rustle softly. The air was filled with the scent of grass and pollen.

She was there with her back to the rock, staring at the open grassland. She wore an informal olive-green dress, held up by thin straps on her well-proportioned shoulders. A matching shawl hung loosely from her neck. The setting sun reflected off her smooth skin, making her glow. Her long, black, curly hair flowed around her shoulders.

He stood there a couple of minutes, savouring her beauty, his heart palpitating madly. He decided to be mischievous: he crept behind her and covered her eyes with his hands.

'*Ta ba yen?*' she asked playfully in the local dialect. From the tone of her voice Leroy knew she was asking, 'Who is that?'

'Someone you've set ablaze,' Leroy answered with a chuckle.

She pretended not to hear. 'Leroy?' She gently pried his hands from her eyes. She looked at him and smiled. 'I thought as much.'

He kicked off their conversation with, 'Why do you come to this lonely spot, Talata? You're always here with your back to this rock. Why?'

'No special reason.'

'My mind has been doing a lot of work since I met you. I've been wondering about you; wondering what kind of person you are. Why don't you tell me a little about yourself? I'm curious.' He settled himself beside her.

She smiled. 'There's nothing to tell.'

'Somehow, I don't believe that. I look at you and I think you're beautiful, intelligent and mysterious. You're out of place in this village. You should be modelling Armani or something. Your command of the English language is superb.'

'I learnt English when I was young. I learned from Miss Fisher. She was a missionary schoolteacher who came to our village. She made me pronounce words properly, the way the Queen does, over and over again till I got it right. She gave me many books on English grammar: Ronald Ridout, Enid Blyton, Oxford English—lots. When I was twelve, I attended the grammar school in Dai-wai, which is the next village. After that, I got a Bachelor's Degree in Sociology from City University, Jos. I did it by correspondence.'

'You have a degree?'

'Yes.'

'Now, I know why you're so eloquent. But I don't understand. If you have a degree, what are you doing in this out-of-the-way village? I mean, you could get a really good job in the city!'

'Well, I was born in this *out-of-the-way* village and I grew up in this *out-of-the-way* village,' she replied, showing she disliked his choice of words. 'I love this village and I really do hate the hustle and bustle you get in the big cities. Besides, I cannot leave home as I have to take care of my father. I'm an only child. My mother died when I was ten. I had to grow up very quickly.'

'You must be very responsible then. Whoever wins your heart will be a very lucky man.'

She laughed. The cool breeze blowing from the expansive, savannah plain drowned out her laughter and blew into her hair, lifting her strings of jet-black curls gently off her scalp.

Leroy studied her. There was not a blemish on her beech-complexioned skin. Not a single one. 'I can't help admiring

202

your skin. It's so smooth; so different.'

'Everyone says that. I'm mixed, actually. My dad is Fulani, my mum was Bedouin.' She stopped and looked blankly at the crystal clear waters of the brook as it bubbled by. She cast a glance at him. 'I've been talking about myself for a while now, Mr Leroy, why don't you tell me a bit about yourself?'

He shrugged. 'Well, there isn't a lot to tell, really. Just the common regular life, you know.'

'Apart from the fact that you dropped out of the sky and survived, I don't know any other thing.'

'Can't you tell something about me? From my face, my gait, my speech?' he asked playfully.

'Looks are always deceptive,' she remarked with a coy smile. 'The fiercest hyenas look like shepherd dogs.'

Leroy laughed. 'Well, I'm American.'

'Now, I know that.'

'I'm in the Air Force,' he lied. It was not recommended to declare being employed by the CIA.

She looked him over. 'You don't cut the picture of a military man.'

'As a matter of fact, I really hate it,' he replied, hoping to change the subject. It was best not to let anyone hammer on his cover.

'Were you flying the airplane that crashed?' she asked excitedly.

'No. I was a passenger, going to Somalia. On assignment. Military assignment.'

'Life is so unpredictable. You were going to Somalia and look what happened: you had a crash and you ended up here!'

'I'm grateful for that.'

'Grateful...for an air crash?' She was puzzled.

'Something good came out of it.'

'What's that?'

He took a deep breath and looked longingly at her. 'You.'

She drew back. 'Me? How is that?

'It's hard to explain. Somehow, I've been so happy since I

203

met you.'

She cast a suspicious glance at him. 'Now, I don't know what to say.'

'Say nothing. Rather than speak, I want you to have feelings.'

'Feelings? For whom?'

'For me!'

'I wouldn't want to say you're crazy, but you are!' she retorted. 'You expect me to have feelings for a total stranger?' *Men! Only five minutes and he's talking about feelings. He has to be a Casanova. A serious one.*

'I'd rather not be a stranger to you.'

'What would you rather be?' She was firm. She had never met a man so brazen and up front.

'A friend. A good friend and if I may stretch my luck—'

'Don't stretch your luck,' she cautioned. 'Let's talk about America.'

'America is a good place to live. Fast, but a good place to live.'

'The image we have over here is that of gangs, gun crime, murder, ghettos, screaming police sirens, and AIDS.' Her eyes pierced into Leroy's as if to spite Uncle Sam. 'AIDS is an American export, you know. From San Francisco.' She placed her face in her palm and rocked from side to side as if to say, beat that.

'I guess you know more about the States than I do,' he conceded, more to avoid an argument.

'And how do you find our village?' she asked, attempting to make a patriotic comparison.

'Well, I'd say it's peaceful, and it's full of very nice people, and I can't show enough appreciation to your village. Especially for producing you.' He knew that was cheesy.

She glanced at him suspiciously. 'Can I ask you something?'

'Sure. Anything.'

'Well, it's more like a warning. I've been trying to have a decent conversation with you but you seem to want to be funny. I sense you have some interest in me…' Her face turned stern. 'It's not going to work. I've never had a boyfriend and I don't want one. I am saving myself for my husband, who ever God provides.'

Leroy was speechless.

'Also,' she went on, 'I think some men like to pull a fast one with undiscerning girls. You know, say a few nice lines and then hope to get into bed.' She looked straight into Leroy's eyes. He felt uncomfortable and looked away. 'I'm twenty-four. I'm a virgin and you are not going to get me, if that's your game. Otherwise, we can be friends. Very, very casual friends.'

His stared at her admiringly. *Twenty-four? A virgin?*

She instantly regretted that her tone had been sharp. But she wasn't sorry. 'Did I hurt your feelings?' she asked, tongue in cheek.

'No,' he lied, forcing a smile. 'I appreciate your honesty and respect your virtues. As a matter of fact, I like the way you talk. You are direct, and sincere. At least, now I know what I'm getting myself into,' he bluffed.

'You're not getting into anything. I'm saying this so you don't think I'm leading you on.'

Leroy forced a beaten smile.

'Now that we've established our boundaries, let's continue our conversation,' she said firmly. 'So, tell me some more about America.'

'Well, there isn't much to tell,' he replied coldly. He knew that *take-charge* trait in women. He was not going to let her boss him about.

'What about New York?' she asked, her eyes lighting up. 'I've heard a lot about New York.'

'That's just what it is, New Yuck!'

'Hmmm.'

'Talata, I'd better be going,' Leroy said suddenly, remembering something he learnt at the CIA Academy: retreat, fall back and regroup. This was the second time he was beating a hasty retreat with this girl. It was getting to be a bad habit.

'So soon?' she asked, tongue in cheek.

205

'Yeah,' Leroy stood up. 'I'll be seeing you later.'

She stood up as well, graceful and elegant. 'Leroy,' she said softly. 'I think I may have said too much earlier, and I may have hurt you. However, in this village, we don't allow friendships to go sour, so, I apologise.'

She stretched out her hand for a shake, her eyes searching to see if she had been forgiven. He smiled, and accepted it. Her hands were baby soft.

'Good night, Leroy.'

She walked away, towards the village, her shawl floating gracefully behind her.

A virgin? An unspoiled woman in her mid-twenties? Did they still exist in this perverted twentieth century?

Now, he was impressed.

45

Ann stood by the kitchen door of The Starving Parrot, staring blankly at the oak trees behind her father's home. This place brought back fond memories of the good times she had with Leroy, right in this very doorway, chatting, discussing, kissing, and planning their dates.

She was not happy. She had begun divorce proceedings against him. Her Dad had urged her on. Today, she'd met up with the lawyers at Harrington & Hergoven for a briefing.

She sighed. *Divorce? How did I get here?*

This was not how she planned her life. When she was a girl her plan was that she would get married to a man she loved. Once. A one-time done deal. Divorce was never in her calculations. Never.

Is it really what I want, or is it what my dad wants?

She hated Leroy for what he did to her...but deep within herself she knew that wasn't true.

The truth was she hadn't been able to hate him, even though she wanted to. Even though she tried. He deserved to be hated. He killed her baby!

But why? Maybe he was so scared of becoming a father... Maybe it was such a big step for him. Or maybe I put him under too much pressure, and he didn't know what to do. After all, it happened so quickly. So, maybe I should try and understand him. Maybe he didn't mean it. Maybe it was a mistake. Maybe...

She stopped. She realised she was making excuses for him. Then a thought crossed her mind; something she never expected.

Why not forgive him?

She could not believe that thought dared to cross her heart. *Forgive him? After all he did? He did something terrible!*

But—

Just forgive.

She sighed. Tears filled her eyes. She pondered a long while. Tears rolled down her cheeks. Okay, she would consider it.

He hurt me but I choose to let it go. I forgive Leroy.

But—

I will not be hard-hearted. No one is really a saint. I forgive him.

That instant, a veil of darkness lifted off her psyche. All the bitterness, resentment and anger she harboured towards him melted away and she found herself feeling happier, lighter and more cheerful.

With the bitterness gone something she used to know returned to the surface: affection. The warm feelings she used to have when they were together flushed all over her. She missed him. She wanted to speak to him.

A rush of excitement flushed through her bones as she reached for her phone. Then she remembered: *Oh no! Dad says he's in Chicago for a month.*

She hung up the phone.

But why hasn't he called me since the last time we spoke?

It's because I was mean to him. I guess he's angry with me. Maybe since I told him it was over, he's accepted that, and moved on. Or why else hasn't he called me again? A man should be concerned for his wife, shouldn't he? He should have called twice or thrice!

Then a thought popped into her head: *Or has he found himself another woman?*

She felt a fit of jealousy just thinking about that.

She smiled as she remembered their unexpected wedding in Las Vegas. That was such a special day. The sun was shining; she was pregnant. She was marrying this gorgeous guy. What she loved most was the fact that it was unplanned. Impromptu. Very private. And they stayed in a suite at *The Bellagio.*

She made a decision. *I'm going to do whatever I have to save my marriage! If it's not too late.*

Her mind flashed back to the idea of Leroy with another woman. She felt uncomfortable with that. What if he has really found someone else? It was that very threat, which pushed her to grab her phone. *I'll call him right now.*

Her heart palpitating, and spoiling for a fight with the imaginary woman that was keeping Leroy, she called his phone. It gave a long continuous beep. *What's wrong with his line? Sounds like it's disconnected. Dad said he's on one of these CIA secret mission things where he's got to remain incommunicado. I guess I've got to wait for him to return from Chicago then.*

The thought that she had to wait made her dejected. She didn't like that. She'd had enough unhappiness over the past days. She wouldn't allow herself to sink deeper into depression. Enough of that. She would wait for Leroy to return from Chicago. Meanwhile, she would get herself a social life. Enjoy herself. On Saturday, she would accompany her dad to that dinner he was having with Peter Rudy, the South African billionaire.

46

The sun dazzled in the sky as Ted Raleigh and Pilot Chuck skimmed over the vast Nigerian interior in the clattering Agusta helicopter. It was ten days since they began the search for the crashed airplane.

Raleigh's walkie-talkie crackled alive. 'AJ, come in for Rodney.' Rodney was the CIA officer co-ordinating the search from a hotel room in Jos.

'Receiving you, Rodney,' Raleigh answered.

'We've got some new information. One of our sources says he's got word that a man fell from the sky in a village called Dan Apali. Maybe you should check it out. It's ten miles off our scope but it's all we got. Do you copy, AJ?'

'Yeah, I copy.'

Raleigh flipped through the navigational maps, which littered the innards of the Agusta. Dan Apali was not on the maps. 'That village isn't on the charts, Rodney.'

'Hold on, AJ. I'll ask for directions.' The line went silent. A few moments later, Rodney called in. 'AJ, are you still there?'

'Receiving.'

'It's a tiny settlement on the west side of Pangpam plains. There's a village called Maigam, bearing ten miles north of your present position. Maigam's on the charts. Locate Maigam, and Dan Apali is three to four miles north-northwest. Do you copy?'

'Yo, Rodney. Roger and out.'

Raleigh worked out the bearings. 'We are here,' he said to Pilot Chuck, pointing to a spot on the map. 'We want to go here.'

Chuck made a mental note, then took the chopper in a steep bank and headed into the clouds. Within minutes Maigam floated into view. It was a small village locked in a valley. What put Maigam on the map was that it had a church. Pilot Chuck reset course north by northwest. Barely one minute later, Dan Apali appeared on the horizon. Situated at the edge of a massive plain, which stretched endlessly to the east. Huge granite rocks and farmland lay to the west.

Chuck brought the chopper towards the village.

'Don't move too close to the huts,' Raleigh cautioned. 'Scout the bushes. I can see the plains from here. There seems to be nothing in it. Hey, wait. Take it down! To the left, Chuck. I see something. To the left, Chuck, to the left.' Raleigh pointed out of the chopper. 'There, to the left, take her down. To the left, at the edge of the bush. Near that farm.'

Chuck took the chopper closer to the ground, its powerful blades created a violent downdraft, which parted the bushes.

'There she is!' Raleigh howled, pointing excitedly into the clearing below. 'There she is, Chuck. There she is, damn it.'

Mangled in the thicket were the remains of N219QY.

47

Pilot Chuck landed the chopper in a clump of grass a hundred yards from the mangled wreckage. There wasn't much left of N219QY except a big semi-circular scrap of metal that used to be the lower half of the fuselage. The top of the cabin had disintegrated, leaving it open to the elements. Slimy green algae had begun to grow on the remains. One of the wings hung off a baobab tree. An engine and various pieces of scrap littered the bushes nearby. A mangled seat was still held to the floor of the shattered cabin. There were no bodies.

Raleigh walked to a conical chunk of metal that used to be the cockpit. Brightly coloured wires dangled from it, leading nowhere. 'Nothing here,' he remarked, looking around. 'No bodies, no personal belongings. Nothing.'

'There's a village nearby,' Chuck suggested. 'We could ask in there. See if they know anything.'

'Right. But the first thing I gotta do is radio in.' He retrieved his walkie-talkie. 'AJ to Rodney, come in.'

'Receiving you, AJ.'

'We have located the wreckage. I repeat, we have located the wreckage.'

A joyous whoop screeched out of the walkie-talkie. 'Confirm you found the wreckage, AJ?'

'Affirmative. Standing in front of it as I speak.'

'Location?'

'Dan Apali, three kilometres north-northwest of Maigam.'

'Good work. What's the situation?'

'Large chunks of debris everywhere. Negative on the rollers.' Rollers was alias for the coded disks.

'Copy, AJ. We're sending a skunk team to help out. The word from yonder is to salvage all classified comms equipment on the airplane. An avionics guy will be in the team to see to that. We're also sending down an explosives guy. The wreckage's gotta be blown up. Do you copy?'

'Copy.'

'Survivors?'

'Negative.'

'Bodies?'

'Negative. There's a village nearby. We're gonna go in and see what we can dig up.'

'Roger. I'll send you body bags and a doctor. In case.'

'Roger.'

'Roger, AJ.'

'Roger and out.' Raleigh switched off. 'Now where is that village?'

'Must be that way.' Chuck pointed to a sandy footpath that led away from the farm.

They followed the sandy path. It led through a few corn farms and a wild orchard that smelt of lemons. The path finally led into Dan Apali.

Feeling every bit like strangers, Chuck and Raleigh entered the village. There was no one in sight but they could hear chattering female voices.

Ted Raleigh brought out four colour photographs. 'Here.' He handed the four prints to Chuck. 'These are the four guys known to be on board. Two pilots and two members of staff. We'll show them to the villagers, see if they recognise anyone.'

The first person they saw was a nursing mother. She sat on a bench in the shade of her thatched hut, fanning herself with a rafter fan. Her naked baby nestled in her arms, his tiny lips gripping his mother's breast.

'*Barka da yamma*,' Chuck hailed.

'*Barka kadai*,' the woman replied.

Chuck was glad she spoke Hausa, one of the five lingua francae in Nigeria, a country in which some 480 dialects were

213

spoken. He held out the four photographs. '*Ka san kowa a cikin wona foto? Girigin sanma ne ya fadi daga sanma.*'

'*Aha! Na san wanna mutun,*' she replied eagerly, pointing out Leroy's print. '*Ka bini. Zein kei ka a wojen da ike.*'

'She knows this one,' Chuck said to Raleigh. 'She will take us to where he is.'

The mother led the way into the village. After a short walk, they arrived at the Roda family compound. It appeared empty save for a few speckled hens, pecking at the dirt.

'*Agba,*' the woman hailed.

'*Agba,*' a muffled female voice responded from somewhere within the compound.

Mama Roda emerged from one of the huts. She stared at Raleigh and Pilot Chuck with interest. She had a conviction that they had come for Leroy. As was the custom, she curtsied.

'*Wan bara mi kosa,*' the nursing mother said to Mama Roda.

Chuck showed Mama Roda the photographs.

Her genial middle-aged face brightened. '*Naka bawa ya kosa.*' She pointed at Leroy's photo. '*Ka'ana.*' She indicated Raleigh and Chuck should follow her.

Mama Roda led Raleigh and Chuck to an isolated hut at the rear of the compound. Mama Roda knocked and entered. Raleigh and Chuck waited outside. A minute later, the rafter mat that served as a door peeled open. Leroy Delgado stepped out. He had been taking a nap. He rubbed his eyes. He wore faded blue jeans. His torso was bare, exhibiting minor traces of what should be a set of stomach muscles. He had developed a dark tan. His eyes popped open upon seeing Raleigh.

'Leroy Delgado?'

'Yes?'

'Ted Raleigh. The Company.'

The Company was an alias for the CIA.

'This is Chuck. He's my pilot,' Raleigh said. 'He doesn't work for our company though.'

Leroy shook hands with Chuck.

'Been searching for you for well over a week,' Raleigh

remarked.

'You guys always take your time, don't you?'

'Man, we tried our best. This place is forty miles off course. How the hell did you guys get here in the first place?'

'Don't know. How did you guys get here?'

'Chopper.'

Raleigh looked around. 'Where are Paul Thorn and the crew?'

'Dead.'

'Dead?'

'Yeah, dead,' Leroy confirmed sadly. 'It was a ghastly crash, man. I'm the only one alive.'

A mournful silence reigned for a few moments.

'The bodies?'

'Buried. The villagers buried 'em.'

Ted Raleigh led Leroy a fair distance from Chuck. 'Are the disks safe?' Raleigh whispered.

'What disks?'

'There were top-secret coded disks on board the airplane.'

'Never seen 'em, never heard of 'em,' Leroy said.

'Do you have any idea where they might be? They are critical to the security of the United States. Paul Thorn had them in his care. I checked the wreckage. Couldn't find anything in there. Think it's been looted?'

'Looted? Shouldn't think it's of any use to them. There's a small hut on the other side of the compound. The villagers stacked all the stuff they salvaged from the crash in there.'

'Can you take me there?'

'Sure.'

Leroy led Raleigh to a small mud-baked hut located next to the livestock pen. It was the only hut in the compound with a solid wooden door. Leroy gestured at the suitcases, bags, clothing, provisions, the airplane's maps and other bits that were stacked against the wall. 'Help yourself.'

Leroy walked out of the mud hut, leaving Ted Raleigh to search for whatever it was he was after.

215

Raleigh emerged from the hut in less than one minute, a delightful smile on his lips.

'You got it?' Leroy asked.

'Yeah.' Raleigh patted his bulging hip pocket. 'Intact. Doesn't look like it's been tampered with.'

Raleigh retreated a few yards, speaking into his walkie-talkie. Leroy knew he was briefing his bosses on his success and taking fresh orders.

'What are your orders?' Leroy asked when Raleigh got off the walkie-talkie.

'I hold on to the goods. It must not leave my person. It will be taken to base to confirm it has not been compromised. A chopper will be coming in soon, bringing our boys. The Air Force is sending a technician to strip the airplane of all sensitive gear. There will also be someone to exhume the graves of Paul Thorn and the crew for reburial back in the States. And also, an explosives man.'

'Explosives?'

'To blow up the wreckage. That plane was a mission plane. It's got sensitive communications gear and stuff on board. Its comms system is probably still intact, including the black box, if it has any. There will be other classified bits that the technicians can't strip off.'

'And you.' Raleigh pointed at Leroy. 'We take you out with the chopper. A special flight will be arranged for you to the Air Force hospital in Germany where you will undergo a full medical check-up. Then you'll board a flight back to the States. Your former mission is aborted.'

'About time too,' Leroy said. At least he was no longer going to Somalia. 'Great. I'll get my stuff.'

At 5.05, the Roda family watched as Leroy packed his things into a black leather bag. Leroy thought of a way to show his appreciation to them. They saved his life and extended amazing hospitality towards him even though he was a total stranger. He turned to Raleigh. 'Got any cash?'

Raleigh handed Leroy a roll of Nigerian bank notes.

Leroy walked up to Papa Roda. He bowed in appreciation, clasping his hands together as he'd learned in the village. He shoved the roll of bills into Papa Roda's palms.

Papa Roda grinned and shook his head, refusing it. He patted Leroy's shoulder. 'We do good deeds because it's good to do them. We do not do it for reward,' Papa Roda said in the local tongue.

To be courteous, Papa Roda led Leroy to the village chief, a stocky man of sixty-five whose face did not betray his age. The chief wore a brown *agbada*, a flowing gown, the traditional wear of many West Africans. The chief received Leroy at the door of his court. Papa Roda informed the chief that Leroy had come to show his gratitude to the people of the village. The chief smiled and waved his staff, indicating his thanks was accepted.

After that, Raleigh, Chuck and Leroy walked to the helicopter, accompanied by the Rodas and about fifteen curious villagers. Leroy cast a parting glance at Dan Apali. He would miss Tila, the mischievous teenage imp. She was not at home now. She was yet to return from school. He would also miss Mama Roda. She was always full of warmth—and also, her delicacies.

Now it was back to the real world as he knew it. Back to America to pick up the pieces of his life. He thought about what he would do. Maybe he would apply to resign from the agency and find something else to do. The crash had taught him a lesson. It was a privilege to be alive, not a right. Life was so delicate; it hung on a thin string—and even that string was too short. Worse, there was only one shot at it.

At the chopper, Leroy hugged everyone. He warmly gave Mama Roda the last hug. He had taken so much to her.

Leroy boarded the chopper, and Pilot Chuck started up the engines. Its massive rotor rotated slowly. The villagers waved frantically.

Leroy felt a huge sense of loss, leaving Dan Apali. In the two weeks or so he'd been here, he had taken so much to everyone.

217

Their way of life was laid back; no stress. He thought of Talata. Such a dish. She was not playing ball, though.

His thoughts took him to America, to Ann, and to Cagley. To Washington DC. To his house. He thought of his car. He had left it in Langley. The agency would have asked a tow truck to deliver it to his home. Cars could not be left in Langley for long. He thought of electricity, ice cream and TV.

The chopper rotor spun faster and faster, creating a small hurricane, which violently swayed the bushes. The choppy roar was deafening. The villagers stood back in awe.

Leroy looked around the chopper with its black leather seat—and at Ted Raleigh with his flaming brown hair, and Pilot Chuck. They all reminded him of the big, wide world out there and its rat race. Dan Apali, on the other hand, was a whole other world…isolated and poor yet its people seemed happy and content. He thought of the beautiful plain that stretched for miles and miles with its swaying tall grasses. He thought of the rock at the edge of the plain. He was torn between remaining in Dan Apali and going back America; between village life and urban life; between the rat race and a low profile existence; between the concrete jungle and the endless grass plain; between Ann and Talata—sophisticated city lady and village princess—both beautiful in their own individual way.

By now, the chopper's rotor had reached maximum RPM. It would lift off in a few seconds. That was when something within Leroy gave way. It was now or never. He made a decision. He grabbed his bag and pulled at the door handle. The back door opened outward with a click, muffled by the roar of the rotor blades. An orange light flashed on the pilot's console. Leroy jumped out of the chopper.

Pilot Chuck saw the 'Door Open' light on his console. He glanced at the back. The back door was open, and the back seat was empty. 'Shit!' Chuck swore. 'The man's gone!'

'What?' Raleigh cried.

Astonished, Chuck looked around for Leroy. Leroy was

thirty feet away, in the midst of the villagers. He cut out the engines.

Raleigh scrambled out of the helicopter and dashed to Leroy. 'Are you okay? Are you okay?'

'Thanks. I'm fine,' Leroy answered.

Chuck scampered over. 'Oh my God, what happened? What happened?'

'I'm sorry,' Leroy said. 'I know you guys have done a lot to rescue me. But I want to stay here.'

Chuck and Raleigh glanced at each other. Raleigh could not accept what he heard, so, he searched for a logical reason. 'You have a phobia of choppers?'

'Yes,' Leroy lied.

Raleigh laughed. 'You should have said so. Okay, dude, we'll arrange ground transport for you.'

'No. I don't want ground transport. I want to stay here.'

'What?'

'I want to stay here. I'm not coming back. I'm sorry, guys, I'm not going back to America. But thanks all the same.' Without another word, Leroy walked away.

Ted Raleigh was rooted to the spot. He turned to Chuck. 'D-did you hear that?'

'Y-yeah.'

'He says he's not coming?'

'Yeah.'

When it finally sunk in, Chuck nudged Ted Raleigh. 'C'mon, man, it's gonna be dark very soon. Get in, we gotta go.'

'B-but—'

'He doesn't want to go!' Chuck yelled. 'Just get in the damn chopper.'

Raleigh climbed back in. As the chopper began to climb, he stared through the windshield at Leroy, now walking away in the midst of the villagers. Ten days. Ten whole days! Labouring night and day, searching for the lousy guy. Finally found him and guess what? The guy did not want to be rescued! It gave him a headache.

48

Leroy did not return to his hut in the Roda compound. Instead, he dumped his bag in a thicket and, shaking off the ecstatic villagers, he raced to the great savannah plain. A mild wind blew from the plains, swaying the tall grasses. He made his way to the granite rock by the brook.

She was there as usual, with her back to the rock. She wore a gold-coloured silk dress. She seemed somewhat downcast as she stared fixedly into the savannah. He watched her for a minute or two. There's a mysterious force that comes to work when you're watching someone, and somehow she sensed someone watching her. She turned and looked in his direction. When she saw him her pink lips parted in surprise.

'Leroy!' Her beautiful eyes lit up, unable to hide her delight.

'You seem so astonished to see me,' he responded.

'I thought you had gone with the helicopter!'

'Well, I didn't. Rather, I couldn't.'

'What happened?' she asked, giggling like a kid.

'There weren't enough seats in the helicopter,' he teased.

'Oh. I see.' Her eyes betrayed an element of disappointment. She forced a shallow smile. 'Is that the only reason?'

Leroy saw the disappointment in her eyes. 'Well, Talata, I didn't go because I couldn't. I felt I was leaving something behind. Something precious.'

'Then you must indeed like our village. You like it so much that you don't want to leave.'

'Talata, it's not the village. It's you. I can't go without you. I don't want to be without you. I admire you; I can't help myself.'

It hit her like a tornado. She gaped. He saw a joyful sparkle

220

in her eyes. Then she regained her composure. 'Don't be silly.'

Her rejection hurt. He suddenly felt inadequate. Maybe he hadn't been romantic enough, but then there were no roses in the village, neither candlelit dinners. All that was available was the spoken word. Besides, he was tired of their little games.

He decided to lay it straight. 'How can I get across to you?' Leroy gestured, deadly serious. 'What should I say? Maybe I'm not saying it right. I keep asking myself one question: why do I feel this way about you? I've tried to find a million reasons why I should not. But I've realised I've got to face the truth.'

She seemed half amused, half confused, but definitely, she was relishing what he had said. 'And what's the truth?'

He looked straight into her eyes. 'I'm falling for you. You know, when I first saw you I was attracted by your beauty. But a woman's beauty is not just her looks; it's something deeper. The other day when you mentioned you were a virgin I began to see your inner beauty. I'm not exactly a saint, I'll tell you that, but when I see a woman of virtue I can't help noticing. It's something I really appreciate. Since then I've been stuck on you.'

She pretended not to hear his sermon. 'So, you refused to go back to America only because of me?'

He nodded.

She sighed. He observed a perplexed look on her face as if she was at crossroads, trying to make a difficult decision. 'Is there a future for you here in this village?'

'I don't know that answer myself,' he answered softly. 'But as far as I'm concerned, you are my immediate future.'

She looked into his eyes, searching for something; trying to read something. 'And the far future?'

'Depends on what happens between us.'

'What do you expect to happen?' she probed.

'A lot. A whole damn lot,' he stated. 'I adore you, Talata. That's a statement of fact. Nothing you say can change that. The fact that I adore you will always be there. There's absolutely nothing you can do about it. Nothing. Your cunning

221

questions won't change that fact. Mocking me does not either. The best I've been hoping for is this: maybe you could just have a small spark of affection for me. Then I have something to hold on to. Something to nurture to a hundred percent love.'

She looked down at the grass. 'Do you know I have a husband?' she asked after a while. She had such a mischievous sparkle in her eyes. It was obvious she was lying.

'That's me,' Leroy exclaimed.

'You?'

'Yeah!'

'No way. Here, in the village, we're betrothed to someone when we're young.'

Now that Talata mentioned the word *husband*, his relationship with Ann and the fact that he was still married to her surfaced in his mind. He should tell Talata about his situation with Ann. That way, she would be in the know, and any decision she made would be an informed decision.

'I've heard of that betrothal stuff, Talata,' he answered, ignoring the prompting. 'It's called *Bakti*. It rarely happens. Tila told me about it. It's an old custom where two families promise their kids will marry each other. It's similar to arranged marriages in Pakistan.'

Tell her about Ann.

She laughed. 'If you know that much about our village, then it's obvious that it's our village you like, not me.'

'I'm not talking about the village, I'm talking about you.'

'Hmmm?'

'Besides, Talata, I know you. You are not the kind of girl to have a husband yet. I sense a lot of intellect in you. I sense sophistication. I sense common sense. You know what you want. I'm certain you don't have a husband.'

'But I do,' she emphasised, chuckling.

Tell her now!

'Okay. So, you have a husband? Now, tell me, what's his surname?' He snapped his fingers. 'Yes, yes, tell me, quick, what's his surname? Where's his house?' It was a trick he'd

222

seen on TV.

'Er…er…er,' she stuttered, unable to come up with a name. She laughed, knowing she had been caught out. 'Okay. I don't have a husband. So what?'

He was silent for a few moments then he tried another approach. The God approach. 'You claim you believe in God?'

'I do,' she said sharply.

'Why would I, Leroy, survive the crash and nobody else?'

'Don't know.'

'Why would I, Leroy, meet you and not some other?'

'Don't know.'

'Why do we seem to understand each other?'

'Do we?' she asked, a mischievous glint in her eyes.

'Perfectly. Don't you think all these coincidences are just too much? Don't you see some supernatural work of God?'

'Okay, okay, I've heard all you've said. It's nice to know I'm wanted. I'm elated. Thanks.' She rolled her gorgeous eyes. 'The answer is still no. I don't want you or anyone else in my life.'

Leroy breathed deeply.

'If I consider your analysis,' Talata continued. 'I think it would have been simpler for us to meet without loss of life. The fact that life was lost doesn't make it look like God to me. It's just chance.'

Leroy grinned. 'Okay. So, you're so smart. But you can't fathom God.'

'Let's not bring God into this. He's too sacred.'

'Fine. So, tell me you'll think about it.'

'About what?' she asked, feigning ignorance.

'About us.'

'Us?'

'Yes. You and me.'

'Okay, so you fancy me. I've heard all that. What exactly do you want?' She was firm. 'Tell me what you want from me.'

'I want a relationship.'

'Relationship?'

223

'Yes. I want to take care of you.'

'Hmmm.'

'I want to marry you!'

Her eyes popped wide opened. 'You want to marry me?'

'Yes, Talata,' he answered, a mischievous smile on his lips.

She stared at him, dazed. 'Why would you say that?'

'Because I love you!'

'You love me?' she cried, alarmed. His new tactic was working. He knew women react to the L word and M word without fail.

'A lot.'

'Men just keep juggling about with the phrase, I love you. Men don't have a clue what it means.'

'If we do, what stops us from expressing ourselves as many times as needed, provided it comes from the heart?'

'Strange, isn't it? You see a woman and simply because you think she's pretty, and you like her skin, and she's a virgin, you claim you love her. True love isn't like that. Think about it: what if she loses that beauty? What if she develops scabies? What if she loses that virginity? Are you still going to be there?'

Her words were deep.

'Don't you think it's some form of infatuation?' she pressed on. 'You don't know me; you don't know my background. You just want to pick up a strange woman by the waterside, and make her your wife? That's not sensible, is it? What if I'm a wicked witch or something? What if I'm your downfall?' She stared at him, her eyes daring him to provide an answer.

Leroy felt somewhat beaten. Her words were true. Good wisdom. She was making him feel stupid. But he wasn't giving up. 'All I know is that you're my soul mate, Talata. You're my better half.'

She threw a cautious glance at him. 'How do you judge that?'

'You're perfect for me. Nobody can feel the way I do unless there's something else to it. We've got chemistry. A spiritual and physical chemistry. You captivate me. For every man, there is a woman somewhere who can tame him. Talata, you can tame me!'

She laughed. 'That's a new one! I haven't heard such powerful chat-up lines before,' she taunted. 'You are smooth!'

Leroy watched as she laughed. She was being amused, having a good time, dancing circles around him. He decided to step up his game. He waited for her to regain her composure. 'Talata,' he called. He paused to allow the mood to cool. 'I have four things to say to you. Please listen.'

She still had the grin on her face.

'There's nothing to laugh about,' he said firmly. 'I'm dead serious.'

Her grin vanished.

'First, I need you to make me whole. You're all I want and I think you're the embodiment of womanhood. Second, I want you to know I'm not joking. I'm dead serious about this. Third, it's gonna take whatever it's gonna take. This means I'm prepared to sacrifice anything for you. If I'm gonna be beheaded in this village, so be it, but I'm gonna do whatever I have to do to get you. Finally, I want you to know that I want nothing but your total love, your warmth, your affection and your companionship. If I can't have your love, whole, faithful and true, then don't give it to me. Don't give me a half portion. Don't pity me. If you will ever say yes, say it only because you're giving yourself to me.'

She stared at him, speechless.

'Don't bother to ask me to be friends,' he pressed on. 'I have enough friends. It's all or nothing. I want a woman I can love. I want a woman who will love me. If I couldn't go back to my country only because of my desire for you then it's more than enough proof of my love.'

He got to his feet, his face dead pan. 'I have nothing more to say to you.' He took a couple of steps then turned around and looked at her. 'Think about what I said. Think deeply about it. I'll be seeing you.'

He walked around the rock and out of sight.

She sat there, gazing ahead. Now, this was serious.

49

Leroy was in a dilemma. Talata didn't seem to have any interest in him at all. Still, he wasn't giving up. He decided to change his strategy. Now, he would attempt to draw out her sympathy.

The next afternoon, as he stepped around the rock he attracted her attention.

She turned, smiled and waved at him. He walked towards her and then mindfully and deliberately, hit his foot on the rock in such a way that it looked like a clumsy accident. 'Ouch. Ow, ow. Oh!' he yelped, hopping on one foot, pretending to be in pain.

She took no notice.

He saw that she was taking no notice, so, he turned up the volume. 'Ooww. Oooww!'

With him making such a racket she couldn't ignore him for long. Her compassion swept in and she quickly walked over. 'Are you all right?'

'I tripped on the rock. I think I've broken my toe. Ouch!'

Now, she was concerned. Signs of worry crept up on her face. She made him sit on the grass and removed his shoes. All the while Leroy yelped and squealed, feigning agony. She responded with soothing words to his fabricated squeals. Then she had an idea. 'Come, Leroy. Let's dip the painful foot in the stream. That should help.'

'I can't walk,' he groaned, grimacing.

'I'll help.' She put one arm around his waist to steady him as he limped to the brook.

'Can you place both feet in the water?'

Still feigning pain, he sat on the grass bank and placed his feet in the brook. The water was warm and soothing. Its natural bubbly flow simulated the effects of a Jacuzzi.

She gathered up her ankle-length skirt and sat beside him. His heart skipped a beat as he sighted her bare legs. They were shapely, well proportioned and smooth as a baby's.

'Which foot hurts?' she asked.

'The right one.'

Now, because she sat to his left, she had to lean over his thighs to reach his right foot. Her closeness excited him. He smelt a flower-scented perfume on her. He had an urge to touch her. Her blue Pashmina shawl provided the perfect excuse.

'Let me hold your shawl,' he offered, 'so it won't drop in the water.' Without waiting for her response he gathered the flimsy material and placed it on her shoulders.

'Thank you.' She gently massaged his toes.

Leroy let out a few phoney squeals. He loved playing the patient while she played the nurse. Lovely.

'Does it hurt so much?'

'Yes.'

'I'll be gentle.' She continued working his toes.

The skin on the back of her neck looked as smooth as ice; lustrous and without wrinkles. He held her shawl onto her back with three of his fingers and with the remaining two he stroked her hair.

'What are you doing?' she protested.

He smiled, enjoying himself. But he didn't stop. To his surprise she didn't push the issue.

After a while, she raised her head. 'Now, that's done. You should feel better now.'

'Ouch! No,' Leroy yelped. 'It's still hurts.'

She worked his toes a couple more minutes. When she felt her work was done she raised her head but Leroy held her down. 'Leroy, what are you doing? Will you let go of me?'

'I hurt the other foot as well,' Leroy chuckled, unable to hide his mischief.

It was then she knew it had all been a scam, and she was being taken for a ride. She playfully slapped his thigh and stepped out of the water, laughing at herself for having been taken so easily. She walked away from the brook and sat with her back against the big rock.

A few moments later, he joined her. 'Thank you so much for the care and massage,' he said mischievously.

She smiled. 'You're welcome.'

He sat on the grass next to her.

'You've given me so much work to do, and now, I'm exhausted,' she said. 'I need some sleep but I don't have a pillow. Since you've been so naughty you'll do just fine.'

She calmly adjusted her shawl then placed her head on his lap and closed her eyes.

The following day, he met her at night. Neither of them spoke. A full moon was out and it brightened the landscape for miles around, bathing the trees in its luscious, golden light. In the village, the kids were listening to ancient tales from the old men. By the brook, two souls seemed to be waiting for a green light.

Talata looked so stunningly beautiful and radiant in an aquamarine dress. It was as if the bride had come to the altar. She glowed and the moon took pleasure in reflecting off her skin.

Her eyes sparkled. They were beautiful, devastatingly alight, and yet they seemed to send a message. She seemed to want something, and didn't know how to ask.

She smiled. He smiled.

He shrugged. She shrugged.

Her flower-scented perfume wafted to his nostrils. That scent kicked his body alive. He couldn't take it any more. After a long while, Leroy reached out for her.

He held her and she didn't protest.

Then they slowly embraced. A loose, formal but tender embrace, her slender fingers rested on his pounding chest, his

228

arms around her waist. After twenty long minutes they drew closer. When they were together they clung to each other as if their very existence depended on it.

She never felt happier. His body gave her the warmth necessary for the chill of the night. It also served as a tower of refuge, a source of strength and a final answer to some secret desire.

The evening wind lifted her shawl, and it wafted in the air current, floating like a flag behind her. It was this third night they ventured to share a first kiss. It was by the brook beside the rock that had become their lonely, private spot. The moon glimmered off the surface of the brook as it bubbled past. As usual, the crickets raised their voices in an orchestra of squeaks and shrieks. As if by some weird work of nature, when their lips touched, the crickets fell silent.

Her lips were so tender.

50

As Talata prepared her father's lunch the next afternoon very warm blood surged through her veins; a contented smile graced her face.

Suddenly, Leroy was all she desired.

For the first time in her life she had been hit by a tsunami, brewed in the depths of the ocean of love. The tidal wave wrought carnage on her defences, swept her off her feet, and indulged her in a vibrant and joyful swim in its waters of love, which left her gasping for breath. Wave after wave, it pounded her shores. Leroy dominated her thoughts.

She had found him interesting the very first moment she set eyes on him as he sat under the pear tree. She began to really adore him when he approached her beside the brook. But she was a woman; she wouldn't just roll over and fall at his feet, would she? She had to put up a bit of a fight.

What good did that do?

This was her first experience of love. She always wondered if she would know love when it came. Now, she knew.

She came alive when he was near, her heart fluttering like the wings of a butterfly.

He exhibited an enormous aura; his kindly brown eyes made her lose control. Sometimes, she simply wanted to run away or hide. It was as if he carried a charm. She could only sway back and forth like a cobra dancing to the flute.

She was living in his world now, no more hers. Everything she did was related to him. When she dressed, she dressed for him; she prayed and she prayed for him. Even when she ate, she avoided fish and onions, so it wouldn't put him off.

Even Buba, her father observed, 'You seem happier these days, Talata.'

'That's how I've always been, Papa.'

She knew it was a lie. She knew she was certainly more radiant. Her attitude had changed. She had always been nice but now, being happy in love, she was extremely sacrificially nice to everyone. Even those she didn't like. All she wanted to do was discuss Leroy with her friends all day long.

Whenever he smiled, her heart melted like butter in a blast furnace.

Whenever he looked away, she thought, *he doesn't like me anymore.*

Whenever he touched her, a thousand volts surged through her body, and she loved it.

That evening, she met him again beside the brook that had become their private love nest. Mother Nature sent forth a playful east wind from the plains. Sometimes the wind was still, inducing pleasant serenity; at times it became mischievous, taunting and massaging the shrubs, coaxing them to dance to its rhythm. Occasionally, the wind flexed its muscle, forcing the little trees to sway in a reluctant samba. For Leroy and Talata, the east wind in all its strength was at best a minor irritant. They didn't have time for the wind. No. Cupid was celebrating a landmark birthday.

They clamped into each other the way a vine weaves into a host tree. Their hearts were in tune as they exchanged their deeper secrets. Everything was said in whispers. Everything was funny and they both seemed to have lost their senses: you could tell from their small, silly laughs. As the night rolled on, their desires multiplied and the menu steamed into bigger kisses and more.

For Talata, it was simply enchanting. So this was love? It was so good, so fulfilling, so vibrant. 'I love you, Leroy,' she said softly when she found her voice, her tender voice amplified by the rustling of the east wind. 'I love you so much. I can't tell why. It's just there. I can't help myself. All I want is to make you happy. I'll only be happy if you are happy. I feel in my heart that you are a man that is good.'

She paused. 'I love you, Leroy. I can't help the way I feel about you. If there's any other word bigger than love, I would say it but its all I know…'

'You know,' she continued a moment later. 'As important as the heart is…it's useless without blood. The heart cannot function without blood. I feel useless without you. All I ask for myself is that you won't hurt me….' Her voice quavered, softened and broke off; it was barely audible. She looked into his face, her eyes searching his, seeking that assurance. 'Please don't hurt me…*Pleeeaaase*.'

He heard her words and his knees began knocking into each other. *The heart cannot function without blood.* Leroy felt vulnerable and helpless. He had wanted Talata right from when he laid eyes on her, and now he had her. Her outpouring of deepest, unhindered passion punched a hole into the depths of his soul. Her words rang on and on in his head, scooping out so much compassion from deep within him, at a depth no one had ever ventured before. No woman had ever declared her love for him so resolutely before. It touched him in the deepest places.

He felt some dampness on his shoulder. He raised her head. Her cheeks were wet with tears. Overwhelmed with emotion, she was crying softly.

He held her close. 'I'll take care of you, Talata, I promise. I'll take care of you. You'll see. Please, don't cry. I won't hurt you. Please don't cry.' His eyes became moist.

They eventually left the brook at 2.00 am.

As Leroy returned to his hut he was racked by guilt. He hadn't been straight with Talata. He hadn't yet told her about Ann, and that legally, he was still married to Ann. The longer he left Ann out of the picture, the more difficult it became to bring her in. He regretted the fact that he had not told her at the last opportunity when Talata was joking about having a husband.

At least then she would have made her decisions about him based on the whole truth. But now, things had moved up a whole lot. She had taken the plunge, and was offering unbridled love. If he were to tell her now…after she had given herself to him, he would be the devil himself, the father of deception. It would hurt her so much and destroy her trust in him.

Maybe it was easier to keep quiet and not talk about it? Hopefully, she may never know. Talata and himself could live here in the village and she need never know. But if the truth were to ever come out...

Still, there should be trust.

Should he force the issue and tell her?

Or was it too late to do that now? Especially now that she had given herself to him?

51

The full moon in the sky lit up Dan Apali. It was quiet in the Roda compound. Papa Roda had gone for a drink with the village chief while Mama Roda had gone with the women to a neighbour's house to chat and sing folk songs. The kids were in the village square, having fun.

Leroy sat underneath a huge mango tree at the rear of the Roda compound, his back against its lacerated trunk. Talata sat between his legs with his arms clasped around her belly. She wore a green and blue, body-hugging dress called an *ankara*. It was dark under the mango tree since its huge canopy of leaves shielded away the moonlight.

She closed her eyes and savoured his warmth. She enjoyed being in his arms. 'Leroy, I'm your woman. I want to be everything to you. I know you expect some obligations from me but can I ask a favour?'

'Anything, my love.'

'If you do this for me, I'll be happy,' she said with a bit of trepidation.

'What is it, Talata, my love. What is it?'

'Promise me. Promise me that you won't force me to go to bed with you. I want to keep myself for you and it's all for you, but can you give me some time? A little time? Till we get married or till I can re-orientate my mind. Please?'

'What do you take me for, Talata?' Leroy answered, staring ahead at the outline of the huts in the Roda compound. 'Our relationship is not for the sake of taking you to bed, it's because I have found a soulmate.'

Her face lit up. 'Then you won't force me?'

'No.'

'Neither will you trick me?'

'No. I promise,' he said firmly.

There was a brief, uncomfortable silence.

'Thanks, Leroy,' she said, relieved. 'I hope I can make it up to you.'

'Having you is enough for me.'

Neither spoke for a couple of minutes. She broke the silence: 'So, now that there's no lovemaking, how are you going to relieve your sexual tensions?'

Gee! Leroy thought. This girl had a way of asking inconvenient questions.

'There's a fine line between love—which comes from deep within—and lust. If I want sex I'll go to those who are willing to give it to me with no strings attached.'

She almost jumped out of her skin. She spun round and glared at him. 'So you mean you'll patronise a prostitute?'

'Calm down.' He laughed and patted her shoulders.

She looked into the distance, dejected, her eyes cloudy. *He would go to women with no strings attached?* 'If that's what you intend to do, then whenever you're ready, I'm ready,' she declared soberly.

'I'm not ready,' he said, observing she was sombre. 'I promised, I'll wait. I will wait.'

'Thank you.'

He nodded.

'You know something else, Leroy? I don't know what's wrong with me, these days. When I hear footsteps my heart jumps. I run to the window, thinking it's you. When I'm trying to decide what to wear, I find I'm trying to impress you. My life is changing. I'm changing. This afternoon, I thought, maybe, this is too much. I don't understand it. Am I all right?'

He held her tight and kissed her ear. 'I have a problem as well, Talata. I can't do anything but think about the girl that I want to meet by the brook—you. But as for me, I'm not complaining.' He tickled her. 'I love it.'

235

'So do I.' She beamed joyfully.

'I wonder how love works.'

'Maybe it's a gift,' she suggested.

'I think so too.'

'What have I done to deserve this? I'm so happy. Can it continue like this?'

He didn't answer. He tickled her again. She wiggled and laughed then snuggled into him. 'Leroy, I'm feeling cold. Hold me close.'

He hugged her tighter. Words often stick in people's minds, and Leroy's words kept ringing in her head. *Go to women with no strings attached. Prostitutes...*

With that ringing in her head, she opted to make a sacrifice; she peeled his right hand off her waist and placed it on her breast.

'Talata?'

'That's where I want it to be. That's the first male hand that's ever been there. I want it there. It belongs to you. I belong to you.'

He didn't speak. A little reluctant, he gently squeezed it. Her breast was very firm. He took his hand off her bosom, and returned it to her waist.

'No.' She placed his hand back on her bosom; this time, both hands on both breasts.

'Come on, Talata, stop!'

Women with no strings attached? Prostitutes? AIDS?

'No.'

She clasped her hands on his, ensuring he did not remove his hands. He fondled her. No one had ever touched her, and her body reacted in a way she never expected nor experienced. A huge surge of desire—all the desire she held back for many years surged through her body like a flood. She had given him access—a gentle squeeze—and now, she found out that what she thought was going to be a gentle paddle in the stream was more like drowning. She found herself on high heat, desperately craving the forbidden fruit. It was so quick that it

236

was unreal. Her breathing hastened. Her heart pounded rapidly. She snuggled into him.

He observed she wasn't calm anymore; she seemed agitated. He knew he had touched a weak spot.

Inside Talata's head, a tiny string of virtue held on. She tried to move away from Leroy but she couldn't co-ordinate her limbs. Now, she knew she was out of her depth. She wanted to say, no, but because her body was saying, yes, it came out like a moan of eagerness.

Can't I just try it?

Don't you know you can get pregnant? a voice in her head warned. *You've never used a contraceptive!*

I don't care, her lusts retorted. The stream had become turbulent. Her body ached longingly. The rapids were round the corner. She couldn't resist.

A deep feeling of regret loomed over her. She was going to lose her virginity. She would be the slut in the village! She shouldn't let this happen, there was too much at stake. Then it came to her mind, those cheesy lines that Hollywood programs into naive women. The empty, meaningless lines she had picked up from western novels and magazines: *make me a woman.*

He's going to make me a woman. He's going to make me a woman. I love him. Why not show him? This is the only way he'll understand.

By now, Leroy was actively massaging her. She surrendered the last bit of virtuous dignity that held her back; she allowed the river of lust to sweep her away. She reached for his belt.

He clamped his hand firmly on hers, stopping her.

She relaxed and tried again. 'Leroy. I love you.'

'I love you too, Talata.'

'Hurry please.' She reached for his belt again.

'No, Talata,' he said.

'Why?'

'We're out in the open.'

'No one will see us. It's dark. Okay, let's go to your room.'

237

'No.'

'Leroy.' She giggled. 'Don't be naughty.'

'No, Talata,' he said firmly. He smacked off her hands.
His firm manner made her simmer down.

'Why?' she whispered.

'Nothing.'

'Please, please. Don't you want me? Don't you love me?'

'I do.'

'Then make me a woman.'

'What makes you think that sex is what confirms you a
woman?'

'Please, Leroy, please!'

'No.'

'Please. I know you want to.'

'Talata, I respect the fact that you're a virgin. I don't care
what the world says but there is serious virtue in virginity. It's
not that I don't want to. I do. I was thinking of it long before
tonight!'

'Then this is the chance.'

'I don't want the chance. You see, when I heard you speaking
about keeping your virginity I was so impressed. It was one
of the things that endeared you to me. I said to myself, this
is the kind of girl I want in my life. I felt more proud of you
than ever. I'll tell you one thing about men. If you open up
freely, we'll take advantage. Freebies, we call them. But when
it comes to marriage men will give an arm to marry a virgin.
Every man respects a virgin. We boast about it to our friends.
You know, my wife was a virgin, we say proudly. Because of
that, I resolved I would try my best to make sure you keep it.
I want what's good for you. I will not want to be the one who
shatters your aspiration, and takes away what you've kept all
these years. I promised you I'd wait. I will wait. I know you're
willing but I won't take advantage of you. Your mind really
doesn't want this.'

'I do, Leroy.'

'Well, I don't.' He frowned. 'When it's over, you'll be full

238

of regret and it can't be undone.'

'I was only joking when I said I wasn't ready. I'm ready. Come on, come on, Leroy.'

'No way.'

'Please, *pleeease.*'

'No!'

It finally sank in. She calmed down, breathing deeply until she got her breath back. The river had refused to carry her away, throwing her disdainfully onto unfamiliar shores.

For a long while she didn't speak. She looked into the distance, feeling rejected. The rejection hurt. But when she got her senses back, she softly said, 'Thank you.'

He nodded inattentively, grim. There were a lot of things on his mind.

She observed the change in his mood. 'Anything wrong?'

'Many things. Many things,' he answered.

He had finally decided to come clean and tell her about Ann. He sought the easiest way of doing it.

'Tell me one of them,' she said, tickling his ribs.

'Okay, I'll tell you one. I wish I'd met you three months ago. There's a reason why I'm saying this. Talata, you're a dream come true. I wanted you and now I have you. But then, I keep asking myself, what next? Where do we go from here?'

'What do you mean?'

'There are a few things you need to know. I want what is best for us.'

'If there's a will, there's a way,' she replied. 'If there is love we'll make it through everything.' She squeezed his hands.

'It's not that easy. There is something I need to tell you and—'

She ran her finger over his lips. 'I have an idea of what is on your mind. The way you talked, it seems you wish to let out all the skeletons in your cupboard.'

'Yes.' He looked into her eyes. 'I have a...uuhh.' She covered his mouth with her palm, stifling his words. 'Hush! I do not wish to know anything—whatever it is. Whatever you wish

239

to tell me can only do two things to me. At best it will make me happy. But then, I'm already happy—I have you. On the other hand, it could make me sad. I hate sadness; I can't bear it.' She looked lovingly into his eyes. 'You may have killed someone before or something like that. I don't care. I like you as you are. Let's not bring up the past, eh?'

'But…uuhh.' Again, she stifled out his words with her palm. 'Ssshh! Don't tell me anything.' She looked over his face then straight into his eyes. 'I don't want to hear about your past. All I want is to be acceptable to you, Leroy. Okay? All I want right now is for you to make love to me.'

She pressed her lips into his.

*　　　*　　　*

John Walsh was on yet another mission. This one was very simple. Simpler still, the victim was only twenty yards away, unarmed and unguarded. Nice. Also, his prey was distracted. Good. The wind blew towards John Walsh, and the moon would soon disappear behind a cloud. Perfect.

John Walsh was known to the very few who knew him as Mamba. He was a thin, wily man in his forties with an oblong face, a narrow nose, and silvery hair. He had bright, genial eyes but if one looked properly, those eyes weren't exactly so genial. They were the eyes of a vicious, seasoned combatant. John Walsh was a veteran of fifteen years in OMATA.

OMATA was a ruthless group of mercenaries who undertook dirty missions without questions. To date, OMATA had been involved in twenty-five hijackings, two hundred and ten assassinations, unnumbered jailbreaks and kidnappings, and fifteen coups. And this was only the first page of their resume. OMATA operated in secret, without an address. The only way to contact OMATA was by placing a property advertisement in *The Times*. Particular ads meant nothing more than accommodation to the public. It meant something else to OMATA. OMATA made the SEALS and SAS look like choirboys.

All around John Walsh were thin stalks of corn that served as perfect camouflage. Beyond the crops were a few dwellings. To his right, crouching in the stalks was the man known as Mucho. Mucho was a former bullfighter. His broad chest was two feet across. He was probably stronger than a bull and definitely more vicious. John Walsh had two other men in his team. One was called Vulture, the other was known as Mill. No one in OMATA answered to real names.

John Walsh surveyed the scene through his infrared glasses. All was quiet. No one in sight except his prey, and his wench. *Easy prey*. All easy prey were always disposed of when they were distracted, when their focus was a woman's body.

John Walsh checked his watch. The time was 20.55, local time. He looked to his left and right. Satisfied his men were in position, he raised his right arm.

Vulture picked up the signal and slid silently into the bushes. He crept stealthily through the foliage. He was the flank man, and his objective was to block off any escape route should their target attempt to flee.

John Walsh's right arm also served as a signal to Mill, a temperamental cutthroat formerly of Israel's Mossad. Mill fitted a stock to his customised Schuster machine pistol. He hit the dirt and crawled on his chest, slithering like a serpent through the corn, towards the target. Not even a person listening out would have heard him approach. He was a true professional. He moved only when the wind wouldn't carry his scent. He advanced only when the leaves rustled. He noted the direction of any lights so as to always remain in the shadows and under the cover of darkness. He monitored the terrain continuously, noting the nearest cover at all times, aware of the quickest exits to his every position. Finally, Mill slithered up to the big tree and flattened himself against its smooth trunk. His dark-blue commando fatigue blended into its bark. The tree was all that stood between him and the target. The target and his strumpet were romping on the front side.

241

'You don't love me,' he heard the woman say.

'I do,' the man replied.

'You only say that. Prove it.'

Mill kept still. Cool, calm and still. He heard the tweeting and smacking of kissing. 'Touch me,' the woman demanded.

Mill shook his head wistfully. When was the last time he had a woman fawning over him? Being a professional, his mind quickly re-focused on his mission. He looked through his night glasses. Vulture was in position, crouching in the corn to the left. Mucho was a few yards behind, sprawled in the dirt. Mill raised his right arm, indicating he was in position. He studied Walsh and waited for his signal.

'Hmmm,' he heard the woman moan. 'Let's go behind the tree.'

A few moments later, he saw John Walsh's signal. It was a go. Mill's killer instinct swung into action. He slipped around the tree. There was a thump as the butt of his gun slammed into Leroy's head. Leroy slipped into unconsciousness without a sound. His arm dropped off Talata's body.

Talata was unaware of anything. She was still in ecstasy land. She didn't snap out of it even as a huge gloved hand covered her nose and mouth. At first, she thought it was Leroy, playing the fool. She smiled inwardly, her eyes gleaming in the moonlight.

Mucho yanked at her and she crashed to the ground, her legs and arms flying around her. He pinned her head to the ground, his huge hands covering her nose and mouth. She couldn't breathe. Instinctively, she reached for Mucho's arm. Both her palms were barely able to go around his wrist, talk less of dislodging it.

Meanwhile, Mill dragged Leroy's limp body a few feet. He heaved Leroy onto his shoulders and disappeared into the bushes.

John Walsh emerged from the bushes. He knew Mucho was choking her. Walsh signalled Mucho with his index finger. From experience, they both knew she would not be able to scream. She would gasp for air for at least fifteen seconds. It was only after she'd recovered her breath that she could think of screaming. Mucho relaxed his grip. Talata gasped violently for air, panting as she breathed. But professionals never allow their subjects to recover, in case the subject is stronger than envisaged. With virtually no effort, Mucho lifted her clean off the ground, and held her in a tight bear hug from behind, pinning her two arms to her sides. Mucho was so broad that he only needed one arm to do this. Using his other hand, he choked her again.

Talata was helpless and dazed in the hands of pros. When her mind regained function she knew one huge man was holding her in a tight vice-like hug from behind. She struggled but it was pointless. It was like an ant fighting a battle tank. Another man stood in front of her. He had fiery eyes and he was a white man. He wore a black commando fatigue; his face was painted with camouflage face paint.

John Walsh brought out his pistol and pointed it at her forehead. Her eyes widened. She trembled in Mucho's grasp.

John Walsh took the pistol off her forehead. He had done that to scare her, and subdue her. Next, he brought out a colour photograph. He held it about eight inches from Talata's face. Even in her half-dazed state, Talata could clearly identify Leroy in the photograph. He was dressed in a dark suit, and he had a big grin on his face. Next to him, intimately close, was a blonde woman. They were about to kiss.

'This bastard's got a wife back in the States,' Walsh snarled. Then he stuffed the photo into her blouse, into her cleavage. Without another word, he turned and disappeared into the bushes.

Vulture emerged from the bushes, his Schuster 50 sub-machine gun panning the area. He whipped out a small white pad from his back pocket. Mucho took his palm off Talata's mouth.

Talata gasped for breath.

Vulture placed the pad over her nose and held it down. Instead

243

of air she breathed the vapour from the pad. Immediately, she felt dizzy. The next moment she went limp. Mucho relaxed his grip on her body. Talata crashed to the ground at his feet, her legs and arms sprawled like one crucified.

'Hope you didn't feed her too much foam,' Mucho remarked. 'Looks like she's dead.'

'What a waste then. Pretty bitch,' Vulture replied.

'What do we do with the body?'

'Leave it. No one will know she's here.'

Walsh reappeared on the scene. 'Move it!' he ordered, and disappeared behind the mango tree.

Mucho surveyed the vicinity. All was quiet. He turned around and melted into the bushes.

Vulture checked his watch. 21.00. He stepped around the mango tree and fused into the vegetation.

At the base of the mango tree, Talata lay sprawled.

A light breeze blew.

In the distance, thunder rumbled. It seemed it would rain.

52

In Dan Apali, it was drizzling. Most villagers had blown out their oil lamps and retired into their huts, relishing a cool night's sleep. Thunder rumbled in the distance. As the thunder rolled away, a distinct, infamous squawk pierced the air. It was faint, yet distinctly audible. Every villager who heard it knew it was the dreaded Black Gagu, a fearsome tyrant amongst birds.

The black gagu was very much like a vulture with its black feathers, erect stance, and long neck. However, the gagu was three times the size of a vulture, far stronger, infinitely more aggressive, and possessed a distinct odour, reminiscent of stale urine. The gagu, by nature, had an insatiable craving for flesh. It was a scavenger only as long as there was a carcass, and it could smell one miles away. Otherwise, it was a most vicious predator. Its serrated beak, four inches long, effortlessly pierced into prey, ripping out their innards. In the old days its beak was used to tip spears. Its two-inch long, scalpel-sharp talons could pierce the hide of an elephant. A starving gagu will attack the first meal that crosses its way, man or beast, dead or alive. The gagu is uncannily silent, until it wants to feed. Then it lets out a peculiar nerve-racking squawk, which incorporates a goose's cackle and a hawk's shriek. It was a distinct cry most creatures prefer to avoid.

A few minutes later, the gagu's ear-splitting squawk shattered the peace of the night again. This time, it was so loud and clear that it had to be from within the village.

Tila heard it.

Is any of the domestic livestock dead? After all, the gagu only called when there was a carcass. She was the person her father put in charge of the livestock. But then her body yearned for sleep. *Let the gagu feed.*

She rolled over on her thatch-stuffed mattress and closed her eyes. She had barely slept one minute when the dreadful ear-splitting squawk pierced the night again. She ignored it. Her father, Papa Roda did not. He detested that creature called the gagu. Even if one of his livestock was dead, a gagu would never turn his compound into a feeding ground. Now, what about that silly girl he had put in charge of livestock? She ought to have heard the noise!

Papa Roda stepped out of his hut. 'Tila, Tila!' he called, his voice reverberating into the night.

Tila didn't answer. Instead, she grumbled under her sheet.

'Tila!' her father called again.

'Yes, Papa,' she finally said.

She stepped out of her hut. It was dark amongst the huts in the compound. A rain cloud had covered the moon, and there was barely enough light to walk around without a lamp. But like most villagers, Tila had keen night vision.

'Did you not hear that noise?'

'What noise, Papa?' Tila peered around into the darkness, feigning ignorance.

'What do you mean by *what noise?* Are you deaf?'

'I didn't hear anything, Papa.'

'If you lie once more, you'll be in trouble this night!'

The gagu squawked again. Loud, clear and ear-splitting.

Papa Roda glared at Tila.

She knew what she should have done. She stepped away from her father, and walked towards the kitchen-hut. She picked up a six foot-long threshing paddle and half-heartedly, trudged towards the livestock pen, grumbling as she went. The goats seemed undisturbed; they huddled together in their shed, their eyes glittering green in the night. The hens were in their roost, asleep. She couldn't be bothered to count them.

The gagu's terrible squawk rent the air once more. It seemed to come from the direction of the yam barn at the rear of the

246

compound. She trudged towards the barn. She looked beyond the compound towards the trees. The usual silhouette was as it ought to be. She returned to her father. 'There's nothing,' she told him, eager to get back to bed.

'What do you mean, there's nothing?'

'There's nothing, Papa. I looked!' She turned and walked towards her hut, eager to get back to sleep.

'Don't go anywhere!' her father boomed.

She turned around. A menacing four-foot cane had conjured into his hands.

'Go back towards the barn.' He pointed the way with his cane.

She obediently trudged to the barn. Any more fuss and the cane would be dancing a stinging samba all over her slender body.

It was dark everywhere but something under the mango tree seemed unusually more darkish. All at once, that darkish patch seemed to move. She crouched low and studied the environs of the mango tree.

The gagu smelt an intruder and let out a warning squawk.

'It's under the mango tree!' Tila shouted to her father.

'What's it doing there?'

'I don't know!' she replied, pacing towards the mango tree. Her eyes adjusted to the darkness and she could now make out the form of the avian cannibal, tearing at something at the foot of the tree.

The gagu saw Tila approaching. It raised its head and let out a horrendous warning squawk. Then it stepped on top of its prey and spread its massive six-foot wingspan, an indication that it was asserting its claim on the prey, and was prepared to fight for it.

Tila didn't stop. She held the paddle firmly and advanced towards the gagu. It was the way children were trained in the village. It was the way they attacked danger. *Never stop, never doubt, lest fear take over.*

The gagu let out another warning cry, displaying its massive

247

wingspan.

'*Kai!*' Tila snapped at the gagu, not stopping.

The gagu took a step forward so that its prey was now shielded behind it. It pointed its beak forward, ready to attack. The nauseous stench of the bird wafted to Tila's nose. She kept on.

The gagu stepped back, intimidated at this intruder's fearless approach. It now knew it really had to defend its meal. It let out a high pitched battle squawk, flapped its wings and soared three feet into the air. With its beak pointing ahead like a spear, the gagu flew forward in attack.

Tila, likewise, broke into a run and advanced towards the gagu. When she was about seven feet from the gagu, she swung her paddle in a wide arc with all her might.

The gagu had good vision. It detected the swing of Tila's weapon. However, its reflexes were slow; it could not re-orientate its massive body in time. There was a dull thwack as the paddle caught the gagu on the neck. Its long neck swung back a full circle as it crashed to the ground, an uncoordinated mass of feathers. Dazed, it let out a barrage of short, agonising squawks as it struggled gallantly to find its feet. It wobbled and shed some smelly feathers. Its narrow eyes gleamed at Tila. It squawked in anger.

A wounded gagu was twice as dangerous. She swiped at the bird once more, catching it on the side. It let out a staccato of painful shrieks and clawed viciously at Tila's paddle. She struck again but this time the gagu ducked. Grunting, she swiped again. The gagu neatly stepped back, flapping its massive wings.

Tila struck once more. The gagu soared some eight feet into the air, displacing a lot of dried leaves. It hovered temporarily, trying to make a decision, all the while shrieking viciously. Tila raised her paddle after it. It soared higher and turned in an arc, heaving its massive body temporarily onto the top of a nearby shrub. Then it took flight, squawking, into the night. This gagu had learned a lesson.

248

Having taken care of the gagu, Tila panted, trying to recover her breath. She curiously observed the prey, and the paddle dropped from her fingers. 'Papa, Papa! It's a person!'

'What?' her father yelled back, dragging himself towards the mango tree.

'A-a woman!' Tila stuttered. 'She's dead!'

'A dead woman?'

'Yes!'

Papa Roda lit an oil lamp then hurried to the mango tree as fast as his ageing legs could carry him. A dead woman in his backyard? 'Who's she?' he asked.

'Aunty Talata!' Tila howled. Papa Buba's daughter. 'She's dead!'

'What's she doing here?' He knelt beside her body.

'I don't know,' Tila shrieked. Then she burst out wailing.

Holding the lamp against the mango tree, Papa Roda looked over Talata's sprawled body. The gagu had shredded her clothes. Ants roamed over her body. There were two big bruises on her arms and a gash on her thigh. Claw marks were clearly obvious on her belly, and they oozed blood.

He put his head to her chest then felt for a pulse. 'Tila. Go and wake your mother and your brother. Tell them to come here.'

'Yes, Papa.' She sped away, wailing as she ran.

Papa Roda knelt once more beside Talata.

'Silly child,' he said, now smiling. 'She's not dead.'

53

Talata's eyes fluttered open several hours later. The bright sunlight streaming into her sparsely furnished room gave her a headache. Her body felt heavy and sore. She felt a sharp pain on her left thigh. She touched it. It stung. There was a huge bandage wrapped around her thigh.

What happened?

She sat up in bed. She observed there were bandages around her arms and around her torso. Where did all these awful injuries come from? She definitely didn't remember anything remotely near this. It had to be a dream. A very bad dream—just like the nightmare she had, in which some men attacked Leroy and her.

Her mind cleared slowly, and gradually, things became more vivid.

Wait a minute. It definitely wasn't a dream. It happened. Her injuries proved it.

And Leroy?

Leroy!

She sprang off her bed. Her thigh hurt so much that she wanted to scream. But that didn't matter. She had to see Leroy. Was he all right?

She summoned all her strength, and got to her feet. Holding her bed, she managed a painful limp. She dragged herself to the door and limped out of her house, groaning with every step. The afternoon sun waxed strong as she galloped the shortest route across the village.

I hope he's fine. I hope he's all right.

She hobbled into Papa Roda's compound. The first person

she saw was Tila. Tila was anxious.

'Aunty Talata, you recovered,' Tila cried in the local dialect.

'Where's Leroy?'

'We can't find Uncle Leroy,' Tila responded, equally alarmed.

'You can't find him?' Talata shrieked. 'Where's he gone?'

'I don't know.'

'Since when?'

'Yesterday night, when we found you under the tree. We looked in his hut. We didn't find him. What happened, Aunty Talata? My father thinks Uncle Leroy has been kidnapped.'

Slowly, Talata recalled the events of the previous night. She had met Leroy...they were under the mango tree...then those men!

She dashed to the mango tree. Tila followed. Talata observed a few black feathers lying around. She also observed shreds of greenish cloth—her greenish cloth. The very one she wore yesterday.

Behind the tree was a clear boot print in the soil. It belonged to someone with very large feet. Further away, there were a number of them. Though it had rained, the prints were still very prominent.

The nightmare was true. She suddenly felt drained.

'Aunty Talata,' Tila called. 'Look, it's Uncle Leroy!' Tila held up a rain stained photograph.

Talata snatched it from her.

Talata's heart somersaulted and then began to thump. She remembered clearly now! One of those men had shown her this photo. She remembered his words, "This bastard's got a wife back in the States."

His vicious voice echoed in her head.

A wife? A wife. A wife!

It rang over and over in her mind.

The very last ounce of vitality seeped out of her. Everything grew blurry. She began to see six images of Tila. The mango tree spun around, and so did the sky. Her knees buckled and

251

she slumped. For the second time in twenty-four hours, she didn't know how she got to her bed.

54

She couldn't eat.

Betrayal.

Lies.

Men!

So it was true. All men were liars.

Play with a cobra before you trust a man.

This bastard's got a wife back in the States!

Leroy was married?

Certainly, he was. The photo, an intimate snap of his wife and himself proved it. She studied the photo over and over till she knew every inch of the woman's face.

Talata hurt to the depths of her soul. All her dreams crumbled. All the thoughts she had nurtured, those precious thoughts of marrying him, having a family, taking the kids to school—everything fizzled out.

Life lost its theme.

She locked herself in her dreary bedroom and wept. 'Why?' she asked the bare walls, but in her mind she was gazing straight at Leroy. Tears poured from her eyes. 'Was I not going about my own business when you came and professed your love for me? If I had known you had a wife, I would never have let you come near me, you tortoise! Now, you woke up my feelings, disorganised my life and just disappeared. Who knows, maybe you've gone back to your wife.

'Before I met you, I was happy,' she wailed. 'I met you and, truly, I was much happier. Why didn't you just leave me alone, eh? Why? After all, you have your own wife! You just wanted to use me. Why are men so evil? You wanted to use me, you evil man. You wanted to know what an African woman feels like. I was a fool. A big fool. Yes, I deserve this pain. I really do. I was foolish. Yes, foolish to have fallen in love with you. I was a dolt. Yes, a dolt. Dolt. Dolt. Dolt. That's what I am: a dolt.'

She got to her knees. 'Oh God, I don't deserve this. Really, I don't. Even if I've been sinning they're only tiny sins. I haven't killed anybody. I don't steal. What could I have done to deserve this? If it is punishment for my sins, Oh God, it's too much!'

Towards sunset, the village chief, Papa Roda and two others in the company of her father called on her. The fact that five elders paid her a visit meant it was being viewed as a serious issue in the village. The elders asked her only one question: what happened?

She gave only one answer. 'I don't know. Leroy and I were talking under the tree when some men crept out of the bushes and held me down. I don't know what happened. I just found myself in my room.'

'Talking?'

'Yes, Papa.'

The elders nodded in wisdom. *Talking*.

The elders sent a party of men into the bushes. They saw nothing except patches of trodden grass and boot prints. They deduced from the boot prints that there were four men.

55

Leroy opened his eyes and found himself gazing at a whitewashed ceiling. He felt an ache at the base of his spine. He concluded it was because he was lying on a very thin mattress. He felt an equally painful ache behind his ear. He touched it to find a hard lump. Though he didn't know how it got there, he had a conviction he had been struck. His left forearm felt sore. There was pinprick on the inside of his arm: bright red with a pinkish mound. He could clearly see the telltale outlines of a tourniquet below his biceps. He was certain he had been hit then drugged by injection.

Without getting up, he moved his head and surveyed his surroundings. He was alone in a room that was about fifteen feet square. It smelt strongly of disinfectant, though he was quite sure this wasn't a hospital. The walls were painted dull white. The small bulb dangling from the ceiling bathed the walls in dirty amber light. There was no window; an air expeller hummed above in the ceiling. A small, ageing toilet was fixed into the wall on the far side. He clearly saw the dark brown grime peeping out under the seat. Beside it was a small washbasin, supposed to be white, but also brown with age. The floor was of plain untreated concrete. The door was across the room from the bed. It was made of thick steel. It looked so sturdy it would need a bulldozer to pull down. There was no keyhole, only a shuttered grill. He coughed and the cough echoed back to him. He heard nothing except a door clanging shut in the distance.

They didn't need to tell him. He was in a prison cell somewhere.

56

Every afternoon, CIA Director Michael Cagley read through a document called *The Director's Daily Brief*. It was a four-page document that summarised the activities of the CIA on a daily basis. It was prepared by Donald Billingham, the Deputy Director (Operations). On page 3, Billingham highlighted a particular portion with a red marker pen.

OPERATION RENEGADE
SUBJECT: DELGADO, LEROY A.
STATUS: APPREHENDED

Cagley read the third line again: APPREHENDED.

He shot to his feet, a massive frown on his face. 'What kind of bumbling fools do we employ in the agency these days!' he yelled at the walls of his office. Alone in his office, he felt like running amuck. Fuming, he knocked over the empty mug of coffee on his desk.

'Can't anybody do anything right in this agency any more?' Cagley's office was soundproofed so no one could hear him. 'Incompetent fools. I gave specific orders. Specific orders. Now, this happens.'

He pressed a button on his intercom. 'Anita, get me Billingham! Pronto.'

He switched off before Anita could say a word.

Damn!

Frowning, and frustrated, he flopped into his seat.

Five minutes later, Billingham entered. As usual everything he wore was Gucci. 'Something wrong?' Billingham asked.

256

'Operation Renegade,' Cagley snarled.

'Done.'

'What do you mean, *done?*' Cagley yelled. 'I thought I told you guys not to do it. I told you to abort that operation. I told you not to bring him back. The boy wanted to stay in Africa. For shit sake, let him stay. The further Delgado is from me and my daughter the better. I don't want him near me. I don't want him in this country.' Cagley glared at Billingham, his long-standing friend and ally. 'I said not to embark on Renegade. You did, Don. Why—why do you guys disobey me?'

Billingham cleared his throat then stuffed himself into a chair across the table from Cagley. He knew how to handle Cagley. He snuggled deep into his seat, undaunted. 'Have you seen the newspapers today?'

'No. What's in them?'

'Nothing. But it could as well have been any of these: *The Washington Post* headlines could have been LOST AGENT SNATCHED BY FOREIGN POWERS IN AFRICA. *The Chicago Tribune* could have been CIA CHIEF'S IN-LAW DUMPS CIA FOR AFRICAN BEAUTY. *The New York Times* could have said, CAGLEY IN NEPOTISM SCANDAL, and *USA Today* would have screamed, CIA DISCIPLINE UNDERMINED: AMERICA IN DANGER.' Billingham paused and stared deadpan at Cagley. 'How would you have liked any of those, Mike?'

Cagley said nothing. He wouldn't have liked such headlines.

'What do you think the President will say?' Billingham scolded.

'About what?'

'About you, Mike!'

Cagley looked away. The squint in Cagley's eyes told Billingham he had hit home. 'You're letting this Delgado boy get to you. You're mixing emotions with business. You're making potentially scandalous mistakes you normally wouldn't. You're leaving gaps you never would have. There's nothing to regret about Operation Renegade, Mike. It's in your best interest.'

Cagley was silent.

'Why on earth would an intelligence analyst and former bodyguard to the CIA Director refuse to return to base? What was he doing in the middle-of-nowhere, deep in the heart of Africa? Was there more to it than we think? Was he selling out? Now, let's assume Operation Renegade had been organised by some foreign power like China or Russia. They would have captured him…and then what? He's an analyst and he was a bodyguard. He knows enough about many things. He knows about our security; you; the Intelligence directorate. Assume they work on him, or worse, they groom him to become their inside man. What would have happened? We left our flanks too wide open, Mike.'

Cagley continued to stare at Billingham. Billingham was right.

'Also examine its impact on staff and morale,' Billingham continued. 'He's the Director's son-in-law for goodness sake, and we let him get away with it?'

Anger flashed across Cagley's grey eyes. He didn't like being referred to as Leroy Delgado's father-in-law.

'He's your legal son-in-law, Mike. Whether you like it or not,' Billingham reiterated despite seeing the displeasure in Cagley's eyes. 'People will say anything and everything. In fact, they already are. We had to bring him back—at least to face trial for desertion, if only to instil discipline in the rank and file.'

'I see your point, Don,' Cagley conceded after a while. 'I liked it better when he was in Africa. He was out of the way, out of Ann's life, out of my life. I didn't see things from that perspective.' Cagley forced a smile. 'Thanks, you covered my ass. I know you've got my back.'

Billingham smiled. 'Forget it, Mike. That's what friends are for.'

'So, how did you handle the job?' Cagley inquired. He was now interested. 'Foolproof?'

Ever since the Church Committee investigated the excesses of the CIA in the seventies, the CIA, FBI, NSA and other intelligence agencies were required to inform Senate of all their covert activities. The way round that was simple: get someone else to do the dirty job.

'Clean. Untraceable,' Billingham answered. 'I used OMATA.'

Cagley's grey eyes brightened up. 'Good. And their payment?'

'In kind. I put in a good word to the Israelis to supply them forty S-10 laser automatics.'

Cagley nodded. 'What about their intelligence briefing?'

'When I learned your boy refused to return, the first thing I thought was that he was dealing with foreign governments. Immediately, I asked Ted Raleigh to recruit informants in that village.'

'Among the villagers?'

'Yeah. Raleigh has a dogsbody called Malik. Malik is Nigerian. He works for us. He went down to the village from time to time in the guise of a crop merchant, buying crops. He managed to recruit an agent in that village. The agent's code name is Soprano.'

'Who's this Soprano?'

'Someone in the village. The identity is secret.'

'Okay. Carry on.'

'So we had up-to-the-minute information on Delgado's activities in that village. In my estimation, it was the girl that kept him back.'

'Maybe.' Cagley shrugged.

Then he realised Billingham had presented him with another shot at putting Delgado away. 'Do me a favour. When Delgado gets arraigned for his antics, can you arrange it so he goes down for treason or something along those lines? I want something that will put him out of circulation permanently.'

'I doubt it, Mike. He hasn't let out any secrets as far as we know. He was just fooling around. At best, he can draw up a dismissal, and maybe some time in jail. Everything depends on the report after he's debriefed.'

On hearing the word, jail, Cagley's mind went to John Hune. 'I like that idea. Can you come up with something so he draws a very long stretch?'

'How long do you have in mind?'

'Twenty years to life.'

'It can be arranged but don't forget he's an analyst; he's got high-level security clearance. He's also received continuous training, which is quite expensive.'

'Don't give me that bull. You call Delgado an analyst? Rubbish. He's too thick for that kind of work. The only thing he's good at was getting into my daughter's undies.'

Billingham paused a while. 'You see, Mike, I really don't want to go down the route of arraigning him for desertion and all that. It's too much rigor. What I actually want is to shake him up and let him have the impression he's in a lot of trouble. Then when he's broken, sober and seeking mercy, we'll send a saviour lawyer to negotiate with him. If he pledges to be of good behaviour, and pledges not to leave the States for two years in exchange for full reinstatement, we'll drop all charges. Then we'll have some peace.'

'That's not what I want. Not at all.'

Billingham rubbed his chin. 'So, what do you want?'

'I'll tell you in a moment. Where is he now?'

'He's in a cell in a safe house in McLean.'

'No!' Cagley snapped. 'Move him. He's too close to home here. Arrange for him to be kept with the Army or the Air Force—at Andrews or somewhere. They have tighter lip control over there.'

'I'll take care of that.' Billingham scribbled on a small notepad.

'See to it they cancel his passports.'

'Okay.'

Billingham adjusted his tie and folded his arms, and stared at Cagley, amused. He had never seen Cagley so passionate about getting rid of anyone. 'But, Mike, what exactly do you want with Delgado? I'm curious.'

'What I want is to get Delgado in a cage then weld the door shut,' Cagley replied.

'Why?'

'He violated my daughter!' Cagley boomed. 'Is that not enough?'

'I understand. I know how you feel.'

'There's something else.' Cagley looked away. 'Delgado owes me big time. I have unfinished business with him. I have never told anyone this. That boy's only brought me misery; his father the same.'

'You know his father?'

'Oh yeah. Oh yeah! Ken Delgado was my Squad Sergeant in Korea. That bastard murdered the woman I loved.' Cagley shook his head sadly. 'She was just a beautiful, harmless P.O.W. Not only that, he made me walk through a live minefield. Look at this scar...' Cagley touched a one-inch scar above his brow. 'I'll never forget that day, sixteenth September nineteen fifty-two.'

Cagley told Billingham his Korea story. When he finished he reached for a cigarette. 'You know...' He shook his fist at Billingham, 'when I was being flown back to the States, that treacherous fool, Sergeant Ken, had the nerve to call me a coward. Me? A coward? After what he put me through?' Cagley sucked in a breath and let it out slow before continuing, 'Not too bad. I couldn't care less. I was going home, anyway. Guess what, he rubbed salt into my wounds, saying, "Don't worry, pie-face, you die and your mother gets an American flag."'

'That's callous. What did you do?'

'What could I do? Nothing. I was in pain. I was dying. All that was on my mind was to stay alive. Can you imagine that? You die and your mother receives a flag. And as a final insult, his son couldn't find any other woman to play games with but my daughter! Can you believe that? Of all the women in the world he goes and impregnates my daughter. The S.O.B.

was supposed to face the rap for that. Instead, he pulled a fast one, went all the way and married her. Can you believe that?' he cried bitterly, thumping the table. 'The smart-ass S.O.B. produced a wedding certificate and walked free. He flung it in my face dammit!'

Cagley lit his cigarette. 'Ann's wedding was something I'd always looked forward to. You know, walking her down the aisle; giving her away to some worthy suitor—with a big garden party and a band, with all you guys in attendance; even the President.' Cagley looked away, forlorn. 'All that was snatched from me. Four years ago I bought a suit from Saville Row in London. Cost me over a thousand. It was in anticipation of her wedding.'

Cagley looked away, sad and angry. 'The father cheated me of the woman I loved, and almost cheated me of my life. Now, the son's cheated me of my daughter.'

Cagley dragged heavily on his cigarette. 'Why won't they leave me alone, Don? I didn't go hunting for revenge. Why won't they let me be? Why can't his son find another woman in America? Why my girl? Worse, he doesn't love her. To him, she was just a fling and when things got out of hand she became a shield. His romp in Africa with that village girl proves it. I'd like to get rid of him once and for all and damn the consequences. Terrible shame he didn't die in that crash. We would have dried our tears by now.'

'I didn't know it was so personal, Mike,' Billingham said softly. 'I thought it was official.'

'It is both official and personal, Don. Can you believe it? His son marries my daughter!'

'Didn't you know? How did he get so close to you?'

'To me, he was just another guard, Skinner or something he was called. I didn't even know who he was until I learned he was messing about with Ann. I had Bosworth do a background check on him, you know, to make sure he wasn't some foreign agent trying to infiltrate. And guess who it turned out to be?'

'So, what are you doing about it?' Billingham was ever ready

262

to get into misdemeanours with Cagley. They'd done many illegal operations together; they had something in common in that they both loathed Congress. Any way to undermine the Oversight Committees was always welcome.

'I'm prying Ann out of his hands. That's working. She's signed her divorce papers; she thinks he drugged her. I think she's gradually forgetting about him.'

'Does she know of his affair with that village girl?'

'No. She thinks he's in Chicago. That's why I want you to move him to Andrews. I'm going to keep him away from her forever. She'll never know where he is.'

'We can't keep him locked up much longer. Very soon the people at Andrews will start asking questions.'

'I know. That's why I asked you to see to it that he goes down for a long time. Get something on him that will stick.'

Billingham thought a while. 'We could cook something up. We could say he was negotiating with foreign agents.'

'That will be too messy. Too much paperwork; too many lawyers; the press.'

'I know. And that way your daughter will know he's about, which is one thing we don't want.'

'She never will. It's for her own good, anyway.' Cagley looked suggestively at Billingham. 'You know, Don, I just wish Delgado would drop dead.'

Billingham knew that deadly, insinuating look. 'That could be arranged. We've got to bide our time. For now, I'll ask Luzesky to work on him. A little payback, perhaps.'

'Luzesky?' Cagley laughed wickedly. 'Luzesky the butcher?'

'Yeah.'

'Good, Good. Let's have some coffee.'

263

57

Sergio Luzesky was dark, sadistic and bald. He was short and stocky with a thick black moustache. He was a member of the CIA interrogation unit. He entered Leroy's cell carrying a brown doctor's bag. His T-shirt was emblazoned with a single word, Scream!

Luzesky had three heroes: Freddie Kruger, Pol Pot, and Idi Amin. His CIA code name was Mengele.

He cuffed Leroy to a chair and directed a bright lamp into his face. 'Time to sing,' he croaked at Leroy, his eyes twinkling. 'Time to sing, pretty boy.'

Then it was down to business. Luzesky's eyes turned dim. His moustache twitched. He was a master of his gory art. Psychological, emotional, drugged or physical torture? He was an expert in every field. He started off with a nerve-racking technique called The Tomb.

'You have high-level security clearance,' Luzesky howled into Leroy's eardrums. 'What is your first obligation in a crisis?'

'Re-return to b-base,' Leroy stuttered.

'True, you were in a crash. True, you were hurt. Why didn't you make an effort to contact base? Assume you were lost, but we found you. And you refused to come home for some reason. What was it?' Luzesky yelled every word in Leroy's face.

'Were you dealing with the Chinese? The Russians? The Nigerians? The Libyans? I intend to find out—peacefully—if you co-operate.' He placed chocolate candy on the table.

'Or painfully!'

He placed an enormous syringe and a bloodstained electrode

on the table beside the candy bar. 'The choice is yours. You can be a smart bird and start singing. If you don't I'll have to extract it from you. And I promise you, pretty boy, you'll sing.' He laughed wickedly. 'You'll sing like a canary.' He dealt a backhand slap to Leroy's face.

Leroy groaned.

'Why did you abandon your duty post?'

'Why did you turn your back on your job and your responsibility?'

'Why did you turn your back on the agency? Are you working for another? KGB, Mossad, DGI, DSS? Who paid you to do it?'

'Who paid you to turn your back on the United States? You discussed aircraft data with that man in the village. How much did he pay you? You discussed the Director's security arrangement with that woman, didn't you? You thought we wouldn't find out? We did! Do you know you're facing a charge for treason?'

'Who offered you money in exchange for information? Or were you offered in kind? Sex? A woman? Aha! A woman! Most of the worst agents are wooed, not by money, but by women. Did they offer you a pretty bitch? Or maybe they took you for a ride and offered you a whore. Dirty bastard. You sold out the secrets of the United States in exchange for a night of pleasure, didn't you? Answer me! Was it by a whore? A pretentious whore called Talata?'

Leroy was stupefied.

Luzesky knew how to work on the mind. He knew how to unlock the crevasses by feeding the victim information that was credible yet, half true, and half false. It often invoked indignation in the victim, coercing them to talk.

'Aha! Talata! We have traced this Talata,' Luzesky bluffed. 'You may not know it but she works for Libyan Intelligence. We've been clocking her for months. We've got a dossier on her. I hope you know she's H.I.V. positive! Or she didn't tell you?'

'Ha-Ha-Ha!' Luzesky laughed viciously. 'She told you she was a virgin, didn't she? Fool. She lied. She's actually a high-class hooker. What did you tell her?' Luzesky rammed a huge spanner into the table. 'Answer me before I kill you!'

The gruelling interview continued for fifteen hours.

58

All men seek success.

It is the manner in which they go about it that makes the difference. Some men labour, while some tear down everything in their way. Some are smart opportunists, while some are merely lucky. Still yet, some are ass-kissers.

Ass-kissers get to the top essentially by cozying up to the boss. They are the masseurs, who constantly massage the boss' ego. They are the yes-men; the boss' cronies, and the boss' ear through which the boss learns of every gossip. The ass-kisser never loves the boss; he loves himself. All the snitching and all the nice-boy façade is with the hope of being rewarded for licking the boss's boots.

Ronnie Ackerman was precisely that kind of man. He was a unit leader in the CIA Office of Security. Ackerman's immediate boss was a guy named Sylvan McKee. McKee answered to Bill Daniels. Daniels reported to Schwartz. Schwartz reported to Cagley who reported to the President. And goodness, Ackerman loved to kiss ass! Starting with Sylvan McKee and going all the way to Cagley, Ronnie Ackerman behaved like a pandering puppy towards his superiors. When any of his superiors was around he transformed into goody-two-shoes, fretting, grinning sheepishly, agreeing to everything they said, all in a bid to charm his way into their hearts. Ackerman took his art a step further: he also kissed the asses of all those in a position to influence his bosses including their wives. Hopefully, they would put in a good word for him sometime.

It was a grey afternoon. Ackerman decided to pick up a new suit at Tyson's Corner Centre, a massive shopping mall west of

Washington. Ackerman had the stereo in his Pontiac blasting Eurythmics' *Sweet Dreams* as he crawled into Tyson's Corner from Chain Bridge Road. He drove to the huge outdoor car park opposite Circuit City and pulled his Pontiac into a slot opposite the entrance. As he switched off the engine a blonde lady stepped out of the mall. She wore a long white trench coat and carried a white handbag.

He knew her from somewhere but he couldn't remember where. She walked briskly to her car. Ackerman continued to watch her, wondering where they'd met.

Then he remembered: she was Ann Cagley, daughter of the CIA Director!

Ackerman's instincts propelled him to do what he did best— kiss ass. One good word from her to Cagley could result in him being favoured by Cagley. It was a golden opportunity he couldn't afford to miss. He scampered out of his car, not bothering to shut the door. He paced in huge strides behind the row of parked cars, hurrying towards Ann. He caught up with her as she opened the door of her Toyota.

'Hey, Annie,' Ackerman called, grinning, oozing extreme familiarity.

She looked at him and smiled politely. She faintly recognised him as one of her father's subordinates. 'Hi. How are you?'

'All right. And you?'

'Very well, thank you.' Ann slipped behind the wheel.

Ackerman politely held the door open for her. At the same time he searched for something to say, something to put him in her good books. He said the very first thing that came to his mind: 'Oh, I had meant to see you. I know it's rather belated but I'm sorry about Leroy's plane crash. I didn't hear about it until recently but thank God, anyway, that he was found alive. Can you imagine all those days in the African jungle? It must have been a nightmare. I can't imagine how you coped.'

Ann's jaw dropped. Adrenaline gushed into her bloodstream, sending her heart pounding at rib-cracking pace. She stared through the windshield, horrified, clutching the hand brake.

Leroy—a plane crash? In the African jungle?

Ackerman stiffened when he saw the radical change in her countenance. She looked like she'd seen a ghost. What had upset her? 'You all right?' he asked, genuinely worried.

'Yes…yes,' Ann squeaked. 'Er, you know, er…it shocks me anytime I remember,' she lied.

'I'm so sorry. I didn't mean to reopen the wound. I'm sorry. I just wanted you to know I share your feelings. Can I get you a drink?'

'Yes, please do. Thanks.'

'I'll be right back.' Ackerman cast a worried glance at her then dashed into the mall. By the time he returned with a can of Coke, she had driven off.

Ann was so shaken and confused that her mind refused to think straight. She drove aimlessly around Washington DC, her mind locked in a state of utter chaos. She had no direction, destination or purpose. All she had were questions. What was going on? What happened to Leroy? Had he really been involved in a plane crash—and been lost for days in the African jungle?

Africa?

But Dad categorically said Leroy was in Chicago doing top priority work!

Ackerman, on the other hand, had seemed so natural and spontaneous, he couldn't be lying. Why would he? Still, Dad sounded truthful enough, too. So…what was the truth? Where was Leroy? Chicago…or was he elsewhere?

After an hour, Ann found herself cruising alongside the tranquil Potomac River. She pulled up by the curb and got out to walk along the waterfront. Did Dad know more than he was telling? Or maybe Ackerman got his facts wrong. But Ackerman said he only learned of it very recently. That meant it had been around for much longer. Now, if something as serious as a plane crash happened within the CIA, Dad was bound to know. Dad had a lot more access to information than Ackerman. Should she go to Dad and ask him?

269

No. That would not work. She knew her father could coax, wiggle, and bulldoze his way out of any tight corner. He had a way of presenting frank, ready-made answers that could not be faulted. Besides, if her father found out Ackerman was her source, Ackerman was as good as dead.

Did Dad know more than he was telling?

What is going on?

59

Heartbroken, Talata kept away from everyone and locked herself in her dreary bedroom. She only left her room to prepare her father's meals. When that was done, she returned to her room to weep. Food was not appealing; she lost weight. She lived only on fruits because they were the only foods that didn't make her nauseous.

It was simply painful living in a world without Leroy. She remembered his assuring eyes, so trustworthy, so warm. She remembered his smile and the way he laughed. It always brought a smile to her face. His smooth voice kept ringing on and on in her mind like a damaged gramophone record. She missed his aura, that magic feeling he commanded, the way he aroused in her the very essence of her being.

But Leroy has a wife!

Or could the man that came to abduct Leroy be lying? He couldn't be. He left a photo, and Leroy was about to kiss the other woman. It had to be true. In a way, she felt hopelessly guilty.

But married or not, wife or no wife, the jaws of love chewed up her heart. What she had with Leroy was perfect. Those precious moments at the brook—simply magic.

She struggled to get him off her mind but it was like a bee pecking at a mountain. Her heart somersaulted whenever he came to mind, and that was practically every minute. He dominated her thoughts.

Will he come back to me? If he loves me, he will. Has he forgotten about me? Will I ever see him again?

She wanted to go find him but she didn't know where to

start. She steadfastly listened to her battery-operated radio. Maybe there would be some news on him.

No news. She wanted to go to the police but the elders had already done that. And still no news. She missed him more than ever. She desired him more than ever. She put it in her mind that Leroy would come back. He would come back. That was why earlier in the day, she made her way to the rock by the plains, the place synonymous with Leroy. She had hoped that by some sheer miracle, he would emerge from the bushes and come to her. He never showed up.

She found herself wishing his wife dead. Then he would come back.

But if Leroy came back I would be taking another woman's husband, wouldn't I?

Snatching someone else's husband? Before she met Leroy that was a blatant abomination. Now, it was something she felt she had to do. Adultery.

'Yes, he should abandon his wife and come back!' she told herself. 'What does his wife have that I don't? He has to make a choice. He has to choose between his wife and I.'

But that's selfish. His wife met him first.

'I don't care! Life is survival of the fittest. His wife is not good enough for him, I am. He's perfect for me. It's me he loves, not his wife! He's mine. We love each other....'

'...And it's not adultery, it's love!'

Seeking answers she reached for a Bible.

60

After two days, Ann finally came up with a plan to extract some truth from her father. It was simple and she didn't know if it would work but she was determined to give it a try.

She took the afternoon off from work. Sometime about 3.00 she put her plan into action.

There was a phone shop right across the street from her office. She went into this phone shop and bought a new cellular phone. She owned one already but for her plan to work she needed a second.

With the two phones in her handbag she got into her car and drove to northeast Washington DC, an area better known as the ghetto. Washington DC looks glamorous on the news— only because the media often show the White House and The Capitol. In actual fact, huge swathes of DC—the part never shown on TV—is deprived. A total slum with high levels of crime, drugs and gangs. The streets were filthy. *Homies* in street clothes and hoods hung around the street corners. Ann drove through its graffiti-laden streets with its dilapidated apartment blocks. When she got to a small road off K Street she saw O'Jay's Pawnshop.

She pulled up beside an overflowing trash can and got out of the car. Trying her best to look tough, she flipped up her collar. Then she summoned courage and swaggered into the shop.

The damp store gave her goose pimples. She calmly regarded the bald 200-pound attendant behind the wooden counter.

'Yes, ma'am?' he inquired politely though studying her with street-wise eyes.

Ann said nothing. Instead, she handed him fifty dollars. A

wry grin built up on the attendant's face. It wasn't everyday a stranger handed him fifty dollars for doing nothing. He coughed dryly then stared at her suspiciously. 'Want anything, ma'am?'

'No.'

'Thanks, ma'am.' The fifty dollars disappeared into the attendant's back pocket.

She brought out another fifty and held it up.

The pawnshop attendant looked longingly at the bill. He was street-wise; he understood she needed a favour. He cleared his throat loudly. 'At your service, ma'am.'

'Do you have a pen and paper?'

He produced them faster than a flash.

She wrote out a small note and handed it to the man. 'I'll call you in about an hour and I'll give you a number. Call that number. An answering machine will come on. Leave this message on the machine.' She waved the fifty dollars between her fingers. 'Can you do that?'

He eyed the bill dangling from her fingers then shot a glance at the note. It seemed harmless enough. He studied Ann intently, trying to decide if she was trouble or not. As a pawnshop owner he knew the streets and he knew street folk, and she was definitely not one of them. She looked too clean and had this wealthy glow. Her blue cotton shirt, striped skirt, and cashmere coat belonged in Congress or Wall Street; it didn't blend into the polystyrene ghetto. Her fingers were trim and manicured, not cracked or dirty, and when she smiled she showed no gold or stained teeth. Also, she spoke with a refined accent. She was definitely not from around here; too posh to be a cop. She was certainly upper crust, another member of the privileged elite.

Again, he eyed the money dangling from her fingers. That fifty would take care of some of his outstanding rent—he was three months behind. 'You mean you want me to call a number then read out this message to the answer machine?'

'Yep.'

'And you wanna pay only fifty bucks for that? Make it a hundred, and you got yourself a deal.'

Ann smiled, and shoved the fifty dollar bill into his twitching fingers.

'You got a deal, ma'am,' the clerk said in high spirits. The money disappeared into his pocket. 'Hey, if you want any other thing, you know...' He turned his voice low. 'Face powder? Soap? Fireworks?' He was subtly offering her coke, crack and guns.

'No. All I want you to do is when I call you and give you a number, you call that number. When the answering machine comes on, just leave the message I wrote on the paper. And sound normal. Can you?'

He grinned. 'You bet, ma'am. You'll be so pleased you'll send me another fifty for a job well done. By the way, I'm Harvey.'

'Thanks, Harvey.' Ann said politely and walked out of the pawnshop.

It was essential to her plan that her father didn't know she was home. Therefore, she drove to a commercial car park, downtown, and eased into one of the parking bays. She switched off the engine but didn't remove the key from the ignition. Instead, she fetched the wheel spanner from the trunk.

Using the spanner, she hit the bow of the key numerous times till the key broke into the ignition. She knew if her father didn't see her car in the driveway he would ask questions. If she told him it had broken down, his immediate reaction would be to send a couple of boys from the office to recover the car. It wouldn't look neat if they started it and it worked. To break the key in the lock was a splendid idea. It was a perfect excuse as only last week her father observed her key was bent and advised she change it.

After this she hailed a taxicab home.

The cab pulled up at the gate of her father's mansion. She walked up to the massive, black front gate. She waved at Bugsy, the bearded guard, who grinned and opened the gates to let her in.

Bugsy thought it unusual that Ann wasn't driving her car. He'd been trained not to ask questions, only to observe and be vigilant. He noted her arrival in his logbook.

She opened the front door and entered the living room. The house was quiet just as she expected. The telephone and the answering machine were placed on a marble stool next to the fireplace. The scrambler was next to the phone. She knew the CIA could easily track any call from their land line, so she got her cell phone and dialled the pawnshop.

Harvey picked it up on the other side. 'Yo.'

'Hi. I'm home. The number I want you to call is this…' She dictated the home phone number. 'Do you get it?'

'Sure, ma'am.'

'Don't forget. Dial the number. When the answering machine picks up dictate the message as it is. Sound normal like you're delivering a personal message. Do it well, Harvey, and there's an extra fifty for you.'

Another fifty? 'Hey, I'm a pro, ma'am. You can count on me.'

'Thanks. I'm waiting.' She switched off her cellphone.

As she sat waiting for Harvey's call, her heart beat rapidly. She couldn't believe she was doing this. However, she was determined to go through with it, propelled by this characteristic, unwavering zeal that women put into whatever they believe in. Ordinarily, she would not have gone to the ghetto unaccompanied. Not to mention visiting a dingy pawnshop.

Back uptown, Harvey was no fool. Having spent all his life in the ghetto, he had learned to eat his cake and still have it. Ann was probably the daughter of a wealthy man, embarking on one of those vain mind games that the overfed people in Washington often indulge in. She was paying a hundred dollars for a phone call that would cost just twenty cents? She hadn't even haggled!

What if she was a cop on stake out? Well, this time, the cops had missed the plot. If the cops wanted to dole out a hundred bucks, hell, he wasn't saying no.

He called his brother to mind the shop. Then he slipped on a pair of gloves and went through the back door into a filthy alley. He hated the alley. Its slimy, green, algae-covered walls made his skin crawl, but for a hundred bucks he wasn't fussy. He emerged on a back street. There was a graffiti-plastered phone booth next to a group of overflowing trash cans. The phone booth smelt of stale urine. Harvey was a smart boy. He would never make that phone call from his shop. That way it couldn't be traced back to him.

Ann wondered why Harvey was taking so long. She was relieved when the phone finally rang. After a few rings the answering machine came on.

Harvey's voice sounded studio-clear over the line. He was perfect. His tone and manner sounded so extremely urgent. The manner in which he raised and lowered his voice was so appropriate that he deserved an Oscar.

Fully satisfied with his performance, she locked the front door from inside and removed her key. That way, her father would find it locked when he returned. Since her car wasn't in the driveway she was certain he would conclude she hadn't returned from work.

Next, she left the door that led from the living room to the dining room slightly open. Another door led from the dining room to the kitchen. She left that open as well. Finally, she opened the white steel door that led from the kitchen to the vast manicured lawn at the rear of the mansion.

Assured everything was in place, she brought out the new phone she just bought and plugged it into the electric socket to charge. Then she sat and waited for her father.

It was a little after six when she heard the gentle purring of a car pulling up in the driveway. A few moments later, she heard the distinct voice of one of her father's guards as he said, 'Yes, sir!'

He was back.

She got out the new cellular phone and dialled her old phone.

As soon as it rang she pressed the answer button. Now, her new phone was connected to her old phone. Anything spoken into her new phone could be heard through her old phone. She placed the new phone in the fireplace, cleverly disguising it with the grate.

She heard a click. She knew her father was putting his key in the door lock.

She took off her shoes—that way she would not make a noise—then hurried into the kitchen. She tiptoed through the kitchen door to the lawn behind the mansion, and shut the door behind her. Outside, she put on her shoes.

She prayed her father would do what he normally did when he returned home: listen to the messages. She put her old phone to her ear and listened. She heard the squeak peculiar to the front door. The trick was working perfectly: she could hear everything going on in the living room.

A few moments later, she heard a muffled thud. She was certain he had dropped his briefcase on the carpet like he always did. She heard the clinking of a glass and then a swish. He was probably drinking either Scotch or water. Then she heard a sigh and his heavy, muffled footsteps.

'What the hell are they waiting for?' she heard him grumbling.

Inside, in the living room, Cagley walked to the window that overlooked the patio.

'Jones! What the hell are you waiting for?' Cagley yelled. 'How long is it gonna take to turn the car around?' He turned away from the window, a frown screwed across his face. 'Dumb ass!'

Cagley glimpsed the flashing red light on the answering machine. He listened to his messages religiously as they were often important. He pressed the *Message* button.

The first message was a request for a game of golf by his friend, Senator Adams.

The second was also a request for golf from Cliff Drummond, chief executive officer of Perrier Electronics, a multinational.

278

'I beat you on Sunday,' Cagley jeered after Drummond's message. The third message was from the Chairman of the Senate Subcommittee on Emerging Threats and Capabilities, informing Cagley that a meeting with the committee had been rescheduled. That suited Cagley fine.

The fourth was from Lizzy, Cagley's Bolivian mistress. She had a smooth, rolling voice, and seemed to be singing as she spoke. She didn't say anything important though. 'Ass,' Cagley gibed after her message.

Then the answering machine crooned, 'Hi. This message is for Ann. My name is Rodriguez. I'm a friend of Leroy's. I received a note from him this afternoon. He asked me to tell you to see him. He says your father knows where he is. He says it's urgent and that he's expecting you. Make sure you see him as soon as you can. Cheers. Bye.'

Outside, Ann held her breath. That was the message Harvey left.

There was deathly silence except for a couple of beeps from the answering machine, which indicated an end of messages.

Back inside, Cagley was stupefied. He looked around the living room suspiciously. The house seemed quiet enough. He walked into the dining room. Everything was quiet; everything was still. He looked suspiciously at the dining table with its big, white tablecloth. He raised the cloth, and looked under the table. Nothing. He walked to the kitchen. The steel door was locked. Satisfied, he returned to the answering machine.

Outside, Ann flattened herself against the wall, listening intently on the phone.

Back inside, Cagley re-played the message.

Ann's heart pounded as she heard it again.

Cagley replayed it once more.

Ann waited.

Then she heard a series of clicks. She knew her father was dialling out. She heard a long beep. He had switched on the scrambler.

'Put Thompson on the line,' Cagley snapped. He looked

279

around cautiously, holding the receiver to his ear. 'Thompson! What the hell's going on here? How did that shitpack get word out?' There was silence while the other person spoke. Then Cagley boomed, 'Delgado! Who else? How did he sneak a message past you? I said he was to remain incommunicado.'

There was a pause. 'Heads will roll, Thompson, believe me!' Cagley slammed the phone.

Next, he removed the micro-cassette tape from the answering machine and put it in his pocket. He picked up the phone again. 'Bosworth, trace all the calls I had on the home line today! Brief me on the callers. Especially a certain Rodriguez. I expect a feedback by tomorrow.' Again, he slammed the phone.

He called yet another number. 'Anita. Produce a comprehensive profile on this subject: surname, Delgado; first name, Leroy; middle name, Alphonse. Top Priority. I want it on my table first thing tomorrow. Also, call Billingham. Tell him to send you the full dossier on Operation Renegade. Also the full updated reports from field agents on subject Delgado, Leroy, Alphonse—'

Ann had heard enough. She switched off her phone.

She waited a few minutes then walked around the mansion. Pretending she had just arrived, she walked to the front door. She adjusted her clothes then rang the bell.

She waited about half a minute before her father opened the door. He looked very ruffled.

'Hi, Dad.' Ann shot him a false big smile.

'Hi. You're back,' he responded. 'Don't you have your key?'

'It's in my car. You didn't even ask about my car,' she protested girlishly, rolling her eyes, pointing to her empty parking space. 'Can you believe it? I went out on valuation, and when I got back in my car, the key snapped in the lock. I had to take a cab back here. I'm starving.'

'So, you've only just arrived?' Cagley inquired, unsure.

'Yes.' Ann stepped into the living room. 'And you?'

'A few minutes ago.' Her father shut the door.

'How was your day?' Ann asked, as she customarily would.

'Not bad,' he answered.

Ann walked into the living room and dropped her bag carelessly on the sofa. She peeled off her shoes, and walked towards the mantelpiece. The answering machine was next to the mantelpiece but she didn't look in that direction. She felt her father's eagle eyes studying her.

Is she aware of that message? Cagley wondered. He was astute in clandestine matters. Strange that the day someone left a message was the very day she had problems with her car. He decided to find out.

'You heard your message?' he asked suddenly, watching Ann's reactions and body language intently.

She was ready for that. 'No, I'm just coming in. I'm so tired. Somebody called?'

'I forgot to tell you. Yesterday, a guy called Rodriguez called.'

He watched her intently.

'Rodriguez?' Ann pretended to think. 'I don't know any Rodriguez. What did he say? Does he want to buy property?'

'He said you should call him.'

'Call him? I can't place anyone with that name. Did he leave his number?'

'No.'

'Do I have any messages today?' She looked at the answering machine. The red light was steady, indicating no messages.

'No,' Cagley lied.

He kept studying her. She acted normally. She showed no signs of tension; nothing was out of place. She switched on the TV, and flipped through the comedies and the talk shows as she always did.

She giggled heartily at *Roseanne's* quips.

She does actually look genuine, Cagley thought.

61

Ann lay on her bed, staring blankly at the night sky.

I should never have given up on my marriage, she thought regretfully. *Once I took the plunge, I should have stuck with it. Marriage isn't about bailing out at the first hurdle, it's about overcoming the biggest storms life can throw at us together. I failed our marriage. I let issues come between us. I was so unfair to Leroy. I didn't give him the benefit of doubt. The only thing I achieved by moving out is that I left Leroy and I, vulnerable and exposed. And it looks like the adversaries— Dad and the powers that be—have seized that opportunity to mess things up.*

She only hoped she hadn't lost Leroy for good. There was absolutely no use crying over past mistakes, she decided. She had made catastrophic blunders, but now, she wanted things to work. She would do everything she could to patch things up with him. *But where is he?*

She was certain now that the answer lay with her dad. Whether Leroy was in Chicago or Africa or with Thompson, her dad knew. How could she get him to come clean? She could simply ask him and expect him to be reasonable. Aggressively confront him and create a scene, or beg him and cry at his feet. Or, she could ask his powerful friends to plead with him.

She knew her father. Whatever way she handled it, he would never budge. However you came at him, he would deny it. He would firmly maintain his stand that Leroy was on top priority assignment in Chicago, and he would go to any length to maintain that stand.

Her dad was like a savage lion. If you didn't have what it

took to overwhelm him in one swift stroke, you shouldn't bother. Wounded, he became twice as dangerous. Her dad was extremely powerful. She remembered an incident a few years back when they showed the picture of a South American head of state on TV. "This time tomorrow you won't be there," her father had declared knowingly. "We've seen to that. Bolero would be president." And sure enough there was a military coup overnight. Not many people on the planet were that powerful. He wouldn't dare use his power on her but he would use it to outmanoeuvre her. She could only keep him off-guard by playing him at his own game.

She remembered her encounter with him after that phoney Rodriguez message. Every syllable he uttered was laden with trickery and lies. 'You heard your message?' he had asked, referring to the Rodriguez message. He had not said, 'You heard your *messages*,' in the plural, as expected in normal conversation.

Another one: 'I forgot to tell you. Yesterday, a guy called Rodriguez called,' he had said. This was another tricky statement, fabricated by him. 'Rodriguez' had called 'today', not 'yesterday'.

Another one: 'Do I have any messages today?' she had asked. 'No,' he'd answered. A blatant lie.

That was his vintage self. Craftier than a monkey, more slippery than an eel. A man who liked to know the truth, but would usually not speak it. He was totally Machiavellian. The end justified the means. For him the law was only good when it served his purpose. And in his position he could manipulate the law. If she was going to tackle him, she would need a lot of leverage, a lot of courage and a lot of luck. She would also need a lot of tact and cunning.

She recalled the instruction her father had given Anita, his confidential secretary. "Produce a comprehensive profile on this subject: surname, Delgado; first name, Leroy; middle name, Alphonse. Top Priority. I want it on my table first thing tomorrow."

So, all the answers and facts she wanted? Her father had them. And they would be on his table tomorrow morning.

But then, his table was in CIA Headquarters, Langley. It was more closely guarded than Fort Knox.

All through the night Ann brooded over Leroy's file. There was only one way she could see that file—and that was by going to CIA headquarters.

How on earth could she hope to get into one of the most guarded buildings in the world? She wouldn't even get near the fence before she was caught. She could imagine the headlines:

ESPIONAGE EXCLUSIVE: CIA BOSS' DAUGHTER
CAUGHT SPYING

Horrid.

Still, she couldn't stop thinking about that file.

At 7.05 in the morning, she made her decision: she would go to CIA headquarters.

It would be risky. But she was beyond caring. She was prepared to do whatever she had to.

She sat on the edge of her bed and formulated a plan. For that plan to have any chance of success it had to fit perfectly into her father's schedule. The day was Friday. He always started Fridays by briefing the President at 8.00 am. He then made the journey to CIA headquarters, arriving shortly before 9.00 am. He usually attended the Friday EXCO meeting at 9.30.

She timed her arrival at CIA headquarters for 8.55 am.

At 8.15 she set off in a rented Buick.

CIA headquarters, commonly known as Langley is located in Fairfax County, Virginia, some seven miles from the White House. It is a concrete and glass complex made up of two major buildings: the Old Building and the New Building. The entire complex linked to Washington DC via the George Washington Memorial Parkway and Dolley Madison Boulevard.

She turned off Dolley Madison Boulevard fully aware that as she drove, hidden cameras on the tall magnolia trees that shielded the CIA compound tracked her. The dull white, seven-storey Old CIA Building loomed ahead. She approached the CIA compound and joined a small queue of cars at the gatehouse. The gatehouse was roofed, and covered like a filling station. Cars drove into the guardhouse from Dolley Madison, and out into the CIA compound at the other.

A slim, uniformed security guard armed with a pistol walked up to her car. The guard wore a wide brimmed hat, typical of state troopers. 'Can I help you, ma'am?' The guard looked Ann over suspiciously like a common criminal. 'You are trespassing in a Federal restricted zone.'

Ann smiled. 'I'm sorry.' She tipped back her blonde hair. 'It's a bit of an emergency. I am Ann Cagley, daughter of the Director—'

'And I'm Bob Marley,' the guard snarled. 'Please turn back!'

Ann forced a nervous smile and handed him her driver's license. 'It's true. Vitally urgent, and very important. Can I speak to Anita, his secretary?' She looked at her watch. 'I have to hurry. He has an EXCO meeting at nine-thirty.' She poured out this information to let the guard know she was an insider.

The guard studied her. His eyes were thin, his face hostile. He reached for his gun. 'Turn back or I'll shoot!'

'Then pull the trigger, please,' Ann responded, blank-eyed.

The guard was dumbstruck. They had their strict instructions, but they were not robots; they had a prerogative. This woman had poured out two vital pieces of information: she knew the name of the Director's secretary. She also knew about the EXCO meeting. Her driver's licence bore the surname, Cagley. Besides, she hadn't panicked when he threatened to shoot.

CIA guards are trained to look at both sides of every story. Ever since CIA officers wantonly turned away a Russian KGB chief who had mountains of vital information, and genuinely wished to defect, they handled cold callers with a little more discretion. What if she was truly the Director's daughter and she had come on account of issues that were relevant to the Director's security or national security? What if what she had to say was vital? Then he could be in trouble for turning her away. The guard gave Ann a good look over. 'Okay, move out

285

of the way,' the guard ordered, waving for her to pull up into a shoulder. 'And don't step out of the car!'

Ann manoeuvred the car onto the small shoulder. The guard walked cautiously around the car. He had a small detector, which picked up electromagnetic waves and laser to ascertain the car was not equipped with any camera or transmitter. He also probed the car with a bomb sniffer. Satisfied, he crossed over to her side of the car. 'You said you're the DCI's daughter?'

'Yes.'

'Why did you rent this car from Flemings?' Already, the security boys had run a check on her car.

'My car has a problem. My father can testify to it. Call him.'

'In a minute,' the guard snubbed. He studied her again then reached for a small radio. 'Two-five to base, can you run an I.D. check on subject, Cagley, Ann? Repeat, subject: Cagley, Ann?'

A conversation transpired between the guard and the base. The guard finally turned to Ann. 'Your date of birth, miss?'

Ann told him.

The guard repeated it into the radio. 'Social Security number?'

Ann recited it. The guard repeated it into the radio. There was a brief pause and then the guard smiled. 'You're telling the truth.'

Ann returned the smile.

'I have to do an I.D. challenge. Code-in, Outback.'

Being daughter of the CIA Director didn't give Ann special privileges but for safety measures she had been issued a secret password by CIA Security. She was to use it if she was in any form of danger, and needed assistance. It also served to confirm her identity to CIA personnel, who would ask her the simple phrase, Outback. She then had to give the correct response.

'Ranger seven-two-four-six,' she told the guard.

The guard walked back to guardhouse. He checked the code word on the computer. The computer confirmed the code word was genuine and also displayed a colour photograph of Ann. A

286

security camera trained on Ann's rented Buick transmitted her photograph as she sat behind the wheel. The guard compared the photos. It was the same person. He got on the intercom and spoke to Security Control. After a brief discussion he hung up.

Finally, the guard fetched a cordless phone. 'Hello. There's a young lady here. Says she wants to see Trident. Her name's Ann. She's his daughter. She's been cleared with Security. Will you speak to her?'

The guard walked up to Ann and handed the cordless phone to her. 'Anita.'

'Hello, Anita. It's me. Can I speak to him? It's urgent!'

'Hello, Ann,' Anita responded. 'He's just preparing for a meeting. I'll put you through.'

There was a mute, then after fifteen seconds the line came alive with her father's voice. 'Ann?'

'Yes, Dad, it's me. I'm in trouble.'

'What?'

'Remember, you said the other day that some guy called Rodriguez called?' She paused to allow her father recollect the call.

'Yes?'

'He called me at home this morning,' Ann lied hysterically. 'He also called my cell phone. Twice. He sounds like a stalker; a crank. He just kept on ranting. I'm so scared. I don't know how he got my number.' Ann tried to sound panicky. 'H-he threatened me. H-he... Oh, no! He said—'

'He said what?'

'H-he said he would rape me!'

'Rape you?' Cagley roared.

'Yeah!'

'Calm down, Ann,' her father said, quickly regaining his composure.

'Calm down? How can I calm down?'

Ann saw that the guard was listening in attentively. She turned her back on him and paced a few yards away. Her voice dropped to an urgent whisper. 'What am I going to do? He's going to rape me! And you want me to calm down? Dad, the guy is stalking me. He told me the colour of the dress I wore yesterday. He said he always had a thing for me and…and if I don't do as he says he would do things to me—bad things. He would hurt me. I'm so scared. Should I go to the police?'

Ann played a prime card by mentioning the police. The police meant publicity. Her father and the CIA hated that.

Cagley thought about everything Ann said. This mysterious Rodriguez seemed to be stalking Ann. He knew the dress she wore yesterday? That was serious. This Rodriguez really sounded like serious trouble. It was most certainly the same Rodriguez who had called the house and left a message yesterday. But how did he get the phone number? Bosworth would have to investigate. Cagley's only worry was Ann's safety. And she should not go to the police.

'Where are you, Ann?' Cagley asked. 'Don't move! My boys will be with you in a minute.'

'I'm downstairs at the gate. They won't let me in. I was so scared… I came here as fast as I could.'

'Okay, stay calm. I'll ask them to prepare a pass for you.'

'Okay.'

'Are you sure you're okay?'

'Yes, Dad. Thanks.'

'Let me speak to the guard.'

Ann handed the phone to the guard. Fifteen minutes later, she was ushered into Cagley's plush office.

Cagley sat unruffled in a leather executive chair behind his mahogany desk. A computer glowed on a side desk nearby. Behind, was an array of six closed circuit colour TV monitors. The office had a light grey carpet. It also had a conference table with eight chromium chairs. There were also two sofas and a knee-high coffee table.

'Are you all right?' Cagley asked, swivelling in his chair.

She smiled. 'Now, I'm all right.'

He waved to a chair across his table. 'Sit down.'

She sat.

'Coffee?'

She nodded.

He poured her a cup of coffee from an electric coffee maker placed on a nearby table.

Ann snuck a look around his table. There were a few documents lying on his desk but there was nothing like a file. And nothing seemed to have Leroy's name on it. Everything looked like letters.

'Here you are.' Cagley handed her the coffee.

'Thanks.' She sipped from the cup.

About then, a sandy-haired guy wearing a brown sports jacket entered Cagley's office. He carried a black folder. He cast a quick look at Ann. Then he turned to Cagley. 'Sorry to interrupt, sir, but the EXCO meeting is at nine-thirty.' He glanced at his watch. 'Just ten minutes. First on the agenda is—'

Cagley cut him short. 'You haven't met Ann. Have you?'

'No, sir.' He nodded courteously in Ann's direction.

'Ann's my daughter,' Cagley announced. 'Roberts is one of my assistants.'

'Hi.' Ann reached out for a handshake.

'It's a pleasure.'

'Did you get the photographs from Williamson?' Cagley asked.

'No, sir.'

'Then do a memo to the Vice President immediately.'

'I've done that, sir,' Roberts said. 'Anita's working on it. She'll bring it in a minute.'

'Okay,' Cagley mumbled.

At that moment Anita walked in. She was middle-aged with a shock of brown hair, and she wore a pair of steel-rimmed glasses. She looked sweet and young in her bright red skirt-suit. She held a sheaf of papers.

Ann watched, sipping her coffee.

In truth, Cagley had forgotten about the instructions he'd given Anita. Now, on hearing about that Rodriguez crank again he decided to sort it out once and for all. 'Anita, where are the documents I told you to prepare for me?'

She handed Cagley the sheaf of papers.

Ann had a feeling those were the papers she wanted.

'Roberts!' Cagley boomed. 'Call Bosworth. I asked him to do some work, yesterday. Why hasn't he given me a feedback?'

'Er, it's in there, sir.' Anita pointed to the sheaf of papers Cagley had in his hands.

'Okay.'

Anita left Cagley's office. Cagley turned a combination lock on his desk and pulled out the drawers.

Ann's mind pitched into a frenzy. Her father was putting away the papers. She had to act. She had to do something fast!

'Ooh, I feel sick,' she groaned, dropping her coffee. It spilt onto Cagley's desk. She grunted and leaned heavily against Cagley's table. Then she sagged to her knees and clutched her stomach, writhing violently.

Cagley was so startled he didn't move. When he got hold of himself he dropped the papers beside the computer and dashed around the table. 'Ann? Ann?'

Roberts was equally aghast.

Cagley dropped to his knees beside her. 'Ann? Ann!' He agitated her arm violently.

'Should I get the medical centre?' Roberts asked.

'Yeah! Hurry. Hurry,' Cagley barked. His face rapidly drained of colour.

Ann grunted, and writhed on the floor.

'Ann? Ann! Aaannn!'

Ann let out a huge gasp and clutched her stomach.

'What is it?' Cagley yelled.

'U-ul-ulcer,' she whimpered.

'Ulcer?'

Still grimacing, Ann nodded.

'Why didn't you tell me?' Cagley demanded, rattled. 'Why didn't you see the doctor?'

'I-I did.'

Ann clutched her stomach and moaned. Cagley was gutted. His baby was in pain. He placed his palm beneath her head and lifted her head off the carpet. She slowly opened her eyes. 'It-it was the coffee.'

'The coffee?' Cagley was startled.

Ann nodded. She looked every bit pathetic and drained. 'I took hot coffee on an empty stomach,' she muttered softly.

Cagley knew ulcer patients were encouraged to eat often, and shouldn't have an empty stomach.

'I'll be fine,' Ann assured him with a weak smile. 'I'm sorry.' She heard Roberts speaking to the medical centre. 'Hey,' she called feebly to Roberts. 'Don't bother. I'm fine.'

She turned to her father, looking childishly into his hard grey eyes. 'Sorry I caused such a stir.' Sluggishly, still grimacing, she pulled herself together and helped by her father, she slowly got to her feet. Her hairdo was ruined. She still clutched her stomach.

'Are you all right?' Cagley inquired, really worried. 'Don't you have any medication?'

Ann shook her head. 'It's at home.'

Cagley helped her to one of the leather sofas inside his office. Ann kicked off her pumps and curled on the sofa. 'I'll just rest a while. I'll be fine.'

'You got me really worried there.'

'I'm sorry, Dad, it's only an ulcer. It gives me a lot of pain at times. I haven't had anything to eat today. I guess the coffee hit it. It's nothing.'

'You were sprawled on the floor, and you're telling me it's nothing?'

'It's nothing, ulcers are very common.' She forced an assuring smile. 'Come on, don't fuss. I'll be fine in a few minutes.' She smiled weakly and lay back on the sofa.

'Now, you lie here and don't move,' Cagley instructed. Worked up, he loosened his tie. It was ages since anyone rattled him this much.

'Don't worry, I'll be fine,' Ann coaxed with a smile. 'All I need is some food. I shouldn't have taken coffee on an empty stomach.'

'Order her some food,' Cagley boomed at Roberts.

'Yes, sir.'

Roberts picked the phone and dialled the canteen. Anita popped her head through the door. 'Everybody's in the house, sir,' Anita announced, referring to the EXCO meeting. Cagley was running late for the meeting and she had come in to remind him.

She noticed Ann on the sofa looking ruffled. 'Hey, honey, you okay?'

'I'll be all right.' Ann forced a smile.

Cagley frowned. 'Why didn't you tell me about this?'

'I didn't want you worrying.'

'You didn't want me worrying? Now, am I not worried?' He placed his palm on her forehead and felt her temperature.

'I'm fine, Dad,' Ann insisted. 'All I need is a little something to eat.'

'What's wrong with her?' Anita inquired.

'She has an ulcer,' Roberts answered, 'and she took hot coffee and it burned on the way down. She's in pain.'

'Oh, honey,' Anita said sympathetically, 'I hope you feel better soon. Used to have it too. Mine, it was terrible.'

Cagley turned to Roberts. 'You ordered something for her?'

'Yes. Is a turkey sandwich okay?'

'Fine,' Ann said softly.

'You sure you don't want to see a doctor?' Cagley maintained, still shaken.

'I've already seen one, Dad. I have medication. It's at home. I caused all this. I didn't eat. C'mon, go to your meeting. I'll be fine here with Anita.'

'The directors are waiting,' Anita reminded Cagley.

'Yes, sir,' Roberts added. 'The Senate Select Committee chairman doesn't like being kept waiting.'

'To hell with him,' Cagley snapped. He turned to Ann and ran his fingers through her hair. 'Are you sure you're okay?'

'I'm fine. You go to your meeting. I'll be fine. '

'Okay.' Cagley poked a finger at Roberts. 'Get one of the medical boys to see her all the same.' He turned to Ann. 'You stay right here. Anita will be here.' Cagley turned to his secretary. 'Anita, you take care of her. Okay?'

'Sure,' Anita responded, happy to play Mother Goose.

Cagley walked to the door. He turned and glanced at Ann. It was a long time since anyone rattled him this much. Ann offered a reassuring smile. Cagley stepped out.

'Take care,' Roberts said. He followed Cagley.

Anita and Ann were all alone in Cagley's office. 'You need anything?' Anita asked.

'Do you have today's newspaper?'

'Sure.'

Anita left the room then popped in a few moments later with four publications. 'Your sandwich is on its way up.'

'Thanks.'

Anita drew the curtains then placed a small cushion under Ann's head. 'A pillow dear.' She smiled.

'Thanks.'

Anita walked to Cagley's table. She noticed the open drawers and promptly closed them. Then she walked to the door.

'Are you okay, dear?'

Ann nodded.

'I'll get myself a cup of coffee,' Anita said. 'One minute.'

'Sure.'

Anita returned to her desk. Ann was left all alone in the office.

The papers she wanted were beside the computer.

62

Cagley returned home at 6.15 pm. He opened the door and walked into the living room.

'Dad!' Ann's hostile voice cracked from somewhere.

Jolted, Cagley turned.

Ann stood by the mantelpiece, a wild look in her eyes. She regarded him disdainfully. 'Are you sure you're my father?' she began. 'Because right now, I'm not really sure if you are. It seems you will stop at nothing to hurt me. No true father would want to hurt his daughter so much. So, are you really sure you're my father?'

He stopped, taken aback. 'That's a stupid question,' he retorted, frowning.

'You haven't answered my question!' she yelled.

He could tell something wasn't right. For once, Cagley sought to keep the peace. He breathed deeply, suppressing the irritation building up inside him. 'What's the matter, Ann?'

'You're holding my husband. That's the matter.' Her eyes blazed at him. 'Why is that? I want you to release Leroy immediately!'

The blood drained from Cagley's face. He stared deadpan at her for a good ten seconds. 'What are you talking about?' he responded, needing time to gather his wits.

'Leroy!'

'Leroy? That fool?'

'Yes, that fool. I know you have him in custody.'

'Custody? I don't have him.'

Ann was astonished at his brazen denial. If she hadn't read the files earlier that day in his office she would have believed him. 'Dad,' she called, toning down her voice and recognising that she had underestimated her father. 'You may not know it but I have eyes and ears inside the CIA... Probably more than you do. There are a lot of things I know. But you don't know that I know these things. I know Leroy isn't in Chicago. I know you have him at Andrews Air Force Base. I know he was involved in an air crash. I know he didn't use ATK on me. A rookie pharmacist at Woodlake mixed up the drugs.' At least, so the files said. 'You've been lying to me all along.'

Cagley's heart skipped a beat. She did seem to have some information. He thought fast, knowing he had to arrest the situation. Having worked so many years in the agency he was adept at psychology and adept at tactics. He knew when to advance and when to retreat. He also knew when to create a diversion. 'Don't ever speak to me that way again,' he cautioned, poking a finger at her. 'You watch your tone of voice.'

Ann suddenly found herself on the defensive. 'This isn't about how I speak to you,' she gasped.

'You're being rude,' Cagley snapped. He had created a diversion; he had cunningly moved the topic of contention to rudeness. 'Where are your manners?'

'Er...er,' Ann stuttered.

'I demand an apology right now!'

'Er... Apology?' Ann blurted, finally smartening up. 'You're holding my husband like a common prisoner and you're asking for an apology?'

'I don't have him!'

'I'm not in the mood for nonsense,' Ann screamed. 'You've pulled the wool over my eyes for too long. You've been manipulating me; lying to me. You messed up my marriage. Now, if you don't want the biggest fight of your life give me my husband. I want my husband back.'

'I don't accept you have a husband,' Cagley retorted calmly.

'What do you call Leroy?' Her fiery eyes pierced into him.

'A pest,' Cagley replied calmly. He looked her straight in

295

the eyeballs. 'A nuisance; no good; a vagabond; someone who doesn't love you.'

'Well, if he doesn't love me, I love him,' Ann cried emphatically. 'I'm Mrs Delgado. Understand? You just have to live with it.'

'Mrs Delgado?' Cagley couldn't bear the thought. Strangely enough he had never perceived Ann by that name. 'You call yourself, Mrs Delgado? You never had a marriage! Two or three weeks? Is that what you call a marriage?'

'Even if it was for a single minute we are legally married. My marriage to Leroy was my personal choice. It is not your business and neither is it the CIA's!'

'It is a CIA issue!' Cagley roared. 'The CIA pays him, you don't. And we pay him to have his eyes on me. Instead, that bastard had his eyes on your ass. He was sleeping with you, damn it. You made me a laughing stock, Ann. Everyone heard you moaning and groaning on tape. Damn you. You opened up like a low class whore. I'm the one cleaning up the mess you left!'

'Killing Leroy was the way to clean up?'

'Kill Leroy?' Cagley paused. 'What the hell gives you that idea?'

'You sent him to Africa. He was in a plane crash!'

'Who fabricated such lies?'

'They're not lies, Dad. I have my sources in the agency.'

'So, you believe some tale from some moron. You don't believe me, your father?'

'A father who lies to me? A man who would stop at nothing to destroy my happiness? I am ashamed to call you my father.' She glared at him contemptuously. 'Look at you, you're not even the tiniest bit ashamed, lying without an iota of honour. You've been interfering in my relationship with Leroy. Look, Dad, if you won't leave Leroy and I alone, it's gonna be disastrous.'

'Are you threatening me?' Cagley asked quietly.

'Call it what you like.'

Cagley poked his finger at her. 'Something must have gotten into your head.'

Ann wasn't fazed. She was long past caring. 'Dad, I'm going to say only one thing to you. Listen and listen well. The time is six o'clock. I'm going upstairs to start getting my things. I'm going back to my husband's house. I'm going back to be his wife.'

'His wife?' Cagley's mind went to the village girl. 'He'll never have you back.'

He'll never have you back? Ann felt a bit of trepidation. Had her father done something to ensure Leroy never got back with her? She decided to call his bluff. 'Maybe and maybe not. But that's for me to find out.'

'Good luck then.' Cagley was indignant.

'Good luck to you as well!' Ann snapped, a vicious look in her eyes.

Cagley had never seen such a threatening scowl on her. She looked dangerous. Everything about her suggested, *I've got something on you.* 'What do you mean by good luck to me as well?'

'The time is six-thirty. If my husband isn't back in his house by eight o'clock, you'll see me on the network news at nine.'

'What would you be doing there?' Cagley's eyes narrowed.

'Talking to the press.' She stormed out of the living room.

After Ann left Cagley paced around the room. 'She knows everything!' he said to the walls of the empty house. 'Ann knows everything. There's a leak in the agency. Somebody's been talking to her. Now she's made a sensational U-turn on Delgado. The same girl that came crying back home, virtually naked is now trying to get back with the same bastard. She wants to go back him! What does she see in him?'

After a few minutes Cagley calmed. 'She will only go back to him over my dead body,' he resolved softly. 'And I'm not going to die.'

He picked the phone and dialled Thompson. There were still quite a few tricks in his box.

63

The narrow underground corridor at Andrews Air Force Base was dimly lit. The reinforced steel door of cell 2B was located half way down the corridor.

The Air Force guard led the two men to the steel door. One of the men was an ugly, thickset guy with bulging frog-like eyes. His name was Thompson. He held a shiny black crowbar. The other was an elderly white-haired gentleman who wore a smart pin-stripe suit and carried a black attaché case.

The guard brought out a huge key from his bunch and pushed it into the lock. The steel door squeaked as it opened inwards. The Air Force guard saluted. The two men walked into the dim, whitewashed underground cell.

'Get on your feet, buster,' Thompson yelled at the scruffy prisoner lying on the steel bed in the far corner.

Leroy cast a defiant look at Thompson and turned away.

The elderly gentleman was a lawyer. He retrieved a set of documents from his attaché case and handed them to Thompson. Thompson shoved them at Leroy. 'Sign it.' Thompson bawled, raising his black crowbar. 'Sign it or I'll break your freakin' fingers!'

'Er...let him read it,' the pin striped gentleman said.

Leroy looked through the documents. Divorce papers. Ann's divorce papers, and Ann had already signed them.

He recalled his phone call to her just before he got on board the plane to Africa. "It's over, Leroy," she'd said. "I'm out."

So she had actually carried out her threat. Well, if that was what she wanted, she could damn well have it! Being with Ann had proven far too much trouble. No woman was worth the hassle, especially one who had no faith in him, ready to assume the worst about him, and bail out on him without giving their marriage a second chance. If a divorce was what she wanted, he would damn well give it to her. With honours.

Leroy snatched a pen from Thompson. He scrawled his signature across the document then flung it at Thompson.

Thompson handed the signed papers to the lawyer.

The lawyer looked through the document. He led Thompson to the far end of the cell where Leroy would not hear them. 'I'm curious,' the lawyer whispered to Thompson. 'How on earth did you get Ann to sign the divorce? I thought her father said she has decided to go back to him.'

'She signed it a few weeks ago when she thought he killed her baby,' Thompson whispered back. 'The boss has kept it since then. Looks like she's changed her mind but the boss isn't having that. He wants them apart, and it's up to us to ensure they stay apart.'

'What are you going to do with the papers now?'

'A lot. For starters, now that he knows she began divorce proceedings, it's upped the stakes. He probably won't have her back.'

'Is that all?'

Thompson grinned cruelly. 'No.'

Then Thompson brought out a .45 revolver. He went to Leroy and jabbed the gun into Leroy's ribs. 'You and I are going for a walk, boy.'

64

Ann's heart pounded as she pulled up outside Leroy's whitewashed house. She stepped out of her car and for a while she stared at what was once was her matrimonial home. She observed its red tile roof, the huge double glazed windows and the relatively young beech tree sprouting in the middle of the overgrown lawn. She still had the house keys in her bunch. Feeling somewhat like a stranger, she let herself inside.

The living room seemed to have passed through a dust storm. The air was stale. The red wool carpet and the furniture all pleaded to be cleaned. Sticky strings of cobwebs networked across the living room, wall to wall. The porcelain vase on the dining table contained a bunch of withered red roses, their lifeless stalks wilted in death. In the kitchen, mould dominated the unwashed dishes. She went upstairs. In the bedroom, Leroy's clothes were strewn all over the seven-foot bed.

She went downstairs. She checked her watch: 7.35. Leroy wasn't here. Was her father calling her bluff?

She switched on the TV in the living room.

Hillary Bosworth's listening device was still functioning perfectly. The transponder worked in two ways. When it was in *Live* mode, Bosworth would park down the street and listen to everything being said in Leroy's living room—live—as they said it. When Bosworth was away he set the transponder to *Record* mode, in which case it recorded everything that was said onto a small disk. When Bosworth came round the transponder relayed everything it had recorded to a tape drive inside Bosworth's car.

Unknown to Ann, Bosworth sat in a car down the street.

'She's back in the house,' he reported to Cagley via his cell phone.

'Do what you have to,' Cagley responded.

'Yes, sir.' Bosworth hung up. He punched another number into his cell phone. 'Dominguez. Get me that junkie bitch. Quick!'

'What bitch is that?' Dominguez asked, miles away.

'The smelly one. The one you used for the Grant job.'

'Arlene?'

'Whatever. Bring her to me.' Bosworth hung up. He turned up the volume on his surveillance receiver. The bug functioned so well that he could hear the TV loud and clear in Leroy's living room. It was tuned to *The Cosby Show*.

Bosworth put his plan into action. He called Leroy's home on his cell phone. Ann answered. 'Hello?'

Bosworth kept mum.

'Hello?'

He kept silent.

'Hello?'

No answer.

She replaced the receiver.

Bosworth called again.

Ann picked it again. 'Hello.'

'Hello,' Bosworth said.

'Hello.'

'I'm Jason Vincent, Sun Insurance. We are offering a wide range of products, which may interest you. We have excellent car insurance, home insurance, travel insurance, life insurance, pet insurance—'

A phone salesman. Ann sighed.

'We also do pensions, marriage insurance, injuries—'

'I don't want insurance,' Ann said. 'I'm well covered.'

'We also have some other products that may interest you. We sell holidays—'

'I don't want anything.'

'We also do books, second hand items.'

301

'I don't want anything,' Ann said firmly.

'Clothing, shoes, handbags.'

'Nothing.'

'Household items, electric.'

'Sorry, I have to go.'

'We have bargain deals.'

'I have to go.'

'Toothbrushes, car stereos.'

'Bye.' Ann hung up.

A minute later, Bosworth called again.

'Oh no,' Ann grumbled, recognising him. 'I don't want anything. Don't call back, please!'

Over the surveillance receiver, Bosworth heard Ann grumbling to herself, 'Silly cow. Next time the phone rings, I'm not getting it.'

Inside the Volvo, Bosworth felt a tinge of victory. That was precisely what he wanted—to frustrate Ann so much that she wouldn't pick the phone when it rang. To be sure, he called Leroy's home again. True to her word, Ann ignored it. It rang five times and then the answering machine kicked in.

Good. Now where the hell were Dominguez and the junkie tart?

Dominguez, Bosworth's Latino lackey and the dishevelled junkie arrived five minutes later. She was about sixteen or seventeen, thin as a rake with dirty hazel hair. She was so exuberant that she had to be on a high. In truth Dominguez, a street-wise greasehead from Los Angeles had set her up with a fix of coke before bringing her over. She wore the same dirty jeans she did weeks ago and the same flowered shirt. She wore ragged sneakers without laces and if one looked properly, they were actually not matching pairs. She giggled non-stop. And she still smelt like a skunk.

Bosworth had to hold his breath. He loved the ladies but this was one girl that could never appeal to him—even if he was paid to. If she touched him he'd go cold. Simply grotesque. Bosworth didn't waste time with her. 'This job will earn you two hundred dollars. Want it?'

'Yes!' she cried. Then she giggled.

Ann made herself some tea as she sat in the living room, waiting for Leroy. It was now almost 8.30 pm. Occasionally she went to the window and looked out for him. Where was he? Had he been released but gone elsewhere or had her father called her bluff and refused to let him go?

The phone rang again.

She figured it could be that nuisance salesman again, so she let it ring. The answering machine clicked and came on. Ann listened. She would know who the caller was when they left a message.

The caller did. Her voice was smooth and silky. 'Leroy, hi. It's Arlene. Are you home yet? I want to say thanks for coming over to my place as soon as they let you go. I'm missing you already…' Her voice turned seductive, and she was virtually groaning. 'Thanks for today, Leroy. I shudder when I think of how you made love to me. Ooohh,' she moaned. 'I can't wait for tonight. I'm waiting. Byyyyeeee.'

The teacup dropped from Ann's fingers.

She didn't stay a minute longer in Leroy's house. Blinded by tears of humiliation, betrayal and confusion, she rushed into her car and drove off into the night.

A few minutes later, Bosworth sneaked into Leroy's house and wiped off Arlene's message. He looked around. He chuckled to himself. The things one could achieve with a bug, lies, and mind games.

At 9.00 pm Bosworth called Cagley. 'Thompson can let him go now, sir. I guarantee she won't be back. Ever.'

That night, a CIA car dropped Leroy in front of his house. He was free again.

Bosworth continued to listen in to everything being said in Leroy's living room. 'That bitch,' he heard Leroy swear. 'To hell with her!'

Bosworth laughed to himself. He was listening in to everything being said in someone's home, and they didn't have a clue. When they swore, he heard; when they fought, he heard; when they did the dirty stuff, he heard.

'I'm a naughty boy,' he chuckled. 'I'm a real naughty boy. I deserve to be smacked. But no one's ever gonna know.'

He giggled like a child.

65

After two days holed up in a hotel, Ann realised the only thing she wanted to do was get away and clear her head. There was a beautiful city she had been wanting to see. It had a most spectacular flat top mountain, lots of beaches, cafes, and history. There was also wildlife, wineries, and probably the world's widest variety of flowers. An old friend once told her a lot about the place. With nothing to hold her back, she bought a ticket and left the next day.

Ann arrived in Cape Town, South Africa, a beautiful, modern city by the sea, at the southern-most tip of Africa. She checked into a suite in the Excalibur, one of the best hotels in the city. It was expensive but she was determined to enjoy herself. There was no better way to get over a man than to get some luxury in her life; spoil herself a little. Her suite was the size of an apartment with a seven-foot waterbed and an excellent view of the brilliant blue sea, so different from the water in Chesapeake Bay.

She walked along the beach, her blonde hair blowing out behind. She mulled over her life. As far as she could see it was a big mess.

Leroy was having an affair. Or worse, more than one affair. *This is the end of the road for us, isn't it?*

What should she do now? Would she let her marriage fail? That would mean she'd let adultery be the ruling factor in her home, not love. Would she give up without a fight?

But fight for what?

Was he worth the trouble? When a man was unfaithful it meant his heart wasn't really there. Or were there other underlining issues she hadn't considered?

Maybe she should let him go. Find another man. Start her life over.

66

Leroy walked into the Rubicorn, a noisy bar on Connecticut Avenue in northwest Washington. Many of the Rubicorn's clientele were city lawyers. You could tell from their dark, pinstriped suits. They were respectable in the office, but transformed into loud, swearing, revellers in the evening. A handful of middle-aged women in skimpy, low-cut dresses stood around, downing cocktails in batches. Their eager eyes trailed any male that ventured past their tables. The jeans-clad regulars lounged at the bar. They were the hard drinkers with thick moustaches and drooping beer bellies. A wide mix of music blared from the Rubicorn's hidden speakers: rock, ballads, rhythm & blues, and hip-hop. The Rubicorn was no place for an asthmatic. Thick cigarette smoke hung above the tables. The artificial haze created by cigarette smoke didn't allow Leroy a clear view, so he made his way between the tables and the winebibbers, looking around for a man called John West.

Leroy finally caught sight of him at the bar, perched atop a wooden stool, sipping lager from a bottle. West had cropped golden hair and looked very much like Donald Sutherland.

Leroy walked over. 'Howdy, man.'

West flashed a big smile. 'Howdy, Leroy. Long time.' West loved urban speak.

'Been ages, man.'

'Yeah! C'mon, man, grab a seat.'

Leroy settled onto the next stool.

'What will you have?'

'Coors.'

West beckoned to the squat, middle-aged bar man. 'Get my friend a Coors.' West's voice was gritty from too many years smoking Marlboros. 'So, how's life treating you, my friend?'

'Not good,' Leroy admitted. 'I'm sure you heard of my hassles with the brass.'

'Of course! Nothing gets past us in Logistics. You've been messing around with old man Cagley's daughter, and he wants you in the obituaries, eh?' West laughed.

'She's divorcing me.'

'Hmmm. That's cold, man.'

West was one of the big players in the CIA Logistics unit. This was the unit that made things happen by handling unseen support activities for the CIA. They provided invaluable undercover facilities for CIA officers and false and genuine passports of all nations to CIA agents. They supplied local currency, made travel arrangements, and knew their way around every country's Customs and Immigrations, facilitating easy, undetected entry for US officers. They also arranged for firearms, safe houses, equipment, cars and transportation; setting up numerous fronts as need be. Because of this West had an enormous network of connections, and so, he was a valuable friend. He also seemed to know virtually everything that went on within the CIA, and more importantly, he did a little dirty business on the side. He could make things happen for trusted people who could pay for his invaluable services.

'John,' Leroy said. 'I need a favour.'

Leroy looked around to make sure no one was within earshot. 'I need a passport, and I need you to tell me how to get out of the country without hassles, and get to an out-of-the-way village in Africa. I'd like to avoid Immigrations, Customs, and US agents. It's quite likely I'm being monitored; I need a clean exit.'

West dragged heavily on his cigarette. He had worked with Leroy on a number of occasions, wangling secure transportation and accommodation for CIA bosses.

'It's gonna cost you,' West declared, finishing his cigarette.

'I'm gonna have to use my contacts outside the agency. It's gonna be one grand, all inclusive. Seven hundred for the passport—it's gonna be a rush job—you get it in two days. Three hundred for the details, you know, the visa and all the nitty-gritty bits that make sure you don't get spooked.'

A thousand dollars for a passport was steep. He knew, however, that what West called the *nitty-gritty details* were vitally important. He was a professional who knew the loopholes, and an expert in smuggling, gunrunning and establishing alibis and covers. That was what the CIA and the government of the United States paid him $80,000 a year for. His advice was invaluable.

'I'll do it.' Leroy fished out a roll of dollars from his hip pocket and counted twelve fifty-dollar bills.

'Give it to the barman,' West said quickly before Leroy could point it in his direction.

Leroy did as instructed.

The barman entered the money into his cash register and closed the till. The barman was West's front. He did his dirty business but kept his hands clean by using reliable intermediaries.

'You'll need a lot more than a passport, Leroy,' West advised. 'Your passport's been withdrawn—I know because we were ordered to do it. What I'm gonna do is this: I'll set you up with a Canadian passport, carrying a Mexican right-of-abode. I'll have to organise the visa of the country you intend to visit from Mexico. That way you can speak English in your accent and the visa wouldn't be from the US.'

Leroy nodded, impressed. This was the professionalism he was paying for.

'You also want me to do a roadmap to your destination without getting spooked? Where do you wanna go?'

'A village called Dan Apali. In Nigeria.'

'Dan Apali?' West made a mental note. 'I'll put it on the computers tomorrow and see what comes up.'

'Thanks. How good is this passport?'

309

'Are you asking if it is genuine?' West laughed. 'Of course, it is. We have huge stocks of every nation's passports in Langley, man. Hey, a passport's a book, just like any other. It's printed. I know the right people who do the printing on security printers. Besides, we have originals printed from the mints of every single country. Don't ask how we get them.' West patted Leroy reassuringly on the shoulder. 'This is my turf, man. I know my stuff. I can get you diplomatic or UN passports if you want.' West finished his beer. 'I'll leave you now. I gotta make a few calls and check out my contacts. Meanwhile, try and get to a twenty-four hour snapshot machine. I'll need a passport photograph of you, clean shaven.'

'Thanks, man.'

John West walked out of the Rubicorn. He never wasted time, and did things briskly if the cash was available, and tonight, one grand was available.

Leroy returned home and switched on the TV. He changed the channel to the 8 O'clock News. Just as the program started, the picture on the TV flickered briefly. He didn't think much of it.

Ann sat alone at a café at the Victoria and Alfred Waterfront, one of Cape Town's major attractions. Behind was the Table Mountain with its flat top. She watched as a fishing boat pulled into the harbour, and unloaded its catch.

A thickset man with curly brown hair approached her table. 'Do you mind if I join you?'

She looked up. He had that I'm-going-to-charm-you look in his eyes.

'I've been looking at you, and you look so sad,' he said. 'Permit me to cheer you up.'

'I don't need cheering,' she retorted coldly, looking away.

'Ah, I think you do. It seems to me you're suffering from a broken heart,' he said knowingly. 'I can see it in your eyes.'

What is it with men? They just can't see a woman and let her be. They just have to chat her up. Yeah, you're damn right.

*I'm just coming out a relationship, and I don't need you or any
other man in my hair. Now buzz off.*

'I'm Peter.'

'And I'm Paul.'

He drew back. She saw the glum look in his eyes. She knew
she shouldn't be so mean. She was taking her issue with Leroy
out on him and everyone.

'Er-I'm sorry, Peter. Bad manners. I shouldn't have done
that. I'm just…you know…sad, as you said.'

He smiled. 'I understand.'

'Please sit.'

Leroy returned to the Rubicorn on Tuesday. John West was
at the dimly lit bar, sloshing down Coors. As Leroy settled
onto a stool West spoke. 'That little village you wanna go? I
checked the agency computers. Your out-in-nowhere village
is actually on it. It's a recent crash site. But there's a problem.
It's not on the map, and there are no directions on record as to
how to get there. The place was accessed by chopper. However,
there are coordinates: latitudes and longitudes provided by
the chopper pilot. You have two options. I set you up with a
passport on a false name and you travel by commercial airline.
In that case the best option would be to cross over land into
Mexico, then catch a plane to Rio de Janeiro. That way you
don't mess about with US authorities. From Rio, you go on
Varig Airlines to Lagos. It goes once a week. Sundays. It would
cost you about two grand.'

'Mexico?'

'You can't get out from an airport within the United States.
You're a marked man, remember? The intelligence community
watch all US airports. I wouldn't recommend going through
Europe. Go through the Third World.'

'What's the second option?'

'Your second option, which I think is best, is insertion.

'You mean…'

'Yes, we drop you in. The same way we insert agents into

311

enemy territory, by parachute. That's the best way to avoid Customs, Immigration, and intelligence surveillance.'

Leroy breathed deeply. That wasn't exactly what he had in mind.

West noticed Leroy's reticence. 'How else can you get to an obscure village that no one's heard of? It's out-in-nowhere, it's not on the map, and has no clear-cut access roads. In actual fact, I don't think you have much of a choice. If you wish to avoid authorities you cannot go via an airport. This is the best way.'

'How's that gonna work?' Leroy knew West was adept at his game. If he gave advice it was good.

West sipped his beer. 'There's a war in Somalia, right? And there's airlifting of food and medical supplies to the war and famine victims, right?'

'Yes.'

'A lot of medical supplies are flown out of the States. Everyday, we have Army and Air Force planes ferrying light medical supplies to Kenya for onward distribution to Somalia. Since the military may move in we need more intelligence for that area, so, we've been putting more officers and equipment into the neighbouring countries, and dropping them in with the supplies. I've been liaising between agency Operations and Air Force transport. Ops tell me what they want and I tell the Air Force what to drop and where. They're pros. They don't ask questions. So, what I can do is this: I'll check the flight pattern of all airplanes doing airlifts tomorrow and look for one closest to your destination. Then I'll simply request the pilot do a covert mission drop. I give them the coordinates and on the way to Kenya, when passing over Nigeria, the pilot deliberately drifts a little bit off-course to the town you want. They use C-130s; they lower the ramp, you jump and zap, you're there! The pilot continues his journey.'

Leroy thought about John West's suggestion. True, the agency sometimes dropped agents into foreign countries by parachute to avoid detection but that was rare.

'It's your best option, man, believe me. You don't even know where that village is. I'll tell you something: many African villages are so remote and isolated that sometimes, even the government may not know it's there. As you know, all we have are the coordinates. If you go by commercial, when you get to Lagos you won't know where to turn, and when you ask around nobody's gonna know a damn thing 'cos it's an obscure village in the middle of nowhere. It's like arriving at Dulles and asking about Little Smallville in Nevada. No one's ever heard of it.'

'Yeah, I see your point. Nevertheless, I'm not sure about parachute jumps. I did a number of jumps as part of my CIA training in Orlando for field operations. Nasty thing, man.'

'How many did you do?'

'Three.'

'Then you'll be all right. It's no big deal. Do the drop, man, it's more direct,' West coaxed. 'You're a CIA officer for goodness sake. A man can only die once, man.' West gulped his beer.

Leroy laughed.

'You'll be fine, man. Believe me.'

'Assuming I even consider doing the jump, I've got no parachute.'

'I'll sort you out with chute. There's not much to it, anyway. It's very simple. You jump out, count to five, pull the string and hold the reins. That's it. It's just that simple.'

They laughed. *It's just that simple.*

Leroy returned home at 7.45 pm. Again, at 8 o'clock, the TV picture flickered briefly.

What's up with the TV?

313

67

Every day, Ann took leisurely walks along the beach in Noordhoek, south of Cape Town, trying to put the past behind her. But as much as she tried, she just could not. Every young man she saw on Cape Town's numerous beaches reminded her of Leroy. And a few older men reminded her of her father. She felt mentally trapped. She badly wished to forget Leroy and her father. The two of them had managed to turn her world upside down, and because of them she was in a foreign country, thousands of miles from home, trying to rebuild her life.

It still hurt whenever she remembered, which was about a hundred times a day—Leroy was cheating.

Then there was her father. Leroy was a saint compared to him. He was the devil. Manipulative and scheming. A man that would not tell the truth. A man who'd destroyed her marriage, almost killed her unfaithful husband, and unlawfully imprisoned him. A man who would stop at nothing to get his own way, even if it hurt her, his only child. It was obvious he had a vendetta against Leroy and it didn't matter that she got caught in the crossfire. How low would he stoop? He would always chase his own agenda, not hers. It would never matter to him if she loved a man unless that man was his choice. The harsh reality dawned on her: he would always be in the picture whatever she chose to do in life.

Violent waves crashed relentlessly onto the beach. The frothy, white surf foamed like detergent.

Also, within the last week, Peter—Pietar, actually, in Afrikaans—seemed to have taken a shine to her. He was charming, dotting, and successful. He was quiet, kind, and handsome. He was a businessman and worth quite a few hundred million dollars. It would be easier to just start afresh out here. A new man; new life. The way she was feeling now, that option was really attractive.

But she realised she hadn't yet gotten over Leroy. That was natural, she reckoned. Her love for him would not simply disappear. It would take time. Love doesn't evaporate instantly, unless it was never really there.

She realised however that whatever she chose to do, whomever she chose to be with, as long as her father was still in the frame, that man could very well suffer the same fate as Leroy.

Well, unless her father wasn't there...

An idea took shape in her head. All her life she had known him to be ruthless. May be it was time to let him know that that streak ran through the family blood stream.

She looked up, resolute. It was settled—and she knew precisely what to do

She dashed away from the beach.

Her father had to go.

68

At ten, on Monday morning, John West called Leroy. 'It's all arranged, man,' West said. 'A C-130 has been deployed from Pope Air Force Base. It's headed for Akron's Field near Baltimore. It will depart Akron's Field tonight for Kenya. Take-off time is twelve midnight. It will stop over in Dakar for a few hours to pick up other supplies. There are five crew, two aid workers and you. Its flight path is about fifty miles away from the village, which is not too bad. The pilot is an experienced covert guy. He knows how to go about it; he'll probably let the plane drift off course or something. You don't have to worry about anything. He'll get you there. I'll pick you up at the junction of Baltimore Avenue and Albion Road at twenty-two hundred hours.'

Before Leroy could get in a word, West hung up.

Leroy had serious reservations about parachuting into Dan Apali. But then he had an overwhelming desire to see Talata—and quickly too. He flopped into his settee and contemplated his options. He made a decision: what the hell? A man can only die once. He would do the jump.

He grabbed a rucksack and packed a pair of tough hiking boots, warm clothes, and a pair of infrared night goggles. Into the rucksack, he threw a torch, food, matches, canned lager, cigarettes, and as much cash as he could lay his hands on. He also packed a Glock 17 with two extra clips—for safety.

By 8.00 pm, he was ready. Since he had a few hours to burn before setting out to meet John West he switched on the TV and watched the 8 o'clock news. The TV had been on for barely two minutes when he observed a flicker across the screen. The picture wiggled then straightened out again.

His instincts were aroused. He recalled the same thing happened yesterday...And the day before—and always at 8 o'clock. Strange. Years of CIA training had taught him to be suspicious if anything seemed odd in any way.

What could be causing the interference? Devices such as transmitters, phones, microwaves, electric typewriters, electromagnetic device, and bugs were notorious for interference.

Bugs? A listening device?

Leroy knew he was a marked man, and this made him a little paranoid.

Bugs were sometimes set to transmit at the frequency on which the TV received broadcasts. It was a trick perfected by the Russian KGB. The TV frequency masked the bug's frequency, making it difficult to detect with a bug sniffer. The listening device would be programmed to record, and then transmit intermittently. If the TV was on, however, it would flicker briefly.

He set about searching his house. He checked the power sockets first. It was usually where the bug tapped the power it needed to operate. A very thin wire would be concealed under the wall paint, leading from the power socket to the bug. He found nothing. He inspected the nooks and crannies of his living room, searching for telltale wires or foreign objects. None. He examined every inch of the dining table, and checked the electrical fittings. Nothing. He checked the back of the sofa to see if the upholstery had been prised open. Still nothing.

Unsatisfied, he got a thin piece of wire and probed it into the sofa in different places. It was when he prodded inside one of the armrests of the sofa that he felt a hard object deep beneath the upholstery. He carefully pried the hard object out. It was a tiny, gleaming electronic device, the size of a dime embedded in the sofa. Its thin wires ran all the way through to the carpet.

He stared at the bug for one long minute, trying to come to terms with the realisation that someone had been listening in on everything going on in his house. Everything he said, someone heard. Every time he made love someone was listening!

He felt violated and exposed; naked.

There would be a listening post not too far away. Probably a van or a man in a car, parked on the street nearby.

Leroy donned a baseball cap and pulled it well over his face. Then he stepped out of his home. The street was empty. He walked down the street, looking earnestly for any car or van that had any occupants in it. Fifty yards away, he spotted a blue Volvo 760 GLE saloon with a huge ginger-haired man behind the wheel. The man was reading a newspaper and eating an apple. He had a little earphone in his right ear. He was so engrossed in his paper that he didn't observe Leroy pass by.

Leroy instantly recognised him. He was one of the goons attached to Cagley's office!

Fuming, Leroy returned home and downed a shot of tequila. That calmed his nerves while he debated on what to do.

It's about time I stood up for myself. It's about time I send a message to Cagley and the CIA. I'm gonna teach this fat toad a lesson or two.

He retrieved his weapon and his blue-handled baseball bat. He kept a close watch on the street till no one was in sight then he marched up to the Volvo. Bosworth was unaware; he sat munching an apple.

Leroy shoved the Glock through the half-open window and into Bosworth's ear. Bosworth froze, still holding the apple in front of his face. Leroy squeezed the trigger once.

The Glock clicked, disengaging its safety catch.

Bosworth heard the click. He breathed easy, relieved, realising he was still alive. Cautiously, he looked through the corner of his eyes. He was staring at a gleaming Glock 17. Leroy stood behind the gun.

'Don't do anything stupid,' Leroy warned sternly.

Bosworth was in shock. For the first time in his life, he was at the wrong end of a pistol and it wasn't comfortable.

'Step out of the car!' Leroy ordered.

'Er, put the toy away,' Bosworth said, sneaking a peek at the weapon in Leroy's right hand. He saw Leroy also held a baseball bat in the other hand.

'Shut the hell up!' Leroy growled.

Blank faced, Bosworth slowly heaved his massive frame out of the car and raised his hands. Leroy prodded Bosworth's underarms with the bat. Just as he suspected, Bosworth carried a gun in a holster under his arm.

'Close your eyes or I'll blow them out!'

Bosworth shut his eyes.

Leroy frisked him, removed his handgun and shoved it into his back pocket.

'Turn around,' Leroy ordered.

Reluctantly, Bosworth turned his back to Leroy.

'Hit the floor!' Leroy ordered.

Now, Bosworth was pissed off with this little weasel who suddenly saw himself as Clint Eastwood. He could tear this little runt to pieces with one hand tied behind him. Bosworth decided he'd had enough of Leroy's tough boy antics. He spun and faced Leroy.

'Damn you, sucker!' Bosworth bluffed. 'You wanna shoot? Then shoot!'

Leroy squeezed the trigger.

Bosworth heard the bang before he felt the pain. The 9 mm slug tore into his left foot. Bosworth yelped as thick red blood oozed from his black leather shoes. But Bosworth was a tough boy from a rough family of sailors. He ignored the pain and lurched at Leroy.

Leroy nimbly sidestepped and swung the bat low. It caught Bosworth in the left shin. He howled, hopping on his right foot. Leroy swung the bat once more, a backhand, catching Bosworth at the base of his spine. Bosworth grunted. It was as if he'd been hit by a tow-truck.

Leroy swung a third time, ramming the cudgel into Bosworth's right knee. Bosworth howled and crashed onto the road.

319

Leroy shoved the Glock into his belt then, grabbing the bat in both hands, he smashed it into Bosworth's windshield. The windshield shattered. Next, he smashed the mirrors, the front and rear lights and all the four windows. Shattered granules of tempered glass rained on to the road and the sidewalk and splattered over sprawled Bosworth. Bosworth yelped as granules of glass cut into his body. He tried to move, but he couldn't. He felt agony like never before.

Inside Bosworth's car, a briefcase lay open on the passenger seat. It contained coils of wire, a tape recorder and a dozen or so tapes—all strewn with shards of glass. Those tapes had to be recordings from the bug in his living room. He grabbed the tapes and shoved them into his pockets.

Finally, he walked over to Bosworth, sprawled, bleeding, and groaning on the road. 'Tell Cagley it's a little payback. Tell him I'm gonna do the same to him when I lay my hands on him.' He delivered a good hard kick into Bosworth's ribs. Bosworth howled like a wolf.

The neighbours had heard the gunshot. A few watched the scene from the safety of their homes. By now they would have called the cops. The police station was less than a mile away; the cops would be on the scene in less than two minutes.

Leroy hurried back home and locked the front door behind him. He grabbed his packed rucksack and tossed it into his back garden.

A siren wailed in the distance.

He stepped out into the garden then shoved the Glock and the tapes into his rucksack and locked the door.

Voices in front of the house announced the cops' arrival. A sharp rapping sounded on the front door.

'Let's take a look at the back,' a gruff voice said.

Leroy snatched up his rucksack and climbed over the fence into the neighbour's garden. He crept through the neighbour's compound and emerged on the next street. As he melted into the shadows he saw police flashlights beaming onto his house.

John West picked Leroy at the junction of Baltimore Avenue in a black Audi A4 sedan. West gunned the Audi towards the Capital Beltway then joined Interstate 95. It was dark and the Audi's headlamps lit up the highway as it ate up the miles. Somewhere on the highway, West slowed and turned into an obscure slip road, which led to a bush track only wide enough for one car. The Audi's headlamps lit up the weedy track. On each side, towering stalks of maize grew so close the fronds swished against the sides of the car.

After a mile, they arrived at a yellow gate. West pushed a combination on a keypad beside the gate; the gate slid open. They drove through and the gate closed automatically behind them.

After a few hundred yards, the droning and whirring of a propeller-driven airplane could be heard. An airfield was near, hidden behind the tall stalks of corn. The dirt track ended at the foot of a huge, tarred runway with large, yellow chevrons. The runway stretched out as far as the eye could see. There were no visible runway lights. West sped down the runway.

A group of aerodrome buildings came into view one kilometre down the runway. Bright orange sodium lamps lit up the buildings. Three Lockheed Hercules C-130's sat on a huge concrete apron. Behind them was a huge warehouse. West brought the Audi to a halt under the massive alloy wings of one of the airplanes. The crew members were checking the controls as a prelude to a flight.

West stepped out of the Audi. 'Come with me.' He opened the trunk and brought out a dull green parachute kit and a helmet. 'Here's your kit; checked and packed. And the passport.'

'Thanks.'

West led Leroy into the C-130. The fuselage was stacked with a few brown cartons, which contained antibiotics. The cartons were held down by massive nets. C-130s only carried light loads or flew empty when crossing the Atlantic so as to extend their range.

321

Inside the cockpit, four crew members sported olive green flight suits, plastered with US Air Force badges. A young, thin pilot sat at the controls. The co-pilot was equally young. There was also a navigator and an engineer. The cockpit shimmered with lit dials, controls, switches and gauges.

'Hi guys,' West said.

'Howdy,' the pilot acknowledged West. He cast a glance at Leroy. 'Are you the drop guy?'

Leroy nodded.

The pilot turned to West. 'We don't have the coordinates yet.'

'They're right here.' West produced a printed piece of paper.

The pilot looked it over briefly and handed it to the navigator. 'There's your seat.' The pilot pointed to a dull green jump bunk at the rear of the cockpit. 'Get strapped in. We'll be outta here pretty soon.'

West checked his watch. 'Gotta disappear.' He winked and tapped Leroy's shoulder. 'Good luck on this mission, man.'

'Yeah, thanks,'

'Safe journey all,' he said as he left.

Leroy settled into his seat. None of the crew spoke to him. Military boys are trained not to ask questions. To them it was yet another covert job—one of the many they undertook to protect Uncle Sam's interests, worldwide.

An hour later, the C-130 shut its doors and its four huge Allison T-56 propeller engines roared to life. It was only when they began to taxi that the runway lights were switched on. They were airborne by 11.45 pm.

69

The Lockheed Hercules C-130 had a top speed of only 375 miles per hour. It took the C-130 thirteen long hours to cross the Atlantic, and it finally touched down at Leopold Senghor International Airport in Dakar, Senegal, at 5.00 pm, local time.

While the airplane refuelled and more supplies were loaded, Leroy and the crew ate a good meal in the terminal building. Well into the night, the C-130 continued its journey, cruising above the night clouds. The moon hung brightly to the left, its brilliant light brightened the tops of the clouds beneath.

Shortly after dawn, the pilot turned to Leroy. 'We'll be in the drop zone in approximately fifteen minutes. The weather is good, no high winds. I've signalled the loadmaster. Get ready.'

The loadmaster entered the cockpit. He was a stocky man of Samoan origin. He wore a green Air Force flight suit. 'Come with me,' he said to Leroy.

'Good luck,' the pilot called out.

'Thanks.'

The loadmaster led the way. They walked between stacks of boxes and supplies in the fuselage to the tail end of the plane. 'Here we are,' the loadmaster said.

Leroy was tense, but he knew he couldn't let fear get to him now. With a little help from the loadmaster, he strapped on his parachute and his rucksack and donned his helmet. Satisfied everything was good and tight, Leroy moved closer to the tail door. He gave the loadmaster a thumbs-up.

'You jump on the green light,' the loadmaster yelled, pointing to a set of coloured bulbs mounted above the tail door.

The red light flashed on. The loadmaster pressed a button

next to the door and it creaked open. Sunlight streaked into the fuselage, followed by a gust of cold air. The droning of the propeller engines was deafening.

The tail door gradually opened into a ramp. The earth loomed thousands of feet below. He could see for tens of miles around. The earth beneath looked like a never-ending green field, folded into a perfect circle at the edges. Huge, green hills loomed far away, their tops lost in dull white haze. Huge rock structures dotted the landscape but at this altitude they looked like big stones. A couple of silvery rivers meandered through the vegetation.

When the door was fully lowered, the loadmaster watched the lights. The amber light came on. He gestured that Leroy should move further down the ramp. Leroy stepped a little further with one foot on the tail door. The wind whipped around his face and tugged relentlessly at his clothes. Leroy felt giddy but he steeled himself as he had been taught in training by breathing deeply repeatedly. He held on to the frame of the fuselage.

The green light came on.

'Now!' the loadmaster yelled.

Leroy psyched himself up. *Go...go...go.*

His heart beating rapidly, he ran down the tail door and jumped. All the air seemed to be sucked out of him as he hurled towards the earth. He felt a churning in his stomach.

His natural desire to stay alive kicked in. As he had been taught, he kept upright and then counted to five. He reached for his ripcord and jerked on it.

Nothing happened.

The air rushed into his face as he plummeted towards the ground at enormous speed. Grunting, he jerked at it again.

This time, the white parachute shot out above him, quickly opening into a massive umbrella, which immediately slowed his fall with a jolt. Steadying himself, he held the reins tightly. He now had to wait out the slow drop down. The cold air blew over his body and filled his lungs. The sun dazzled brilliantly in the sky, but the helmet visor protected his eyes. As the ground loomed closer, he looked down to see where he would land. It wouldn't do to get splattered on the rocks. He tried to gauge how far he was from the ground. He looked down. He could see the tall blades of grass.

Any moment now.

Moments later, his boots slammed into the earth, and he toppled into the thick grass. The parachute dropped like a massive bedspread over him.

He regained his senses and realised he was still alive, and it was all over. Relieved, he lay back on the grass for a minute or two and just enjoyed the fresh air, and strong scent of chlorophyll emanating from the grasses.

After a few moments he got to his feet. There was nothing but green grass and shrubs for miles around. He loosened his parachute and let it drop. He felt somewhat good to be back here. The atmosphere brought back memories. Fond memories. He opened his rucksack and brought out a beer.

He trudged across the plain to find Dan Apali, sipping his beer in high spirits.

The early morning sun beat down full strength as Leroy trudged along, carrying his rucksack. His rugged mountain boots were totally plastered with green paste from the million or so blades of grass he'd trodden upon. He pulled on a Yankees baseball cap to shield his face from the dazzling sun.

It was now an hour since his drop. But where the hell was Dan Apali?

70

Michael Cagley was attending a security meeting with Canadian Intelligence in Ottawa. The meeting had just ended when Donald Billingham telephoned from Langley.

'We have a situation,' Billingham said. 'Delgado.'

'Delgado? What's happened now?'

'We don't know the whole story, but he had a run-in with Bosworth, yesterday evening. Shot him, then worked him over with a baseball bat. Bosworth's in hospital. Two broken bones and a shattered kneecap.'

Cagley was silent for a while. 'Who took Bosworth to hospital?' he finally asked.

'The cops.'

Cagley cleared his throat. Cops were bad news, especially since Bosworth had been doing an illegal assignment. By law, the CIA was not allowed to operate on US soil except in special circumstances. 'Did they question Bosworth?'

'We took care of that. I had a word with the police chief. Besides, Bosworth knows better than to complain.'

'And Delgado?'

'We don't know where he is. He's disappeared.'

'He could be holed up somewhere or trying to get out of the country,' Cagley suggested.

'Quite possible.'

'Put out an APB to all ports. Contact our people worldwide. He should be apprehended on sight.'

71

It was a little after five in the evening when Ann placed a call to the United States. Bob Weiser, a sixty-year-old Washington veteran took the call in his two-bedroom apartment in Alexandria, Virginia. 'Hello.'

'Hello,' Ann replied. 'This may sound odd, but my name is Ann Cagley. Would you know me at all?'

There was a pause. 'Ann Cagley? I'm sorry I don't know anyone by that name.' Bob pondered a while. 'The only person I know with the name, Cagley is a pathetic little man in Langley.' The bitterness and resentment as he mentioned the name, Cagley was evident in Bob's tone.

Ann was not fazed. 'That pathetic little man is my father.'

There was a long pause. Then Bob slammed the phone.

She had reckoned that would happen but she wouldn't be put off. She rang back.

Again Bob answered the phone. 'What do you want from me?'

Bob Weiser was the foremost candidate campaigning to represent the Democrats at the last presidential election. Cagley and Bob were arch enemies. It kicked off when Bob offered to buy a drink for an unaccompanied woman at The Perivale Golf Club in Bethesda. The woman was Lizzy Bottagano, Cagley's mistress. Cagley had always kept his relationship with Lizzy quiet. He didn't like Bob hitting on his woman, especially as Bob was a known charmer. Worse, Lizzy was giggling raucously at everything Bob said, obviously falling for his lines. Sitting at the other end of the clubhouse, Cagley put a stop to it by calling her cell phone.

'Who's that bozo?' Cagley demanded when she answered.

She turned and saw the displeasure on Cagley's grim face. She got the message. Bob followed her gaze and saw Cagley looking murderously at him. Bob Weiser knew immediately that he had incurred the wrath of Cagley, thereby making himself a powerful enemy who would do anything to stop his march to the White House. On the other hand, Cagley knew that if Bob got to the White House he was out of a job. Bob Weiser could not be allowed to become President. On a campaign trip to Chicago, DEA dogs sniffed out cocaine hidden in Bob's luggage at O'Hare Airport. Bob denied all knowledge. The drugs were later deemed to have been planted by unknown people but by then it was too late. Bob's reputation was tarnished. The Democrats could not afford the baggage and he was dropped as a possible candidate. He ended up in debt and had to sell his mansion in Bethesda. Now, he lived broken, with high blood pressure in a mid-scale two-room apartment block in Alexandria. He always believed Michael Cagley had something to do with his troubles. Despite this, he was still well-connected in Washington.

'Please hear me out!' Ann pleaded. 'I need your help. I know you believe my father framed you. This is precisely why I called you—'

'Is this a trap?' Bob boomed.

'No! Please just hear me out. I know my dad was very likely responsible for the drugs found in your suitcase. I can help you get justice.'

'What?' Bob was all ears.

'The reason I got to know is because he has this habit of thinking out loud. Especially when he's relaxed at home. On this day they showed you on TV, he muttered to himself, "You'll be going down soon." You were arrested a few days later.'

'I knew it!' Bob cried. Then he exercised caution. 'Why are you telling me this?'

'You're not the only person he's hurt. He hurt me too. He

328

ruined my marriage. It's time he's brought to his knees.'

Bob heard her sobbing. 'So, what do you want from me?' he asked, still not convinced.

'I want him stopped. I'm willing to do whatever it takes.'

'What do you have in mind? Your father is extremely powerful. Stopping him will require determination.'

'I know. I have an idea. What I really need is to contact the one person who can deal with my father: the President. If you could give me the fax number of his secretary I would wish to fax a few things to him.'

Bob had always fancied an opportunity to get even with Cagley and now it was being handed to him on a golden plate. But this seemed too good to be true. Being an experienced Washington insider he wouldn't allow himself to be trapped. This could even be an underhanded one from Cagley himself. On second thoughts he doubted if Cagley would use his daughter. Or expose himself so easily.

But Bob still had to be cautious. 'Leave me your number, my dear. I'll think about it and call you back.'

Bob called a friend in the National Security Agency. After a few hours he confirmed that the call came from Cape Town, South Africa. Cross checking with Immigrations and the airlines confirmed Ann had gone to South Africa.

Bob called Ann back. 'So, what would you like me to do for you, my dear?'

'The President's personal fax number, please.'

He gave her the number. That was the fax in the office of Mary Dean, the President's personal secretary. Its number was top secret.

'Should you need help in cutting him down to size, I am very available,' Bob said.

'Thanks. I'll keep that in mind.'

'I'll be interested to know how you get on. Should you really wish to demolish Michael Cagley then you and I can work together. Fax me whatever you have.'

He gave Ann his own fax number.

Ann ended the call to Bob.
Then she dialled another number.
'Jayne Macintosh Attorneys?'

72

The savannah grassland stretched for miles and miles in all directions. There was no village or settlement as far as Leroy could see. He knew what had happened: the C-130 had overshot the drop zone. This was an inherent and common danger in parachuting.

He was lost.

But getting lost was the good part. He hadn't considered the bad part until he heard a deep growl. He turned round and saw a full grown male lion staring straight at him. The beast was as huge as a motorbike—Leroy never knew they grew that big. Its head and mane was as huge as a car tyre. He froze. Heart pounding violently, he yanked out his pistol.

The beast didn't seem the least interested in him. It had probably just made a kill. It stared at him for a few tense moments then yawned and trotted the other way. Shaken, Leroy broke into a hurried trot, looking over his shoulders every few steps. *Lions?* What had he let himself into?

He had no sense of bearing as he fled. It was that sense of danger that forced him to think. He recalled that the huge grass plain in Dan Apali stretched towards the east into the rising sun. Working on this fact, he headed west.

After two hours he sighted a corn farm. A farm meant there would be a farmer. If there was a farmer, then a settlement wouldn't be too far away. He had never been so relieved.

He followed the footpath leading away from the farm. After a few minutes Leroy saw a group of mud, cement and thatch huts interspersed between the plains and a thin forest. As he walked closer, the scenery became uniquely familiar.

He stopped, turned around and looked towards the east. Now, the plains stretched before him and a range of distant hills bordered the horizon. This was unmistakably Dan Apali! This was the plain that stretched out from the bubbly brook where he had met Talata.

There was no one in sight. He decided not to enter the village and instead, walked through the tall grasses towards the spot where he always met her. His heart pumped hard as he approached the granite rock beside the brook. He stopped. This was the spot.

Their spot.

73

Mary Dean looked out of the White House window; over the manicured lawn and flowers that surrounded the White House. The coffee machine beeped. She poured some coffee into a mug and carried it into the Oval Office for the President. He liked his coffee black and sweet.

'Thanks,' he said, not looking up from his work.

The sun streamed into the Oval Office. She drew the blinds halfway so the glare wouldn't disturb him.

'Thanks,' he said, again not looking up.

She observed the President was squinting as he read a document. She handed him his glasses. He hated wearing them but she knew he needed them to read. He just couldn't be bothered to get them.

'Thanks,' the President said again. He put them on.

Mary Dean had been the President's secretary all the way from his days in the Minnesota House of Assembly through his tenure as governor, and finally as President. They were like a glove in a hand.

She returned to her office.

The President's personal fax machine came alive.

She watched as it churned out several pages. Mary Dean picked up the printed fax. It read:

IN THE UNITED STATES DISTRICT COURT
FOR THE DISTRICT OF COLUMBIA

Ann Mary Cagley   (Plaintiff)

Michael Cagley (Defendant)
The Central Intelligence Agency (Defendant)

COMPLAINT
PLAINTIFF DEMANDS TRIAL BY JURY

1. At all times hereinafter mentioned, plaintiff was a resident of 1262 Maple Avenue, Chevy Chase, Maryland.
2. The first defendant is currently resident at 1262 Maple Avenue, Chevy Chase, Maryland, and being a US government official.
The second defendant is a US Government agency, located at Dolley Madison Avenue, Fairfax County, Virginia.
3. The jurisdiction of this court is invoked pursuant to 28 USC 1331...
4. The first defendant at various times embarked upon a variety of offences of which the following constitute a few:

I. On or about the 15th August 1991, the defendant unlawfully kidnapped and imprisoned the plaintiff's Husband, Leroy Delgado.
II. The defendant arranged to plant illegal substances, notably narcotics on the Democratic candidate, Bob Weiser on or about April 1988 to alter the outcome of a general election.
III. The defendant conspired with the President of the United States and other officers of the U.S. government to illegally overthrow the sovereign government of the country of Bolivia on the 27th of November 1986.
IV. The defendant engaged in numerous illegal

activities, which are sensitive, and will be revealed
to a Grand Jury.

5. Wherefore, plaintiff demands a trial by jury, and custodial
punishment as the court may deem appropriate.

Signed
Ann Mary Cagley
Currently at 122 Ocean Drive, Noordhoek, South Africa.
Jayne MacIntosh Attorneys LLP
Plaintiff's Attorney

Mary Dean's heart beat rapidly upon reading it. She was
used to dealing with crises in the Administration, and this fax
promised nothing but trouble.

A court complaint. Michael Cagley, the President's trusted
lieutenant was the subject. Anything that affected him would
no doubt smear the President politically. She was especially
concerned with the allegations in the fourth paragraph. All
were poisonous to the administration. Kidnapping? Setting
up Bob Weiser? She remembered that case. It had received
so much press coverage. And it was only because Bob was
out of the way that the current president won the election. It
could mean the President's election was a farce! What would
the public think of that? The third allegation was the worst. It
specifically implicated the President.

At first, Mary Dean panicked. But she forced herself to
calm down.

Her first reaction was to dash in to show the fax to the
President. But that was not how personal secretaries to the
President worked. She had to get as much information as he
could need.

Who was Ann Cagley? She had never heard of anyone by
that name. She knew Michael Cagley very well. He briefed
the President every day.

She dialled the President's chief of security. 'Andy, hi. Can you find out about someone called Ann Cagley?' She looked at the fax. 'She could be related to Michael Cagley, CIA. Could be a family member. They share the same address.'

'Ann Cagley?'

'Yes.

'Okay.'

Mary Dean hung up.

A few minutes later, the chief of security called back. 'Ann Cagley is Michael Cagley's daughter. His only child.'

'Okay. Thanks, Andy.'

Next, Mary Dean called the Attorney General. 'Hello, Bill. The President needs advice right away. Urgent. I would say it's an emergency.'

That was enough to set Bill Ainsley into a fit. 'I'll be with you right away. '

74

The sky was bright blue without a single cloud. The late afternoon breeze rustled the tall savannah grass.

As she often did, Talata walked to the rock that stood by the plain. She had never expected to see him again. She froze as she came around the rock, and saw him sitting there, staring out at the plains. She covered her mouth to stop herself from screaming.

At some point, Leroy sensed someone was watching him. He looked around. The sun was setting in the distance and it shone into his eyes, obstructing his vision. Someone was there. He knew it was a woman since her dress fluttered in the wind.

He stared at her.

His heart jumped hard.

For almost a minute, they simply stared at each other.

She had changed. She looked thinner.

He found his feet and walked up to her. She wore a blue silk dress and a matching shawl. He stopped temporarily. Without a word, he reached out and drew her close.

He sensed she was a little reluctant. He drew her regardless.

Although she had been hesitant at first, when they came together she held him tightly.

He smelt the faint, flowery scent in her hair. 'God, how I've missed you.' He buried his face in her hair.

She didn't say a word. Instead, she broke down and wept into his chest. 'Y-you didn't tell me you were married!' she spluttered between sobs. This was all she could say. That was where it hurt. That was the betrayal.

He felt somewhat ashamed. He saw the anguish and the pain

of betrayal in her eyes. He opened his mouth to speak. Her eyes locked into his, questioning and searching for the truth. Her dim, wet eyes spoke for her. *Tell me the truth, Leroy,* her eyes demanded. *Please tell me the truth. Is it true?*

'I-I...' Leroy stuttered. Nothing he could say could ever be enough.

Talata saw the guilt in his face. It was true! Yet, she saw that he was deeply and genuinely sorry for letting her down.

She drew away from him. 'I can't do it, Leroy. You're someone else's.' Tears streamed from her eyes. 'Go back to your wife.' Her voice was barely a whisper but her pain was palpable. She turned her back to him.

'I love you, Talata,' Leroy said softly, holding her shoulders.

'I love you too, but Love is not enough. This is not about love. I-I'm talking about your wife... Me... This love triangle—the whole mess.'

'Yes, it's a big mess, and I'm really sorry. But as of now, I'm no longer married. We can finally be together.' His words came out hurriedly, desperate to convince her.

'What?'

'By the time I got back home, Ann had served papers on me. She's left me, Talata. So, you see, I am now a free man. You and I can...' he rattled on desperately.

'Why didn't you tell me about her when we first met?'

'When I had the air crash, I didn't even know if I was still married. Yes, I had a wife, but we split up before the crash. So, at that time I was beginning to consider myself as being single again. However, deep in my heart, I thought there was a remote possibility she could come back. So, I was in a dilemma. I was beginning to get involved with you then. I wanted to tell you my situation that night at the mango tree but you said you didn't want to know of any skeletons in my cupboard.'

She remembered vividly. Truly, that night she had sensed he'd say something heartbreaking, but then she had been euphoric. She had not wanted anything disturbing her joy. No ants in the honey pot. So, she had not let him speak.

'Why were you kidnapped? What happened? Some people—especially the elders and the village chief—think you're a criminal, that you're on the run. They say that's why a group of gun-toting men came to arrest you.'

He laughed flippantly. 'I'm no criminal. I'm a good man.'

'But guns?'

'Remember I told you I am in the military?' He still could not reveal his CIA status.

'Yes?'

'Remember, I refused to return to the States only because I wanted to be with you?'

'Yes?'

'Well, in the military, that's called desertion. They came to arrest me. I was jailed.'

'Oh!' Now it made a little sense to her. She was relieved he was no criminal. All her worries had been put to rest. Still, she folded her arms and walked about twenty yards away. She sighed heavily.

Leroy saw she was burdened. He walked up to her. 'What is it, Talata? What is troubling you?'

'I know I love you, and I think you have a degree of affection for me as well. But as I said, love is not enough. I don't think...' Her voice trailed off. 'I don't think we can carry on from where we left off.'

Leroy frowned. 'What do you mean?'

'I...just can't carry on. You see, I used to think I was strong, but now I realise that I really am not. The kidnappers left a photograph of you and your wife. Every night, I looked at you in the picture, and I felt so warm within.' Her voice became softer. 'Then I would cry. I cried for love.' Again tears welled in her eyes. 'But then I looked at your wife and I cried again. This time, I cried for pain. Looking at her tore my conscience to bits.' She burst out crying. 'I always felt like a thief...taking someone else's property...someone else's husband. I wanted to die. I blamed myself for splitting up a man and his wife. I felt so bad. And now, it has affected me so much that whenever I

339

think of you, I think of her as well. She's always at the back of my mind. She'll always be there.' She looked into his eyes. 'I'm psychologically damaged, Leroy. I need to heal.'

Tears welled to his eyes. 'I-I'm sorry, Talata,' he stuttered. 'I'm sorry for the pain I put you through.'

'It's all right. It's all right.'

'I'm here now, Talata. I'm here to stay. We can make this right.' He touched her shoulder tenderly. 'I know I might be asking a lot but do you still have any feelings for me?'

She sighed and her eyes became cloudy. 'I do. B-but...it's not just about the feelings.'

'What is it? Why can't we be together? I want to help you heal. Is there another man?'

'Another man?' She stared at him as if he was crazy. 'No.'

'Then what is it? Why can't we start afresh? Why?'

She paused a while then spoke: 'First, there's the issue of your wife. I can't put it behind me no matter how much I try. I can't live with the guilt. Now that you've mentioned you're divorced, I can't stop thinking that it's all my fault. Please understand that, Leroy. I just can't get over that. It happened to my grandmother when my grandfather got another woman. She never recovered. I grew up knowing her pain. The sweet woman I used to know gradually degenerated into a spiteful, bitter woman. I saw the destruction it does to families. I decided from then on that I would never ask a man to leave his wife for me. Never! I don't want it done to me, and I won't do it to someone else. I loved you so much that at some time I was willing to compromise. But I think I'm stronger now. I'll move on; find my own man.'

'Okay?'

'There is another reason.'

'What is that?'

She looked fixedly at him. 'It is written that a man shall leave his parents and cleave to his wife, and the two shall become one. Besides, what God has joined together let no man put asunder. It is also written that a man shall not put away his wife save for adultery, and he that goes with a married person commits adultery.'

He knew she was quoting portions of the Bible. 'Spare me the sermon.'

'It's not a sermon, it's my new way of life. That's the only good thing that came out of everything that happened to me. Well, really, the best thing. I grieved so much and I found the Bible. It was my companion through those times. It was what helped me. In it, I finally found the Truth. I found peace. It has taught me to do the right thing. I have decided to follow Jesus.'

That was when Leroy realised what was so different about her. She had climbed the moral and religious high ground. She spoke with such strong conviction. He knew at that moment that her mind was made up. He would never persuade her. It was like speaking to the Great Wall of China.

'You know something, Leroy? A man's greatest misery is worrying about what he doesn't have while forgetting what he actually has.'

'What's that supposed to mean?'

'A man's greatest misery is worrying about what he doesn't have while forgetting what he has.' Tears welled from her eyes. She tried to force it back, but could not. 'The grass is never greener on the other side, Leroy. Your wife is what you have. Go to her. Take care of her.' She looked deep into his eyes. 'Y-you have to go back to your country. We don't belong together.'

Her own words wrenched her heart because she still loved him so much. If only things were different. She would never love another man like she loved him. But she had chosen her path. It was the path of goodness and virtue. She was giving him up. It was a sacrifice for decency, goodness and for Christ.

341

75

The President stared, horrified at Bill Ainsley, the Attorney General. 'She's bringing down my whole government!' he cried. 'This is no longer Cagley's problem; it threatens my whole administration. Can you imagine if this gets around Washington? The daughter of the CIA Director insisting her father did some dirty business in conjunction with the president. Whether it is ever proven or not, millions will believe the story.' He paced for several moments behind his desk. Then he stopped. 'So, what do we do now?'

'The Federal Rules of Criminal Procedure could be rather unfair in the sense that if someone makes a complaint, procedure demands a warrant is issued for the defendant's arrest,' Bill answered. 'Whether or not the complaint is valid or irrelevant.'

'We can't have that surely. An arrest? That will make the news.'

'There is a way round that, sir. We can get an attorney to make an application to the court to issue a summons instead.'

'Then what happens?'

'It will buy us time. I'll call her lawyers and set up a meeting. See if we can talk.'

'Thanks, Bill,' Mary Dean said, keen as ever to protect the President. She was not a high-ranking member of the administration but she was in on matters that concerned the President's reputation.

'Another thing we must do is containment,' Bill said. 'Keep those in the know to a minimum.'

'How many people know about this anyway?' the President

asked.

'Counting now, we've got Mr President, me, Bill, Ann, and her lawyers,' Mary Dean answered.

'No one else outside this room gets to know,' the President warned.

'Yes, sir,' Mary Dean answered.

'I'll come down on her lawyers,' Bill offered. 'I know Jayne. Her office is downtown. I'll ask her to keep this off the record; get it off her files. She knows better than to let this go to trial.'

'Where the hell is Cagley?' the President asked.

'On a flight back from Canada,' Mary Dean checked her watch. 'Due to arrive at Andrews in an hour or so.'

'My guess is he's not aware yet,' Bill said. 'There is usually a period of time between the complaint and the arrest. They'll probably go to his home tomorrow.'

'Should I raise him on the air?' Mary Dean asked.

'No. Leave a message in Langley,' the President answered. 'He should come in as soon as he lands.' The President pondered a while. 'My gut feeling is that we need to talk to Ann.'

'I agree. Strictly speaking, we ought to go through her lawyers. I could take a risk by circumventing her lawyers and call Ann herself. I'm sure she has a reason for doing this.' He pointed a finger in the air as something dawned on him. 'Something is odd here.'

'Odd?'

'Judging from the number on the fax, this was sent from South Africa. In all likelihood, Ann sent this in personally, not through her lawyers who are based here, in the United States. Usually, her lawyer should file the complaint in court on her behalf, and the court would get the cops to arrest the accused. The question is: why send it to the President? He's not the accused, Cagley is. My guess is she wants the President to know; she wants to be heard. She's trying to put pressure on Cagley.'

'I see your point,' the President said, relieved.

343

'But we don't have much time. I have the idea Ann seems to be ready to follow it through.' Bill warned. 'If this news spreads, the administration is dead.'

'I'll call Ann right away.' Mary Dean dashed towards the door.

'Do you have a number?' the President asked.

'No. But I'll send a fax back and leave my number. Let's hope she calls.' Mary Dean walked out of the oval office.

'What the hell's wrong with Mike?' The President charged at Bill, frustrated, now that they were alone.

'He's always been a bit of a nut case, sir,' Bill answered. 'But a useful nut nonetheless. He's been there for us, taking care of the messy stuff. I wouldn't want to cross him. But we can't forget he's had his uses.'

'I know. But next year is election year for goodness sake. We don't need this kind of scandal.'

Mary Dean dashed back into the Oval Office a few moments later, flustered. 'You won't believe it. I just got a call from Paula Baxter. Ann sent a copy to the Senate Leader as well.'

'She's really trying to screw us,' Bill lamented. 'How many people has she sent it to?'

'Get onto her right now,' the President ordered.

Mary Dean scrambled out.

76

Michael Cagley walked into his office at CIA headquarters at about 11.00 am, having just returned from Canada.

Roberts, his personal assistant stepped in a few moments later. 'Mary Dean called from the White House, sir. Raven wants to see you as soon as you arrive.' Raven was the current code name for the President.

'Damn!' Cagley swore. He was worn out from the series of meetings in Ottawa. He had been looking forward to spending time with Lizzy, letting her work her magic. Cagley was pensive for a moment. 'Okay. Call her. See if he can accommodate me this afternoon.'

A minute later, Roberts returned. 'She says Raven wants to see you right away.'

'Right away? What's so urgent that can't wait?'

'I don't know sir. Maybe an update on the Middle East.'

'It must be,' Anita added. 'This morning, he asked for an intelligence estimate on the disposition of the Israeli cabinet in view of next week's peace meeting in London.'

'It can't be. Billingham was supposed to brief him this morning.'

Cagley paced to the window. What could the President want? Some covert work overseas? Not likely. The current President made do with his daily briefing. He never asked for more, never asked for less. What was it that couldn't wait?

Something was cooking.

He turned to Roberts. 'Tell 'em to get ready,' he ordered, referring to his driver and escort.

'Yes sir.'

Cagley walked to the door.

'Would you need any special briefing?' Anita asked.

Cagley shrugged. 'Just stay by the phone. If I need something I'll call in.'

'Yes sir.'

Tired, Cagley stepped out of his office. The Commander-in-Chief was calling.

Cagley arrived at the White House shortly after noon.

The Head of the CIA was a powerful figure, and Cagley was ushered straight through to Mary Dean's office.

'How are you, Mike?' Mary Dean asked, warm and receptive, as usual. By now, she was over the shock of the complaint. It was not her place to discuss the situation, however.

'How was your trip?'

'Awful,' Cagley mumbled. 'And how are you?'

'I'm all right. I'll let him know you're here. He's got a few senators with him,' she whispered conspiratorially.

Mary Dean pressed a button on her intercom. 'Mike Cagley is here to see you, sir.'

'Ask him to come in.'

Cagley entered the Oval Office.

Normally, when the President needed covert advice, he saw Cagley alone. On security issues other security chiefs were in attendance. Today, the President had three senators with him. They sat on the sofa, opposite a big TV. The three senators were members of the Senate Select Committee on Intelligence. The Senate Committee had oversight of the CIA, NSA and other US government security agencies concerned with Intelligence matters.

'Mike,' the President said, acknowledging Cagley's presence. The President wore a navy-blue suit.

'Hello, sir.' Cagley nodded at the three senators.

'Hello, Mike.' Carlton Hughes saluted. Carlton Hughes was the chairman of the Senate Committee. He was a four-term senator, and was once head of Army Intelligence. Now ageing, Hughes was more of an amiable compromising gentleman, no longer a regimental stiff body.

'Hiya,' Cagley replied. He noticed the mood in the room was somber. He waited for the President to speak.

'I asked you to come down, Mike,' the President began. 'As you know, we are politicians and some people in this town don't like us, and always want to drag us down.'

Cagley sighed. He should have known. Another Washington mud-slinging session.

'The sleaze never stops,' the President continued. 'It comes with the job. But the elections are coming soon. So, we need to tread carefully.'

'Mike, we are sorry to have to drag you down here,' Hughes began respectfully.

'That's all right,' Cagley responded.

Cagley was comfortable with Hughes and this committee. A few members had been involved with the military and security at one time or the other and they realised the nature of the intelligence game. They hardly gave bad reports, and always corrected issues discretely.

'We really couldn't be bothered with this thing,' Hughes continued, 'but it seems your enemies in DC are stirring the hornets' nest. They made a complaint to the court, and sent a petition to the President, and to us, and to the Senate Leader. One was also sent to the head of the Lower House. It is obvious they are trying to crack some bad eggs.'

Cagley shrugged, unruffled. The first law in Washington was *get used to the sleaze*.

'Mike, I am firmly behind you,' the President said. Cagley was an unscrupulous but valuable ally. He recalled the time some moron blackmailed his daughter when she stupidly got herself filmed indecently. Cagley made that problem go away. 'What I want to do is to keep this contained and persuade them to back down, and see if we can do some bargaining.'

So, what is it, this time? Cagley wondered. *Another moron making yet another allegation?* His enemies had made hundreds of them over the years. He couldn't be bothered. He

347

was too well protected by the agency to get his hands sullied.

'Okay,' Cagley agreed with a sly smile. That was the way things worked in Washington amongst the big boys. They watched each other's backs. Thousands of issues never get into the public arena because they are quietly dealt with behind closed doors. He remembered the Iran hostage crisis in the seventies. Whilst the media and the public made a lot of noise, the big boys worked the phones, cutting deals. And the time when some loan shark threatened Bill Ainsley? Cagley called John Hune who called some goons. The loan shark promptly disappeared. He appeared two days later bearing a gift. 'Let's hear what they have to say.'

Hughes held up the TV remote control and pressed a button. That instant, the TV produced a clear colour picture. Seeing the image, Cagley shot to his feet.

'What are you doing on there?' Cagley howled at the image on the screen.

'Testifying,' came the reply from the TV. 'Evening, Daddy.'

It was Ann. And she was the enemy. The one making allegations against him. He stared at her. Her face was unyielding. Uncompromising and vengeful

Cagley dropped into his seat. A severe headache ravaged his head: deep inside; by the side; behind—everywhere.

'Where's this from?' Cagley muttered.

'Cape Town, South Africa,' Hughes answered. 'We're linked by satellite. Tele-conferencing.'

'What's she doing there?' Cagley growled.

'I don't know.'

Cagley glanced again at the TV. He still couldn't believe it. Ann was taking the stand against him? Ann! Ann, his only daughter. What was she testifying about? What had she said?

'We were thinking,' the President said softly. 'Maybe you and her can talk it over. Obviously, this is a family issue.'

Cagley sank into his seat, his face burning. Sweat cropped from his brow. He could not look the President in the eye. It wasn't that there was much Ann could say. He was absolutely certain of that. But it didn't matter what Ann had to say, truth or lie. It was just that very simple fact that Ann, his very own daughter, was testifying against him. It was just like the wife of the Republican Presidential aspirant campaigning for the Democrats. It was a big question to his credibility. How would the grapevine in Washington react to that? The Head of the CIA—and your own daughter took the stand against you before the President and the Senate Committee! Cagley was broken. Humiliated.

'I don't want to talk,' Ann responded indignantly from the TV.

'What do you want, my dear?' the President asked warmly.

'I expect to see that he's prosecuted,' Ann declared. On a desk behind her was a fax machine. 'In the least he's fired.'

'Your daughter has filed a criminal complaint with the district court,' the President informed Cagley.

Cagley raised his head and glared at Ann.

'Have you got any evidence of these allegations?' Hughes asked.

'What allegations?' Cagley growled, cutting in.

'Lots,' Ann replied, answering Hughes. 'I will be a witness. I've got lots to say. My dad is one of these people who think out loud. He sometimes blurts out comments. I remember when WMTA estimated Saddam Hussein's F-15 jet fighters at twenty-five, he said, "it's forty, you morons."'

Cagley knew he'd done that. He wasn't a dimwit, he only allowed himself to do that in the safety of his own home. Couldn't a man be safe in his own home anymore? Did he have to worry about moles within the family as well?

'Notably, I remember five years ago when they showed the picture of Pablo Gonzalez, the president of Bolivia on TV, my dad didn't know I overheard when he said, "This time tomorrow you won't be there. We've seen to that. Bolero would be president."'

The President shot a dirty look at Cagley. How could Cagley slip up so badly?

For once Cagley was shaken. He had left a chink in his armour. That chink was his daughter. His trust in her. Never in his worst nightmare had he expected his daughter would use such comments against him.

'I trust my lieutenant completely,' the President said, defending Cagley, nevertheless. 'He would never be involved in such things. You'll need a lot more than hearsay, Ann.'

'I would call that a confession, not hearsay,' Ann contended, eyes ablaze. She knew the President was siding with her father. Neither of them was easy meat. She turned up the pressure. 'Getting rid of President Gonzalez would not have anything to do with the leases on the gold mine in San Simon, would it? Especially, as both you, dad, and you, Mr. President have got shares in it. I bet the public would love an explanation on that.'

Cagley and the President exchanged troubled glances.

'You father and I have investments in gold, Ann,' the President accepted amiably. 'But it's perfectly legal.'

'But you bought your leases only after Gonzalez was deposed and Bolero was installed,' Ann retorted. 'You got it cheap from Bolero.'

'Getting things cheap isn't an offence. If the Bolivians want to sell their gold at a billion, fine. If they want to sell for a cent, fine. It's *their* gold, after all.'

'That would be interpreted as remuneration for getting Bolero into power,' Ann contended.

'It can be interpreted any way they want.' As the President spoke he cast a warning look at Cagley.

Cagley knew that dangerous look. It meant *better sort this out*.

'Your dad is valuable to me. Why do you want to destroy him?'

'He wrecked my marriage, wrecked my life and imprisoned my husband. Isn't that enough?'

'That's why the two of you have to talk, Ann. You know what? Why don't you come see me when you get back? Withdraw you lawsuit. Come see me say, next week. We'll have lunch. Then I'll broker a talk between you and your dad. I promise you, I'll fix this.'

Ann knew the president wasn't playing ball. She ramped up the pressure. 'Have you asked how I got your fax, number, Mr President?'

'How?'

'I got it from Bob Weiser.'

'Bob Weiser?' Cagley suddenly felt vulnerable. Ann was now conspiring with his enemies! What did she know? He recalled his last meeting with her when she confronted him on that bastard, Delgado. Ann had claimed she had eyes inside the CIA, and true she did seem to know some stuff. Suddenly, Cagley was no longer sure that he'd kept clean tracks. Maybe she knew a lot!

'If I don't get a response in five minutes, I'll be sending my next fax, Mr President,' Ann warned. 'Yours was the first. I sent the second to the Senate Leader, and the third to the Senate Committee on Intelligence. The fourth went to the Speaker of the Lower House. I promised I would send Bob Weiser something this morning. I'm sure he'll be grateful to have my sworn statements. He'll know what to do with it. Thereafter, I'll send one fax every fifteen minutes till I've gone through everyone in Congress.'

'You can't do that,' the President bluffed.

'With all respect, sir, watch me.'

So they could see her, she fed her court complaint into the fax machine and punched in Bob Weiser's fax number.

She pressed the send button. The first page fed into the fax. The President and everyone looked on, horrified. Cagley had gotten over his shock. Hard as ever he stood his ground. He only frowned. He was unrepentant; unperturbed.

The President and everyone glared at Cagley. Was he going to let that happen? Was he going to stand by and let his daughter screw the whole administration?

Cagley caught the President's glare. It meant only one thing: jump or be pushed. He was not going to sacrifice his presidency

351

for Cagley, or indeed anyone. No honour amongst thieves.

Cagley knew that unforgiving look. He also saw the shear horror on the faces of Mary Dean, Bill Ainsley and the senators.

'Okay,' he muttered grudgingly, throwing up his hands. He got up and walked to the door then stopped. He turned round. 'You shall have my resignation within the hour.'

Cagley stormed out of the White House.

Ann heard her father's remark.

By then the fax had begun scanning the page.

She pulled out the plug.

77

Leroy arrived at Dulles Airport in Washington DC aboard a United Airlines plane from London using the passport he procured from John West. It was a genuine passport though under a false name, so he had no problems passing through immigrations. A gale blew over DC but Leroy barely noticed it.

He had spent the past week getting out of Nigeria. All that time he kept wondering about Talata. How could a woman claim she loved a man and yet be so resolute and unyielding? Why didn't she want him anymore? It was a real conundrum. He had spent hours and days trying to woo her and convince her that he was back for good but she adamantly refused to continue their relationship. He knew she was heartbroken, and she distrusted him—no matter how much he tried to explain his situation. "We have no future together," she insisted. She was his true love, he concluded.

Without her he felt empty. All the adrenalin and hope that drove him back to Nigeria—all the meetings with John West; acquiring a false passport; being smuggled out of the States; the dangerous drop into the plains of Dan Apali—it had all been a waste. He felt hollow, unfulfilled.

He hailed a cab from Dulles straight to his home in University Park. During the whole trip, he didn't look up once. Not even with the gale force winds rattling the cab window. His heart ached. He had never known such heaviness.

The wind howled viciously and displayed its relentless power by uprooting a couple of small trees outdoors. Leroy barely noticed. He entered his house. The house was silent, cold and empty. He didn't belong here anymore, he reckoned.

He belonged in Nigeria.

He flopped onto his sofa.

Talata.

Talata.

Talata! I need you!

He grabbed a beer from the fridge.

He sipped his beer. He hadn't eaten much in a week. He'd lived only on beer and cigarettes.

What am I doing here? I want her. I need her. I have to go back and get her. I have to convince her. I'm going back to find her.

He got to his feet to make a move. But the last ounce of reason within him made him sit down again.

Or maybe I should become a serious Christian as well. Then she will accept me. After all, there's nothing to lose. In fact, maybe it will sort the mess that's my life out! I could even become a priest! Father Leroy. That would be good.

Or maybe when I receive my divorce certificate from Ann I could return to Nigeria; show it to her. Then she would change her mind.

He lit a cigarette. He'd been smoking like a chimney ever since Talata broke his heart. Forty sticks a day. Now, his fingers trembled constantly because of the high levels of nicotine.

A gust of cold air whispered across his neck. The high wind had probably forced one of the windows open. He turned around.

Ann stood at the foot of the stairs.

He stared at her, too stunned to speak. A million swear words ran through his mind but none made its way out of his mouth.

'I went to Cape Town to get over you. I met a man who would give me millions of dollars if I wanted it,' she said softly.** 'I tried to fall in love with him, to get over you. But I couldn't. My mind was always with you. I finally realised one thing, I love you. I gave up on you and I realise I made a mistake. I married you. That gives me the right to claim you as mine. I've decided now, that any woman who wants you will have to come through me first, whether it's Arlene or the village girl.'

Leroy drew back. *Arlene? Who was Arlene? The village girl? Talata? How would she know about Talata?*

Ann saw his baffled expression. 'Yes, I know about Talata. I read it in the CIA files. They say you had an affair with her.'

Leroy blushed but he said nothing.

'It's my fault that happened. It's my fault because I let us down. I walked out on us. I didn't trust you as I should. I'm sorry I doubted you. But I've learnt my lesson.' She walked up to him. 'It's you I love, Leroy. Only you.'

Leroy thought a while. Maybe Talata was right. *A man's greatest misery is worrying about what he doesn't have whilst forgetting what he has.*

'I've learnt my lesson too.' He reached out and held her fingers. He looked into her eyes. She was beautiful. 'My duty is to take care of what I have—and that's you. I'm wasting my time worrying about what I don't have. The grass is never greener on the other side. The grass is green so long it is watered, nurtured and cherished.' He smiled. 'From now on, I'll cherish you and I'll take care of you. I promise.'

** This story is in *The Phantom Rogue* also by John Golden